THE
VELVET
SLEDGE
HAMMER

sort of a novel

EDWARD SAVIO

BABELFISH
PRESS

BABELFISH
P R E S S

8 The Green
Dover DE 19901

ISBN-13: 978-1-63124-027-0

For reprint permission: permission@babelfishpress.com
All other information: info@babelfishpress.com

Most of this is true.
As for the rest...I couldn't say.

1

MY FATHER, THE ASS PICKER

Somewhere over the Atlantic
December 1993

I DON'T KNOW how I got to be here. The height of my career. The height of forty-one thousand feet, heading into a storm. And not the meteorological kind, although one of those is on its way, too. On my way to Geneva. On my way to change the world.

And there's something else I'm not really sure of: How I got to be pretty much the best in the world at what I do, which is, well, *argue*.

Two weeks ago. Saturday night. My girlfriend and I. We go out for an elegant dinner, then come back to my place to cozy up. Laura and I are in bed. One of those perfect moments. Warm fire. A good bottle of red. Moist skin against moist skin. Her body is under me. I'm deep inside. A slow grind.

"Billy..." she says breathlessly.

"What is it, baby?" My voice a low, sexy growl.

"I think it's time."

"Yes, baby." I *love* when it's time.

She moans, which never fails to send a rush through my body.

"I really want to have a baby with you," she purrs.

I wouldn't have pulled out of her faster if her pussy was about to explode.

"A..a baby?"

"Yeah. A little mix of me and you." There's a smile on her face.

"You have to be married to do that," I semi-shouted, not meaning to. Somehow, I have this old-fashioned notion that children and marriage go hand in hand. For a guy who's slept with as many women as I have, I can be a prude sometimes.

"You don't *have* to be, but my parents would probably insist on it."

Ah, Laura's parents. If I married into that clan, I'd be the underachiever in the family.

"A baby?" I ask again, not really conceiving the whole concept.

I mean, why now? When everything between us is going so great.

Why *now*? Two weeks before the biggest, most important negotiations of my career.

Why now? When I finally have her handcuffed to the bed.

"Laura, you wanna *marry* me?"

Instead of recognizing my stunned, incredulous tone for what it is: total fear, shock, anguish and disbelief, she reaches out and tearfully says, "Yes, yes, oh yes," only her hands barely made it a few inches before the metal restraints stop her cold.

One of the more anti-romantic misproposals.

I have seven days to sort it all out.

Bring to a close the longest, most comprehensive negotiations in the *history* of mankind, get one hundred and sixteen countries to unanimously consent to the agreement, and, if the fate of the world economy isn't enough pressure, I need to answer the two questions burning a hole in my head since the Saturday before last when I *inadvertently* proposed to my wonderful girlfriend: One, am I ready to be married to one woman for the rest of my life, forever, till we're put in the ground dead, and two, am I even remotely qualified to raise a child.

Seven days.

Seems impossible.

Especially, when you realize where I started.

THIS IS ALL I REMEMBER:

My mother on the couch reading a book, excusing herself for the flatulence she was pumping daintily into the air, "Those G.D. vegetables...I tell you..." my father in his *underwear*, T-shirt tucked inside his whitish briefs, dark socks and shoes—yes, shoes—standing in front of the TV, picking at his ass till he couldn't get his wrist up it any farther and looking over the tops of his glasses to view the glowing screen, clueless to the fact he was impeding adequate absorption of our drug of choice.

"You make a better door than a window, Sam," my mother would say, just before ripping another one, followed by a barely audible apology, "Umsorry."

"Jesus Christ, Mary! You're rotting inside," was my father's customary response.

This was my childhood.

These were my Ozzie and Harriet.

Which, I guess, might be one of the reasons I'm so good at what I do.

U.S. News and World Report calls me "the only member of the Cabinet with the guts to tell the President the truth." *Business Week* says "the U.S. Economy is safer, healthier, and stronger" because of me. *The Economist* calls me "an insufferable bully."

I'm not simply an arguer. I'm the United States Trade Representative.

I'm a *professional* arguer.

I've had a lot of practice.

See, my father would stand there in front of the TV for something like three minutes. Just long enough for the rest of us to have missed the crucial scene or piece of dialogue that allowed the entire show to make any sense.

"Dad, just move to the right...three feet. It's one step," I'd say in an attempt to open negotiations.

Profanity-laced mumbling would proceed a move of maybe an inch by my father. The dime-sized hole in his baggy, no longer tighty or whitey briefs—where he had, over years of hard work, tunneled through the fabric—drew your attention as he moved that minute distance whether you wanted it to or not.

"Could we maybe compromise at a foot and a half?" I'd say, countering his first, unacceptable offer. "We'll be able to see and you'll be able to hear cause I'll finally shut up."

"Christ, you people drive me crazy!" Then he'd storm off.

Victory is sweet.

Unless you're sitting within five feet of my mother after a plate of broccoli.

. . .

OF COURSE...HE'D be back.

My father was only about midway through his nightly audit of the house. Checking the airflow passing through the windows in the summer, the thermostat in the winter, extinguishing every light, inside and out, we couldn't get to first.

For several years, while he got the brainy idea to heat the house with coal, the ceremony included shoveling two scoops of the solid black fuel—making this sound like someone puking nuts and bolts and a P.A. system—into a pair of small Chapée stoves, one in the living room which forevermore made useless the charming fireplace and hearth I had so often sat in front of as a young boy, and one in the cellar that did what, dad?, heat the basement? No one lived in the Goddamned basement.

"No," he'd explain, "it heats the floor."

As if that made any sense.

The outer rooms, mine included, hovered around fifty-two degrees in the winter while my summer clothes and last year's schoolbooks were doing just fine in the cozy tropics below ground.

"I like warm feet," he'd say whenever you questioned his logic.

"Wear some socks," I screamed at him during one of our many disagreements on the subject.

What pissed me off even more was that my feet received no benefit from this obsession. No, my room was built not over the basement, but over a concrete slab in what was once the garage.

For many years I thought of my dad only in this way. As the man who brought coal into our home, yelled a lot, and picked his ass in front of every episode of M*A*S*H.

The final moment of his nocturnal rounds came as he reached out and lowered the volume on the television so he could sleep.

Oh, not all at once. It was a process.

An excruciating, ludicrous rite that happened every evening nearly, if not exactly, the same as the night before and the night before that. Turn down. Listen. Turn down some more. Listen. Turn down again.

"Dad, we can't hear!"

"Jesus Christ!"

We'd negotiate a slight increase in volume. We, the ungrateful wards who did not, could not, but someday would, appreciate the sacrifices he made for us. He would tweak the knob down one last time, and retire to his room. Lie on the bed for about thirty seconds. Storm back out. Then scream, "I'm gonna turn this fucking thing down or I'm gonna put my foot through the damn thing! Which will it be? I gotta get up in the morning and I need my Goddamn sleep!"

My father, six foot three, two hundred and twenty-five pounds, was the epitome of *The Princess and the Fucking Pea*. Couldn't get his rest if his surroundings weren't exactly—and I mean exactly—as he wanted them to be. He often threatened to build a little shack for himself deep in the backyard away from the house because he couldn't stand another night of our noise. Only the Princess gave up on that threat when he realized we were all in favor of the idea.

"You promise?" I'd say, sweetly, daring him.

And that would segue into yet another of our many arguments.

More than once, I've been in the middle of a marathon session when some nub sitting across the table from me from Japan or Europe or East Bumfuck starts thinking, if they just make life a little more uncomfortable for me, they're going to be able to dump a million more truck engines or CD players or extension cords on the U.S. market. Only the poor bastard doesn't understand that short of nuclear war there isn't much I can't handle after my childhood.

Scream at me. Call me names. Throw knives at me.

I've seen it before.

So, who is responsible? Who can take credit for who and what we are?

Parents? Or the world?

Is it the astronomer who discovers the star or the poet who gives that faint flickering light meaning by weaving a tapestry of words?

All I know is, I hate poets.

I have to admit that, in some ways, I've inherited my father's peculiarity—as any woman I've slept with more than once will tell you. Sound. Too much, not enough, not the right kind will annoy me until I track it down, locate it, and destroy it. A ticking clock is like Chinese water torture. It rings in my skull till I want to smash it. A fan is soothing and helps me sleep, although, most women I've dated don't seem to think it's as cute an idiosyncrasy in the middle of January as they do in the middle of July.

There are some females who feel the same way about sound. I, however, am not dating one of them.

If any of you out there are funny, pretty and have a fan on at night or gadgets by your bed issuing forth ocean waves, spring rain, or babbling brooks, track me down. My girlfriend might have something for you. Sorry, my *fiancée*.

Two weeks and I still can't get used to that word.

My dad couldn't close his door to stifle the sound, of course. There was a certain flow of air he needed to have in order to sleep. He was big on airflow. In the house, in the car, in his clothes. He could stand in one spot for ten minutes, tracking the air movement from a fan or heater with his hand, starting at the source and moving his arm, his whole body back until he couldn't feel the breeze anymore. While driving, a hand would slowly extend toward us into the back seat of the Volvo or the Ford as he measured the current. He'd adjust the direction, the speed, the angle until he drove us completely insane. Once, he nearly caused a ten-car pileup on Interstate 95 because he couldn't get enough air into the fucking car.

"I can't drive like this! I'm suffocating in here," he roared as he almost plowed into the side of a Saab. My dad loved those cars. "Best cars ever made!" Only the two Saabs we owned when I was very young, had three cylinders and needed oil in the gas tank like it was a Goddamn lawnmower.

I hated those cars. He loved them.

I was three.

It was the start of our differences.

So, the volume was turned down to make the television more or less useless. The rest of us, my two brothers and my sister, became excellent at reading lips and interpreting body language. A skill I still possess today. I've used it to my advantage in trade negotiations as the men and women on the other side try to whisper secrets to one another. Last year I was able to get the Japanese to import three times as many Jeeps because I knew they were bluffing.

But we, the unappreciative offspring, did win out in the end. All we'd have to do was wait fifteen minutes till the Princess fell asleep, and then, we could do pretty much whatever we wanted...including shutting his door.

Although, we'd pay for it the next day.

Airflow.

·   ·   ·

I HAVE SOMEHOW, up until a few weeks ago, avoided thinking about things like this while crisscrossing the Atlantic or the Pacific or the North Fucking Pole at altitude. Now, I can't seem to stop the raging waters of the past from flooding my brain.

I wonder if the people I'm with, my friends, Laura, my fellow travelers, have any idea I'm thinking these things. I wonder if they ever think this way.

If they don't, I'm a little scared.

If they do, I'm terrified.

And the plane only makes it worse. It has something to do with the sound. The whoosh the jet makes. The rush of air recirculating in the cabin. Like a giant version of the fan in my bedroom. It unlocks the deepest, most fertile, dream-like parts of my brain, regardless of whether I want it to or not. Usually, I employ this idiosyncrasy for good. When I need to write a speech or plot a course of action for negotiations, I turn on my fan, or a faucet, or tune an AM radio all the way down to the end where there's nothing but static, just to get me to that place, that place high above the clouds.

But this kind of thinking, this rehashing the past, this is the dark side of opening your mind.

So, why am I doing it?

In a word...

Terror.

My fiancée—that word again—thinks I'm the sweetest, kindest, most talented person. My President thinks I'm a hero and "a great American." He actually *said* that. But me, I know the truth.

I'm a moron.

How about another word...

Children.

The word alone is enough to make me encase myself in Saran Wrap.

This sudden push toward parenthood is why I'm torturing myself with the likes of Tina Moore, Christmas Holocausts, and the sordid details of my childhood.

It's not that I don't want kids.

I do. I really do.

I just don't want them now. I don't have any training for this.

Maybe when I'm ready.

Laura's response to that: "You're gonna make a great father."

"You wanna bet? Have you seen my role model?"

She's met the Princess, but she hasn't seen him in all his ass-picking rageoholic glory. This is my ace in the hole. My trump card. The one and only weapon that might cool her desire to tie me to her so tightly.

Still, preparation is half the battle. So, I've been poring over everything, trying to figure out how this whole *raising a kid thing* should work. It should be a simple equation, right? I'm a "brilliant strategist able to tame complex problems with elegant solutions" (so says *The Washington Post*), I should be able to reason it out.

Only I can't.

The problem is: I'm on my way to the final negotiation session for the Global Agreement on Tariffs & Trade's Uruguay Round, something that in comparison to children is child's play, and it seems to the world that I've evolved into this relatively normal adult. Which, of course, is *not* the problem. The actual dilemma comes in knowing all the fucked up things in my past, all the painful memories locked inside my head that are lying in wait like ticking time bombs—no, worse, like land mines I know are out there, somewhere, but I have no idea exactly where.

I may never step on one, but how likely do you think that is?

And every trip, every time I hear the President thanking me for a job well done, every time Laura tells me how wonderful I am, I think, today, today is the day. Today, one of those little bombs is gonna get mailed to me and BOOM!, the world will know the truth.

So far, that hasn't happened. Might have something to do with our crack team at the postal service. Lost in the mail, perhaps.

But how long do you think that's gonna last?

You can never go home again, they say, and I say, thank God for that!

Only sometimes you're forced to go home and when you get there, no matter what's happened in your life, no matter how many successes you've had, it's like you never left. You're still the same little shit who set fire to the neighborhood fort because you wanted to know if burlap was flammable.

It is, by the way—burned it to the ground.

Still the same idiot who fed different kinds of rocks to each of the neighbors' dogs so you could tell which one was shitting on the front lawn, forcing you to clean it up. (It was the cockapoo, ironically.)

That's why I hate going home.

. . .

MY FATHER'S nightly review wasn't a question of security. No one in our neighborhood ever locked their doors. It was simply ritual.

The house, which sat in the middle of a quiet street at the edge of a forest, was built by Sebby and Annette, my grandfather and grandmother on my mom's side.

Sebby, who is my favorite person in the world, was a carpenter until his knees gave out. He was a good carpenter. But he was no architect. He didn't have any grand vision of building his dream home just the way he wanted it. In fact, he didn't have any vision at all. He got the plans for the house God-only-knows-where for free, which is why we have the only flat-roofed single-family residence in New England. It's a California *desert* home, stuck right smack dab in the middle of Connecticut. The fact that this didn't seem strange to Sebby is probably the only defect I can find in my grandfather's lucid and usually keen wisdom.

Besides looking like we'd lost half our house in the most recent Nor'easter, having a flat-roofed house had several other notable distinctions. When the summer sun pounded down onto the thick, black gooey tar, being inside was like stuffing your body into the oven and wrapping yourself in tin foil. Even worse, during winter, when the storms got heavy, I'd have to dig out the ladder from under a foot of snow, climb up, and shovel the roof.

The *roof*.

It's hard to grow up having to shovel your house and not have that affect you negatively in some way.

Sebby and my gramma Annette built the place themselves at night and on weekends. The only help they received was from a few friends lifting the ceiling joists into place one Saturday and from her brother, an electrician, who put in the wiring as well as the plumbing.

Which is why the hot water goes to the kitchen sink and the cold to the toilet before it ever gets remotely near the shower.

Many a morning, I'd be awakened to the sound of a pig being slaughtered as my mother absent-mindedly washed out her coffee cup while the Princess was taking a shower.

"Sorry!"

That it was Sebby's house always annoyed my father, even though my grandparents only lived in it two years before selling it to my parents at a ridiculously low price. Had it been his father, it would have been fine, but it was her father and that made all the difference in the world.

Our house wasn't so much a home as it was a proving ground for sarcasm, quick wit, and obnoxious comebacks. Those with the mental bravery and the physical capability to survive dinner at the Gerricks came away with a new understanding on the meaning of life. It was at these times when the family shined in its own odd way.

Every word was cutting, funny, and downright entertaining.

My dad, the brute, the ass picker, the Fat Track destroyer, became cool guy, hip, the have-a-drink-with-you gentle giant.

Some may have faulted my father for his performance in the company of others as disingenuous and duplicitous. Some may have held a grudge that guests fawned over my father, and if they only knew better...

Not me.

I was all too happy to put up with the *Incredible Chameleon* as long as he didn't embarrass me in public.

Sure, a few of my closest friends would get an earful once in a while.

But they understood.

It was the toll one had to pay for being entertained most other times.

It's taken me most of my adult life to dig myself out from under my "happy" childhood. I'm not going to do that to my kid. Uh-uh. No way. Only I have no idea how *not* to. Where was that class in college? PARENTING 110, NOMANSONS 2B. I mean, I had to take a seven-week course to get certified to swim underwater twice a year with an air tank. At the very least, people should have to pass a simple multiple choice quiz before they can spend the next eighteen to twenty-five years directly influencing a being that's going to eventually move out, operate a motor vehicle, and be able to legally purchase a semi-automatic rifle with an extra capacity clip.

If there was ever something people should have to pass a test for, parenting is fucking it!

"Please cover your left eye and read from the top of the chart."

D-O-N-T-B

E-A-N-A-S

S-H-O-L-E

So what about my offspring? What am I supposed to do with them?

I'd read one of the fifty-thousand books on the subject, but what the hell do these people know about anything? One woman who's written dozens of these holier-than-thou how-tos has got two kids, a son and a daughter, playing a round-robin tournament against the world's most elite detox centers.

I'm supposed to listen to these idiots? I don't need to pay $24.95 to figure out how to fuck my kid up that good. I can do it for free.

Do I apologize in advance?

Tell them, kids, all the stupid, asinine, screwed up things I'm going to do to fuck up your lives, well...they're just not my fault.

Say, "Hey, sorry about that. Just disregard everything I say. Overlook anything I do. Read a book, maybe it'll help."

And besides, you'll get over it.

Maybe.

If you have any ideas, write me:

William Gerrick
Office of the United States Trade Representative
600 17th Street, N.W.
Washington, D.C. 20508

Actually, I have this theory I've been working on since this morning. It's deceptively simple.

I'm gonna figure out all the stupid shit my parents did, write it down, and do exactly the opposite. If I'm really meticulous about this and examine the whole situation, the absolute whole situation top to bottom, and just not do anything they did, my kid could turn out to be Emperor of the Universe.

I CAME up with this theory while I was having my fourth glass of o.j. at Bellina's in Georgetown at six A.M.—something I often do when I'm not in some far off country. Everyone else in the place was jacked up on the All-You-Can-Drink überjava they fire up each morning, a mix of caffeine and sludge they scrape off the pot bottoms of all the other coffee shops in town, that has more beans per ounce than once thought possible using conventional physics.

Some sort of proprietary caffeine infusion process.

These people come in the door nearly comatose and sprint out like they've just swallowed a barrel of jet fuel, their jaws flapping faster than a duck winging away from buckshot.

Coffee has never held for me the same allure as it does for most people. Perhaps it's because I lost my father to a pot of joe at the corner Dunkin' Donuts for half my childhood. My father would drink twenty-four cups of coffee a day. Twenty-four. Think about that.

They say the average adult male is sixty percent water. Well, my father was seventy percent Viennese blend.

I'll never forget the time he told us he had cut it down to fifteen cups a day, "Doctor's orders," like we were supposed to be impressed or something.

So, I'm sitting there, watching these people and I see this one woman. She has straight blonde hair to her shoulders, a few strands of it falling into her face. I watch her because she's pleasant to look at, and she's the only person still working on her first cup, and even then, she's hardly touched it. She's writing in a leather-bound book, which I realize is a journal.

My recent tirades aside, I've never been one to analyze my past or my childhood. I've gotten through life, succeeded, in fact, by ignoring these things. Crazy thoughts on planes over the Arctic, sure, talking to myself when I'm alone in a car at three A.M. and warmed by a few Martinis, Absolut®-ly, but truly scrutinizing my psyche, self-reflection? No. And writing it down, never. Especially not in a form that could be traced back to me.

Dredging things up is a messy business. Just ask anyone who's ever dragged the bottom of the Hudson. Lotta skeletons in that water closet.

But there she was, writing away, laughing at some memory she was committing to paper, then suddenly, without explanation, she's crying.

I couldn't stop watching her.

So when she looked up, she looked up to find me staring.

I'm not a very shy person, at least, that's what everyone keeps telling me, but, personally, that distance...that ten or twelve steps across a room to a woman in a bar, in a dance club or even a coffee house, is the farthest, most treacherous stroll a man can take. I'd rather walk a minefield. Because at the other end of that walk is the distinct and most likely probability that you're going to have to turn around and march right back to wherever you came from.

She didn't look away. But then again, she didn't smile at me either, but there was something...

Finally, she lowered her eyes and returned to her journal, her pen immediately back to its previous tempo.

With my curiosity getting the best of me, I got up and started to cross the chasm between my table and hers, navigating the sea of tables and chairs and people with their to-go cups.

It wasn't far, but it seemed like forever. I feigned confidence.

If you never do anything that scares you, you never do anything great.

Halfway there, my phone started ringing.

I answered it. Sheer reflex. "Billy Gerrick."

"I love it when other women check you out." It was Laura.

"What?"

I start looking around, like a bank robber looking for cops on his way out the door with a cool million in small bills. Was she here? Was she looking in from the street? I couldn't see her.

"I was just thinking, you're going to be seeing Rafael and all the rest of your groupies. And whenever you come back from these trips, you have that...I don't know...that strut you get."

"I don't strut."

"You strut."

"I don't have groupies."

"Ah-huh," she said, not believing a word.

She gets like that sometimes. Sometimes I like it. Sometimes it makes me wonder if she understands.

"Listen, Laur, I'm getting my last decent glass of orange juice before Europe."

I could hear her give a little cozy moan. She was still in bed.

"I know. I just wanted to tell you to have a safe flight. And that I love you."

"Me too."

She let out another comfortable sigh. "I've been checking out wedding places," she said, casually.

I froze. "You agreed not to tell anyone till I got back," I said in a whisper, although I don't know why—it wasn't like I was being followed by the press.

"I promised not to tell any of our *friends or family*. You didn't say anything about a wedding planner."

So casually.

"Actually, I believe I said, *anyone*."

Laura was silent.

"Fine," I sighed. "Wedding planner. As long as she doesn't know anyone we know."

"You're good husband material, Gerrick."

"You think?"

"I love you. Have a safe flight. Call me when you land."

"I will."

I hung up the phone and almost headed back to my seat when the pretty blonde looked up at me from her journal again. No going back now.

I somehow traversed the minefield that lay between us and put my hand on the empty chair across from her, but didn't sit down. She was even more beautiful up close, the morning light mixing with her hair, making it come alive. But mostly her beauty had nothing to do with her smooth skin or almond eyes and everything to do with what lay behind them.

I said something moronic like "Hi," and she said something witty like, "Not since I switched to decaf."

We made it through that first awkward moment, how, I don't know. I wish I did. I'd write it down, put it in a book and sell ten million copies.

It amazes me that we've sustained the species this long.

I mean, back a million years ago it was all much simpler. Bonk on head. Drag back to cave.

Now, I'm not advocating this sort of Neanderthal behavior. Although, I don't believe women are equal to men.

I find them superior.

So, I sat down and I asked her what she was writing.

"Personal things."

There was a moment where I thought this whole episode was going to blow up in my face. I nodded my head, told my muscles to stand. Looked back at my table, receding into the distance. Long way back.

"Why do you ask?" she said as I was getting to my feet. "Are you curious or are you just *interested*?"

I was impressed with her subtle wording, her clever probing of my intentions.

"Curious," I answered, watching the light dance in her eyes. She was not inviting me in with her glance. There was a subtle coolness in her manner—she was keeping her head about her—but she was much more open than I expected someone to be after my intrusion.

She caressed the leather cover as she told me her father had died several months ago. Not unexpectedly, he'd been ill for some time. And toward the end, she had asked him about his life. All the moments he could remember. His childhood. The War. Where he had met her mother.

"A coffee shop, perhaps?" I said, feeling like an asshole as soon as the words had left the jumbled mass of neurosynaptic pathways in my skull by way of my mouth and blasted into the open air.

Her look was more than kind.

What a fucking idiot, Gerrick. She was feeling something deep, something important and I, I was unable to wrest control of my lips from millions of years of breeding that forced me—in the face of everything— to pick her up. (Well, I guess now that I'm engaged, I won't be getting to the "up" part anymore.) Sometimes it amazes me that anyone would want to date me, let alone bear my children.

She let the moment pass.

"They met in Norway. His unit was helping remove land mines the Nazis had laid."

Then she explained how her dad had seemed so happy looking back, even during the painful moments, the sad times, that after his death, after she had put together the pieces of his life, she decided to give the same gift to herself.

"He came alive again while he was talking. The day before he died, he thanked me for making him look back."

And that's what she was doing in the coffee shop in which I met her. Writing in her journal.

I was still smarting from my stupidity and I almost apologized, but then thought better of it.

I remember my Grandfather, not Sebby, but my dad's dad, Robert, saying to me once, "Kid, excuses are for the weak." I don't think I ever heard him apologize for anything. I'm sure he did at some point in his life —he was married. Wives don't stay wives for long without an occasional *mea culpa*. Then again, his first wife, my grandmother, died twenty years before he did.

Robert Gerrick was the stubbornest, orneriest, most charming son-of-a-bitch I've ever met. Of course, this is a man who thought the world revolved around him...and come to think of it, he may have been right.

In fact, over and over and over again the doctors said, "He'll be dead by morning." And over and over and over again, he'd wake up yelling at the fucking nurses because they wouldn't let the fossil smoke in the ICU. He'd have a Goddamned oxygen tube hanging from his nostrils and he'd want to torch up a cig. "You'll set the whole place on fire. Put out that damn flame!" they'd yell at him.

He'd grumble out something through tubes and an unlit cig (he wouldn't let them get away with taking that, they'd have to disconnect life support to do it) about how they'd figured out how to crack his chest, cut out his heart and sew it back in without assassinating him, but they couldn't figure out how to have the ICU not explode because he wanted a Goddamned Lucky Strike.

He made no excuses.

And when I'm at the negotiating table...or the coffee table, neither do I.

I reached out and gently tapped my finger on the back of her hand. "You're a lot braver than I am. I'm not very comfortable examining my past," I said.

She nodded, understanding. "It definitely feels weird at first. Kind of a cross between claustrophobia and motion sickness."

I laughed, recalling the nauseous, confining feeling I'd been suffering off and on for the past two weeks.

"It made me realize some things about myself," she said. I kept watching her lips as she spoke. "You'd be amazed at how much you've forgotten until you start digging."

"Well, I can assure you *my* father wouldn't be thanking me for bringing up the past," I said. "It's best to keep mine buried."

"I thought so too, but...you can't learn from it if you don't remember it."

I thought about that statement for a moment. I was about to say something when she spoke again.

"So, what is it about your past you're afraid of?"

"I don't know exactly. I guess that's what I'm afraid of."

She looked at me, studying me, and then said, "You don't seem like someone who's afraid of too many things."

We talked for a moment or two more. Then after finishing my orange juice, I got up and left Bellina's, and left Sydney, that was her name, sitting at the table, explaining my abrupt exit by saying I had to catch a plane to Geneva.

"If I had a dime for every guy who gave me *that* line."

I told her I hoped we'd run into each other again, although, I knew even if we did, we'd only nod a pleasant, somewhat distant greeting.

"I hope I didn't bother you too much."

"You did, but...now, I have something else to write about."

In an instant, I was gone, allowing her to return to her journal and the private thoughts I had invaded.

AS I WAS PACKING my bags, I thought about what she said, that you can't learn from the past if you don't remember it, and how animated Sydney looked, thinking about her own past. How she seemed so open, so comfortable with herself. And how she told me her father had worked for the D.C. bomb squad, earning numerous commendations during his career.

I remember thinking as I walked away from Bellina's, how ironic it is that bomb squads prefer to explode a possible device rather than a) leave it alone because they're usually fake, or b) defuse it. It's safer that way, they say.

Consequently, here I am, strapped into a 767, on my way to the most important trade summit ever, trying to blow shit up.

Unmapped landmines from the past.

I figure if I do it now, I might avoid having my offspring hit with shrapnel later.

LIKE I SAID, we're winging our way to Geneva. This is the ninth "final" negotiation session for the Uruguay Round of trade talks, a dialogue that's been taking place for almost a decade. A negotiation I've been working on all but exclusively for the last three years. Hopefully, there won't be a need for a tenth final session. This is the last hurdle to replace the nearly fifty-year-old Global Agreement on Tariffs and Trade with an instrument more encompassing, more open, more enforceable, and for most countries, more scary as well. It will be the most far-reaching agreement undertaken by mankind. Ever.

The summit is ostensibly being held at the GATT headquarters, a small, relatively powerless overseeing body that's been operating on a provisional basis for nearly five decades. It's situated in a corner of one of the UN's offices in Geneva.

Geneva is this lovely city by a lake. That's about all I know. I've been there twenty-seven times.

I know what the inside of the Intercontinental Hotel looks like. That's where most of the meetings will actually be held. They have wonderful chairs there. My father would be very happy to park his ass in one of the Intercontinental's chairs. If it seems that my father's ass is of great interest to me, let me clear this up. It isn't. It was for him, however, to the exclusion of almost anything else. I don't think anything ever happened to my father's ass that I, my family, and half the neighborhood didn't know about *in detail*.

"I'm going to have this fucking boil lanced if it's the last thing I do!"

My mother would respond, "Geez, Sam, stop talking about it and just do it!" Which, I believe, is where my next-door neighbor, an advertising man, came up with the slogan that won him that running shoe account. By the way, no one on my track team ever paid for sneakers.

"I can't even sit down! Jesus Christ!" my father would shout back about two seconds before he'd lock himself in our only bathroom for forty-five minutes.

This from the man who seemed to want to personally ingest the entire nation's daily requirement of fiber. Wheat germ, soy germ, psyllium husks, you name it, if it had the effect of a bulldozer, my father wanted it in his bowels. There was more roughage pushing its way through my father's lower tract than there was going through a Metamucil factory. You would think with all that bulk he'd be safe. But, alas, as we all learned often and loudly, such was not the case.

As a kid, I never quite understood what my father did. My birth certificate lists his occupation as IBM Computer Operator. That was way back in the early sixties when that was like saying you worked on Mars. All I know is that one of the man's primary jobs was to monopolize the one and only bathroom we had for an hour every morning before the rest of us could get anywhere near the thing. My father needed complete and total access to the bathroom. Never mind that he only spent ten minutes of that hour actually in the bathroom, and not all at once, either—the rest of the time he had to have it clear, on reserve, booked, withheld for that singular moment when he'd need to take a seat on the crapper, shower, or shave that face of his. And he didn't even shave, although I didn't know it at the time. One stroke, two strokes, and he'd be done. For someone as big as he was, he had the softest beard. He could go for weeks on one blade. Me, I rip my face off if I go more than three shaves on the same razor.

Like the evening pre-bed ballet, there was ritual in the morning.

First the shower, then there was the cooling off period where the fog was allowed to dissipate from the mirror. He couldn't just wipe it off. That left streaks, and you couldn't have that. No, he had to have the entire bathroom freed up, liberated, till the breeze removed the fog naturally (see above re: airflow).

"Can't I use the fucking bathroom in peace?" was the battle cry heard nearly every A.M.

"Sure dad, you can use the bathroom. I'll just take a crap out here in the kitchen."

What made the whole thing so absurd was that our house, like I said, had one bathroom. When I was nine, we put in an extra sink so the rest of us could get ready faster, since my dad's bathroom greed left us with scarcely enough time before the school bus came. Of course, only the spot where the original sink had been had a mirror in front of it, rendering the other sink virtually useless as well as unused.

My parents spent over a thousand dollars redoing the sinks and couldn't bring themselves to agree to buy a fucking fifty-dollar mirror that would have made it worth the price.

A few months ago, I asked my mother why they had wasted their money on a sink that no one used. You know what she said? "Everyone used that sink, all the time."

I tried to explain to her that soaking my brother's dirty underwear because the neighbors down the street no longer let him use their bathrooms after he stopped up several of their toilets did not constitute actual use as a sink. That's what the sink by the washer in the basement was for.

There is a running theme to my parents' home improvements. And at some later point maybe I'll explain why we no longer have a flat roof at Casa Gerrick. And why there are now six bedrooms instead of four, even though almost no one lives there anymore.

Only one of the reasons being to give my father more rooms in which to pick his ass.

2

DYING FOR A CIG

BY THE WAY, that *Business Week* article about me, I was on the cover. Under the headline, "Trader or Traitor."

Being the United States Trade Representative makes me a lightning rod for special interest groups who for one reason or another, some of them valid, most of them not, want to derail the march toward free trade and globalization. Somewhere, someone is protesting something contained in some part of this new GATT agreement to somebody. Some of these someones would burn me in effigy if they had the slightest idea what I looked like.

Well, thanks to *Business Week*, now they do.

DID I happen to mention that the woman across the aisle from me is not wearing any underwear? I know this because she has gotten up thirty-four times since the stopover in London.

I'm not sure what she's trying to get out of her bag, but several of us in the area are glad she hasn't found it yet.

My assistant holds out a faxed note in my direction. Allison's been with me four years now. A record for me. Before I found her, I went through eight assistants in one year. Not a record for me. Of the myriad qualities that make Allison a perfect fit, the best are that she, 1) has a sense of humor—it can get grimly harsh in the heat of things, and 2), she is comfortable—even enjoys—being around power, but is not in the least bit impressed by it.

Allison is attractive, irreverent, smart and seems to know what I want before I want it. It's not an exaggeration to say she's one of the main reasons I still *am* the United States Trade Representative.

"Nap time's over," she says as she pushes the note at me.

I can already tell I'm not going to like it. She's usually more disrespectful when no one can hear.

I look at the piece of washed out, flimsy paper.

No, not gonna like it at all.

The Malaysian Minister of Trade & Industry is this short, weasel-faced cousin of the King who lives in one of the most lush countries in the world and is, ironically, allergic to every flowering plant known to man.

He is, at this very moment, on the ground in Geneva attempting to rally support against my proposal to discuss labor standards at the APEC meeting in Indonesia next month.

Not rallying against any *particular* labor standards, but rallying against the proposal to even discuss them...at all.

Let me come clean about this. I'm not trying to raise wages for his people because they're slogging through twelve hour days, six days a week and barely making enough to survive. I feel bad for them, and I do what I can, but his people are not my primary concern. I'm trying to raise his country's standard of living so maybe, just maybe, a few hundred thousand Americans will lose their jobs to unfairly cheap labor instead of a few million.

I tell Allison to have one of the "babies" from our delegation buy up every package of Benadryl and Sudafed in the hotel and surrounding stores, and then send twelve dozen of the most beautifully fragrant roses to the trade minister's room.

THE PILOT HAS JUST COME on and is telling us we're now cruising over Germany at thirty-seven thousand feet and some fucking thing is off to the right. I tend to prefer it when my pilots stick to their primary job, which, I think, is flying the plane. Far too many of them want to be my tour guide. I mean on a cruise ship, the activity director is not the one steering the boat.

I think that's Munich down there or, at least, somewhere near it because I see what looks like the tented acrylic glass roof of the Olympic stadium. I can't help but think about the Israeli athletes who were taken hostage, then killed, not only because of the tragedy for the men and their families, but because that tiny sliver of history was one of those defining moments, a sea change if you will, like Kennedy's assassination, that has brought us to this point where we think nothing of being searched or having our bags scanned and probed and our underwear checked. Thank God, I don't wear any.

I wonder if I can see where Gunter's relatives lived. I think of these things sometimes when I'm flying, then consider how the hell would I know the home of one of Gunter's ancestors from a pretzel factory at this height.

I met Gunter in sixth grade when five elementary schools dumped a few hundred blooming adolescents into one big caldron called middle school. What idiot came up with that idea?

Gunter's parents were exactly the opposite of mine. It was widely assumed around our school his mother had been SS when she was young. Never mind that she would have been about eight when war broke out in Europe. Didn't matter, the rumors persisted. At Gunter's house, his mom was the boss. Not that mine wasn't in some way in charge, but my mom was boss like a lion tamer is boss. You whip, you threaten, but in the end, it's really the lion that decides your fate.

Whenever I visited him as a kid, and his mother was around, I would stand at attention like four feet of bamboo had been rammed up my ass.

When Gunter came over to my house, he didn't even knock. Rather, he'd knock, he just wouldn't wait for anyone to answer. He'd come right in, go to the fridge and open it.

"Hi, Mrs. G," he'd say as he leaned in to find something to snack on.

You would never do that at Gunter's house. It wasn't that you weren't invited to take such liberties, you were actually warned against them. The unspoken gist left no doubt you'd get sent to a gas chamber by the Commandant if you did.

"Put zose down!"

"Keep za hanz off za strudel."

"I didn'z hear you zay pleaze!"

GUNTER'D GRAB something to chow on and stuff it in his mouth. Usually, a piece of cheese, Land O' Lakes, that he'd consume with a lot of smacking and gnawing and gulping. Talk to my mom for twenty seconds, then ask, "Hey, Mrs. G, where's Billy?"

"He's in his room, Gunter. If you can find him."

My room was 9 x 10. Had a bed, a drafting table, a television, a huge lazy boy, a thirty-six speaker sound system my dad had built and then busted up in a fit so that only *nine* of the speakers worked, and a piano. That the room was cozy and not crowded, is a testament to my prowess as a spatial genius. "It is all a wonderful illusion, a sleight of hand." That's what *The New York Times* said. Not about my room, but my trade agreement between members of the Organization of American States. It could have been about my room, though. Maybe that was the genesis, the beginning, where I learned to put things together, compromising here to make room over there and why I now spend my days traveling the globe trying to get two sides to agree on something neither one of them wants. Mostly, I've worked for companies, but for the past four years, I've worked for the Government because the President of the United States called me on the phone, himself, as I was just getting out of the shower, and asked me to serve my country. There's a lot of people in this great nation of ours who might scoff at being a public servant and giving up the lucrative private sector for a government salary, but the truth is, it's a privilege and an honor to "serve at the pleasure of the President." So, at the end of my seventeen-second conversation with the President, while I was still dripping wet, I said yes.

After an intense background and security check, an even tougher confirmation hearing, I would become the youngest cabinet member in United States history.

Four years and I don't know how many miles later, I'm still working for the man.

We hit a bit of turbulence and the seat belt sign comes on, along with the No Smoking symbol, which is useless, since smoking isn't allowed on any flight going to or coming from the U.S.

I don't smoke, never have, well, maybe I'll have a cigarette or two a year, always after getting lit at some bar.

I had to take a Turkish Air flight a few months back, which pretty much took care of my allotment of tar and nicotine for the next solar orbit. Me and Allison were the only two people on the plane that weren't smoking. Oh, there were some babies that weren't puffing on a cig, but the mother's they were breastfeeding off of were toking up a storm.

Nothing tastes better than smoked mother's milk.

I wonder what my grandfather Robert would have done to a flight attendant who dared to tell him to put out his cig. Especially a male flight attendant.

My Grampa Robert was notorious. After his eighty-third birthday, my grandmother (my second grandmother—like I said, he outlived the first by two decades), she worried he'd collapse somewhere in the street, so she decided he could no longer take his morning stroll around the neighborhood.

That must have been a constructive discussion. Her giving him all the reasons why he shouldn't, him telling her to mind her own damn business.

"The neighborhood's not the same anymore, Robert."

"Shuddup."

Him heading toward the door, feet shuffling as fast as they could. Getting there in an hour and a half.

"You're not as young as you used to be."

"Shuddup."

Ants beating him to the exit.

"You could fall and hurt yourself."

"Shuddup."

Then, in something far slower than a flash, he'd be out the door.

See, even though the neighborhood he lived in had gradually changed so that the unfavorable sections of town were beginning to encroach on his—they were within a few blocks now—my grandfather had the idea that he could still kick the shit out of any neighborhood street punks that crossed his path. In fact, he'd talk trash to them as they hung out on the corners a few blocks from his house.

Yell at them, "Get a job" and things far less subtle as he shuffled by at less than a mile an hour.

Funny thing, the punks seemed afraid of him. Oh, you'd hear an occasional, "Shut up, ol' man." But most of them just nodded to themselves, perhaps taking his sage wisdom to heart. Or more likely, knowing as everyone did, Robert had been a decorated fireman who had saved the city's long-time and current mayor's life when he was but a wee little aspiring politician.

It wouldn't be taken lightly by the cops if the mayor's savior was beaten to a pulp.

Finally, realizing that her husband was as stubborn as a jackass, and knowing that he'd try to go out whether or not he could walk, my Gramma Helen bought him one of those three-wheeled, half wheelchair, half Indy car jobs so he could tool around the neighborhood.

He was a punk's worst nightmare: an angry fossil with a lit cig in his mouth and an oxygen tube up his nose who could spew out hateful epithets at forty miles per hour.

"You lazy sons-a-bitches!"

Zoom, he was gone.

It was almost laughable. I mean, really, what the hell could they do to him? Kill him? Cut a month off his life?

Like he gave a shit.

He'd been a flyer in the war, a fireman, he'd been shot down, had buildings fall on him, had three heart attacks and two quadruple by-passes. He was sick and tired of sitting around the house all day. His only pleasures were Lucky Strikes, Mutual of Omaha's Wild Kingdom, and kicking a little ass. He wanted action. Knowing him like I do, I swear, he wanted those punks to bother him, take a shot at him just once.

But they never did.

Every once in a while, when I'm in deep with a tough one, a negotiator who's getting the best of me, I think of the old crag tooling down the sidewalk. What would gramps do? What would he say? Would this nub be beating the shit out of him?

That's when I look across the table, dead in the guy's eye and tell him, in the most diplomatic way I can:

No, no, no, and I don't give a fuck.

3

SWISS NEAR-MISS

FRANCESCA THOMAS, whose elbow is resting against mine, has been observing me observing the pretty blond Swiss Miss sans underwear. She actually hit me once somewhere over France. "I'm gonna tell your girl-friend," she said.

I handed her my satellite phone. "She'll have one question. 'Do you think the woman wants my man?' She likes to know she took a hot item off the market."

Francesca doesn't take the phone. She has no interest in telling Laura anything, except maybe, "Honey, I've stolen your man."

Ms. Thomas leans her seat back farther than mine and unconsciously touches her skirt. It's now riding up her thighs, showing the lace top of her thigh-highs.

Allison pretends not to notice, but I can see her roll her eyes.

Francesca has been with me on six missions abroad, so she knows, she knows what she's doing. She stopped wearing pantyhose after the second trip when she overheard Allison telling a very funny story at my expense. It was about Rafael Perrieux, the French negotiator, with whom I... Well, I'll get to that.

Francesca has beautiful legs and a very pretty face, but personality-wise, she's not my type. If I weren't in a serious relationship, it might be different. She and I by now would have most likely had "missionary sex" as it's called amongst the trades and dips—apt abbreviation for diplomats—who are always being sent on missions to far off lands without any chaperones. But that's all it would be. Hit and run. A little secret between you when the heat is on at the table. Nothing more.

In fact, before I began seeing Laura, I made a major pass at Francesca in Lisbon. She turned me down flat, didn't want to have anything to do with me, didn't find me attractive at all. And now that she can't have me, she flip-flops on me. Claims she was drunk that night.

I mean, what does that say about me? Inhibitions low, libido high. Still, no go.

It's easy to see how missionary sex can happen in Bangkok when you're running from hotel to hotel in the pouring rain, eating food that makes your ass feel like an entire fourth of July fireworks display has been shoved up your colon. Food like that causes your head to spin and the rain mats down pretty hair and makes dresses cling and causes lips to be so much more sensitive to a kiss.

Actually, when you really think about it, it's hard to see how missionary sex doesn't happen *more* often.

Six months ago, I took my lovely fiancée—who was simply my lovely girl-friend then—to Thailand where we were hammering out the ground rules for a new Pacific Rim agreement that won't even be negotiated for another year. Sheets of water were falling from mystical stormy skies and the Japanese assistant-sub-deputy-under-secretary to the deputy minister's aide was holding things up because he was "disturbed" by the fact that the Japanese flag would be on the far side of the "circle of flags" and not next to the United States and Chinese flags up front. That the flags, as is customary, were to be set alphabetically from the attending countries, China being first, the U.S. being last, didn't seem to matter. Japan should be up front. It's a trade super-power. I snuck out my phone, dialed the hotel and told Laura to stand on the corner by the main street market. I told her not to bring an umbrella. She started to say, "There's a monsoon going on outside," when she stopped and, I guess, remembered me telling her my thoughts on Bangkok and rain.

She would be there, wet and waiting.

I hung up the phone and put it away. The Japanese trade was still prat-tling on. Hoping to terminate the discussion—a wet woman was waiting for me—I quieted *Angrysan* when I told him that from inside the confer-ence hall, the Japanese flag would be directly in front of the main doors. And every time anyone looked out from the lobby, which was where everyone would spend hours upon hours, not just seconds walking in, they would see not the Stars and Stripes or the Red Star, but the Rising Sun.

I was out in the rain within six minutes where I picked up this sexy soaking wet American off the street and took her back to my hotel room and told her to hike up her skirt and show me her world.

THE PLANE TOUCHES down in Geneva. It's a good landing, or so the American one row up informs us as he unbuckles his seatbelt before the plane comes to a complete stop, receiving a glare from the flight attendant. He's a seasoned flyer, he continues, not just to us, but to the pretty blond Swiss Miss sans underwear. I'd like to season him and put him on a barbecue spit. He's the reason people around the world can't stand Americans. What do we look like, goofy teenagers on our first flight? I have logged the fourth most miles ever flown by an American official. And when the plane puts down in Dulles after this trip, I'll move up to third.

The American is fishing out his luggage as the plane hits the gate—literally—sending his moronic skull into the open compartment door. I can see the flight attendant giggle.

The Swiss Prime Minister is waiting for us on the tarmac at the bottom of the stairs. He's wearing a sash and looks like he has a stick up his ass.

I like the guy. I feel sorry for anybody who's forced to wear a sash.

The pretty Swiss maiden smiles at me and says, "*Bienvenue en Suisse.*" She poses at the top of the steps, then gracefully takes each step. She has my full attention all the way down.

She turns at the bottom and says goodbye to me, so sweetly, so coyly.

"*Au revoir.*"

There's another woman I will never touch, never taste, never have to pay alimony to.

Francesca bangs me in the head, knocking me out of my brief, but impressive fantasy.

She's just pissed I won't fuck her.

Not to say I don't have sex on these missions. I do. It's just "table for one." I'll be at the social gatherings they always schedule for us trades so we don't blow a fuse. I'll be well dressed, looking good. I'll be shaking hands, "How do you do?" Then forty-five minutes later, I'll be back in my hotel room using those very same, well-manicured hands to jerk off for the third time since lunch and I've still got a cocktail party and a dinner left before the night is through.

I guess other men think about sex and fucking and oiling Swiss maidens up while they milk goats in the hinterland, but Jesus Christ! enough already.

I know that I will pay for my crimes someday. Oh, I won't have to wait for God to punish me, won't have to wait till I step up to the Pearly Gates for my chastisement, no, just till my as-yet-unborn daughter hits sixteen and starts dating.

Nobody has a fucking sense of humor like God.

4

PENETRATING QUESTIONS

NOW, do you really think that when God created the Universe, he was, some fifteen billion years ago, putting in place a mechanism that would, after all these explosions and this matter crashing into that matter, eventually yield handheld satellite phones and Fizz Bang mouth candy?

I mean, the gift shop in the Intercontinental has twenty-two kinds of batteries. Hello. If there was a master plan here, all we'd need is one fucking size.

Not to say that God was wrong when he started this whole Time thing. Life is a good idea in theory.

God is kind of like Henry Ford. Henry built the Model A, gassed her up, stuck one in every driveway in America, but that doesn't mean he had any idea what your teenager is going to do with, or in the backseat of, his creation on Saturday night.

So, here we are at a pit stop in time, a quiet period, if you will, where all this matter has decided, for the moment at least, to remain relatively stable.

And what have we gotten for humanity's struggle to survive?

Civilization.

We have, what? five thousand years of recorded history? You'd think in all that time, being that sex is something of an integral part of our purpose on this planet, someone, somewhere, would have figured out how to explain it to kids so we don't run around thinking we're gonna die when these hormones coursing through our bodies turn a completely wonderful, loving child into a raving mass that breaks out, blows up, and jerks off.

There is something inherently wrong with that.

Let's take a page from my folks' sex manual, shall we?

Let me explain what my father, Keeper of the Knowledge, said to me the first time I asked him about anything to do with sex.

I was ten, just barely. I was sitting in my room, in the dark. I had, months ago, discovered that the more I pulled on this thing between my legs, the better my mood became. Pull. Pull harder. Pull some more. Good mood.

So, I'm there. Lying on the floor, feet in the air, tugging away, not really understanding what I'm doing, thinking, I must be doing permanent damage to myself, but, okay, I'll do it just a little bit more, then I'll stop, I promise. Just a little longer. Okay, in a second, I'll stop. Just one more—

And then WHAM!

The most incredible feeling washes over me. My whole body is tingling. My toes are singing *Ava Maria*, my fingers are—

Wait a second. I'm bleeding. There's blood on my stomach, I can feel it. I'm terrified now. I get up, run for the light. Shit! That's bright. My eyes recover. My body is all prickly and my head is spinning, sparkly things are whizzing past my eyes.

I finally gather the courage to look down.

There is no blood.

There is only this white, sticky, stringy liquid on my abdomen. I have no idea what it is, what I am looking at, although it looks like egg whites— ah, how close I was.

Whatever it is, my cock, which only a moment ago was very hard, is limp. I think, oh my God, I've killed my penis. I've killed my penis.

Permanent damage.

I put on a pair of underwear. I've got to talk to someone. I run up into the living room.

Thank God! my mother is lying on the couch, snoring delicately. I hear her rip one. "Excuse me," she says in her sleep.

Perfect, I can talk to the Princess alone. I head for my parents' room. The door is three-quarters shut, just the way the Princess likes it. I have to be careful, I don't want to wake my father too quickly. I'm only ten, I want to see eleven.

I open the door maybe an inch, it doesn't creak, not even a little bit.

"Jesus Christ, Mary!"

How could he even hear that?! It was like a fucking pin drop.

"It's me, dad. I need to talk to you."

He flicks on the light. His hair is at all angles, but his T-shirt is still neatly tucked into his underwear and his dark socks remain, protecting his feet from—God only knows what. He sits up and puts on his glasses.

I come over to his side of the bed, the far side, the west side, the side the Princess likes. I make the trip around the foot of the mattress, moving toward him. I'm already pulling on the elastic waistband of my Fruit of the Looms, exposing my cock to an overhead view.

He sees me, sees the worry on my face. The Princess, the ass picker, the screamer, the Fat Track destroyer, looks at me, his eyes are softer, more gentle. "What's wrong, Billy," he says to me. His voice is so smooth, mellow with the sound of sleep.

"I was..." I lie. I don't know exactly what I said, but it definitely wasn't that I was yanking on my pud because it felt good.

He swallows my lie and seems to believe it. And why shouldn't he? Who pulls on their cock except me?

I pull down my underwear so he can get a better look. Man, am I glad mom is asleep in the other room.

"What is it, dad? What happened to me?"

I touch the liquid. Almost hit him in the face with a gob of it as I lift my hand up to show him. I need an answer. I need to know if I'm going to die.

He looks at my hand, at my cock, then glances up at me again. Here it comes. The truth, the enlightenment I seek.

"It's just a strain, Billy. You strained yourself."

A strain.

I...I had strained my cock. Like I had twisted my ankle or sprained my knee. This was the sage advice, the wisdom my father bestowed upon me. For nearly the entire next year, as I continued to whack off as much and as often as possible, I lived with the colossal fear that soon the "strain" would get to be too much and I'd have to put my dick in a sling. And there I'd be, my dick strapped and bandaged to my body, harnessed like an old man in a truss, and people would point at me and say, "Oh, look he strained his little thing," and everyone would know what I had done, everyone would know my deepest secret.

But for now, it felt too good to stop. I knew someday I would have to.

Someday, the sick, twisted pleasure would come to an end. I just was hoping it wasn't soon.

I'm still waiting.

When I finally found out, months later, this was the way cocks were supposed to behave, I nearly punched my father in the face. The only thing stopping me was that at the time he was a foot and a half taller than me and weighed twice as much. I did, however—knowing now my father's unease about the subject—for a week straight, come into his room in the middle of the night, my dick in hand, saying, "I think I strained it again. Why does this keep happening?" He would fumble through lame explanations night after night, until one evening, he gave me a look that let me know he knew I was fucking with him.

A small victory.

DOES anybody ever ask our opinion? Ask us if *these* are the parents we want. Of course not.

I know there are some people in the world who are just so happy and thankful and blessed to have been given the parents they were born to, but who really cares about these Barbie and Ken dolls? They're the ones at parties who everyone else is trying to run away from. Imagine being in "It's a Small World After All" when the ride breaks down. Picture what you'd feel like after you've heard that refrain for the five-hundredth time. All I can say is, I'm glad I don't own a gun.

Listen, God sits there and shuffles the cards, and BOOM!—you're dealt what you're dealt. What you make of the hand you're given means more than anything.

And boy, did I get a pair.

Between my father's advice on strained penises and my mother's always useful recommendation, "Billy, please don't have sex," I don't know how I got out of my teens without seven kids and a raging case of V.D.

"Billy, please don't have sex."

What is that? I mean, what is any self-respecting teenage boy going to do? He's going to have sex. That's a direct challenge. You can't turn your back on shit like that.

When I give that order to my pretty sixteen-year-old daughter, there will be no "please" preceding the command, and I'll be prepared to enforce it with an electrified fence and sophisticated tracking devices.

Forget Big Brother. Big Daddy's watching.

No MATTER, after my first self-communion, my obsession with sex was cast. There was nothing either one of my parents could do.

And once I discovered there was a whole industry that would cater to my needs (I discovered this industry in the top drawer of the Princess' dresser), I set out on a quest for knowledge in the pages of these magazines and books. I would stare at the pictures of these naked women, tits and pussies staring me in the face, women who had posed with a camera focused on their bodies solely for money. I got off more than a few times to that thought alone. That these women I was leering at had stripped naked for cold, hard cash.

It made me hot.

They sounded so innocent in Playboy, not so innocent in Penthouse, and downright nasty in Hustler, Gent, and Whammies, but all of them had to know that teenage boys around the world were whacking off to the sight of their pretty little hot paid-for boxes on display.

I would say, imitating what they would proclaim loudly and freely, "Oh, fuck my pussy, fuck me, baby, just come over here so we can fuck. My pussy needs to get fucked."

I'm not sure if today's kids are luckier or not. I mean, we had someplace to go. What can you say or do now? Who can you fuck that someone might be shocked? Your mother? Been done before. Your father? Been seen on Oprah. Twice last year.

It's the coming of a new age, and it's a bit scary. If you think the Baby Boomers are bored with middle age because they've done it all, wait till my generation or the one after that hits their Golden Years. What's it going to be like in a hundred years? Can a cunt-cam live from inside the vagina of the hottest pop singer be far away on MTV.com?

Here's Venus singing the remake, "I Can't Get No Satisfaction."

Well, of course, she can't with that camera shoved up her twat.

Listen to me now, you'd think I was this vulgar all my life. The truth is, I just don't care as much anymore what other people think.

For years, being the polite, non-sexist, locker room-talk-hating, woman lover that I am, I wouldn't say any of these "dirty" things to a real female. Then as I got older and dared to utter a little spicy attribute, I found that women wanted to be pushed up against the wall, have their hair pulled...and get this...SPANKED...spanked? Who would have thought that? All that crap about respect and tenderness and wanting a sensitive man and I run into more than a few, no, more than a lot of women who liked it on the ass at least once or twice during a session.

The more you love, honor and cherish a woman, the more dirty, nasty, sex-crazed things you can do to her.

It's weird but true.

Nice girls who turn bad behind closed doors.

Although, you must be aware that at any moment, at any given time, the woman you're tying to the bedpost may look up at you and say, "Sometimes, I just wanna be *held*."

THE RIDE from the airport is relatively routine. I'm shuttled to a late model Mercedes limousine along with Allison, my bodyman, and Francesca, who gets the privilege because she's one of my deputies. The rest of the team and the balance of the security detail are loaded into several identical vans, if you can call them that. These European-designed vehicles seemingly lack the size and structure that would allow them to survive anything but a low-speed crash with a small Fiat.

Think VW Bus without all the luxurious trimmings.

The conversation in the back of the car is hushed and casual and none of it directed at me. I'm poring over research and analytics.

One of my concerns about the current draft of the trade agreement, which is thousands of pages long, is the issue of cross-market pricing. There are two main problems.

One is cost-shifting.

Say a multinational corporation builds dishwashers in the U.S. However, they import the water pump from a subsidiary in Mexico.

The water pump, which actually costs three dollars to build, is sold to the American subsidiary for thirty dollars.

Since the multinational corporation is really paying itself, they've moved profit out of America and into Mexico, where corporate taxes are lower.

It can work the opposite way. This time the dishwasher is built in

Mexico. The computerized control panel costs thirty dollars to make in the U.S. but is sold to the subsidiary in Mexico for three dollars.

Again, profit has been shifted out of the country with the higher taxes.

Even worse, companies use these figures to argue to American workers that they need wage and benefit concessions to cut labor costs because they're not making any money.

The other problem is *Grey Marketing*.

Corporations, for legitimate reasons, price their products lower in poorer countries, everything from cameras to pharmaceuticals. Sometimes the products are exported out of and then back into the same country. It's cheaper to buy American-made drugs in Canada than it is in the States. I'm determined to address the issue in the trade agreement before this problem becomes an epidemic.

Pretty fucking interesting stuff, huh?

Well, kids, it paid for that comfy crib you're sleeping in, so get ready to hear a whole lot more of Dad's ramblings.

As I STEPPED out of the back of the car, ahead of Francesca, ahead of Allison, but after my body man, I could see the trades marching in and out of the hotel, their game faces so fixed, so determined that a casual observer might not notice the stench of fear emanating from them. That smell would only become worse once the real bargaining started.

These trades cared too much about the outcome to ever be of any real use to their homelands and their people. It's sad, but the most inexperienced negotiators often come from the places that need the most help.

"Have you written the speech?" Allison asked as we headed toward the loud gathering of protestors arcing across the Intercontinental's portico.

I tapped my head. "It's all right up here."

"So you're saying you haven't written it."

"No, I'm saying it's in my head. Percolating."

"Okay, Mr. Coffee, you're giving the speech *tonight* and you've got sessions all day."

"I've had a lot on my mind."

"Yeah, I know, she wasn't wearing any underwear. Try to keep it in your pants."

"You know, I am a member of the Cabinet. Show some respect." I lowered my voice. "At least in public."

"*Try* to keep it in your pants," she suddenly took on a tone of deep respect, "Mr. Ambassador."

"Much better, thank you. And I keep it in my pants."

"Really? Can I just say...Rafael Perrieux."

"*Seriously*, I have enough on my mind."

Allison understood and dropped it.

We were escorted by my Secret Service detail past the protestors shouting conveniently pat slogans and waving anti-globalization signs.

I needed to forget about Laura and marriage and kids and beautiful women without panties and focus on my job, on what I came here to do. And I did...for three seconds. Till I saw—among the swaying "People Not Profits" and "Earth Not 4 Sale" placards—one protestor holding up a banner that said, "*Our Children Are Our Future!*"

I actually went out of my way to scream at him. "That's what I'm afraid of!"

MY BODY MAN POLITELY, but firmly, re-aimed me for the door, and like passing through an inter-dimensional portal, I moved from one world to another, into an environment wholly unlike the scene outside.

The atmosphere inside the hotel was just as charged with energy as the street, but it was not one of anger, but of anticipation, nervousness.

The lobby was filled with people, most in Western business suits, but some in traditional dress native to their countries.

I stood there, watching for maybe a second or two, although it seemed much longer, and the feeling I got was like those moments just before a highly anticipated boxing match. The last-minute preparations. The VIPs and their entourages. And finally, that very human mix of excitement and apprehension that comes from knowing you're probably going to see some blood.

The difference was that, here, there wasn't going to be a brawl between two large, sweaty, brooding men in a ring. This would be a fight between at least a half-dozen political heavyweights that spilled out into the crowd, into every corner of the hotel, and even into the street.

When I thought about it, it seemed more like professional wrestling. At any second, you might be surprised by a folding chair to the back of the head.

Immediately, I felt at home.

· · ·

ONE OF THE negotiators for the U.S. in Geneva—actually the current permanent (I love that oxymoron) U.S. envoy to GATT, Tom Bowman, a guy who's been one of my best friends for years, long before I began working for the President—walked up to me and firmly shook my hand.

"Welcome, Mr. Ambassador," he said to me formally, deferentially, mostly for those watching and the press that were taking pictures and video, but also with a hint of friendly needling.

Tom was older, more distinguished, more experienced in government-to-government negotiations, yet significantly less powerful than his younger friend. Even though he presided over the day-to-day operations at GATT for the U.S. delegation, I drove the policy.

I knew it annoyed him from time to time, but he never let it intrude on our friendship.

"Tom," I said, just as formally, voice deeper, handshake firmer than normal, as a few pictures were snapped.

Through a pleasant and well-practiced smile, he muttered under his breath, "Why is Laura calling me, asking me how tall I am?"

One of my last memories of Laura before leaving on this trip was watching her cut out paper figures, writing the names of people she wanted and those she thought I wanted to be in the wedding party, and arranging them by height.

I grumbled, "Later," through a smile.

The first session with the top negotiators present—my peers, not Tom's—was mostly a rehashing of the last eight years of the Uruguay Round. Like we needed that.

I looked around at the men and women with whom I'd soon do battle. And I wondered, what had they learned over the years? What strategies were they preparing?

I had a professor at college, Andrew Beckett, a Brit actually, who was at the time, the preeminent authority on international trade. The man who coined the term "Win-Win."

I remember sitting in my dorm room at Wesleyan reading through his book, which shaped my beliefs tremendously. Read it not once, but three times.

This dense, six-hundred-page treatise would become the foundation of American trade policy for over twenty years. Filled with ideas on every aspect of trade, it was sprinkled throughout with his rules for negotiating.

He was proud of his work and quoted from it often.

"Compromise is the only way to guarantee an outcome," he'd say, tapping his index finger on the lectern. "Know the consequences of your actions before taking them." Another of his favorites.

Like many established professors, he'd interject these tidbits into the lecture as if they'd been born right there before your eyes out of the spontaneous discourse. You could almost believe he was having a thoughtful, living, breathing exchange of ideas, even though he had said these exact words, in the exact way, countless times before.

"Demonstrate your care about the other party's needs."

But of all his viewpoints, the axiom he most often cited—this in reference to the power of America—was, "The biggest stick is sometimes the hardest to wield."

One afternoon, I strolled into his third-floor office overlooking the grassy quad filled with students, and slammed *Good For All: Achieving the Win-Win Scenario* on his desk. The sound of the book slapping the wood top made a satisfying echo in the hall outside his cramped office.

It wasn't an unprovoked attack. He had called me his best student in class that day. And I thought it was time to clearly dispel that notion.

"*That* right there," I said, pointing to his book, which did not move, even though he stared at it as though it might, "is the reason we're getting our asses kicked in global trade by countries the size of Rhode Island!"

He swept up his shock, then calmly glanced at me with the gaze of someone to whom Presidents have listened.

"We are the shopping cart for the world," he said.

"What?" I said. Shouted really. "What the hell does that even mean?"

He started to open his mouth, but I had heard or read everything he had to say on this subject, and I tapped hard on the book in the way he tapped on his podium. Whatever words were about to come out of his mouth got swallowed.

"Listen, you can fail me. You can kick me out of class. You can write me up to the Dean. But I'm not going to have you tell me that *this*," again tapping hard on the book cover, "is what I should believe."

I had been about to walk out. I didn't need or want to show him up anymore, or arrogantly tell him what I already instinctively knew, that his ideas had paralyzed U.S. trade. But he couldn't let me go. Couldn't let his prize pupil out the door without one last lesson.

"Then you will have failed to learn from the past."

I stopped and turned back, glancing at the book.

"That *is* the past."

I went to class. Kept quiet. Used the time to develop my own theories on global trade. I answered his multiple-choice tests "correctly," adding addendums like, "if we want to become the whipping post of the world" or "in order to lose the trade war" onto the answers. In the essay book on my final, I wrote the words, "WHY YOU ARE WRONG" at the top and used the rest of the pages to debunk every one of Beckett's theories.

I didn't share these thoughts with the rest of the class, not because I was afraid of being ganged up on or that I'd lose the debate. I didn't breathe a word because, I thought, why tell these fairly smart, well-connected classmates of mine what's right when I might very well be on the other side of the table from them at some point in the future.

Which, in fact, I have been on several occasions.

Instead, I made up my own rules.

I say, *Compromise is no way to win an argument.*

I say, *If you wait until you know the true consequences of your actions, somebody else has made all the money.*

I say, *If you care too much about anything, your opponent will use it against you.*

I say, *Somebody's got to get hit with the big stick before everybody else is afraid of it.*

The Japanese have a saying, "Business is war."

If that's true, and I believe it is, then trade negotiations are peace talks conducted with bullets whizzing overhead.

I have one week to figure this all out.

Technically we're supposed to be voting the agreement up or down in three days—we'll blow through that deadline like we've blown through the previous dozen. The *real* deadline is in five days. Around dawn here in Geneva. That's when the law that grants the President, *my* president, Fast Track authority to negotiate trade agreements sunsets. Every person here knows, if we don't have a deal signed and submitted by Sunday 11:59:59 P.M. Eastern Standard Time, the U.S. Congress gets involved.

And if that happens, it could be a year or more before we get this close again.

But I said one week, didn't I? Seven days. Well, two days after that, Laura and I will be joining her five best friends and their recently acquired husbands in Hawaii. By dinner that first night, whether or not I've gotten her a ring and asked her *properly*, she's gonna announce the secret she's been impatiently keeping at my behest for fourteen days and counting. That she and I are getting married and will soon be passing on our fears, idiosyncrasies, and bad habits to another generation of humans.

So, to recap, I have a week to settle the most important, complex, and dangerous negotiations ever attempted, that is, the when, where, and how much it's going to cost (and I don't just mean monetarily) of getting married to Laura. And the even more important side agreement detailing the if, when, and *why* of having children.

Oh, and I need to basically get the entire world to agree to a comprehensive, binding trade agreement, which every country really, really wants as long as they don't have to be the ones to open up *their* borders too much.

"SEVEN DAYS," I said out loud, surprising myself and a few others sitting near us at the table.

"Five days," Allison whispered in my ear, correcting me.

"I know," I mouthed.

She shot me a worried look. Climbing off her chair that was just slightly behind me, she crouched down between me and Tom and pretended to hand me several important papers which were just her list of things to do. Most of which were variations of *Get BG To Do _____* .

Get BG to Write Speech.

Get BG to Read Latest Draft.

Get BG to Call...

You get the idea. Apparently, BG is a difficult person.

"What?" she said as she leaned in. It wasn't so much a question as it was a demand. Tom tried his best to appear like he wasn't listening.

"It's nothing." I paused. "It's just..." Another awkward moment passed, then I added, "Laura."

"What about Laura?" she asked, more worried now. Each word separate and distinct.

"Nothing. It's nothing." I glanced along the table, somebody from some insignificant country was speaking. I then turned back to Allison, lowering my voice further. "Just...apparently, we've been fucking this whole year for no apparent reason. Now, she legally has to have one."

She opened her mouth to speak, but several members of the Japanese delegation were staring at her.

"Of course, sir," she said, then slipped quietly back to her chair.

I had a pretty good idea what Allison was thinking. I could feel it on the back of my head, burning into my skull.

I know I said I didn't care what people thought about me. That's not altogether true. I'm just saying that living in fear of how someone might regard you or what might happen if you took a chance, or said something a little edgy in bed or at the bargaining table...well, it just smothers the spontaneity, the beauty of life.

I make decisions for a living. That's what I do.

I take risks. And sometimes I'm wrong. Sometimes I fail, horribly. But I don't fear making mistakes. You can't live that way.

In fact, I'd venture to say that no one who is King or Queen of their mountain, whether it be a business person, a basketball player, a race car driver, a politician, an entertainer, or even a trade negotiator, believes that Fear is their friend. Except when you make other people feel it.

Oh, a certain amount of fear is good, keeps you sharp, but I'm talking about the kind of fear that acts like an anchor.

It's a lesson that doesn't come easy. You usually have to pay for it, have to lose something special before you fully understand. I know I did.

The trick is not beating yourself up too much, spending so much time on self-recrimination that you fail to learn from the mistake.

A fool isn't someone who does foolish things. A fool is someone who doesn't learn from the foolish things he's done.

I've been a fool many times.

On occasion, I've learned from it.

One summer night, a night so long ago, yet less than half my life away, I was schooled about fear and not taking chances.

I was taking some summer courses at Wesleyan University on economic politics, trying to make up for my less-than-stellar high school transcript with some college credits. So far, every school I applied to—including Wesleyan—had said, "Great SATs, wonderful essays, but geez, do you really think college is right for you?"

I spent three hours a day trying to answer that question.

I did extremely well in the class, even though I was working a full-time job. I chalk up my success in college to the lack of any real authority figures to rail against—no principals, no teachers who cared if I applied myself or not. It's a quirk in my personality: a contempt for any authority that demands my respect without earning it.

I guess I stood out because the dean of the economics department came by one day and encouraged me to apply to Wesleyan. "I already have," I said, "and was told that perhaps a state school would be better."

He told me he couldn't get me into the school, but he could get me set up as a non-degree undergraduate. I'd have to work hard and I'd be limited in the credits I could bring over if I ever got full admission, but it would get me a foot in the door.

But this was before that.

Wesleyan University has a well-known Summer Arts program that brings together young actors, writers, dancers, and artists who share their talents with each other in a way that helps them see art as a whole, and not just as words on a page or apples in a still life.

An acquaintance of mine from high school had written an existential play, where all the characters were dressed and made up as avant-garde clowns. Within the play were three distinct acts. Separate stories, different settings, different genres. But the characters throughout all of them had the same relationship to each other. He had developed it further at the Summer program. It was to be the grand finale of the big Arts Festival Night they put on at the end of the summer session. One day, the guy I knew stopped me on campus and asked if I would play one of the parts. I was shocked and flattered. I mean, there were so many actors in the session. Why not them, why me, a trade-in-training?

"Because the role is sort of based on your dad," he said.

This guy had been to my house a few times, seen my dad in rare form maybe once or twice. I was amazed my father had made so strong an impression on him.

I agreed immediately.

I remember the play, remember the character of the "Father Figure" with the permanently arched brow (ah, make-up). My friend didn't have it right—my father—how could he? He wasn't the man's son.

But it was still fun, and I threw in a few of my father's signature mannerisms—picking his ass, eyes peering over his glasses, the distracted, faraway gazes whenever he wasn't directly involved in a conversation—that made the thing play even funnier.

I had no idea what I was doing, but when the lights went up that summer night, we were all in a zone. Sometimes that happens, where you're in a moment, where things around you seem to move in slow motion, where you can lazily take the time to soak up all the details and still have plenty of time to react. Like when you see a glass fall off a table and you get your hand under it before it hits the ground.

We clicked. And the audience loved it.

Of course, they would. They were actors and writers and dancers and artists.

After the play, everyone was milling around on the lawn surrounding the stage, sharing some food and desserts, saying their last goodbyes to the friends they had made over the summer.

And somehow, some way, I don't have any idea how, one of the top five smartest, wittiest, most beautiful people I have ever met, strolled up and started talking to me.

I don't remember her name exactly, maybe because it's too painful. Jenna or Claire, I think.

We ended up talking on the grass for two and a half hours.

She was a dancer with stunning legs, a beautiful body, and a great smile. She sat in front of me, her legs spread out completely. She was stretching as we were talking, of course. It seemed as natural as breathing for her.

We talked about acting (she liked the play). We talked about parents (her father was just like that). We talked about politics and dancing and dating and all that.

And then, when the night was through, and the last people were packing up to leave, she kissed me on the mouth and gave me her phone number on a torn-off scrap from a paper cup, then walked into the darkness to her awaiting chariot, which was a '74 Pinto, if I recall.

I went home that night, put the fragment of paper cup entrusted with her number on my desk by the phone, then climbed under the covers and dreamed about Jenna/Claire, dreamed about walking with her on the cool grass, hearing her laugh when I told a joke, then watching her dance underneath me in bed.

For three weeks I stared at that number, trying to figure out why she had given it to me. Surely, it wasn't for a date. Her? With me?

For three weeks, I didn't call.

When I finally did gather the courage to dial her number, she was so fucking pissed at me, she nearly hung up the phone. She couldn't believe that I hadn't called, after all that had passed between us on the lawn, after all we had talked about.

She was so mad at me. Just completely ripped.

"I thought you were dead! Or at least lying in a coma somewhere unable to reach a phone, unable to speak. Because that was the only way I could believe you wouldn't call me!" After a few more chastisements, her voice grew softer. She told me she had really liked me. "I really thought we connected."

"I did, too," I told her.

"Then why didn't you call?"

I had no answer. Because the truth was too embarrassing. That I didn't think it was possible for a girl like her to like me. That I thought she might laugh at me when I suggested we see a movie or something. That I was terrified to pick up the phone and dial seven little numbers.

"I was waiting for my phone to ring. Not sitting by it, but every night when I came in, I'd ask my mom, 'Did a Billy call?'"

But there were never any calls from a Billy.

She and I talked for six hours on the phone. We clicked even more that night than the night on the grass. Every fiber in my body told me this girl was something special. Something very special indeed.

Which made it even worse.

About a week before I called she had met someone else. Someone who "called me back," as she put it so gently and yet with the force of a bat to the head. And as much as she really, *really* liked me—did she have to stress that word till it nearly snapped?—she wanted to "see how things would go with him." It was only fair to him, she said.

I told her, "I thought we clicked."

"We did."

"We *do*."

"We do."

"Then, then why are you going with him?" I asked, hoping to plead my case.

"Because he took the chance and made the call."

I HAVE on occasion punted and not gone the extra mile to win a woman or a contract or a trade point. I've occasionally not dialed a number I've been given, for a million reasons, mostly because I wasn't really interested enough in the person on the other end of the line. But I have never, ever, from that day forward ever not went for a woman, or a job or anything I really wanted simply because I was afraid of not getting it. Never.

Don't get me wrong. I'm not saying I always get what I want. I've been turned down by more women, in more countries than I care to admit. I've lost contracts, gotten my ass kicked at the bargaining table. But at least I try. Hockey great Wayne Gretzky once said you miss one hundred percent of the shots you don't take.

I think about Jenna/Claire now and then. And not in some longing, regretful way, but in...a sort of...awe, because that one missed opportunity that would have been so very fun, so amazing at the time, has saved me from missing out on almost every great thing in my life, from my career to my relationships to asking Laura out for a date, knowing she was one of the most sought after, most eligible women in D.C., and way out of my league.

If Jenna/Claire only knew the effect she's had on my existence.

5

RAFAEL, THE ETERNAL FLAME-OUT

I WAS WRONG.

The Intercontinental Gift Shop has only twenty-*one* types of batteries. It's run out of the AAA size that I need to power my digital voice recorder, a device that I can't seem to live without (I still haven't finished "writing" my speech). However, if I had the need to power up a Russian pacemaker, I could get that battery.

Fresh from not finding a suitable power source, I find Rafael Perrieux gliding across the lobby, her elegant, perfect dress flowing behind her. She's thought of this outfit for days, planned it out to the last detail, hosiery, jewelry, lipstick. She's been trying to get me to notice her. Only the joke's on her because I've been noticing her since the day we met. Rafael is France's lead negotiator. She and I once had two weeks of unbelievable sex, passion and arguing several years ago when I wanted to end a relationship I was in and she wanted to export more wine.

We both got what we wanted and a little more.

When Vanessa, the woman I was dating, found out I had slept with Rafael, she picked up the TV—I swear—and threw it at me. It was still on. The last thing I remember before the screen knocked me in the head was Vanna White turning six "T"s on the puzzle of a famous song. And as I slipped into unconsciousness, I realized it was "The Night The Lights Went Out in Georgia."

As well as the night my lights went out in Georgetown.

I didn't press charges, of course, partly because the nurse at the hospital stared at me as if I was one of those guys who gets shot or cut or beaten by a woman fighting back after years of abuse, and mostly because it'd be in the papers. But I did send her my portion of the hospital bill. Which she paid with the note, "*best money I ever spent.*"

I don't think I've ever ended a relationship cleanly. Don't think I've ever had this conversation:

"You know, *Blank*, I really haven't been happy these past few *blanks*, and I think that maybe we should stop seeing each other."

"No! Billy, I love you. And I promise, I'll try harder."

"*Blank*, I can't. It's not going to work. We're not right for each other. We see things very differently. You never want to *blank*, and I always do."

"I mean it, Billy, I'll let you *blank* anytime you want."

"I'm sorry, *Blank*, it's over."

"I understand."

Never, not once. They usually sound more like...well, like the sound of a crowded street market in New Delhi as it's trying to scurry out of the path of a runaway train.

EVEN THOUGH I'VE been in a relationship for over a year, the longest monogamous liaison I've ever had, even now, engaged, successful, and apparently on my way to having children (sorry kids), I look out my window when I'm driving or over at the Swiss Miss in the next aisle when I'm flying and see a female leg showing just a bit too much skin or the hint of a bra and that caveman instinct takes over. I want to touch, need to touch that sweet creamy skin. There are times when I'm talking to a beautiful woman when she makes it clear that I could go back to her room with her and do anything my little head desires.

But I don't.

Because when it comes to women, I'm like an alcoholic. Having a drink every once in a while isn't really gonna hurt anyone. But one drink leads to another, leads to another, leads to having another drink thrown into your face.

So, I must repress two million years of evolution. Subvert the bad boy lurking beneath this pleasant exterior. It's as difficult as it is surprisingly easy. The two sides waging war inside me, canceling each other out. At least, that's what I tell myself as I masturbate while thinking about the cute waitress at the Denny's by the airport who served me two eggs and some sausage.

Over easy, baby. Over easy.

It's true, I get to travel all over the world and sit next to pretty women who find me interesting and incredibly understanding. "Yes, I'm responsible for the current trade pact with the EC." "Me? Just getting back from the G-Seven Summit in Tokyo." "Why yes, I do believe some trade barriers need to be maintained in developing countries." And if they have any idea of what the hell I'm talking about, they usually lean forward and, unconsciously, of course, show a bit more leg or cleavage or smile, something to reaffirm my decision those several years ago to stick my head up my ass and become a dual poli-sci/economics major. Of course, I did have a third major in college—women's studies. Something I still seem to be majoring in, even though, like I said, I no longer pull my pencil out during tests.

P.S. I have standing orders from Laura that if I *am* going to have sex with another woman in a far-off land, I have to call her so she can listen in. I'm told this would be a turn-on for her because she knows I don't love another woman even if I might love another woman's body. The thought makes her hot, and she tells me this every so often, followed seconds later, minutes later, hours later, by a tectonic-level orgasm. I also realize that my fiancée understands how much I hate phone companies, hate to give them one cent more of my money than is absolutely necessary. I suspect she knows I would be thinking the entire time about how much the call is costing me and never really enjoy what I'm doing, which would be fucking a beautiful woman in an exotic locale.

The woman is brilliant.

AND IT'S NOT like the feminine sex doesn't have issues of their own. Women find a nice guy, a friend, a partner, and they dream of being conked on the head, dragged back to the bedroom, and wildly fucked so hard it hurts to walk the next day. Rewind one million years.

Or take the other side: A woman goes with her instincts, finds a strong, hair-pulling Neanderthal, and after a few years, she starts fantasizing about the short, timid guy in accounting who brings her coffee in the morning and remembers her birthday with flowers and a card.

Remember, sometimes she just wants to be *held.*

We are, without a doubt the only species on the planet that can't simply enjoy what we have.

One of my fellow trades spent six years pursuing his wife to the exclusion of almost everything else in his life and now that he has her, he's cheated on her five times with women who look exactly, and I mean, exactly, like her. He actually said to me in all seriousness when I questioned him about this, "A person's gotta have *variety*."

Well, I guess...

If you call a six-pack of beer variety because you're drinking from different bottles.

For humans to find stability, we have to change. We have to inflict change on others. Tell me the last time the elephant changed. It eats, it sleeps, it charges. Pretty much that's what it's been doing for the last ten thousand years. And, until we slaughter every last one of them because we think it's really neat to have some yellowed carving sitting on our mantle, that's what they'll be doing for the next ten thousand years.

RAFAEL IS a thorn in Laura's pretty little side. The one person for whom her "Reach Out and Touch Someone" speech does not apply, no matter how big the phone bill.

It has little to do with my having fucked Rafael. If Laura were agitated by former lovers, we'd have to emigrate from D.C. and move to Idaho. And it has nothing to do with the fact that seemingly wherever I am, there Rafael is. It's her job. We run in the same circles.

No, it has to do with Rafael herself.

See, Rafael hasn't learned the boundaries most women seamlessly and unmistakably erect between old flames burned down to old friends. Her hand could as easily be on my thigh as on her fork during a working dinner break. It's harmless to the French, whose national pastime seems to be fucking those-to-whom-they-are-not-betrothed. They think we're underdeveloped and childish and lack passion. Maybe so. But at least we bathe.

Anyway, it's moved way beyond using her feminine wiles to wriggle a few extra deal points out of me. She knows me better than that. If she was to depend on getting me to capitulate because I was going to get a little sex on the side, she might come up on the short end of the stick, so to speak.

Well, not that short.

It's something personal with Rafael now. Not personal in that way that personal might mean something—love, lust, passion, or any of that. No, not that. There's a component of pleasure-seeking to it, for sure, but it's getting me to give in to her, to cave on our agreement, to surrender Laura for even one moment. Because it's not like I couldn't slip my hand under her airy skirt, flip it up, and slide myself into that pretty body that I know inside and out. I've been there before. The borders, like with Canada, are mostly unpatrolled when it comes to old lovers. And it's not like I've hated her hand on my leg after a long day battling it out over wheat, wine, and what constitutes domestic content.

Tom smiles as he sees Rafael strutting for me. A few months ago, when this conspicuous assault by Rafael began, I found myself alone back in her hotel suite and maybe six minutes from ground zero before I got my wits about me. I told Tom about the incident, which was innocent at the same time it was nearly cataclysmic, and he said, "Billy, when you play with matches in a room full of open barrels of gasoline, don't be surprised when you blow yourself up."

Tom is a wise and learned man, much more mature than the few years he has on me. He's the guy who hammers out the fine details after I've blown into town, carved out a general framework, and hopped on a jet to another hot spot. He'll also most likely be appointed the first U.S. Ambassador to the Multilateral Trade Organization or GATT II or whatever the hell we'll call it—we're still negotiating the damn name—that is, if we ever get this thing signed.

"*Bonjour*, Billy," she says with that lovely accent of hers. "How are you?"

"Good, Rafael."

She kisses my cheek, first the right, then the left, then the right again.

"You look nice."

"*Merci bien*."

She has dressed perfectly for me. Not like Francesca who had gotten all the pieces right but just didn't put them all together correctly.

No, Rafael has nailed it, and she knows it.

"How've you been?" I ask.

"Verrrri gud, Billiee. I was excited for a week knowing you would be here."

I'm human, my heart skips a beat at the thought of her anticipating my arrival.

"I'm looking forward to hammering things..." I stop, my mind freezes. All my professional trade responses are sounding like cheap sexual innuendo in my head.

She looks at me and knows. She just smiles.

It's going to be a long week.

"Perhaps, one evening we could enjoy," she says gazing at me with those perfect eyes I used to stare into for hours, "a bite to eat."

A long, long, long, long week.

6

THE INTERCONTINENTAL, ROOM 631

I GET up to my room relatively unscathed. Just a few inappropriate touches that I'll forgive.

I fall back onto the bed. God, I hate hotel beds. What do they make these things out of? Recycled cardboard, old Q-tips and shredded secret documents?

There's a movement in the hotel industry: luxury beds, more comfortable than anything a normal person could afford. This region of Switzerland isn't part of that movement.

My bags have been brought up, opened, my suits have been hung in the armoire. The rest of my clothes have been neatly placed into drawers. Americans live in such a self-service, do-it-yourself world, we've lost the ability to graciously accept hospitality. It took me a couple of trips to Geneva before I felt comfortable with having someone rummage through my things. First time, didn't go so smoothly.

"What are you doing?"

"I yam putting your bags away, *Monsieur.*"

"Do I look like I'm an invalid?"

A long pause.

"I gave the last of my cash to the porter. All I've got are traveler's checks."

"It's a pleasure to serve you, *Monsieur.*"

"Oh."

I felt like such an asshole that I asked the guy to have a drink with me from the minibar, which made him think I was trying to pick him up. He told me to call Franz in maintenance to get help with my problem.

I was ignorant. I was green. But at the time, I had less than a half a million frequent flier miles, just about all of it in the States, and I had been burned so many times by "service staff" in places like New York City who pick up your bags, move them six feet, then stand there with their hand out waiting for a gratuity. And then roll their eyes if you give them anything less than a five. That's eighty-three cents a foot, or ten dollars a minute. The federal minimum wage for an entire hour is $4.25.

I actually stayed in a hotel in Florida where one guy parked my car for me, brought me back my keys (sort of *like* a valet, only they park your car, but you have to go get it when you leave, having no fucking idea where they put it). Tip. Another guy took my bags from where I was standing stupidly holding my keys, and brought them to the front desk. Tip. Still another brought the bags, and me, up to the room. Tip.

I had to find an ATM on the way to my Goddamn room.

Such hospitality. I felt like I was serving them.

I've since made it a point to understand local norms wherever I go because when it comes to tipping, or greetings, or how close you stand, or how loud you speak, it's a mishmash of traditions and expectations.

It's one of the difficulties with getting everyone to reach a consensus on trade practices. We have different ways of doing things.

There are places that tip, and places that bribe.

By the way, it's not that you never tip in Europe. It's just that the price of your *filet mignon* actually *includes* the cost of the waiter bringing it to you.

Europeans go to a restaurant and want to be left alone. I go to a restaurant and get annoyed if the waiter doesn't check on me every five minutes to see if I want something—because I usually do—*but* I get totally weirded out if I can't pump my own gas.

Perhaps, it's the last vestige of the hunter mentality.

I was in Manchester, England a few months ago and had to stop for "petrol" along one of the "motorways." Not only was I, and everyone else around me, driving on the wrong side of the bloody road, but when I pulled up to the pump, there wasn't one of those "insert and remove your card quickly" gadgets, which have, thank God, eliminated all human contact with service station employees.

I stared at the pump for I-don't-know-how-long, vainly trying to find something to stick my Visa card into.

I had no idea what to do.

Suddenly, from out of—where, I don't know, one of those bullet-proof sound booths?—this goofy-looking English lad came over and asked, "Whaddaya wont mate?"

Hamburger. A Budweiser. What do you think I want?

"Gas," I stammered. "Um, Petrol...*Fuel*."

" 'ow many Quid?"

Fucking speak English!

I mean, didn't we kick the shit out of you a couple hundred years ago? Speak our language, Goddammit!

"Just fill it."

"Aw-ight."

As he pumped the fuel into my rental car, the last great English car, the Volkswagen Golf, I stood there, leaning against the VW, watching him work. I had no use for myself. I was a redundant system. I felt even more stupid because in America, if you can't pump your own gas, you're either a rich pompous ass, handicapped, dressed for a wedding, live in New Jersey, or a complete loser.

When I looked down, I could plainly see I didn't have on a tux, nor was I in a wheelchair, nor was in the somewhat misleadingly named Garden State, nor was my bank account likely to make me a candidate for the Forbes 400, so that left...oh, yeah, loser.

There is zero reason I need to have some bloke run the pump for me. I'll let you in on a little secret. I've never been with a prostitute. Why? I don't like paying anyone to do anything I can do myself.

The President said, "a great American," just remember that.

SINCE EVERYONE'S been so busy doing everything for me except the one thing I need them to do, which is, find me some AAA batteries so I can listen to my notes and write the speech I should've completed before I left D.C., I have nothing to do.

I look for the ubiquitous pen and paper set. It takes me about two seconds to find it. By the phone, on the desk.

It wasn't hard. All hotel rooms are the same. You can go halfway around the world and the only tenable difference you can find is the language on the paper strip they wrap your toilet seat in so you can feel confident that it has absolutely been "Sanitized For Your Protection."

Most hotels, especially the bigger ones, bolt the headboard to the wall —like I'm gonna steal that—and have maids that knock on your door regardless of what the sign on the handle says, KNOCK KNOCK KNOCK "Hozkeping," because wherever maids come from *Privacy Please* means *Come Right in and Vacuum as Loud as You Can While I'm Trying to Sleep.* Most hotels still cover the beds with spreads in annoying floral or geometric patterns to hide semen stains more easily. Walk into a room with a black light and you'll be walking right back out. Doesn't matter where you go, there it is.

Only thing you can say is, the ritzier the accommodations, the more likely that sperm has a trust fund.

I'm in one of the most picturesque cities in the world. I could be in Cleveland for all I know.

So, I sit back on the bed in the...

...yeah...the Geneva Intercontinental...and I try to scribble down some ideas, but all I can think of is the woman at Bellina's who, except for maybe Laura, is the one mostly to blame for all this ranting and raving.

Learn from the past. Yeah, right.

"HEY, SWEETS, I MISS YOU," I coo into the phone.

"Who is she?" Laura asks.

"What?"

"I had a vision of you staring at someone on the flight over."

"I thought you like it when I check out other women."

"No, I like it when other women check *you* out."

"She wasn't wearing any underwear, honey, I couldn't help it."

The *I couldn't help it defense* has a long and distinguished history among men of every age, era, color, and culture. Women are always getting on us when we use this argument. "You can't help it? You have a brain, don't you?"

"Well, ah, duh...I dunno."

"I mean one with *some* impulse control."

Actually, I find it ironic that women dismiss our *innocent by reason of hormones defense* so easily. Especially since women have been trying for centuries to get men to forgive the emotional roller coaster most females inflict on their mating partners, the bad moods, the comments about our friends, and so on and so forth because, *"It's that time of the month."*

I mean, didn't a woman get acquitted of *murder* because she had a bad case of PMS?

I happen to think that me having sex with another woman—never mind just gawking at her on a plane—is a crime far lower on the sentencing scale than killing another human because you ran out of Midol.

"You're saying I'm moody?"

"Oh, no honey...not you."

There's a moment where all I can hear is the pale static of an international call, the hissing silence made longer by the delay in the distance between us. Then Laura lets out one of her cute little laughs. When she speaks, her voice has a warmer tone.

"Well, I'm glad to hear you had a pleasurable flight."

"Yeah, well, it was just a glimpse."

"That's too bad," she says, genuinely.

She pauses. A package is slipped under the door and I go over to retrieve it.

"I miss you," she adds as I flip through the contents of the envelope. Inside are transcripts of wiretaps and surveillance audio of several of my fellow trades all marked TOP SECRET. The words of the Japanese minister, EU officials, and several others are here. I have to assume they're trying to listen in on me right now.

"Me too, baby. Very much. Although, I'm glad you didn't come. It's gonna get nasty around here before we're through."

"Well, we're gonna have a whole week together in Hawaii to relax. I can't wait to tell everyone."

"Mmmmhuh."

Six and a half days and counting.

More items marked For Eyes Only, Classified, Confidential, boring, boring, boring. Then I come to the last few pages. TOP SECRET is handwritten on them with a large question mark at the end. Definitely Allison's hand.

As I flip the page, I leave the CIA and enter *Bride Magazine* in the form of several washed-out pictures of bridesmaids' dresses.

"Did you get my fax?" Laura asks.

I would bet money she's already spoken to Allison to confirm its receipt.

"I know you've got a lot on your mind, but I really liked the platinum ones."

They all look platinum after squeezing into the fax machine and getting screeched through the international phone cable.

Allison, doing what she does, getting me everything and anything I could ever need to make a decision, has ripped pages from a French fashion mag with similar dresses in platinum to show me the color. She couldn't help herself and has written, *Definitely these!* next to the ones marked platinum on the fax.

It's unanimous.

I can feel my blood pressure going up.

"Laur, we gotta talk about this wedding thing… Just not now."

"I know. I know. You're dealing with some last-minute something that's important. We just need to set a date before all the best places are taken. I think April would be nice."

Hold on, hold on.

What's this about April? I put down the CIA papers and pictures of taffeta skirts—I need to focus.

"April? Four months! Isn't there, you know, some sort of mandatory waiting period? Like buying a handgun?"

"No, honey, there isn't."

I believe there are three things everyone should have to be trained and licensed for:

Getting married.

Having kids.

Buying a gun.

And I'm flexible on the gun.

My mind still can't get around April. "You really think we could pull something together that quickly?"

"We better. I was thinking about going off the pill next month. There's no way I'm walking down the aisle any more than three months pregnant."

Somewhere in my head, a tactical nuke explodes.

I find myself saying, "No, I wouldn't…I, no, of course…not. I gotta… Allison's motioning, you know, for me. The Japanese are going…going nuclear over California rice again." I even motion to the empty room to sell the lie.

"Okay. I love you." She pauses a moment. "And no, *playthings*. You're gonna be a daddy."

Then she delivers her parting thought. Six thousand miles away and modern communication technology allows her to whisper sweetly into my ear that she hopes our first child is a girl.

Meanwhile, God's up there thinking, that's right, just you wait, Gerrick. A girl. That's gonna be fun to watch.

7
OVER JILL, OVER GALE

I GET off the phone with Laura and the thoughts rush my brain like a pack of wannabe sorority girls. I mean, why can't we just keep things the same? Where did this kid thing come from? Apparently, her biological clock has been ticking for quite a while, only I couldn't hear it because I sleep with the fan on.

I lay my head back on the pillow. I need to work on my speech. I am highly motivated by a need to avoid being embarrassed. I do my best work when utter humiliation is a real possibility.

Only I can't focus.

A thought crosses my mind. The timing of Laura and I getting together. The fact that she could have any man. Maybe Laura's working for the EU. They'd love to see me fail, crash this thing, get one of the cadre of yes-gotiators that have been spoon-fed Beckett's Win-Win codswallop their entire careers to take my place.

No, this is personal. She wants a baby. She may even want it more than she wants me.

A girl.

Even if she only gets half of her looks from Laura, she's going to be beautiful.

I'm gonna be sitting there, staring across at my daughter's boyfriend, knowing exactly what he's thinking, what he's thinking *with* and where he's thinking about putting it.

I was there. In the other chair. I know.

There are just some things you don't forget.

You remember your first bike, your first fight, the first fight you won, your first first-place finish in any sport at any level at any time, your first time getting under a girl's bra, the first time you got into her pants, the first time getting the pants off, and the first time you had to buy condoms.

Oh, yeah, and the first time you got to actually use one of those condoms. Which hopefully was on some hot date sometime before the condom's expiration date.

And of course, there's the first time you woke up in the morning wondering, if you got in the shower immediately, poured bleach all over your genitals could you arrest the disease you possibly acquired the night before from what's-her-name?

That *first time*, that mystical event that so many movies, romance novels, and wet dreams are made of, is something most girls—not all, but most—save for that special someone. Usually their first real boyfriend. They want to feel safe and loved and cared for. They wanna make it special and memorable.

Guys just want to get the fucking thing over with.

Oh, I tried the romantic thing. I had a girlfriend I really cared about. We went out for a while, moved at a comfortable pace. I used to ride my bike over to her house on the other side of town in the middle of the night. I will drive for sex. I will fly for sex. I will bike for sex.

We even tried to have sex on one of those 2 A.M. visits, but it ended up not *fitting* into the evening's plans.

Now, I'd been having sex for quite a while actually. Even longer if you counted before anyone joined me.

I'd been naked with several girls, all sorts of heavy petting, oral sex, but actual intercourse, true penetration? Hadn't happened. And as I found out that night, wouldn't happen that summer either.

Pretty much like everything else, mostly my father's to blame.

Because while the Princess was busy picking his ass, something far more interesting was hiding just around the corner...

...his cock.

My dad has a monster crank. It's huge. I remember when I was nine seeing the thing, I mean, just enormous!, this woolly mammoth, thinking, no wonder he takes so much fucking time in the bathroom, he's gotta empty that monstrosity out.

Fortunately, or unfortunately, depending on how you look at it, I was endowed with something a little less freakish. Still, it posed enough of an obstacle that the young women—who were willing, but not able—could not or would not let my cock anywhere near their virgin territory. I was stopped at the Mason-Dixon line more times than the Confederate Army. In fact, I have never had sex with a virgin. Not one.

So, I dated and dated. Wonderful girls, smart, funny, pretty, sexy, who would do anything for me, except put my tiger in their tank.

"Billy, I really want to wait and do it with someone who I just really, really...think will fit."

That was pretty much the consensus, give or take a few words.

Summer was turning to fall. I was getting nowhere. So I did what anyone should do about any problem. I stopped worrying. It wasn't easy, but I let it go.

And true to the peculiar software that runs our world, a few days later, I started getting these notes on my car window. They always said the same thing: "Hey, Baby, wanna make a movie?"

I'd pick the note up—there was one every few days—and look around to see who was in view, hoping to recognize someone that had been nearby the other times I got notes. But no one stood out.

The messages were obviously written by a female. The E's and A's that looped and the lollipop I's were a giveaway. Still, I thought someone might be fucking with me. Maybe it was some guys—friends or foes, they don't act all that different in high school, except for the intent—who got some girl to write the notes for them. Or maybe it was just a couple of girls messing with me.

Then the notes started to change, ever so slightly. They still said basically the same thing, but the wording and intonation were altered.

"Hey, Baby, c'mon, let's make a movie."

"I wanna make a movie with you, Baby."

"Baby, mmmm, let's do another take."

This was not, of course, a female Francis Ford Coppola, anxious to explore the dominant art form of the twentieth century. The meaning was relatively clear, even for someone as thick as me. You must remember, this is the man who, in less than a year, would completely miss the subtle hint of having Jenna/Claire do the splits right in front of me for several hours, hand me her phone number, press a lingering kiss to my lips, and still think, *she probably just wants to be friends.*

I started to ask around about who could be leaving the notes. I found a lot of blank faces, but I also found some of those blank faces pinked up when I asked my questions. No one would tell me anything, but I was beginning to focus in on which clique this budding filmmaker hailed from.

I finally nailed it down to a small group of girls, and since I had known all of them since at least fifth grade, I figured I would have picked up on something from one of them in those intervening years.

All of them except one. Jill Dohemann.

Jill's family had recently moved into town, sometime during the summer. She was new, had no history.

She was my best guess.

The next weekend I saw Jill at a party. Sometimes you just know when you look at someone that a spark is going to ignite, that the barn is going to burn.

Neither one of us mentioned a thing about the notes.

But at two in the morning, the Princess in bed, my mom asleep on the couch, I snuck her in the back door, which is about six feet from the door to my bedroom.

Jill tried to tell me she was a virgin. I could believe I was the fourth or fifth person she'd been a virgin with, but the first, no way. To start off with, she was waaaaay too relaxed. This wasn't some rookie. She had been to the show before. Knew how the movie began, the whole second act, knew the climax, the ending, the credits, and how if you were patient and stayed in your seat, you'd get to see the movie again in about fifteen to twenty minutes.

We had sex six times that night in the course of about three hours. Maybe less. That's a record, in terms of turnaround, I have yet to break, although, I don't know if putting my dick inside, stroking her ten or twelve times then coming, is actually something to be proud of.

Hey, I was used to having only one person to please.

Adding another person in the room complicated things exponentially.

SIX YEARS AGO, I was asked to speak at my first trade conference. This nothing little meeting down in Buenos Aries where I was to be the principal draw. These poor bastards. There were no global implications, thank God. Wasn't anything I could really screw up. I mean, it was the *Southern Hemisphere* for Christ's Sake, who would even know? But still, I was anxious.

I fumbled around, had a couple of false starts, went through the whole thing too quickly, peaked early, and let it drag on too long.

It was very much like my inaugural romp with Jill.

Come to think it, I didn't satisfy those people either.

JILL AND I would end up having sex on two other occasions, the last one a special Graduation Night send-off. Which I think she enjoyed the most of our three encounters. Thankfully, I had factored her into the equation by then.

The trades at my next two conferences weren't as lucky.

FOR FOUR AND a half years—*four and a half years*, I started trying early —I had been diligently, and I mean relentlessly, searching for that one girl, that one special girl that would let me pass into manhood through her. Then finally, I had gotten it over with.

Just like that.

It was a shock to the system, this sudden change in status. You don't realize how much of a burden you've been carrying around until it's gone.

They say—as I'm finding out—that women in their thirties start getting anxious if they haven't had any kids by then. That biological clock starts ticking louder and louder. Not as well publicized, a guy's alarm starts sounding at about thirteen or fourteen and doesn't go off until we go off inside the softest part of a woman.

I'm telling you, four and a half years of *tick tick tick tick tick*.

And then less than a week after my little "*wanna make a movie*" girl and I spent the night, another girl willing and able would come and, literally, pick me up and take me home and take me to bed.

The floodgates were open.

I had met Gale Hauser at a party a few weeks before sleeping with Jill. We exchanged phone numbers and had spoken a couple of times on the phone. We decided we'd go out to a movie or something. It was the "or something" that I was most interested in.

This is why I'm going to get a little girl. Payback.

Jill and I had no real connection outside of bed, leading me to put an end to our intimate relations after the second time—I emphasize *after*. Believe me, that was a hard thing to do. After tasting the fruit, it only made me want it more. But I knew if I let it go on, I would just end up hurting her. Only problem was that other than Jill, things had not been going my way in this area since the unsuccessful border crossings of the summer. I was going to have to play it cool.

Well, playing it cool might be a little misleading.

I was punishing my body by running seven miles a day during Cross-Country practice.

Cross-Country is a wonderful sport. Sort of like track only instead of running on rubber-coated asphalt, you run through cow shit, bees' nests and snow-covered mud. I was actually very good at this. I guess I had gotten proficient at dealing with so much bullshit and pain throughout the years of Gerrick home life that cow shit seemed like a vacation.

And we didn't jog seven miles, we ran. We ran because our coach, who was more than twice as old as us, could run *nine* miles. It pisses teenagers off when a middle-aged man can outdistance you.

I credit Coach P with forcing me to dig deeper within myself. I credit him with giving me shin splints (this really cool injury where the muscle rips away from the bone). And I credit him with running me so fucking ragged that I barely had the energy to play with my dick myself, let alone bother finding someone else who wanted to play with it.

Instead, I would go home, soak my body and focus on intense pain.

Then one day, I got the proofs back for my high school yearbook photograph. They were not good. The pain did not help me forget this. I realized that if I had any hope of ever succeeding anywhere at any time at anything, I would not only have to keep the pictures sent to me from ever being seen, I would have to break into the temperature-controlled vault and burn every negative as well as any record of them ever having existed.

You know those idiotic faces that you think to yourself, "Geez, I hope I don't make a face like that." Well, that is the exact idiotic face I made as the camera shutter clicked.

Pop.

My mother asked me, "What were you thinking when you posed for this picture?"

I told her, "I was thinking, I hope I don't make a really stupid face."

Now, was I being paranoid? Worrying that a high school pic might affect my future success? Maybe. But I've seen too many of these geeky photos gleaned from the yearbooks of now-famous people get disseminated all over the free world. It's a favorite tactic of late-night talk shows, tabloid newspapers, news magazines, and sketch comedy programs, showing the infamous what-were-you-thinking with that outfit/hair/dorky expression high school yearbook shot, and I would be Goddamned if I was *knowingly* going to let something so obviously wretched be broadcast over worldwide television.

Okay, I had big aspirations even then.

In defense of the more famous that have come before me, at the time those goofy photos were taken, the subject of these pictures reasonably assumed that they looked as hip (which would later turn out to be "as goofy") as everyone else.

One look at my picture and I didn't need twenty years to tell me I was gonna look like an idiot. I looked like an idiot right now.

So, like several of my classmates, some who had a similar disastrous experience with the "official" photographer, others who simply wanted something a little more interesting to immortalize their high school years, I went to a well-known, highly recommended photographer that specialized in more personal portraits.

Most of the great photos in the last few yearbooks had been taken by this guy.

Instead of it being one...two...three, click, one...two...three, click, and you're done, he had blocked out an hour for a studio shoot with me where he would click off a couple of rolls of film, which meant I actually could choose from a selection of photos greater than two.

This was a wonderful idea, in theory. What actually happened when I went to his studio, which was, in fact, the basement of an aging two-family house, and the photographer finally showed up ten minutes late from another shoot, was that the guy's trusty canine, seeing a "suspicious character" loitering outside his master's dungeon, decided to acquire, at least, attempted to acquire, a substantial portion of my crotch.

Now, I am not afraid of dogs. I've lived around dogs, large and small, all my life. But no matter how much love I had for the canine species, I wasn't gonna let one of its members capture my flag.

Women can't truly understand scrotum protection, they don't have a zone quite so fragile hanging off their bodies. I realize women have breasts and it hurts when someone runs into them, but it's just not the same. And yes, birth hurts more, but a) you have nine months warning, and b) you can get an epidural well in advance.

No such warning and no such agony alleviation exists for men.

So, over the millennia we've developed this internal radar and avoidance system to safeguard our naughty bits and anything else in a twelve-inch radius therefrom.

When something—the foot of a young child, a ball coming off a bat, or the jaw of a rabid dog—comes within the no-fly zone, our bodies scream: warning, danger, prepare for impact!

When my alarm balls went off, my body automatically sprang into action. First, the hands and forearms instinctively formed an "X" in front of my dick. Next, my legs sprang into action, quickly jumping back so that I would be out of reach of the snapping jaws of little Cujo.

This was where I—and nature—made a mistake.

Right behind my head was an archaic, never-been-used, about-to-be-condemned fire escape, covered in eighty-two years of rust and decay which flaked off when anything touched it.

My head, my skull, the container which holds the brain I am so fond of, smacked into the most corroded corner of the fire escape.

Blood began trickling from my head.

The photographer was genuinely worried about me. However, he seemed more concerned about the possible lawsuit I might file, than the probable brain damage I may have suffered. He proceeded to tell me that not only did he *not* own the building (he gave me the name, address and telephone number of the landlord), but that he had on numerous occasions told said landlord about the danger of having rusted fire escapes for this very reason: That some photographer might be late, causing some client to stand around and do nothing until some dog attacked the client, forcing that client's head into the decrepit, oxidized metal, and cracking that client's skull open.

I finally told him to, please, shut the fuck up and get me to a hospital.

He looked at me, blankly.

"Oh, you need a hospital?"

"Are you fucking kidding me?" I said, pulling my hand away red with blood and rusted metal.

He stuffed Cujo into the back, the dog growling at me the whole way, and drove me the mile to the hospital and another half mile up the driveway to the actual door of the hospital.

I have never quite understood hospital emergency rooms. For a place whose very existence is solely set up to handle extreme crisis situations, nobody seems to be in that much of a hurry.

I've seen post offices with quicker service.

There're always these television shows about hospitals, where gurneys are busting through double doors, then rushed into trauma rooms.

Never seen that happen.

Never sat in an emergency room and thought, now *this* is compelling viewing.

I was sitting in the registration chair, I swear, my head bleeding onto my face, and this admissions clerk was asking me questions like:

"Mother's maiden name?"

"Zilano."

"Father's occupation?"

"Alcoholic." She glanced up at me. "Computer technician."

"Nature of injury."

"I don't know, why don't you tell me," I said as blood dripped down my cheek.

I was parked out in the waiting room (aptly named). The photographer hung around as long as my photo shoot would have taken. I guess he only had so much time scheduled that day for compassion. He informed me that he had to return to his lair to perform services for another student —did I know Ken Simpson? From Middletown? Sadly, I did not.

He instructed the nurse at the desk to forward the bill to him, but I noticed the name and address he scribbled down was the same one he had given me earlier, that of the landlord.

And so I waited some more. The steady stream of blood gushing out of my skull didn't seem to cause much alarm amongst the staff. This was early on a Friday evening and, as they explained to me many, many times, they were preparing for the normal cocktail of GSWs (gunshot wounds in hospital speak), stabbings, and drunk driving accidents. Minor head wounds it seemed did not make headlines in the ER.

I finally got a doctor to see me, after I had lost about a pint of blood, and after a woman with a Coke bottle stuck in her vagina got that taken care of.

It's not the Real Thing, honey.

A very competent and attractive doctor and a very competent and handsome nurse stitched me up. They were sympathetic and kind and obviously having an affair. My skull became yet another venue for flirtation. They completed the suturing in about two and a half minutes. Apparently, they had a rendezvous in the storeroom immediately following my procedure because both appeared very troubled by the low level of supplies in the ER and wanted very much to restock them.

Four hours of waiting for two and a half minutes of doctoring.

I really believe hospitals should expedite patients who can be patched up in just a few minutes, kind of like how shoppers will wave through a customer with a single loaf of bread at the checkout line.

The doctor slapped a couple of painkillers into my hands. The nurse handed me a glass of water and told me to take the meds. And then after I swallowed them, told me I wouldn't be able to drive myself home because of the painkillers I had just taken.

They promptly headed for the storeroom to refill supplies.

I complained to the desk nurse. They had to let me drive home. She explained that I couldn't be released until someone came to claim me.

I was like dry cleaning.

I guess my faculties had been affected by the blow to the head because I continued to argue with the woman for ten minutes until, when she was just about to agree to discharge me, I remembered that my car was not in the parking lot, but on the street in front of the photographer's, about a mile and a half away.

This realization convinced me that perhaps I shouldn't attempt to operate a motor vehicle.

The nurse once again told me to pick up the phone and call someone.

So, I did.

The Princess, as always, was unreachable.

Even now, after I've given him over the years for birthday and Christmas presents every technological communication device known to man—a CB, a pager, a number of cell phones—my father remains untraceable. Last year, I presented my father with a beaded car seat cushion, a deluxe version of the kind he has bought in various styles for the past twenty-five years. Inside the cushion, I was going to have sewn a five thousand dollar homing beacon—I'm not kidding—utilizing GPS technology and a state-of-the-art satellite phone system. I was gonna have it installed into his car and hooked up very discreetly to the cushion. It would, at any given moment, give me the location of my father's car within a hundred feet. Which ninety percent of the time would be within a hundred feet of him. Combining a massively complex mapping software program with the GPS data being transmitted from right under my father's ass, then translated into coordinates that could be plotted on my PowerBook, I'd be able to tell exactly where my father was at all times.

Even with him having a cell phone, I have been able to track down my father's whereabouts when I needed him a total of three times in the last five years. I realized that even if I bought the GPS system, I would be lucky to increase that number to three a year.

Then I'd be pissed that for five thousand dollars, all I could tell you was that on June 8th, September 16th, and December 3rd, at approximately 1 P.M., 8 P.M., and 11 A.M., respectively, my father was within a hundred feet of the Dunkin' Donuts on Main Street.

The drunk that sleeps out by the payphone could've told me that for a donut and a cup of coffee.

The other three hundred and sixty-two days, my father would avoid detection like he always did.

I had an often-pondered notion during my childhood that my father was some secret agent for an unknown, off-budget covert agency within the intelligence community. The only thing that has kept me from completely believing this is not that my father isn't smart enough, because he is, and not because of his drinking, because spies are always having a couple of martinis before heading out to save the world from tyranny, no, I am convinced he couldn't be an instrument of the intelligence community for one simple fact.

He is a world-class mumbler.

One of the reasons my father is so good at talking to beautiful women is that they are accustomed to males being unable to speak in their presence. In fact, the only people who can understand what my father is saying on a regular basis are stunningly gorgeous females. Something, which, to this day, pisses my mother off.

As an agent, my father'd be out in the field gathering sensitive and urgently needed information. He'd find it, immediately pick up his satellite phone—the one I gave him last Christmas—call the head of whatever agency he was a part of and say, "Mmmmph rrummpllhh hhmmmya!"

And that would be the end of most of NATO as we know it.

LACK OF A TRACKING device effectively knocked my father out of the running to come get me. My brothers and sister were not old enough to acquire pubic hair, never mind driver's licenses. And my mom wasn't home, which I knew the instant my grandmother picked up the phone at my house.

Now, my Grandmother has a license.

She passed her driver's test with a perfect score—so I'm told—something like thirty years earlier.

She has been behind the wheel of a car exactly one time.

When she took the test.

For some reason, she has never driven again.

"Grandma, can you come and get me?"

"Who is this?"

My Gramma Annette has talked to me a thousand times on the phone. She has no idea who I am from my voice. Of course, years later, she would stare at herself in the mirror and ask my mother, "Who is that?" So, I guess I should be grateful for all the years she did recognize me in person.

"It's Billy."

"Billy? What are you doing? Shouldn't you be home by now?"

"Yes, Grandma. But I'm at the hospital and I need someone to drive me home."

"At the hospital? I thought you were getting your picture taken."

"I was trying to get my picture taken, but there was a problem." My head was beginning to pound. It was the conversation I was having rather than the blow to the head.

"Of course there was. They don't take pictures at a hospital. Except X-rays."

"Grandma, can you please put on Dean or Max?"

Max got on the phone. "What are you doing at the hospital? I thought you were getting your picture taken."

"Max, I have a pounding headache from having this very same discussion with Grandma. Do me a favor. When mom comes home, just tell her that I need a ride from New Britain General Hospital."

"Are you okay?"

"I'm fine. I just need a ride home."

"Okay. I'll tell her."

"Thanks, Max."

I ran down the list of my friends who had cars. Dialed them up. None of them were home. How did we live without cell phones? I thought about calling my dad's dad, Robert, who lived nearby, but decided against that since hearing the story about the last time he had taken the car out.

No one had actually been killed mind you, but there was widespread panic, anarchy, and looting left in his wake.

And then I remembered about Gale's phone number in my wallet.

I dialed.

"Hi."

"Hey. It's Billy."

"Billy. Mmmm, I didn't expect to hear from you today." She sounded very coquettish. Yummy. "So are we on for this weekend?"

"Absolutely. Tomorrow night okay?"

"It's a date."

"Perfect. But I have a favor to ask you first."

I wasn't able to get two sentences out of my mouth when she said, "I'm climbing in my car right now and coming to get you."

Twenty-five minutes later, there was a pleasantly petite brunette strolling into the emergency room.

The nurse finally gave me back my personal items. She looked at us disapprovingly. We were, of course, teenagers and therefore considered a pain in the ass until proven otherwise.

GALE'S CAR had what at the time must have seemed like a technological breakthrough. A semi-automatic transmission. The brain trust over at Honda Motor Co. came up with the brilliant idea of making a car you can shift without a clutch. Now, I know there are race cars and high-performance vehicles that incorporate this type of technology, but how this hairbrained idea ever made it into production on a six thousand-dollar gnat with four wheels is a complete mystery to me.

This contraption combined the absolute worst attributes of a second-rate automatic transmission and those of a stick. It had no power *and* you had to *shift*.

A couple of miles from my house, she "down-shifted," then turned onto a road leading away from my home.

"My house is *that* way."

"But *my* house is this way."

And at *her* house, no one was home.

Perhaps the only way to get a woman to fall for you easier than having the cutest fucking dog on the planet is to bang the shit out of some part of your body.

When Gale got me home, she laid me down on her bed, went back upstairs and made a little ice pack for me, then came down and tended to my wound.

Within ten minutes, she said—I can't quite remember, something like —"I know one thing that might let you forget about the pain. Let me kiss your head and make it feel better."

When I began to pull away the ice pack, she said, "I had something a little farther south in mind."

From the instant Gale's lips touched my skin, I knew I was not with a virgin. Which immediately made me very, very, very happy.

She dragged her lips down over my stomach, then further still as I ran my fingers over her shoulders, descending to her nipples. The feel of a women's nipple passing across my open palm is one of those incredible gifts of nature.

After a wonderfully long session of foreplay, she finally parted her legs and let me slip inside.

It was wild sex. The kind you'd have on a cattle ranch with the boss's daughter after a long day in the saddle and an hour and a half in the tub.

I'm not exactly sure what it was, perhaps the pain medication, perhaps having my skull sliced opened, maybe it was simply that semi-automatic transmission that was making me hot.

Or maybe it was a pain/pleasure thing. Because while I was sliding deep inside my newest favorite girl in the world, the top of my head was banging into her headboard.

This wasn't Jill. This wasn't thirty seconds and done. I was enjoying myself tremendously, right up till the moment Gale's mother walked into the bedroom and sat down on her sister's bed directly across from us.

There's not much you can do in these situations, but try to move as little as possible, hoping that a) the covers stay on, and b) it doesn't make too much noise when you inevitably slip out.

I kind of deduced from that first moment that Gale's mother was different. She appeared conservative in her dress and the way she carried herself, but let her open her mouth and she was spewing New Age-y tenets before there was such a thing.

There were no locks on the doors at Gale's house, a fact that would begin to bother me as we saw each other more and more.

Her mom just opened the door, came straight in and parked herself. No knock. No warning. Just a maternal face waiting for an answer.

A long moment of silence followed. I half expected her, after the pause, to take a breath and whisper, "Let us pray."

Instead, she asked us to put on our clothes and come upstairs (Gale's room was in a finished basement) so we could discuss this at the kitchen table like *adults*. She said that, "adults." Now, my first thought was, if we're all adults here, why do I feel like I've just been scolded.

Her mom's biggest problem was not that I was fucking her daughter, which would have been my first guess, if anyone had asked me—which, thank God, nobody did. No, it was that she felt constrained, prevented from freely moving about her house, restricted from unencumbered communication with the fruit of her loins because we were behind a closed door.

What!?

Never mind that her mom had never *seen* me before in her life.

This was either the biggest load of bullshit in the history of parenting or this woman had met her husband at a love-in. I had learned only moments before, that Gale's mom had given her the pill, starting when she was fifteen, so, 1) I didn't need a condom, and 2) the bullshit/hypo-critical theory was losing a little steam. She actually believed this crap.

I don't know which was stranger, the fact that her mother was seem-ingly upset about not being able to freely commune with her offspring or the fact that I sat there naked with her daughter's pussy surrounding my cock and calmly said, "Okay, we'll be up in a moment."

I've never been one to panic. I'm very good under pressure, very composed in circumstances most people would find exceedingly uncom-fortable. Maybe I was born with it or maybe it has evolved over time. Probably a little of both. Someone will slam a door and I'll jump, but open the door while I'm slamming your daughter, I won't even flinch. It's not that I don't care. It's just, what the hell am I gonna do? Jump up and run around?

Not the diversion I'm looking for.

In the intervening years, I have been caught by Gale's father, Terry's mother, almost caught by Leslie's homicidal brother, caught by a farmer while I was fucking in his cornfield, a cop, a librarian, a Gap saleswoman, a projectionist at a movie theater, a conductor (train), a conductor (sym-phony), and by the manager of a radio station as I was having sex with the number one late-night DJ in Chicago that by coincidence happened to be his girlfriend.

Some might say I have bad luck regarding sexual encounters. I guess it's all in how you look at things.

I prefer to think of it like this: if you do something enough times in enough places with enough people, *eventually* someone's going to see you.

Speaking of people seeing me...

I almost missed the deadline to get my picture into the yearbook, but they gave me more time, given the circumstances. I ended up rescheduling my photo shoot with the photographer, his rabid dog, rusty fire escape, and studio in someone's basement. And you know what? Even now, fifteen years later, I flip open my yearbook and still don't cringe when I come across my picture.

Which is a good thing, because that picture has been broadcast on television, and splashed across newspapers around the world.

I look at the clock and realize I've done nothing for the last hour but think about old girlfriends, and fight the urge to call the one in this hotel and go to her room.

I grab some bottled water—I always try to have plenty of water brought to the room. I usually carry a case or two on the plane.

But it has to be *drinking* water.

I hate Perrier and the rest of the sparkling waters, hate spring water like Evian as well, because if I wanted spring water, I'd go outside the Intercontinental and suck some directly out of the Lake.

That's water from the fucking Alps.

I say leave the spring water where it is. In the spring. Something like a billion little green bottles come out of *Source Perrier* every year. Don't they need this water? Next time there's a drought in France, and they come crying to the MTO or whatever hell we call it, that their farmers need to be subsidized, I'm gonna say, why don't you just gather up all those pretentious little bottles you send all over the world and pour *them* one by one onto your fucking crops.

8

BATTERIES NOT INCLUDED

I FINALLY GOT one of the permanent staff at the U.S. mission in Geneva to find me some AAA batteries somewhere in the city. I'm not sure what he thought I needed them for, but he brought eight four-packs to my room, thirty-two batteries, enough to last me until *1995*.

Fresh batteries installed, I began to plot out my speech.

I love this part of the job.

I hate it as well.

I love getting up in front of a thousand people from nearly a hundred and fifty countries and commanding their attention for half an hour. For a non-pol, I'm pretty good at it too, if you overlook my debut in Buenos Aires.

The part I hate is writing speeches.

Not so much because I have to *write* them—I've got more than an enough to say about the subject of trade—but because of what I *can't* write. I can't simply get up there and say what I think. I have to be controlled, deliberate, conscious of every word so as not to offend.

Sometimes I'd just like to take off my shoe, pound the podium with it, and tell some of these countries that we've been the world's most open trading partner since forever, so stop whining, get off your fucking soapboxes, and open your markets. Some of these countries, like Japan and Germany, wouldn't be half of what they are today without the U.S. We are perhaps the only victors in history to help rebuild the enemy's economy with no designs on controlling their land. It was the right thing to do at the time. It led to a more stable world, but it's time to play fair.

I had to be delicate, but that didn't mean I couldn't scare them a bit. And suddenly, what had been percolating, brewed.

The speech poured out of me, effortlessly. I was cruising, the words were flowing. Till I caught a glimpse of the stack of unopened batteries on the desk, and my family's yearly Christmas Holocausts came to mind.

For some people, it's snow, for some the scent of burning logs on a hearth. For me, nothing says Christmas like a megapack of AAs, fresh ones, spent ones, a lone, discarded cylinder on the floor in the corner. Mainly because we never had enough batteries to power all the new toys we'd get, and we'd have to share them, steal them, plunder them until the stores reopened the next day and we could badger my parents into getting more.

Which wasn't easy.

"Sam, could you pick up some milk?"

"Jesus Christ, Mary. I don't have time to waste fighting crowds at the grocery store."

"It's only milk, Sam. You can pick it up at the corner market. And get some batteries for the kids, will you?"

My father hated picking things up. He wanted to be free. Didn't like the pressure of having to remember one fucking item, let alone two.

"Jesus Christ, I've got things to do."

What my father had to do was pick up some beer, drink it, drink some coffee, piss, and drive all over creation. That's his phrase, *drive all over creation*. Where "creation" was and why my father was flattening it under his wheels no one, including him, could reliably explain. Normally, a man's home is his castle, but with us in the house running around, asking questions like, "Why do birds fly?" home was more like a sadistic prison torture chamber to him. No, his castle was his car. First a Saab, then a VW Bug, then a Pinto station wagon, then *another* Pinto station wagon, then finally, a series of Honda Civics. That both my parents now have Hondas drives me crazy. I've spent years trying to get the Japanese to open their markets and import more American cars. So now they build a few Accords in the U.S. with Japanese parts and ship them back to Tokyo. Not really what I had in mind.

So, there was my father, behind the wheel of whatever car he was driving at the time, with a beer between his legs, listening to a stereo system worth nearly a third of the car's value with a hundred watts per channel, level meters, graphic equalizer, power-boosting amp so he could listen to what? Rock, heavy metal, even crisp renditions of Bach and Beethoven? No. Easy Listening music.

WEZY.

There is perhaps nothing worse on the planet. Being burned at the stake—child's play. Lock me in a room with John Tesh playing, and within an hour, I'd give up the few state secrets I know.

But John Tesh was what blared from his three thousand dollar car stereo system.

In his eyes, my dad had it all. A kingdom that rolled. That was mobile. That didn't have to stay home.

See, this was the old days when drunk driving was not only legal but a National Sport.

"I was so shit-faced, but I still made it home in under ten minutes."

This quote was from Chester Woods, my high school's Resident Alcoholic, the day after driving home from a party, normally twenty minutes away, *if* you ran the stop signs, with about ten beers in him.

Chester, who was called "Harvey" by everyone for no apparent reason, other than it seemed to fit him better than Chester, drove a car with a hole in the floor like Fred Flintstone's, which poured noxious fumes into the vehicle.

Horrible, toxic, deadly gasses.

It explains a lot of his behavior.

My father would have never said anything like that. Admit nothing. Deny everything. The Princess was always "fine to drive."

Oh, I have to admit, my father was a professional drunk driver, better behind the wheel smashed than my mother stone-cold sober. He's retired from the sport now. Oh, he still drives to God-only-knows-where, but he just does it jacked up only on coffee now. He used to put thirty-five to forty thousand miles a year on his car (it's down to around twenty-five now), only we lived ten miles from his office, where he labored for eight to nine hours a day.

We not only couldn't figure out *where* the hell my father would go, but how and *when*.

"I just like to drive. Is that a problem?"

No, but did you happen to pass a store along the two hundred miles you drove today, while I sat here—forbidden by state law to operate a motor vehicle because I'm not old enough—incapable of procuring dairy products, staring at a dry bowl of cereal, which I finally spooned into my mouth without so much as a drop of liquid?

I learned two things, then. One, that you can't always count on people to do what they say they're going to do, and, two, Raisin Bran sucks without milk.

"You ungrateful—" My dad never called me "son" in that patronizing way that fathers are supposed to. Neither would he hail me by my first name, except when he was in the mood to, which was rarely. In fact, for a long time, I don't really think he knew my name. Mostly I was known around the house as simply "The Big Sonofabitch"...not because of my size—I would eventually come in at a hair over six feet, which is three inches shorter and about fifty pounds lighter than my dad. No, I was "The Big Sonofabitch" because I wasn't one of "The Little Shits" as my two brothers and sister were collectively Also Known As.

See, I was born five years before Dean, the next oldest, six before Max, and seven before Anna. We used to have this heartwarming little custom in our house. We shared everything evenly. I got fifty percent and they got fifty percent. When they were old enough to comprehend the inequality of this, they used to complain daily that I always got more than they did.

But I earned every fucking particle. I forged, I cleared, I cut out the path in the jungle, then paved it. When it came to discipline, curfews, etc., our mom was completely broken after me.

Which meant, "The Little Shits" had pretty much free rein.

NEEDLESS TO SAY, I was going to have to wait till mom picked up some batteries before I could once again play with the most incredible gift I had ever received—before or since—the Mattel Hot Wheels Fat Track Indy Car Racing Set.

I was nine. It was right about the time I had discovered diddling my dode. The Fat Track was about the only thing I found nearly as interesting.

It was great. Three rechargeable Hot Wheels cars with tiny engines spinning around a thick black track. I had already powered through an eight-pack of D batteries by the end of Christmas Day. I needed an alkaline fix.

Now, having my mother run an errand was no sure thing either. When my mom wasn't clearing rooms with her gastrointestinal afflictions,

"Those G.D. vegetables," she was forgetting something or other. Be it her children's names... "Dean...Anna...Max...I mean Billy." (I once got called the dog's name, which strangely enough was Flapper. We actually had three dogs named Flapper, all of them German Shepherds, one right after another. We also once had a cat called "Bob," but he lasted only about two weeks. Ran away after the two-hundredth time Max played "Police Copter" with him, swinging him by the tail and then letting go.) Or be it the punch line of a joke she just spent the last ten minutes telling. Which was usually a good thing, because I've laughed at exactly three jokes out of the two thousand, three hundred and six my mother's told me.

But if we hounded her enough, eventually, she'd remember, and the batteries would appear, ready to be drained.

Did I happen to mention I loved that Fat Track? Best present my parents ever got me. There were crashes, there were spinouts, there was victory, and there was defeat.

For seven whole days, I played with that toy. I'd race my little brothers, who would lose, of course, because I would trick them into picking the slowest cars again and again and again. A little bit of juice from the giant "gas pump," and I'd be off to another victory.

Finally smartening up, my brother Dean asked, "Why can't I use the Ferrari?"

"It's broken."

"No, it's not. I wanna use it this time."

"You can't."

"Billy won't let me use the Ferrari," my brother Dean shouted into the other room, hoping to get a reversal on appeal. It was New Year's Day, and we were getting in a little extra playtime before the turkey dinner was served.

"It's *my* toy."

The decision was handed down almost immediately. "Billy, let your brother use the Ferrari," my mother said as she clanged some silverware down on the table in the kitchen.

"But maaah-om..."

I heard rumbling from downstairs in the cellar. My father was trying to find some fucking tool on the workbench, why, I have no idea, he never fixed anything in our house. "Jesus Christ, who moved the Goddamn Phillips-head?"

Things were going according to plan. Dinner was about to be served, and my father was revving up his engines like a dragster ready to peel out. I don't think the Princess ever actually finished a holiday meal as far as I can remember. Something, somehow, some way would cross his path and knock him out of orbit. The best you could hope for was to avoid colliding with him. I had long ago staked out my seat at the table, the one across from my mother and diagonally away from dear ol' dad. There was a dishwasher I had to scoot by on one side and two walls and two brothers blockading the other. There were just too many obstacles for the Princess to climb over before he could get to me, which was the point—because I was The Big Sonofabitch, remember? And no matter what the problem, I was surely somehow to blame.

So, on these solemn occasions, Thanksgiving, Christmas, New Year's Day, Easter, Mother's Day, and sometimes the Fourth of July, my father would end his involvement in the meal by throwing or breaking something or both, then tearing out of the driveway to some exotic locale like Dunkin' Donuts or Friendly's, which is sort of the illegitimate New England child of a fountain shop crossed with a Denny's.

On such days, these places would be populated by pitiful, lonely people who didn't have families, and by pissed off employees, whose only solace was getting paid double-time.

Into this world of hopelessness and gloom, the Princess would stride, happily, for a cup of coffee or twelve. He reigned supreme in the donut and coffee shops of Central Connecticut, always the smartest person in the place, always the most admired, usually the only one with more teeth than fingers, and absolutely the only one who had some place else he could be if he wanted.

This is another of the differences between the Princess and me.

I always wanted to be the dumbest person in the room, surrounded by people who knew more than me, were more skilled, more successful. In that way, I could learn from them, study them, take whatever I thought worthy and go about building the person I am today.

And every time I start to look around and think I'm the smartest one in a room, some true genius or stunning woman walks in.

Either way, I become a complete dolt.

The holiday "cheer" as we used to call it, nine times out of ten, would begin something like this: "That Big Sonofabitch," my father would scream, while I was standing less than ten feet away, "blah, blah, blah,

blah." Pretty much, what was shouted subsequently started to all sound the same.

I was the devil.

Mom was the nag.

My father was the poor, persecuted soul.

I often thought my father missed his calling. Acting in Greek tragedies, he would have been a star. If only he'd have been born twenty-five hundred years ago.

If only.

BUT THIS ONE New Year's Day, the day of the Fat Track Incident, the Princess was in especially rare form.

I guess I didn't come to the table quickly enough—I just loved playing with that thing—when my mom called me for dinner.

"Be there in a minute."

Dean and I were in a battle for top racer of the day. He'd gotten better at picking cars.

A few minutes went by and my mother called me and Dean again.

"Okay, coming," I said as I crossed the finish line first, even though I had let Dean have the Ferrari.

I heard a "Jesus Christ," from the Princess.

I was probably throwing my father's schedule off. Holiday dinner was usually at 1:30. He would spend the next fourteen minutes and thirty seconds gathering food and stuffing it down his throat, then he was supposed to be pissed off by 1:45 because no one would pass him some damn thing. And he'd be out the door by five to two, which meant he could be at Dunkin' Donuts by 2:15.

Like clockwork.

My dad could get pissed off at just about anything. Oh, sometimes his wheat germ was moved in the fridge two inches to the left, sometimes it would be that we didn't get him something the millisecond he screamed for it, and sometimes he'd just fly off the handle because he couldn't hold his fork, "My fucking hands," or see well enough to rethread a screw that had fallen out of an appliance, "My fucking eyes," or a combination of both, where he couldn't hold on to the screw, nor see well enough to find it, "My fucking body's falling apart!"

But here it was 1:44 and the man hadn't even gotten a single morsel of food into his mouth. A man's gotta keep a schedule.

So, one minute later, as I was putting away my Fat Track, I heard the immortal, "That's it!"

The next thing I knew, my father's foot was coming down on the plastic high-banked turns of my Fat Track, over and over, shattering them into tiny shards. The gas pump-shaped charger was punted across the room—one of the batteries is *still* missing in action—and two of my three cars had been sent to the compactor, crushed under his weight. The third, which had been attached to the charger, exploded into pieces as it hit the wall.

It took all of about five or six seconds.

I don't remember doing it, or how I got there—did I leave while all of it was happening? I think so—but I crawled deep into the corner of the closet in the living room, so far to the side that no adult could get to me without emptying eighty percent of the contents of shoes and boxes and coats and clothes. And I screamed and I cried and I pleaded to God to return my own personal Indianapolis Speedway to me, to send me back in time ten minutes, so I could avoid this Fate.

Over and over I kept repeating, "I was putting it away. I was putting it away."

I don't think I ever had anything in my childhood that I really loved that wasn't smashed, broken, damaged, taken away, or thrown in the garbage. Some people get upset when they hear this, but for me, it's served me well. Because from that day on, I've never cared about anything so much that I couldn't bear losing it.

But at that very moment, as I sat in the closet crying, nine years old, the world collapsing around me, I just wanted things back the way they were.

I PUT another set of new batteries into the voice recorder, and an hour later, finished writing the speech.

9
A BRIEF HISTORY OF TRADE

"IN THE YEARS after World War II," I paused. "So I'm told," a few people in the room laughed. "The overriding concern of U.S. foreign policy was containing Soviet expansionism." The Cuban delegation shifted uncomfortably in their seats. "This concern guided the strategic decisions..."

Of whom to bomb and whom to kill and whom to basically ignore.

I spared them that.

"...as well as decisions relating to international economics and trade in particular. The United States often sacrificed its own economic interest in deference to the geopolitical demands of fighting the Cold War. We tolerated, even encouraged, the development of economic havens where our allies cultivated competitive industries behind protectionist walls. We often allowed other countries access to our home market, without gaining comparable access to theirs. As the dominant military and economic power in the world, and having the added benefit of a nearly self-contained economy, we could afford to be magnanimous. Our strategy allowed industries in Europe, Japan, and developing nations to grow, which helped build a middle class and promote stability in these regions. The political and economic structure we created stood firm for forty years. Our strategy worked. Today democracies and market economies are the rule rather than the exception. The Soviet threat no longer exists."

But then a funny thing happened on the way to World Peace. The Cold War ended and we were getting our ass kicked all over the globe by places like fucking Taiwan. I blame Beckett and his win-win bullshit.

Now, I have nothing against the little islanders, but how can forty percent of the products in my house be made there? It's the size of Hawaii. The only thing I have in my house from Hawaii are pineapples.

I diplomatically cut that out of the speech and instead said:

"But the world has changed. The Cold War is over. Economies and currencies are interdependent. America still seeks to promote global growth and stability..."

I said nothing about what I thought could possibly be the biggest threat to future world stability. Maybe not in a decade. Maybe not in two. But someday. China. The Chinese weren't even here. Not officially, at least. They weren't a member of GATT, just an "observer" country. They would take over Hong Kong from the British in three years. That oasis of pure capitalism had already enticed the communist leaders in Beijing to create the Shenzhen Special Economic Zone, which in thirteen years of existence had not doubled or tripled or quadrupled the sleeping giant's Gross National Product, but multiplied it by a factor of *eighteen*. The People's Republic could someday become the Profit Republic.

"...and to raise the standard of living for ourselves and our children, and their children. But we will not convince the American people that expanding trade is good for the world and for them by saying, simply, 'trust us.' We will only convince the American people by continuing to fight for their interests. We will only convince them by negotiating fair deals and insisting on shared responsibility with our trading partners. Our President has fought hard to do that. We have fought hard to do that. It's been and will continue to be the driving force of our trade policy. Future prosperity—at home and abroad—depends on our continued success.

"Thank you."

There was applause. From the Americans, Canadians and Germans—rousing. From everyone else—polite. I had rallied the troops. I had hopefully sent a warning shot across the bow of the competition, letting them know, I wasn't here to play footsie with them. I was here to fuck. Straight up. No bullshit.

I glanced at several of the more important negotiators, including my Japanese and Brazilian counterparts. Hutseo gave me a nod. Diego looked bored, like he'd rather be at a *futebol* match or thinking up new methods of deforestation.

Rafael smiled as I came off the podium. She got up and pretended to head toward the bathrooms, but instead changed direction at the last minute and stood at the back door as I was making the customary "Walk of Shame" where everyone gives enthusiastic applause to a less-than-stirring speech. Applause which immediately dies the instant the speaker walks out the back of the room. There are rarely any encores in political public speaking, except maybe when it's Castro. Then again, he carries a loaded sidearm.

You better damn well cheer.

More commonly, the speaker bores everyone to tears, then thankfully, gets away from the microphone before permanent damage is done.

Luckily, I was able to walk down the center aisle straight out the back door like Presidents do at the end of the State of the Union to a joint session of Congress.

I got handshakes, pats, congratulations, thumbs up, a whistle, and then I was out the door.

And there she was.

"I 'ave seen you give better. At least you didn't put Diego to sleep," she said.

Diego Costa was known to take a snooze during conferences. The only way you could tell this—he could stay motionless for hours at a negotiation without stretching, needing to walk around, or go out for air, could delay or completely ignore the need to go to the bathroom, then sip water from a straw, just to make you suffer—the only way, was that his normally labored, tuberculotic wheeze, turned into a foghorn.

"Thanks, Raf." More than a hint of sarcasm, which the French get only slightly better than the Germans, which is to say, almost not at all. I looked at her dress. "I've seen you in better."

"But it's good enough to get you to sleep," she said without adding the unspoken 'with me.'

I laughed one of those casual, sarcastic laughs you give when someone says something you can't possibly admit to. Something you, the person, and anyone else paying close attention knows is far too close to the truth for comfort.

Rafael moved in close and kissed me on the mouth.

This was a clear violation of protocol and of several agreements we had hammered out over the last few years. No more touching. No more giving me a peek at any body parts she wouldn't show to the President of France...during a State dinner. (I had to add that last part). Which, incidentally, didn't narrow it down all that much.

The hotel manager walked by and smiled as she finished the kiss. I've been to this place over two dozen times. The man knows me, knows how I like my suits and shirts, very little starch, what liquor and wine I want in my room, what flowers I want brought in when Laura joins me on a trip, and here he's just witnessed a very public display of the very private behavior I had outlawed.

"Why the hell did you do that?" I said, wiping my mouth, but unable to wipe away her scent from my skin.

"Because I chose you."

SHE SAID those very words several years ago in Florence.

Indeed, I had been selected.

I was to become part of an elite group of men. A much smaller group than you might think. Rafael was nothing if she wasn't picky. And she was many, many things.

It was merely two weeks. Two unbelievable weeks.

There had been a few times after that, here and there, where Rafael and I would slip off for an hour or two, but those liaisons weren't nearly the same. She had touched something in me in those fourteen days, and maybe...maybe I had done the same in her.

It was subtle, the difference, but after Florence, we were slightly guarded, not distant, just a half a step back from the edge of the cliff.

And every time we fell into bed, I would tell myself, *last time, I won't sleep with her again.*

Not for any reason other than it was softening the memory of those two wonderful weeks. And I didn't want that picture in my mind to be dulled.

I don't exactly know how it ever happened, but it would. Even after I promised myself. Even after we agreed. I mean, she knew just the right buttons to push and I let her press them. It's that whole Canadian border thing. It's just too easy for people to slip through.

It wasn't some moral dilemma or preprogrammed guilt that ate at me, even though I had usually been loosely dating someone or other at the time—before Laura, before I had rules about that kind of thing—it was that I didn't have any control over it.

If I were some other man, some man who didn't make his living being in complete control, or at least, as near to it as possible, it might not have bothered me at all.

But I'm not some other man.

I got the feeling Rafael *wanted* to dull that time in Florence, wanted to make it seem like one of the other things the French are so famous for—*l'affaire.*

"I need to go upstairs," I said, causing Rafael to smile. "*Alone.*"

So, I went up to my room, removed my clothes and calmly got into the shower where I just wanted to let the water, the warm essence of it flow over my body.

Just wash over me like a warm Spring rain.

What I got was a tsunami.

The shower head was missing, causing the water to come shooting out of the uncapped pipe in a torrent the instant I turned on the faucet.

I TRIED THE FRONT DESK, who put me to engineering, who put me through to the hotel manager, who I'm sure assumed I had broken it off in some wild sexual encounter with Rafael. But all he told me was that there had been a rash of shower head thefts.

I looked at the phone.

Actually pulled the phone away from my ear and glared at it.

I had no response.

I had no idea what to make of that sentence, so I simply said, "Okay," and hung up the phone. I mean, what else could I say? Does this happen often? Is there an international ring of shower head thieves causing a worldwide shortage?

What the fuck did people do with a used shower head, when there was money and jewels and lamps and TVs to be stolen?

The truth is, I didn't want to know the answer. I think the possible explanations scared me more than the gushing hot water that had scalded me.

Now, I'm really not one to make trouble, but it seems to me if the Intercontinental Hotel can charge me three hundred dollars a night, they can afford to get me another fucking shower head. I may seem to be making a big deal about the shower head, but believe me, you want to know how serious I took this, unscrew *your* shower head and sit under it for a while.

You can give me a call and tell me what you think.

So I was standing there, trying to dry off, and I find that along with the inoperable plumbing there seems to also be a linens shortage. I like a good air-dry as much as the next guy. Unfortunately, it was the next guy who was walking in the door.

He was tall, blond, angular, German most likely. Didn't look like he was a trade. More like a businessman or maybe a lobbyist.

"Excuse me," I said.

He looked a bit confused. He glanced down at the room number written on the folder housing his keycard, then up at the number on the door. "I believe you're in my room."

I looked around. "Ah, no, this is my room."

"Six thirty-one," he said, pointing to the folder, then the door. "I just opened it."

I went over to him, grabbed the keycard out of his hand, and pulled him into the hall. I didn't even care I was naked. I closed the door, slid the card into the slot.

"The maid was just here, she probably—"

The green light went on, and the lock clicked.

He looked at me. "My room. The last one they had," he said. He snatched back his card key.

Definitely not a lobbyist.

I went inside and picked up my card off the bed. I was going to demonstrate to this nub his obvious mistake. I pushed him out of the way, slammed the door and put my card in the slot.

Red light.

I tried again.

Nothing.

"Let me," he said.

"No, this card opens this door. Trust me." I jammed the card in a third time. "I hate these things. I feel like I'm sleeping inside a fucking ATM!"

That's when it happened. I didn't mean to do it. The force I used was too much for the thin piece of plastic. It snapped off deep inside the slot.

Now, not even the German nub's card could unlock the door.

As I stood there naked on the sixth-floor hall of the Intercontinental Hotel, yelling at the door, I heard the ting of the elevator as a collection of females got off.

Now, I'd like to say that one or more them offered to take me to their room. Didn't happen. Not even close.

One of them did scream, "Oh, my God!"

The German guy was right, by the way, there aren't any rooms left in the hotel. I know this because when I went down to the front desk, dripping wet, skin peeling off my shoulders, clad only in a towel I was able to get from a shocked maid working the sixth floor, the very polite clerk confirmed this very unfortunate fact. Not to be paranoid or anything, but who should be sitting in the lobby enjoying an espresso from a *doppio*-sized cup, but Rafael.

"So nice to see...so much of you," she said as she walked over with this evil little grin on her mischievous pretty face.

"I'm trying to be more relaxed," I told her, wiping a little bit of shampoo out of my eyelashes, which was sort of surprising since I figured most of Lake Geneva had been heated then dumped on me.

"You have some —"

"I know, I know. What are you still doing down here? I would've figured you'd be upstairs trolling the conference room by now."

"Nobody up z'ere. At least, not anyone I want to play with more than you."

"Thanks, that makes me feel so much better."

"You're verrrry welcome, *mon chéri*."

"You didn't, by chance, happen to have bought all the excess rooms in the hotel?"

"If you need a room, you can stay with me."

"Oh, no, no. I don't think so."

"I promise, I will not touch you." She looked at me, sincerely. "I will only touch myself."

Rafael has never played fair.

"At least with me, it would've been a lot more fun getting wet."

"You know...you are really starting to bother me."

"Yes, I can tell."

And she could because at that moment she had her hand along the inside of my thigh, which, I don't need to tell you, didn't make it any easier to attempt a getaway in my towel.

She's even tougher to negotiate against.

French women really annoy me. Unfortunately, they annoy me in an extremely satisfying way.

For the moment, I was going nowhere.

10
WHY THE FRENCH REALLY HATE US

AFTER ARGUING, one of my family's greatest gifts is the ability to export madness to those outside our clan. Spending time with my family is like jumping out of an airplane. You're scared, it's dangerous, you may not survive, but it's definitely a rush. To that end, my mother was not satisfied with spreading our charms around our town or even Connecticut alone. She was hell-bent on serving us up as an American host to foreign students.

"We need to share our way of life with those of other cultures," I remember her saying.

That my great-grandparents were from the very same places these students lived, posed no irony for my mother.

They were foreigners. We were not.

Not that either of my parents are xenophobes. On the contrary, my folks want to devour alien culture, dissect it, and sift through the rubble until they understand what it's like to be French or German or whatever.

Unfortunately, they never do. Understand.

I often felt pity for them, these experience seekers, as they got off the plane and were greeted by us, for I knew these kids spoke two or more languages, had traveled to numerous countries, experienced different cultures, but nevertheless were as unprepared for what lay ahead as an infant taking the SAT.

These poor people, four in all, two males and two females, one each summer, were simply not ready for life in the Gerrick household. That after spending time with my family one of these fine young Europeans offered me a chance to visit him, still remains one of life's sincere mysteries.

We picked up Dominique, the first of the four, at Bradley International Airport, just north of Hartford.

I speak four languages now, understand two more, although I rarely speak anything but English at the bargaining tables. I learned this not from any relative, but from the Japanese. They always let their interpreters translate for them, even though every single one of them can speak perfect English, and many have studied in the States.

It's a power thing. It's like how most things are traded in U.S. dollars. It's not because everyone likes paying for oil with George Washingtons, it's because we've been, for most of the last century, the biggest, baddest trade partner in the world.

The Japanese are just trying to say, hey, we're huge too.

But back then, I could only speak enough French to get myself beat up, arrested or slapped. In fact, I never really learned how to speak a foreign language until I needed to pick up on French girls. Strange how certain things in your life lead you to your destiny.

Dominique was a good-looking guy, almost two years older than I was. And we had a great time that summer, even though I think he was slightly—only slightly—disappointed with his surroundings. He was a gracious guest, but I could tell he was used to a little more in terms of creature comfort. He liked my room very much, even though it was small, because I had made it into such a lair. And he was grateful for the six weeks I slept on the couch. He also liked my younger sister very much— she was nine then—I think mostly because he had never had a sister and partly because she just adored him.

We had a great six weeks of taking him places and letting him meet my friends and going to summer parties. We connected, he and I. It was my first experience with someone outside my small sphere. A Frenchman who lived in France, not an American with French ancestors. Something happens to people once they pass through Ellis Island and its modern equivalents, something profound. Because once you see the land that brought together so many different types of people from different parts of the globe, and see the meshing of cultures and foods and genes, see the words on the Statue of Liberty, you realize that for all its faults, all the negative things you've heard about America, it's one fucking awesome country.

The year after Dominique's visit to America, I received an invitation to spend the summer with him and his family in the city of Nancy, located in northeast France.

My parents scraped together enough money for my ticket, and just after my sixteenth birthday, I left my home to embark on what would be one of the greatest trips of my life.

If only my father could get me to the damn airport.

"Goddamned JF-fucking-K!" he screamed over the blaring horn as another car got in his way. "You know why this city is in the shit-house?"

"Why don't you tell me, dad."

"Cause they don't know anything about traffic control in New York. Look at this mess. I can't fucking drive in this shit. I knew I should've put you on the train in New Haven."

My father had locked inside his sizable head all the secrets the ancients had been hiding from modern man. All of society's ills had been eradicated, rectified, wiped away within the walls of his skull. That no one outside my house or Dunkin' Donuts has heard these theories haunts mankind to this day. The fact seemed to slip my father's mind that he had to build a third driveway for his car because he couldn't handle the traffic problems that were caused when I got my license and started to share my parents' other *two* driveways. Most people got along with one driveway, not the Gerricks. Nope, we had three.

I often wondered if my father's solution for New York City traffic would include a nine million lane highway.

"If you had gotten home on time, you could've put us on the train, " I said, "but you didn't, and we would have missed the flight."

Time was something of a mystery to my father. He would tell you he was going to pick you up after practice at 5 P.M. in front of the school and he'd drive up at 6:45, then leave you stranded if you happened to be at a payphone trying to track him down and didn't get into his car within thirty seconds of his arrival.

That night, I was flying with the son of a family friend, Gino, who was sitting in back enjoying the banter and even egging the Princess on by asking him questions about traffic flow. Gino and I had met many times over the years, at parties, get-togethers, holiday drive-bys, but we didn't really know each other well. On that flight, that flight from New York to Paris, with a stopover in Hell, we grew quite close. Primarily, because it was the first time I was ever on a plane.

When I get nervous, I get funny. I was very funny that flight.

Gino and I were both heading to France to stay with families. He would be going to someplace outside Paris. I was going ninety kilometers east.

I have been to Europe, God, maybe a hundred times now, but on that night, I was going to a place of wonder and history. I was heading out on an adventure no less fantastic in my mind than Magellan's or Cortez's. Well, okay, maybe I wasn't an intrepid explorer...I had the number—thanks to mom—of every American Embassy, Consulate, and corporate office she could round up.

She actually gave me a map of France with all of the American Express offices marked on it. I guess, in case I happened to decide to storm the beaches of Normandy and needed Traveler's Checks.

My father weaved and swore and circled and cursed as we made our way through the maze that is JFK. "These fucking people. Don't they know anything about designing fucking airports?"

If you've never been to JFK, and it's only marginally better now than it was then, let me try to explain what my father, somewhat justifiably, was screaming about.

Picture an airport. O'Hare, Dallas-Ft. Worth, SFO, LAX, Heathrow.

Any of 'em.

Throw it in a Cuisinart. Then add a highway, any highway, but preferably one that's curvy, constantly under construction, and wraps back around on itself.

Puree.

What you'd come up with would be approximately twenty-four point-five times better than JF-fucking-K.

Unlike most airports, the terminals at JFK aren't centrally located, but instead, are spread out like Polynesian islands all over the place. I have always pitied travelers having to change airlines. In fact, the only thing that is centrally located in JFK is the spaghetti-like maze of overpasses and underpasses, potholes, concrete and tar where New York's tourists spend much of their visit.

Finally, somehow, we arrived.

The Princess said his goodbyes at the curb. His love of airports was only slightly outpaced by his hatred of parking at airports, so when he asked me if I wanted him to come in (I knew he wanted to see the 'pane, pane' take-off, he was like a child in his awe of trains and planes and automobiles) I simply had to say, "I heard the parking at JFK is screwed up."

"Screwed up? It's a nightmare! They could fix it, of course. They could build enough parking right next to the terminals, but they won't. You know why? The fucking unions."

"The unions?" This was a new one.

"Taxi and bus drivers. They don't *want* you to park here."

"Just..." I stared at him for a moment, "drop us off at the curb."

So, I kissed the Princess's scratchy face, and Gino and I made our escape.

Once we got inside, we got our first clue that, perhaps, our wonderfully cost-conscious mothers had made a mistake in putting us on an airline no one had ever heard of.

The clue came in the form of a sign that was handwritten on what was once a manila folder that had probably contained documents pertaining to one of many lawsuits brought against the airline.

Written on the torn-in-half folder in big green Magic Marker letters was the airline's name: evergreen. Small "E" in this person's rendition.

I have since learned that Evergreen is a cargo carrier and that it has exactly one plane it uses for Charter flights. One plane with seats.

One.

I had no idea of this at the time. I was more concerned with what other things they were skimping on if they couldn't afford decent signage. Nuts, bolts, flaps, an experienced crew?

It's funny to think now that I was sixteen years old when finally taking my first flight and, did I happen to mention, terrified?

In fact, I didn't really start to enjoy flying until just a few years ago, when I decided I better fall in love with something I'd be doing a dozen times a month.

That's being in a plane an average of once every two and a half days, every week, every month.

But back then, I enjoyed flying as much as having my head drilled.

That we had to wait six hours because of a "technical problem" with the plane didn't make me feel any more confident about the outcome of my trip. (One passenger kept asking, "Why don't you just send another plane?" Answer: Because we don't have one.)

The only thing that kept me going was the knowledge that I wouldn't have to deal with the Princess for six whole weeks. Now, you might think, young Billy, first time away, he'll be homesick.

Not for a minute.

Because that was the year my father began growing African violets in the cellar. Hundreds and hundreds of plants sitting warmly under the bluish-violet glow of three dozen Gro-lights. Some men spend their weekends watching football players tear up the turf or basketball players crash the boards. My father watched plants grow. I am amazed by the simplest things in the world, a tree, ants, the ocean, but never have I ever been less excited than observing African Violets bloom.

It's not that they aren't somewhat pretty—they are, I guess. Growing them, grafting them, coddling them just seems a monumental waste of time. I mean, roses, maybe, but scrawny little things that look more like mutant, colored four-leaf clovers? Who needs them?

My father often couldn't pick me up from track practice because the hybrids were "germinating."

My mother loved those things. Loved them. That was until she had five hundred of them blocking the washer and dryer.

The Princess is not one to be concerned or efficient with other people's space. He'd confiscate a few more feet, and the number of plants would grow. Oh, he stacked them, built contraptions (another of his favorite words, along with concoction) to light them and water them like plant high rises, but by the end, the man was jonesin'.

He swore he only wanted a hundred. Soon a hundred seemed like nothing. He wanted two hundred. Once he reached that, he wanted three hundred. He finally ran out of room after about five hundred.

See, my father had the idea that the flower shops of the world were clamoring for African Violets. And he would be the one to supply them, as many as they needed. He had actually gone as far as to talk to some local nurseries.

Now, you might think from the enthusiasm of the Princess that these nurseries were actually interested in receiving African Violets from a man who grew them in the area between his washer, dryer, and extra freezer.

You would be wrong.

I'm not gonna say that they had *no* interest whatsoever, but I think it was a combination of common courtesy and morbid curiosity.

Like many things in the Gerrick household, the African violet saga— like the Fat Track, and holiday dinners—had a tragic and violent ending.

It started when the Princess couldn't find something that was, he realized later, in the trunk of his car where he put it, and ended in a fit of anger after my mother had the nerve to question my father about why our electric bill had tripled.

That afternoon was the day he destroyed every last African Violet.

I hated those plants, kind of like I hate coffee, Saabs, Hondas, and malt liquor. They were things that occupied my father, took him away from me. But still, that day, the day he trashed his flowers, I was strangely saddened by the loss. I don't think I was mourning the passing of the little brightly colored "shamrocks," although I do find them slightly more attractive now than I did when they occupied our house. No, I was more upset for the Princess because as it has happened so many times for so many people in so many places, a momentary flash of rage ruins years of past work and years of future pleasure.

He grew some flowers after that, but it was never the same. His heart wasn't in it in the same way it used to be.

But on the other side of the Atlantic for six whole weeks, I would be free. Not that I wasn't free at home, because I was pretty much able to do whatever I wanted as long as I could outlast my mother's resistance.

But this was different. This was true freedom.

The French don't let teenagers drive until they're eighteen and even then they can't go faster than 90 kph (about 55 mph) the first year. You're actually required to slap a magnetic decal onto the back of the car you're driving. It has the international "NO" slash over the number "90." That's freedom, you ask? Ah, but see, for that, you get something in return. If you can reach the bar to ask for a drink, you can buy a drink. Not as much damage a drunk bicyclist can do.

In a way, the theory is brilliant. The young men and women get to do something they are most likely going to do anyway, and they also get some experience testing their alcohol tolerance before climbing behind the wheel.

THE MOST LASTING lesson I learned dealing with Evergreen Airlines, which has come in handy over the years, is that you should never, never, ever get on a plane hungry. Forget not shopping hungry. Or the stupid myth about not going into a pool after eating. *This* is advice worth listening to. Believe me when I say this, you will not feel better after your in-flight meal, even if you're sitting in first class, which just so happens to be the most expensive two-star restaurant in the world.

After more than six hours of waiting, buying food from the Automat and not eating it (I always thought an Automat was either a place to do laundry, or the thing underneath your feet in a car. As I found out, it only tasted that way.), feeding all the quarters we had into the little black and white TVs attached to the armrests of the waiting area seats (do you know what was on TV in New York at three in the morning in 1979 before cable and satellite became ubiquitous? Nothing.), and finding it impossible to sleep on the cold polished floor of the terminal—even if you could let your guard down long enough to try—after all that, we were finally told we could get on the plane.

Rounded up and herded onto the plane would describe it more aptly.

It took another two hours to get the engines started.

I offered to get out and push.

Finally, at eight in the morning, an hour after getting off the ground, and twelve hours since my last meal, I was handed my first taste of Evergreen cuisine. If I had eaten tree bark and rocks, I would have been more satisfied.

I longed for the Automat.

SOMEHOW THE COWBOYS in the cockpit got us to Paris without any scars, at least, physical.

Following stops in Dublin and London, I stepped off the plane at about 10:10 P.M.—this is night to me—and yet, the sun was just setting. This may not be strange for those people along the Arctic Circle, but I was in Paris. Paris, France.

It was a bit unnerving. I had no idea the sun could set this late for anyone who didn't live in an igloo.

Dominique had stayed home to study for exams, so I found his parents waiting for me at the gate. Two people who spoke as much English as I spoke French at the time. Which left a few gaps in the conversation. We gestured with our hands a lot, and picked up my luggage from the baggage carousel, and then with a great deal of smiling and nodding made the ninety-kilometer drive to Nancy as the night faded into—finally—darkness.

I sat in the back seat of their Peugeot as it screamed down the "highway," which was little more than a two-lane road with plastic reflectors in the middle—oh, that'll keep a wined-up businessman from crossing into oncoming traffic.

I was scared shitless in the back of that car.

I'll discuss more about driving in France later.

Other than that, my trip was wonderful.

The first thing I'm gonna do when my kids turn sixteen is put them on a plane and send them to Europe: France or Spain or Italy. Okay, maybe Germany if they really, really beg me. And after I've forced them to listen to German and Italian language CDs side-by-side. There's just something very romantic about the Romance languages and the people that speak them.

The Germans know how to make a car, but they don't know shit about romance.

I said before, French women annoy me. They irritate me because I can't seem to keep my hands off them. I become too easily enamored with them for my own good. Rafael is only the last in a series of *femme fatales*. In fact, French women are the reason I fly all over the planet to try and sell more American goods and services.

Well, one French woman, in particular.

A girl, actually.

Her name was Patrice. I met her through Dominique on my visit. She had short chestnut-colored hair, an athletic body, and long, beautiful legs. She spoke English well—her father often traveled to New York on business and practiced speaking with her. She was an accomplished fencer, competing against nationally ranked twenty-five to thirty-year-old men, even though she was only sixteen.

She was also Dominique's best friend's girlfriend.

This presented somewhat of a dilemma for me since I was very attracted to Patrice, and she was apparently attracted to me. That was not the dilemma. The predicament was that I really liked her boyfriend, Loren, thought he was cool, and knew that I would have to spend two weeks hiking in the wilds of Corsica with him and Dominique and seven other guys.

Overt moves on his girlfriend could end with me at the bottom of a ravine.

Still, it was difficult to ignore the way her body, the touch of her hand made me feel. It charmed me, the way she would dance with me when her boyfriend was facing us and how as soon as he turned away she would press herself close against my body.

I don't think we were being particularly discreet. Just enough, I suppose. I made it off Corsica alive.

I think he knew. He had to. But then I guess that's the way of the French.

One day, while Dominique and Loren were completing their *baccalauréat*—the test they take at the end of high school—Patrice and I had six hours alone together. It is still one of the most erotic six hours of my life.

We weren't having sex. We were fencing.

Feint. Parry. Thrust.

She was teaching me a sport I had always been fascinated by, a sport which took on new dimensions with her as my opponent.

Afterward, exhausted from the competition and from the heat between us, we sat on the floor and simply touched. Her hands showed me a way of caressing that even with all our clothes on was like having sex. She taught me like no American girl could about the power of faint breath on the neck and what that could do to a lover.

She made me curious about the world outside America, which led me to learn French, Japanese, and German (all of which I speak badly, but understand perfectly), which led me to study global politics, which led me to macroeconomics, which led me to international trade.

She also taught me how to duel with charm and how more than one side can get what they want.

She kissed pretty well, too.

As RAFAEL CONVERSES a few feet away with a handsome member of her team, touching his arm in that way that is designed to remind me again of what I'm missing, I'm handed a note from the big blond oaf behind the desk.

"What's this?"

"A message," he says, oafishly.

Now, I haven't gotten an actual *paper* message from a hotel clerk since I got stuck in Cairo at this little hotel my former travel agent told me was "quaint" and had a "local feel."

I now know what that means. One bathroom per floor. One phone.

In the lobby.

I get dozens of messages. Most of them voice mails from Allison telling me of the dozens of messages I have.

What made the note stand out so much, was not that it was on paper, not that it was taken while I had been sitting on my bed two feet from the phone, but that it was from my grandfather.

Sebby rarely called me. It wasn't as if my maternal grandfather hated talking to me, it was that he was uneasy and somewhat suspicious of technology.

I should clarify that. He didn't *despise* progress in principle, as long as it didn't change the world *too* much.

He was happy with the way things were, that's all.

He always felt inadequate when it came to using technology. He was one of the smartest men I've ever known, but street-smart, not book-smart. My Grandfather Robert, on the other hand, was comfortable with new things, advancements, the latest development. He passed that on to my father. The Princess is well known for his stereo acumen. In his bedroom and in the cellar were two of the finest audio systems available in the world. Four hundred watts per channel on the setup in his bedroom.

I'm not kidding. Four hundred watts.

Nobody makes a speaker that can handle four hundred watts. Not one that can fit through the front door. If we took a wall out maybe...

Four hundred watts per channel is meant for studios and small concert halls, or for powering ten pairs of speakers throughout an entire house.

Not a bedroom.

But that's what he had.

For two speakers.

"Gives you amazing clarity. No hum," my father would say.

This techno-lust, I have inherited. I realize this makes me like Robert and my father in some ways, but I don't mind that part of me being from them. I know I'll always be at ease with whatever comes at me in the future.

You only get old when you give up learning.

And yet, there is something about people who can interface with computers and gadgetry so easily. I think it betrays a certain coldness in ourselves.

Sebby has never been cold. His crooked smile is warm and disarming, his face, his eyes, his touch, everything about him, exhibits a certain radiance.

Unfortunately, I'm not all Sebby. Thankfully, neither am I all Robert. I don't mean to say that everything about my father's father was bad because that's not at all the case. It's just that some of his most striking qualities—extreme intellect, piercing logic, extraordinary perseverance—were also his most remarkable faults.

I've mentioned a number of ways my grandfather Robert has influenced my ability to deal with some of the more sinister techniques of pols, dips, and trades—stonewalling, distortion, trying to get under your skin, but it's Sebby that brings to me the patience, kindness, and wisdom that assuages those harsher traits.

Sebby doesn't preach like too many people who fancy themselves teachers, mentors, and gurus do. As occasionally I do when I'm talking to my troops, or giving a speech, like that podium pounder I gave earlier.

No, Sebby has always been a man of few words. He teaches by example, by showing you the technique of using your hands, not telling you.

He was a carpenter. A man who learned his trade during the depression, building bridges under the auspices of the WPA.

In his forties, when his knees began to give out, he quit doing carpentry full-time and went to work, along with my grandmother, for the state, becoming houseparents at the Connecticut School for Boys. We'd call it a youth correctional facility today.

Neither of them had any formal training, unlike those who would come after them, which is perhaps the problem with today's Youth Authorities. These well-schooled, well-meaning people are not cut from the same cloth as those they try to help. They've spent too much time delving too deep into the science of behavior that they sometimes lose sight of what is in front of them.

A kid.

In trouble.

In need.

Even though many of these kids were black or Puerto Rican, my grandparents, who grew up in the depression, could relate to them. They understood being poor, having tough childhoods, and being from immigrant families. Kids pick up on that. They know. They can tell the difference when you're talking out of a book or from your heart.

"Social engineers" tried to figure me out in second grade, when I was a "troubled child" as they put it to my folks.

The school wanted to "help." Only I didn't seem to fit any of their categories. Not that they didn't try.

There was this one guy, a school shrink, that had me take tests and stare at inkblots and on and on and on for three days straight.

I was seven years old, too young to outsmart an adult—or so these morons thought.

I stared at the spots, tried really hard to appear to be thinking, and then, like a gift from God, I had a vision. And in that moment, the most perfect answers rushed into my head, and I simply couldn't resist.

I had to stifle a laugh as I looked him dead in the eye and said with all the pride and excitement of someone finally seeing the truth.

"That one looks like an atomic mushroom cloud." "A duck, with a brain tumor." "Jesus with a handgun."

God only knows what he wrote in my file. I never saw him again.

MY GRANDPARENTS' new job included a house on the grounds of the school, which is how I came to live in the home they built. It was only a few years old when they began working for the state and sold their flat-roofed pride and joy to my parents.

Their new residence was at the top of a hill, overlooking brick buildings and picturesque fields of green grass and mighty oaks. The exterior reminded me of a mini-Monticello, Thomas Jefferson's grand home in Virginia. It had a stately look about it, although it was not made out of granite or marble, but a reddish rock, the color of rust and earth mixed together.

Inside was rather small. A serviceable kitchen and a modest bedroom with two twin beds, a dresser with a white doily draped over it, and a picture of Jesus. There was a third room, uncharacteristically large, that was part living room, part den, part dining area. It was almost as tall as it was wide, and it's most striking feature was a light that hung down from the ceiling over my grandparents' small, steel-edged, cloth-covered, pre-Formica-veneered dining table.

The light was attached to the ceiling by a long tube that had been painted over so many times I wasn't sure if it was made out of metal or paper mâché. The tube terminated a few feet above the table, blossoming into a most amazing lamp, with colors and textures I had never seen before, that I have since observed only in the most ornate homes, palaces and consulates of the world.

The fixture stood out from the rest of the room, which was rather drab.

There were attempts made to brighten the place up, mainly two fringed lampshades that sat atop floor lamps, making them look like a couple of anorexics boozing it up at the Cotton Club.

Only the light over the table distracted the eye. Under its brightness, Sebby and I and my grandmother played thousands of hands blackjack, war, poker, and mostly gin rummy. I can't tell you, can't begin to explain or even comprehend how these afternoons spent saying things like, "I'll take two" and "I call" became some of the greatest moments in my life.

There are no words to describe the quiet wisdom that I would gain sentence by sentence spoken between the picking up and laying down of the cards in a game of rummy.

"When you beat someone," Sebby said while reordering the cards in his hand, his focus totally on the task. "The important thing is...not to gloat." He slid his thumb over the fanned corners of the cards, checking them one last time. "Don't apologize. And," he said, as he started putting cards down on the table, "never ever let 'em see your cards..." Groups first. A couple of three-card ones, and a four-carder. Then sequences. Actually, there was only one sequence this game. "...till the very..." A twelve-card run in hearts from the deuce to the king. "...last second."

He snapped the king down, his last card, then gently rapped his knuckles on the table.

"Knock," he said, winning the hand. The sound echoed off the high ceilings.

Of the things I cherish most about myself, the things that I have tried to cultivate, the things I am ultimately not as good at as Sebby, are the things like tolerance and family and duty and hard work and honest effort that he taught me while fixing a window, or putting up storm doors in winter, or the screens in summer, or simply during a hand of gin rummy.

Sometimes, my grandparents would take me down to the "cottage" they supervised. I was always amazed at how these young offenders treated Sebby and Annette. Treated them with respect. It could only be because my grandparents earned that respect.

They were stern. They were disciplinarians. But they were fair.

There is this story that my grandfather tells every once in a while at family gatherings. Several of the boys in their house got into a fistfight one afternoon. My grandmother told them repeatedly to stop. When they refused to listen to her because their blood was boiling, and their anger was already up, she grabbed a large cast iron frying pan, lifted it over her head and cocked her arm, ready to throw it.

My grandmother, even years before age began to cannibalize her body, maybe weighed a hundred pounds. To see this slender woman raising cookware probably one-third her body weight in a threatening manner may have caused some people to laugh. Everyone who hears the story laughs. But not those boys. They froze in place their fists inches from their targets. And as their hands dropped to their sides, all they said was, "Sorry, Mrs. Z."

Sebby would tell the story with a mix of laughter and awe, and even some tears, proud of what they tried to do—to give meaning to wayward kids—and proud of his wife.

Hearing the recitation, my grandmother would simply nod. And sometimes, only sometimes, she gave a quiet, "Yep."

That was all the emotion she usually gave.

It's not as if she's a cold woman, far from it, but it's difficult to conjure up an image of my grandmother crying or laughing. Seen pictures of it. Have vague whispers of these moments in my mind. Yet nothing on the surface. Sebby is the one who wears his emotions on his sleeve. Whether it was talking to my father, trying to get him to recognize his responsibilities, or to me when I needed some guidance, or to "his kids."

These boys had scars on their faces, and eyes that looked much older than their years. They had seen things, things that I didn't see at their age and many of which I still haven't seen, thank God.

I was only a few years younger than these kids, but they seemed like men to me. Most of them towered over my grandparents, which made it more amazing to see these boys look up to them.

To see any of these young men on the street—and these weren't even the worst of them, the violent offenders, murderers and rapists, they were kept in a high-security area with fenced-in buildings and fenced-in basketball courts, razor wire at the top—even these more minor offenders would be frightening. But for some reason in the presence of Sebby, under the vigilant gaze of Annette, they were friendly, smart, even funny.

They acted more like kids.

After the School for Boys was integrated into the School for Girls—that was an intelligent move, putting troubled teenagers of opposite sexes within sprinting distance of each other (trust me, you don't ever want to see two pregnant juveniles having a brawl in a cafeteria)—my grandparents moved to an apartment and drove each morning to the co-ed facility. I only remember visiting them once at this other campus. It wasn't home then, it was different. I think the kids felt differently, too. When you live amongst them, there is a trust, a respect, a family that is forged.

I once asked Sebby, "How come these kids have to stay in jail?"

"Because they did things that were wrong."

"I'm always doing things that are wrong," I said. "Why do these kids end up here and not me?"

"Because they come from places that are hard. Where nobody cares about them, at least not enough."

For a moment, I felt special when Sebby said that, then I felt sad for the other kids, then a bit embarrassed, because I realized, I didn't always appreciate what I had.

What was right in front of me.

"WHY DIDN'T you put this through?" I said to the big blond oaf. I was upset I had missed Sebby's call, and even more angry that it had come in while I had been in my room.

"We 'ad you listed as checked out," he said in his most annoying French accent.

"I just checked in!" My voice boomed in the cavernous lobby. The few people that weren't already staring at me turned their heads. I lowered my voice. "Have you people gotten in my room yet? All my clothes, all my papers are in there."

The oaf looked at me. "Geofrey," he says, only he pronounced it *gufwha*, "is upstairs trying."

I wanted to slap him.

"He 'as 'ad to call the company that installed the system. We 'ave never 'ad a card break off in the lock before."

No, I wanted to knock him over the head.

"THEY GAVE AWAY MY ROOM."

"There must be another room in the hotel," Laura says from the other side of the Atlantic.

I'm still wet from my skirmish with the shower head-less spout. No longer dripping, just a nice, uncomfortable dampness.

"I'm in a towel. I'm pissed. Believe me, there aren't any more rooms in the hotel. Apparently, besides hosting every fucking trade in the world, the IOC is fielding bribes to choose the next site for the Olympics."

"The Great Billy Gerrick—my *man*—can't negotiate one room out of them?"

"Your Great Billy Gerrick is wearing a towel in the lobby, yelling his head off. If there was a broom closet available, they would have gladly shoved me into it by now."

"So you're going to bunk with someone?"

"I guess." I rub my head. I've now got the protection of a phone booth, so I'm not so self-conscious about being clad only in terry cloth. "And which person are you thinking would be appropriate for me to bunk with?"

"There must be a half-dozen women at that conference you've already slept with."

This is Laura's way of telling me she knows all about me.

"I think it's closer to ten, actually."

"I don't doubt it." There is an audible pause. "Rafael offered to let you sleep with her, didn't she?"

I try to explain that it was just a kind gesture, an empty offer.

"It was some kind of offer, all right," she says.

"Okay, gotta go now...and find myself a cardboard box. I love you."

I hang up the phone.

RAFAEL BRIBED SOMEONE, I was sure of it. Or maybe she just whispered really nicely into the ear of the oafish desk clerk in that voice of hers, but no matter. There was no point in trying to win him or anyone else over, if that's what she had done. I simply didn't have enough ammunition.

I still had nowhere to stay.

There were obvious choices. None of them great. Tom had a house just outside the city. He also had a brand new baby girl. In fact, he had asked about getting a room for himself, so he could get some sleep. There was Allison. Not a good idea. Besides, her suite was our team's command center. I'd get no rest there.

Doug Powers, Tony Genaldi, Ken Strazinski, were already sharing a room because space was so tight. Having the U.S.'s senior negotiator sleeping on a cot would not be good.

For my back or our negotiations.

Karen Ko and Francesca. Nice thought.

No.

I kept running down the possibilities.

All the options were either unworkable, inappropriate, or gave the appearance of impropriety.

It may sound weird, superstitious, even a bit pompous, but little things like this can give the appearance of a team out of sync, slightly disorganized. Not only do you want to be mentally at the top of your game, you also want everyone else to think, "Don't fuck with him today."

Now, on the other hand, the rumor of sleeping with the most coveted woman in Geneva wouldn't necessarily be a bad thing.

I usually did very, very well the day after spending the night with Rafael.

It might be their envy or my confidence, or maybe it was just that I'm a helluva lot more grumpy, tense and distracted when I haven't gotten laid.

I'm a very simple man.

"OKAY, BUT NO TOUCHING," I say to Rafael, setting the ground rules as firmly as possible. "I mean it."

"Of course. I told you." She pauses. "I will only touch myself."

"See, no, you cannot say, do, or think things like that tonight. Agreed?"

She nods. I can picture her crossing her fingers behind her back, only I don't know if the French do that.

"Perception," I say, and she nods again, knowingly. "is truth. Perhaps, if we do this discreetly, properly, it will appear...good for both of us. I'll just call Laura and..."

"...explain why you are sleeping with me?"

"Near you. I will be sleeping near you."

Rafael smiles. But then as she continues to look into my eyes, I see hers betray a deeper feeling. A slight sadness, as if she's playing a game that she doesn't want to play. Maybe she's tired of these battles.

"Florence was nice, wasn't it?"

I look at her and sigh.

"I think I'm gonna sleep at the consulate. It'll look like I'm getting last minute instructions."

"I will be verrry, verrry gud."

"That's what I'm afraid of."

"You, Billy, are not afraid of anything."

Yeah, except maybe a seven-pound, three-ounce diaper wearer.

Terrified.

I sigh, rubbing my eyes with my fingertips, looking around at a lobby that is deserted even though there's not one free room, which means the low-levels are still in session, which means only one thing. "Raf, I don't think things are as finished as we've been led to believe."

For the briefest instant, Rafael Perrieux, the skilled negotiator makes an appearance as her face registers what I said. But that Rafael is gone as soon as she notes the thought.

She plays with my fingers, resting at my side.

As if she does this all the time, she smoothly hands me her room key.

I glance up at her. "Maybe." I let my fingers linger in her grasp, then pull them gently away. "I have to go. I need to go over something sensitive."

"Me, too," she says, running a finger over her shirt right where her nipple should be. And there it is. "Call me before you come up, so if I'm busy with someone, I can ask him to leave before you arrive."

I don't know why, but I feel a tinge of jealousy.

11

SEBBY, THE ARCHITECT

SINCE I HAD NOWHERE ELSE to go that wouldn't get me in trouble, I decided to look in on the low-levels who were battling it out in what was normally a very elegant ballroom.

It might be a little insulting to call these highly-educated professional negotiators "low-levels," especially since this is where the actual letter by letter wording of the agreements are worked out, but hey, that's what everyone calls them.

THE ROOM WAS ORDERED PANDEMONIUM. Assistants running back and forth with documents, reference materials, drinks, aspirin, Valium.

I could see Tom was agitated.

More than agitated.

"No, no, no, no!" He was sitting in his chair, teeth clenched, trying to keep from shouting. "Can't you see how ridiculous this practice is? It encourages a de facto tariff we have no control over. You might as well just tear up this whole document! It'll be worthless."

I got Tom's attention before the top of his head blew off. He excused himself and came over.

He took a look at the towel.

"That's a good look for you. You trying to curry favor with island nations?"

"What's going on?" I said, ignoring the remark. I had embraced my just-got-out-of-the-sauna look.

He took in a deep breath, let the air out slowly, then peered back at the table. "Some of the Europeans are going back on their promise to cut the bribery tax deduction."

"You're fucking kidding me."

"Oh, I'm serious. And some of our Latin friends are backing them up."

"Of course, they are," Doug Powers said, joining us. "Didn't Cubrero get a million dollars from Deutsche Telekom last year?"

I searched the room and found him immediately. Cubrero was cloaked in an expensive suit that was definitely English, most likely Henry Poole. "*Half* a million. His Prime Minister got the million."

One of the most profound challenges America faces is how to remove impediments to markets outside the United States. I've talked about some of these barriers, but one increasingly prevalent practice has been largely ignored, and even implicitly accepted—bribery and corruption in international transactions.

They have often been accepted as a necessary means of doing business, as "cultural phenomenon."

In 1977, the United States passed the Foreign Corrupt Practices Act. To this day, we are the only nation on earth who holds its citizens accountable for engaging in this kind of behavior.

We're not talking about slipping hundred dollar bills to customs officials at the border. We're talking bribes worth hundreds of thousands of dollars, sometimes millions, cutting U.S. companies out of what's estimated to be something like one hundred to two hundred billion dollars in business each year.

Each year.

Tolerance of this is a worldwide problem. You see it in the economies of Asia and Latin America, even in our historic trading partners in Japan and Europe. Believe it or not, in some countries in Europe you can even deduct the costs of bribery on your taxes.

Let's see...I drove my Mercedes twenty-one thousand kilometers for business at 0.50 Deutsche marks per, leased fourteen computers for the office in Hamburg, and bribed the President of Paraguay with ten kilos of gold bullion.

That's my tax return. Send me my refund.

This is what Tom is frothing at the mouth about. We had negotiated over a year ago that the EU would force its member countries to prohibit the tax deductibility of bribes to foreign officials. We were not even at the point yet of asking them to *criminalize* bribery as we have. We're just talking about abolishing the preposterous tax write-off here.

"We are not going to table this," I said to Tom. "Tell them I said that."

I WAS FORCED to purchase clothes from the gift shop because they still couldn't get into my room.

I was standing by a lovely fireplace, watching Tom tell the trades at the table that the removal of tax deductions for bribe money was not negotiable when the word came. It came via fax delivered by a very nimble porter.

Sebby was dead.

I couldn't breathe.

My grandfather, my favorite person in all the world, was gone.

The porter, thankfully, must have read the contents of the dispatch and did not give me the chance to reach into my brand-new pocket for a tip. It's the small kindnesses you remember.

I thought about the missed call again. My blood rose in anger and frustration fueled by sadness.

I stared through the flimsy sheet, seeing nothing but a blur.

We were two days before the crucial vote on the agreement. Two days from the moment I had been working and planning and studying for for the past four years, that my predecessors had spent eight more years trying to complete.

The shape of trade and the global economy for the next half-century and beyond was being forged over the next forty-eight hours.

Sebby would have wanted me to stay, which was exactly why I had to go home. He was more than my grandfather. He was a mentor, a confidant, someone I had more in common with than either of my parents or even my siblings. And yet someone who was so completely different than me.

There was no way I was going to miss Sebby's funeral. No way I was going to be kept from getting up and eulogizing him. Because he, as much as, or more, than anyone else, was responsible for what I have become. I could not sit here, questioning how to raise my own kids, without acknowledging his incredible influence on my life.

But even if I jumped on a plane immediately, flew back to Connecticut, stayed only for the services, and jetted back, I would miss the vote.

It wasn't like I absolutely had to be here—Tom could cast the ballot—but it was perception first and foremost. And perception is truth. The U.S. took this agreement seriously, and our top negotiator, the United States Trade Representative—I—needed to be here. And then there were the customary last-minute emergencies and wrangling that goes on, like the bribery tax break. Things that always threatened to derail the vote and even the agreement. It was the strategy of several countries to engage in laborious negotiations, finally agreeing to a compromise that makes the vote possible, then at the last minute, sometimes, literally, the last minute, come back with some outrageous demand.

Unfortunately, it has been quite often successful, which has caused an erosion in the process as others use the tactic.

And I know that I said that we'd probably blow this first deadline, rendering the vote a meaningless exercise, but it'd be just like some of my colleagues to use my absence as an opening to introduce new proposals that might start to take on a life of their own before I could get back to put a bullet in them.

The stakes were high. If this agreement passed, America would be on a more level playing field with the rest of our trading partners for the first time in history, instead of being the only open market in a world of closed doors and locked fences.

There would be danger, certainly, but doing nothing would be worse.

I had to be here.

And I had to be at Sebby's funeral, too.

"Can you believe this shit?" Tom was heading over with Francesca in tow. "They think they've got us over a barrel. That we want an agreement by the Sunday deadline at any cost. The President's legacy, blah, blah, blah."

Allison arrived after a pit stop at the front desk. Her look told me they hadn't gotten in my room yet. Tom was still railing against the EU.

"You know what," I said, interrupting him. "Fuck 'em." I turned to Allison. "I need you to get me a car." Then to Francesca. "I need you to leak something to a reporter." Finally, to Tom. "I need you to give me your black coat."

"My coat?"

"Yes."

"I love that coat."

"You really shouldn't get too attached to things."

I handed the fax to Allison. She glanced down at it casually. I saw the look on her face as she read the words, even though she tried to hide it from the others. Her reaction almost did me in. But I held it together.

I slipped on Tom's coat.

Without me asking, as if reading my mind, Allison handed me a secure phone. Her face was tight. She was trying desperately not to betray any more emotion. I don't know if she *could* read my mind, but I thanked her in my head anyway.

I reached for Allison's wrist, then glanced at her watch as the phone rang for the fourth time. A female voice answered. "How may I help you?"

"Seven-six-two-nine, please."

"Yessir?"

"William Gerrick, three-nine-alpha-six-four-two."

"One moment."

Another voice answered, this time a man's. "C-O-S."

"Craig, It's Billy, is he in?"

"Let me check."

When the President's Chief of Staff, Bobby McClain, answered the phone, he sounded much too chipper for this time of night, then I realized that it was only a little after five o'clock in Washington.

"Billy...I hope you're calling to tell me some good news. We need a little today."

"Well, actually I'm calling with not-so-good news." I heard him sigh. I continued, "I wanted to ask you something."

"Shoot."

"Was the President serious when he said I could play hardball with these dipshits?"

"I can affirm that recollection is a fair reading of his comments. However, to the best of my knowledge, I don't believe the President ever used the word 'dipshits' to describe our international trading partners."

"Duly noted," I said, answering his tone of mock seriousness.

"What's the problem?"

"It's not so much the negotiations. Despite some last-minute fucking around, they're mostly on track." I paused. "It's my grandfather, Bobby. He passed away earlier today."

"I'm sorry, Billy."

"I appreciate that." I was quiet for a moment. What I was about to ask was monumental. "I...I really need to be home for his funeral."

"Billy...this agreement is incredibly important."

"So is my being home."

Bobby McClain is a person that I've grown to know fairly well during my time in this administration. He is a kind, sympathetic, and understanding individual. He is also loyal to those he likes. He is, however, most loyal to the man that sits in the big chair in the Oval Office. They've known each other since the fifth grade where a young Bobby McClain punched the lights out of a bully who had tripped the future President on the playground, causing the budding politician to split open his lower lip. A scar he still has today.

"So, tell me," Bobby said. "I wouldn't be getting this call unless you had a plan."

I SAID I had to get one hundred and sixteen countries to unanimously agree.

That's not entirely true. Everyone who *wants* to be part of the treaty must agree. But it's not like Malta could say, "no" and the whole thing falls apart. That would be ridiculous. Malta would just be removed from the treaty and not reap the benefits.

Now, if one of the major players or one of the big trade blocs didn't sign on, that *would* effectively destroy the agreement.

"Hold on a second," Bobby said after I finished telling him my idea.

The phone went silent, just the echo of an international call. They sounded better these days, bouncing off satellites, or speeding through the three new fiber-optic transatlantic cables put in over the last two years, but you could still hear the subtle difference. There were minuscule delays in the conversation.

When Bobby came back on the line five minutes later, he didn't apologize for the lengthy absence.

"He said, do it."

I was already halfway to the airport before he gave me that answer.

. . .

THE LIMOUSINE I'm in pulls onto the tarmac and comes to a stop alongside a waiting military plane. Its paint job is a simple, very unmilitaristic, white. But the words in big block letters, UNITED STATES OF AMERICA, are hard to miss on the fuselage.

I pull Tom's coat over the gift shop clothes.

I step out.

A bitter wind whips through me. I pass a lone cameraman and two photographers that seem so out of place without the protection of the herd.

I make my way up the stairs leading to the military plane's door.

At the top of the steps, I pause briefly, giving them the perfect photo op: I glance back over my shoulder, a solemn look on my face.

Several flashes go off, and I disappear inside.

I COULDN'T SLEEP on the plane.

Something was bouncing around inside of my skull, something I couldn't quite put my finger on. Rafael was part of it. Even though she was the picture of chastity when I told her I wouldn't be sharing a room with her. She didn't ask me why or attempt to repeat her earlier beguiling manner. Instead, she wore a sympathetic look of concern. She knew something wasn't right, but she didn't know what it was.

The playful interactions with Rafael were bothering me much more than they usually would.

I guess, for a moment as I entertained the idea of sleeping in the same room with Rafael, I let my mind wander a little further than the usual male fantasies.

I would have gone up to that room with every conscious intention of having nothing happen between Rafael and me, but somewhere deep inside, I knew my subconscious wanted to slip into that bed, under the covers, and inside of her.

Some idiot, somewhere, somehow came up with the statistic that the average adult male thinks of sex at least once every twenty seconds. Now, how the hell anyone could have come up with that figure is simply ridiculous. I mean, how does one even begin to quantify that?

"Tell me, are you thinking of sex now?"

"Ah, well, I guess I am."

"How about now?"

"Ah, sure."

"And now?"

"Now that you mention it..."

It's a moronic assertion. But let's for the sake of argument agree that on average the typical male thinks more about sex than the typical female. This isn't to say that women don't think about sex a lot. It's just different. And for women, it ramps up over the years.

We, men, find ourselves stepping into the *longer* line at the grocery store because the checker at register six is much hotter than the ones at five, seven, or nine, and definitely more appealing than the three hundred pound butcher in lane eight that's been called up to the front to help out with the after-work rush.

We do this unconsciously, without thinking about it. Sometimes without even knowing it.

Think I'm kidding? Next time, check out the lane with the cutest checker. See how long her line is.

But I wanted to sleep. I didn't need these thoughts rattling around in my head.

Perhaps my insomnia was because I kept thinking about Sebby's call. I didn't call him back immediately because I was standing naked and in the middle of the lobby.

I just...figured I'd...call him tomorrow.

Maybe he knew he was dying. Maybe he wanted to talk to me, to say something, say his goodbyes. It was almost too awful to think about.

So, instead of dwelling on it or on Rafael any further, I planned and built a series of ridiculous and outrageous proposals that I would have Doug Powers spring on the world community tomorrow afternoon in the middle of finalizing the agreement, which would throw the entire convention into disarray. Using Doug would throw everyone off even more, leaving them to wonder why I had left and why Tom hadn't made the statement in my absence.

Was the U.S. serious? Was it so dissatisfied with this agreement that it would walk away from it?

We, of course, would blame our actions on those several countries who have, in the past, and I'm sure by then, dropped a few bombs of their own on the proceedings. If that's the way they wanted to play, well, the U.S. would oblige them. It would also give me a good thirty-six hours to spend in the States, even more if we could goad France into thinking we were going to review their agricultural exemptions.

Rafael might take my unwillingness to spend the night in her room not for prudent behavior, but for deception.

Sometimes you have to play the hand you're dealt.

One of the pilots came back from the cockpit and handed me a note. It simply said: *Chaos*.

I DON'T KNOW who sent the note, most likely it was Tom.

When I finished sketching out the plan of attack, I laid back and closed my eyes. What was bothering me? It was more than just Sebby. It wasn't Rafael. She was the symptom, not the cause.

I closed my eyes tighter. I didn't want to see it, what it really was.

Laura.

All this talk about having kids...we were going about this completely backwards. Somehow, I have this idea that, first, I would ask a woman to marry me on a pristine tropical beach at sunset with warm clear water lapping at our feet, not seconds after my shocked *coitus interruptus*— which wasn't a proposal but a rhetorical question—then after a wedding, a honeymoon, a couple of years of fun, sex, and good times, *then* we'd talk about having kids.

Maybe I was being too inflexible. Maybe I was just afraid of being a parent—although I really do want children.

I wished for five more minutes, five minutes so I could talk to Sebby, ask his advice. He would find the words somehow that would lead me, even if it wasn't immediately, to some understanding.

Sebby adored Laura. Her dark hair and dark eyes reminded him of his sister when she was young. He liked all the things about her that I liked.

And yet, just before I left, he said something very strange to me.

Like I said, Sebby was a carpenter by trade. The knuckles on his hands were thick and malformed from working too many hours for too many years. Even after he sold the house he built with my grandmother to my parents, it was somehow always his.

I had gone up to my parent's house after having meetings in New York with key members of the Mercantile Exchange. A calming talk before these final negotiations. When I arrived, I found Sebby on a ladder, tearing out a rotted awning support.

"Billy...hand me that level," he said as if my presence wasn't a surprise, as if I was always at his side.

I handed Sebby the wood level, the same one he'd been using for probably forty years. I watched him press it against the wall, half his lower lip folded into his mouth as he eyed his work.

"Laura and I got engaged last night...sort of," I just blurted out.

"You think you can hold your side up?" he asked. I wasn't sure what he meant until he motioned to the other end of the level. "What's 'sort of' mean?"

"It's hard to explain." I stretched my arm to keep the level steady and in place. "She's amazing. This is where the relationship has been heading, but...I'm not sure the timing is right. I mean, I want to...at some point." I tried to hear my words as Sebby would hear them. They didn't sound convincing. "This isn't public knowledge at the moment, so..."

"It'll go with me to the grave," he said, marking a line across the level with a pencil.

"And Laura wants kids. Now. The thought of that terrifies me. I don't think I'm ready."

"Nobody's ever ready for kids. Strange how people keep having 'em." Sebby nodded for me to take the level and put it on the ground. "Give me the three-penny nails."

Sebby took the half dozen nails I gave him and pressed them between his lips on the left side of his mouth, sharp ends sticking out.

"I like Laura," he said, without losing one of the nails, an amazing feat.

"Me, too."

He hammered the first nail in a fresh cut two-by-four that would become the new awning support. Took the second out of his mouth and started hammering. One, two, three, then he stopped. Staring at the nail halfway into the wood, he said, "Although I always picture you with someone like that ballet dancer you told me about. You remember her?"

How could I forget her, Gramps? "Yeah. I remember."

He finished knocking in the second nail. Took another and banged it in. Then he paused again, this time looking straight at me.

"Even now, you have this..." he motioned to his eye that sparkled even though it was dulled by hard work and age. "...this look when you talk about her."

Sebby always spoke his mind, always spoke it with kindness. But this was out of the ordinary for him. He rarely stuck his nose into my personal business, especially when it had to do with women.

Sebby came off the ladder and unceremoniously pulled out his gold watch and put it into my palm.

"What are you doing?" I said.

"My father gave me that watch when he said I'd finally taken on the responsibilities of being a man, having a family. His father had given it to him when he truly became a man. I only have a daughter. I'm giving it to you."

He gently, lovingly slapped my face.

"Gramps, I can't take this. I'm not ready."

"I know," he said, kindly. "But I can't wait any longer."

I LOOKED at the watch that I had been carrying around in my briefcase— the only thing of mine not locked in room 631—an object that now meant something so different to me, something so much more important, and I realized I hadn't called Laura to tell her of Sebby's death.

I picked up the phone in the armrest of my seat and dialed Laura's apartment. "Hey, you're home early," I said when she answered.

"You're up *late*. How is it going?"

"Laur..."

I don't know if she heard something in my voice or the unmistakable sound of a call from forty-two thousand feet, but she immediately said, "Oh, God, what is it, Billy?"

I told her.

She began to cry and tell me how sorry she was. She knew how important he had been in my life.

Thinking about all the times I had helped Sebby, I remembered the summer we replaced the back porch, which was rotted and damaged by rain and snow and sun and the years, like the awning support had been.

My mom actually put her foot through one of the decaying boards while hanging laundry on the clothesline. It was one of the oddest sounds I've ever heard. My mother has a laugh that'll get a pack of hyenas rolling in the aisles, and a sneeze that can trigger an avalanche. But this particular sound, I had never heard before. Scratch that, never heard come out of a human.

If the sound of hot water hitting my father's skin in the shower was like a pig being slaughtered, then my mother falling through a rotted plank of wood was the sound of a piccolo having an orgasm.

I swear to you, my dog, Flapper (#3), heard it first. The initial reverberation was well beyond the hearing of any normal person.

After we extracted her from the gaping hole, which was not that easy since my mother is probably the world's foremost authority on acting like dead weight, Sebby came over to look at the damage and informed my mom that she needed a new deck.

Dry rot.

We built a new, larger, sturdier structure that still stands today. We worked side by side building that. Dean helped, too. He was too young to do any lifting, but he did what he could. And even helped us solve a few design problems.

There is something ancient and magical about construction, building something where once there stood nothing.

It's easy to destroy. It's so much harder to create.

I rested my head against the seat back and finally fell asleep.

THE PLANE LANDED at the small air base next to Bradley International Airport just outside Hartford. An annoying crosswind makes landings here much more hair-raising than they need to be.

I hate this fucking airport.

Allison, who I understand "gives great head"—thank you, Hank Richardson, from Commerce for that little tidbit, such a tool, like I really needed to know that or picture her yanking on Hank—had arranged a flight up for Laura. She was waiting for me when I arrived.

An airman saluted me, then presented me with an envelope addressed by hand as I stepped off the AirStairs.

Laura ran up to me and threw her arms around me. I kissed her and held her for a long moment, not sure who was comforting whom.

As we were escorted toward a waiting limousine, I opened the note, handwritten in a scrawl that leaned far to the right. I have received many notes from the man, but none drafted by hand before, yet I instantly knew who it was from.

Dear Billy, I am sorry to hear about the loss of your grandfather. I

understand it is him that I should thank for all these years of a job
well done. —B.

"What is that?" Laura asked as I folded the card from the President
and put it into my jacket pocket.

"Just a note."

IT WAS a little before 6 A.M. when I got to my parents' house. Normally
things would be quiet at this hour. My mom'd be up, and the Princess
would just be readying to take possession of the bathroom for the rest of
the morning.

Sleep was a very important thing in the Gerrick household.

And in the morning, especially on those days we had to go school, we
wanted more of it.

My mother would sometimes have to bang a pot right over the head of
her children in order to get us up in time for school.

I remember numerous times her having to rip the bedspread and
sheets off me to even make a minor dent in my slumber.

I have calculated that my mother spent approximately one-third of her
total daily caloric output trying to wake up her kids.

But the house was anything but quiet this morning. All of the lights
were on and I could see people walking back and forth inside as the limo
pulled into the driveway, looking out of place. It appeared that there were
more than five people pacing in the house. My grandmother had spent the
night in my old room. My grandfather's two sisters had driven over at
about 5 A.M. to help my mother get the house in order.

I have never found it difficult to express my emotions to my friends and
to my lovers. I don't have any difficulty being sympathetic and attentive—a
good listener. But when it comes to my family, I have something of a block,
a Berlin Wall, if you will, that leaves a tiny but noticeable chasm between us.

I had no problem expressing my sorrow and grief to my grandmother,
just like I never had problems expressing how I felt to her husband. As I
went to hug my mom, who began crying the moment she saw me, as if
somehow reminded by my presence of the loss of her father, when I put
my arms around her, the weight of the situation allowed me to close that
distance and be completely there for her.

It was one of those moments, an instant in the course of a life, that defines a relationship. It was suffocating for me to imagine no longer being able to see or speak with Sebby. I couldn't begin to understand how devastating the loss was for his only child.

I held on to my mom for a moment longer.

After Laura pulled my mom aside to comfort her, my siblings and I took a walk down the street.

It was a warm and pleasant day for this time of year. The sky was clear and the sun was rising over the trees. We spoke in shorthand. About how Grampa would give us money, or play the ponies, or teach us how to fix something around the house.

Then, with our remembrances put away, we divided up the responsibilities, who would take care of mom, and Grandma, who'd make sure that the house was set up for the guests.

My job was to write the eulogy.

I have often had to write important speeches, some of them for trade conferences and policy events, a few of them for more personal gatherings. I find that the more meaningful the speech needs to be, the more personal and dear to my heart the subject is, the more difficult it is for me to construct a coherent text.

When I tried to put together my memories for the high school yearbook, I had so many people I wanted to mention and so many things I wanted to say—likes and dislikes and dreams and ambitions—I just couldn't narrow down my words to something that would fit in a two-inch column of text.

So, what I ended up doing was waiting to the last minute—big surprise—and instead of making the tough decision of who to mention and who to leave out, I chose to write a poem, shunning entirely the format that all of my classmates—except me and two others—used.

Sebby's eulogy was much more difficult because the subject matter was infinitely more precious to me than my high school days. I was going to sum up eighty years of a man's life in five minutes, less than four seconds a year. That's impossible to do for any man, and my grandfather was not just any man to me.

I went down to my old room, and Laura and I silently changed into our finest mourning wear. I looked in the mirror, tying my tie. A Double Windsor.

I closed my eyes and Laura came over to me.

I felt the loss.

"He taught me how to do this," I said.

WE ARRIVED at the wake and filed out of the cars quietly and solemnly. I tried to console my mother who was weeping. The Princess was doing a good job of taking care of my grandmother. He was always exceptional in situations like this. I may not always do it, but I like to think of him in this manner. The way he was at these times.

My father walked with my grandmother, talked with her, and tried to keep up her spirits. She didn't cry as much as my mother did, didn't display the kind of emotion I knew Sebby would have shown.

I think she had shut herself off. Clearly, she was in shock and there was nothing, not even the sight of her husband's lifeless body lying in front of her that could convince her what was going on was real.

I knelt before Sebby's coffin and paid my respects, lingering there for several minutes, not wanting to get up, not wanting any of this to really be taking place. I let myself touch his hand, his oversized knuckles. I could feel him, but not there.

I felt more of him in the smooth wood at the edge of the casket. And like he had done a thousand times beating me at gin rummy, I tapped the mahogany with my knuckles and whispered, "Knock."

I finally got to my feet and went over to the far end of the front row, as far away from the procession of mourners as I could get. Here, somewhat isolated in the presence of so many people, I finally began to write about the man who had meant the world to me. I had attempted to pick up a pen and jot down some ideas on the plane, but nothing came out. I tried to write down some thoughts at the house...nothing.

Even as everyone was leaving, even after everyone had begun to head over to the church for the services, I sat there sobbing, pen in hand, tears dropping on the paper in my lap with the body of my grandfather just a few feet away, scribbling down some pitiful words to define a most wonderful soul.

I don't like death. I don't like it at all. I don't think it's fair or just or right. Why give us this mind, this heart, this soul, this sentience, only to take it away?

I try late at night to close my eyes and wonder what it would be like to no longer have consciousness, but I can't seem to fathom it.

As I stared at the paper, at the drops of tears, I could hear my brothers calling to me, telling me to hurry, parroting my mother's words, that we were going be late to the church.

It was at that moment the words came to me.

"WHAT CAN I say about my grandfather, my Grandpa, my Gramps? Without a doubt, he was and always will be my favorite person in the world. And the one I most respected. When everything else was cloudy and gray, when times were tough, I could visit him, in person or in my mind, and feel a sense of strength and stability.

"Many times as I've traveled around the globe, it's been the times he and I spent building porches, fixing doors or windows that I look back on to draw some wisdom. And he was wise. He rarely preached, he rarely spoke with fanaticism, he used simple words to form simple ideas which spoke volumes.

"Don't get me wrong, he was not simple. And from this man, this carpenter, who had no more than an eighth-grade education, I learned more than any teacher or professor or scholar ever taught me. He was the architect of the me that stands before you.

"Being so far away was difficult for me as well as for him. It was only when the family was all together that he truly felt at ease.

"And for me, I would sometimes not call or write, not because I didn't want to, but because the calling or the writing only reminded me of the distance of that part of me which remained so far away.

"I am not sad—not as I thought I would be. It's strange, but I feel a sense of joy that he—up until the end—had lived his life the way he wanted: independent, playing bingo, and with his wife.

"Before leaving Geneva, a dear friend asked me how I was. And I realized I was okay. I was sad that I would never again on this earth be able to speak to him directly, and I felt sorrow for my mom and especially my grandmother—who has known only a life with him since the age of sixteen. But for me, I felt at peace. He had been my rock through a rocky childhood, my mentor when teachers seemed to hold nothing for me. And he was my soul when I thought I had none. And as I turned to my friend, I said to her—I have him in here, inside, he is in my soul and he will be there always.

"He found joy in family, in working with his hands, and helping other people, the basics of life.

"Seeing him at the wake left me thinking something was missing: the life in his face. The animation of expression. The face of love.

"In my life and that of my family, all that we touch will somehow be touched by him.

"And this one man, this one special man—father, brother, grandfather, husband—like a single raindrop in a pond will expand out from the center, and his ripple will affect a hundred lives, a thousand and so on. Forever."

I WAS in tears as I closed the small, blank-paged book where I had written these words, and gathered myself enough to walk away from the pulpit and down the marble stairs without collapsing.

As I made my way back to my seat, I saw my mother's face, the pain, the loss in her eyes and I had to choke back my emotions, had to keep strong, for if she saw tears, she would lose control completely. She could never stand to see me cry.

I tried to listen to the sermon, but it was hollow. The priest didn't know the man I knew. Barely knew him at all. They were just words.

At the grave site, those who gathered were encouraged to toss a handful of dirt onto his coffin. I had done this maybe a half-dozen times in my life for relatives or family friends that had gone before Sebby. But like the words of the priest, those other times had not affected me.

This time, I was profoundly stung by the feel of the cold dirt on my skin and the sound of it landing on Sebby with a muffled, unnerving thud.

AFTER THE FUNERAL, the first thing Laura said to me—the *first* thing —was, "Who is your *dear friend*? Rafael?"

I just stared at her.

I didn't bother to tell her it was the woman I've spent more time with than any other woman: Allison.

When we got back to the house, the house that Sebby built, I helped my grandmother out of the car. She was still in shock. We stood in the middle of the front yard and stared at my home. I held her close to me, squeezing her against my side as we both faced the formerly flat-roofed house.

She had built this house as well. Her own hands had held the wood, the nails, carried the bags of cement. Sebby and Annette, together, side by side. She and Sebby spent most of their time with each other. They worked together, built together, lived together. And someday, she would join him in death together. Side by side.

"You did good, Gramm. You and Grampa."

"Yeah," she said quietly. I knew what she was thinking.

I knew.

She wanted the Fat Track back together. She wanted things to be back the way they were, the way they had always been.

12

THE PRESIDENT, LINE ONE

THE PEOPLE CAME. They ate. Talked about Sebby. They laughed and cried, then wiping the tears from their eyes, laughed again.

People always have nice things to say about a person when they're dead. It's the great equalizer, death is. We are all the same in its grasp. But with most dearly departed there is a certain revisionism that takes place. Maybe it's closer to editing. Things are left out or left unsaid. The faults are forgotten, the imperfections overlooked, at least for today.

I hope that's the way it will be for me, that those people left behind will overlook my faults.

Only with Sebby, there was no adaptation, no reworking of his past. I have never met anyone who has ever had an unkind word for Sebby.

Not one.

Even those kids, now men, who had been parented and punished and patrolled by my grandparents, came to his funeral *fifteen years* after he retired, and had nothing but kind words and tears in their eyes for Sebby.

Finally, everyone but the immediate family and my grandmother had left. Laura went off with my cousins so that we could have some time together. And we sat in the kitchen of the house that Sebby and Annette built, and picked at the leftover desserts, and talked about the man who had been father, grandfather, mentor and husband.

I WENT to sleep in my room which hasn't changed much since I left home, even though Dean had moved into it after I left, and then Anna after that. I was in my room alone. My mother has this annoying rule about unmarried people sleeping in the same bed under her roof.

"Aaaaaah, Jesus Christ. Don't you think that's a little ridiculous? You had all your children by the time you were my age."

"We were married. And don't use that language in my house."

"I'm not going to have sex with her. I just want to sleep with her."

"There isn't a difference for me."

"You know, I could show you some video of us that might change your mind about that."

So, Laura was upstairs in the part of the house that didn't exist when I was growing up. It was only 9 P.M., but I needed to try and get some rest. Maybe it was for the best, not having Laura next to me. I couldn't seem to sleep anyway.

After a while, I got up and looked into the closet, which had a combination of Dean's and Anna's and my stuff all crammed into it. I pulled down my high school yearbook, the one from the year I graduated, and began flipping through the pages, staring at the faces of people most of whom I had spent at least seven years with, many of them twelve.

A few of my classmates were in the D.C. area, and on occasion, we would get together. But for such a large group of human beings—even though my class was small by most school's standards, two hundred and fifty people, a thousand in the whole school—so few of our lives have intersected after we threw off our caps and gowns.

I thought about how many people I would speak to and see in an average high school day. There were the students in my classes, the girls and guys that had lockers near mine, the guys I played sports with.

I thought about how large a circle of friends and acquaintances, teachers and administrators (of whom I saw quite a bit) were in my life at that time and how those numbers have slowly dwindled over the years to a smaller and smaller group of close personal friends.

I'm luckier than most. I'm surrounded by an entourage of people whenever I travel. I come in contact with negotiators and politicians and civil servants by the hundreds. And because this circle of people treks from place to place, a veritable movable feast, I run into them often.

For a while this upset me. That my pool of friends had become less deep. That we slowly close ourselves off to more people, the circle squeezing tighter and tighter until you're left with just a nuclear family and a few select friends.

But then I began to realize something. Maybe it's not that the number of people I know has declined, maybe it's that the criteria I now have for calling someone a close friend is much higher than it was in high school, in college, or even in my early twenties.

And yet, I'm not sure if that's good or bad.

I COULD HEAR my father marching up the stairs from the cellar cursing some part of his body for failing him. He is in month three of sobriety, having finally given up the sauce.

I am, so my mother tells me, extremely lucky to have missed months one and two. For some people going on the wagon clears up a lot of their problems rather quickly. Most are not as fortunate and need to work through a transitional period. Still others, like my father, actually deteriorate the first six or seven months.

The Princess was usually a very good drunk. He was social. He was fun.

Sure, he broke shit, stomped around, cursed and all that, but for the most part, he was manageable. There was a certain pattern and order to his actions.

On the day alcohol was removed from my father's system, his body completely went berserk (another favorite word of my father's). His entire nervous system went dark, his muscles rebelled, and his brain started to notice things that had been dulled by the smooth edge of alcohol.

There were a number of reasons why my father chose to drink, so when he stopped, he began to grow acutely aware of all the things he'd been drinking to forget.

He passed by my door and went up into the main section of the house. I heard a few things rattle and clang. Nothing broken. I went back to my yearbook, back to the faces and the dreams of my classmates.

I heard the phone ring.

A moment later, my mother came to the door, pale, looking as though she was going to faint. I thought someone else had died.

"Billy..." she stammered, "it...it's for you." She handed me the phone.

"Hello."

"Mr. Gerrick?"

"Yes."

"I have the President on the line."

13

THE GIRL MOST LIKELY TO

THE CAPTAIN HAS JUST COME on and told us that we will be experiencing a little more turbulence in a few moments and that it could last a hundred miles.

This disturbs me, and not simply because I don't like turbulence. I never enjoyed it when one of my friends shook the maple tree in front of my house while I was up at the top. I am disturbed because I've been holding on to my armrests for the *past* one hundred miles, thinking *that* was a rough ride.

I try to put the flight out of my mind.

I'm alone. Laura stayed at my parents for another day, in case they needed anything.

The phone call from the President was short and to the point.

"Is the funeral over?"

"Yes, sir."

"I'm sorry about your grandfather."

"Thank you, Mr. President. I got your note."

"You all right?"

"I'm fine."

"Good. Then get back to Geneva."

"I agree. But I think we should talk first, sir."

I CLOSE my eyes and try to find a peaceful place in my mind where I can recharge. I know I won't get any sleep tonight. As soon as the plane lands, I'll be taken to the White House for an all-night strategy session.

It's hard to imagine that the same kid I was staring at in my yearbook a couple of hours ago is, in less than forty minutes, going to walk off this plane and immediately be flown from Andrews Air Force Base via Marine helicopter to meet with the President of the United States.

I had lofty goals back then, but that's still a long way to have come.

Before I was interrupted by the President's call, I was reading over the memories, the ambitions and dreams and good wishes of my classmates. And I was struck by an awesome sense of continuity, the march of time, and more than a bit of sadness.

We were so full of hope then. Our lives were ahead of us. Anything was possible, and everything looked probable.

I knew some of these ambitions and dreams had come true. Many hadn't. Irregular briefings from friends told me that. And of all the people I didn't know about, I wondered, which ones had succeeded, who had failed?

When you pore over numbers in a trade analysis study, you see the count of jobs lost in one sector and gained in another. It's my job to make those two things balance as much as possible. Tip them in our favor if I can.

Only those are statistics. Just because one person gains a job while another person loses one, doesn't make it even.

As a young kid, growing up during the Vietnam War, I remember watching Walter Cronkite on the CBS Evening News every night. He made me feel, no matter what, that everything would be all right.

For as long as I could remember, the world fascinated me, even when I didn't fully understand what it was I was watching.

Every night, the numbers would get put up on the screen over a background of gray fields with gray trees and gray grass. It was the number of soldiers killed that day. Americans: 26. Vietcong: 368.

I used to play cops and robbers, and cowboys and Indians. I knew what war was.

I didn't have any idea why we were there. What we were doing.

All I did know was that we were winning.

Americans: 26. Vietcong: 368.

Those people in that yearbook, they weren't slices of a pie chart or numbers flashed on a screen. I knew better now. They were living, breathing beings. People who lived, fell in love, married, had babies, moved, changed jobs, grew old and passed the torch to the next generation.

The first pocket of severe turbulence hits the plane, and as the seat belt sign comes on, I want to know the fate of everyone in that book. And of the fates I did know, there were some I wish I could change.

Especially one.

Krissy Simon was my first real crush. It began in seventh grade—even though we had met in sixth—and continued on, well, forever.

There'd been others before her. But they were flashes in the pan in comparison.

My first was in kindergarten, Tina Moore. It was rather serious. I was going to marry Tina and raise horses with her. We were about five years old at the time and raising horses seemed to us the most logical way to make money, which is kind of like thinking raising children will bring you income. Her family had a farm with horses and a few empty stalls, so we had that covered. And marriage? Seemed as fine a time as any to take the plunge.

My mother would ask me, "Why do you think you can raise horses? You can't even take care of Flapper."

"Flapper is a dog."

"And where would you two live?"

"Either here or over at Tina's."

"I see," my mother would say.

See, at five years old you have no concept that your parents aren't going to take care of you for the rest of your life. That eventually—and sooner than you think—you have to take care of yourself. Then after a while of doing that, which is annoying enough, you have to start taking care of *other* people, little ones at first, who get bigger and cost more and want to hang around as long as they can. Coming full circle and ending up where those parents who were diapering you, will have to be diapered themselves.

My mother tried very nicely to explain that, no, once you get married, you can no longer live with your parents. This came as quite a shock to me. Up to this point in my life, my mother had denied me many things but never a place to sleep.

"Okay," I said, "then there's another reason to raise horses. Tina and I can live in the barn." It was more than big enough for horses and us and all the cool stuff that we wanted to get.

I didn't quite understand the process of registering for gifts—it's like a letter to Santa, right?—but I knew that people who just got married received a lot of presents. A lot more than I ever got from Old St. Nick, and certainly more than I got on some random Saturday in June, and that's when my birthday is.

Marriage seemed like a pretty good deal.

Having briefly discussed the financials of such nuptials with Laura, I realize that even if everyone gives us the most expensive gift they could and I return every one of them for cash, I will still end up twenty thousand dollars in the hole.

Eventually, Tina and I decided that perhaps we should wait.

But, being the bastard that I am, I didn't wait. By third grade, I had discovered Deb Stanislausky.

Deb was cute and sporty with caramel skin and short hair and a mole on her cheek that seemed to me the most incredibly adorable thing I'd ever seen. Her laugh endeared me, made me want to make her laugh more. She said the funniest things. And she could outrun all the boys.

Not me. I'm fast.

Or maybe she let me catch her.

The marriage thing didn't even come into play. By third grade, we were all so over marriage, I couldn't believe I had even considered tying myself down with Tina.

I could tell Tina felt the same way, which kind of annoyed me.

So that was Tina Moore and Deb Stanislausky. Crushes for sure.

But then in seventh grade came...Krissy.

All the guys loved Krissy. And why wouldn't we? She was smart, pretty. She developed breasts earlier than any of the other girls. And she just seemed to be a step or two out of our league.

Years later, as we were getting ready to graduate high school, she would be voted Most Likely To Succeed. She would earn science scholarships and win awards from around the country for her work in mathematics. She would be Captain of the cheerleading squad, a good sprinter, excellent in English and debate. She would graduate in the Top Five of our class. She would learn to play a great game of tennis, make the varsity squad, and she would do all of this being a farmer's daughter.

Now, where I come from farmer's daughters are not quite the same as they are in the wheat belt or the corn belt. What we, in New England, call a "farm" most people in Missouri would call a garden. Fifty acres, a hundred acres, something like that. But it's still a "tough row to hoe," maybe even tougher, since it's hard to make a living off of fifty acres unless you're growing pot.

Oh, I forgot to mention she would also be the Homecoming Queen.

She looked incredible in her gown. In fact, she always managed to look great, even though we all knew her folks didn't have much money. Neither did mine, but I didn't have to buy a different gown every formal dance that came up.

Money wasn't a problem for most families in our town. Mostly middle and upper-middle-class. But even for those who fell below the median income, there wasn't a real discrepancy between the haves and the have-nots. At least, the gap wasn't that noticeable then.

Used to be, in America, we wanted to keep up with the Joneses. Wealth was quieter then. Now, it's splashed across magazines, on television. Now, too many people want to keep up with the stars, the celebrities, the ostentatious. When you try to do that, you start to become keenly aware of the differences in how much money you have.

KRISSY CAME AMBLING down the main hallway on the first day of seventh grade, and me and just about every other guy watched her the entire way.

She and I had spent all of sixth grade together in the same English class, but I never really noticed her. But then something happened over the summer. Two things actually.

Her incredible tits...that's only one thing, by the way.

The other something was the way she walked, the way she acted. Somehow, someone, somewhere informed Miss Simon that she was now a woman, and women carried themselves very differently from girls.

Miss Simon heeded this advice. Heeded it well.

Over the years, we became friends, me and Krissy.

We were both outsiders in a way. I didn't hang out in just one clique. Maybe because when I was younger, no clique would have me. I didn't grow up in one of the neighborhoods where all the kids lived. Later on, it worked out to be an advantage for me. I knew everyone, was invited to the parties of all kinds of people. I always had a few very close friends, some of the coolest people, but I wouldn't call myself part of any group.

And Krissy, well, Krissy, she was an outsider because she was so far ahead of the rest of us that she was all by herself. I don't mean she thought she was above us. She didn't.

She didn't put herself on a pedestal, everyone else did.

Our being outsiders made us understand each other.

It's sort of like the Beauty and the Beast. People keep their distance from both, for far different reasons, but the result is the same.

You are set apart.

You are alone.

Even years later, nearing graduation, she was even more of a woman, the only woman, in a sea of girls. Bright girls, mature girls. But not women.

By eighth grade, everyone looked up to Krissy. The girls wanted to be like her. They were jealous of, yet respected, the way she handled guys and the way guys handled her. And the guys, well, we looked up to her for all of those things I mentioned earlier, but above all, because she was the prize. The Holy Grail. The one that none of us ever got. She teased us, dating guys who were just a little bit older than us, giving us hope that when we got to be that age, she might date us. But by then she was onto guys just a little bit older than that.

Pretty much from the moment seventh grade began, from the moment she strolled down that hall, hips swaying, smile shining, eyes glistening, I developed a very serious crush, more like a long-term infatuation, with Krissy Simon.

I would fantasize about her...while sitting next to her in class, while on those long bike rides I would take to visit my friends. I would daydream that she was my girlfriend. I would imagine scenarios where we would go out on dates and to parties, and even into the back seats of cars.

Everyone talks about how kids today are more sexually aware, but in seventh grade, I was aware of one thing. That Krissy Simon was the girl I wanted to be inside of most.

Twelve years old and I knew I wanted to pull off those white cotton panties of hers and slide inside of her every time and anytime I desired. It wasn't only about sex, either. Okay, it was a lot about sex, but it was about something bigger.

I would dream about being an only child with parents who had to travel often. Parents who by my thirteenth birthday would let me stay home alone as they jetted to someplace fabulous.

Freedom, sex, love, a house to ourselves. This was an adult relationship, not some childhood fling.

In some ways, because of how detailed and exact my fantasies were, I felt as if I *had* slept with Krissy. I even acted like I had. I don't mean I went around implying in the locker room or when hanging out with the guys that I had fucked her. I never said a thing about Krissy, even when others brought her up. Partly because I truly cared about her. Partly because I didn't want anyone else to know my deepest thoughts, my secret life with Krissy.

I knew it wasn't true, this alternative history I had created, but the fantasy gave me an internal confidence. It may have been an illusion, a delusion of grandeur, but those dreams got me through those first few years of adolescence, after the hormones began to rage and before I learned the discipline and restraint to control them somewhat.

I never did get to sleep with Krissy. And maybe that's a good thing, because that...that might have spoiled it.

Over the next few years of high school, we would talk to each other and have a glancingly deep relationship, the kind where we knew what the other one was thinking. We didn't talk all that often or do that much together. It wasn't that kind of friendship. But whenever we would spend time with each other—working on a project in class, hanging out in the deserted halls after school, talking in some corner at a party—we understood each other completely.

We were the outsiders. The ones set apart. We were totally alike and entirely different.

When we spoke, it was as if no time had passed since the last deep conversation. I was one of the people that she could tell things to, confide in. Why? Because I wasn't afraid of her, she told me. I wasn't scared or apprehensive to pose the tough questions that most guys wouldn't dare ask. And most girls wouldn't either.

Except for two other guys she also trusted, every other pubescent male within a thirty-mile radius was under the misguided perception that they might still get in her pants someday.

I had already been there. In my mind.

It gave me the freedom to be comfortable with her, the freedom to be myself, to be intimate.

AFTER I WENT AWAY to school, I would hear about Krissy every once in a while. My mother would send me newspaper clippings of anything that just about anyone who ever remotely crossed my path had done. I'd get the rest from her verbally, info gleaned from the "grapevine" as my mother would put it. Since no one my mother knew, knew anyone that I knew, I never knew what the hell she was talking about.

"Remember, Tamma Hawkins?"

"No."

"Sure you do."

"I assure you, I do not."

"She was the one in your Kindergarten class who had the, you know, *bladder problem...*"

"How do you remember this shit? I was there, and I can't remember any of this."

"You may be an adult, but you don't have to use that kind of language with me. You get that from your father."

No fucking shit.

I sigh, "I don't remember her, mother."

"She always wore her hair in a ponytail."

"Mom, half the girls in my class wore their hair in a ponytail."

"But how many of them had," she whispers it again, "a *bladder problem* as well?"

"I'm hanging up now."

Every so often, I'd get a clipping about someone I actually knew. This is how I got news of all the awards and national scholarships Krissy won. Like me, those scholarships were the only way she was able to afford to go to college. Her parents did what they could, but it would have never been enough.

I heard through friends that she was dating this guy from our class, a nice guy, one of the cool guys from the stoner crowd.

This is nothing against him, but he wasn't nearly as smart as she was, not even close. I'm not quite sure what she saw in him. Maybe it was simply that no matter what she did or achieved or didn't do, he would be in awe of her. I think, for Krissy, the bar was set so ridiculously high, the pressure so great, that she wanted someone to love her just for herself. Her weak, fragile self. Not this mythological creature that had been created by teenage boys and girls alike.

Like I said, she was voted the girl most likely to succeed. She embodied the hopes and dreams of her parents, to be the first in her family to graduate college.

These were no easy goals. There were no uncomplicated decisions for Krissy. Even when she partied and goofed off, there was a limit to the pleasure she allowed herself. She shouldered the weight of awesome responsibility.

I thought about her sometimes, wondered what would happen if we saw each other again. What we'd say to each other.

I HAPPENED to be home one day. I took a semester off from college—I was going to school in D.C. by then—and made a pit stop for a few weeks at my parent's. The rest of the time through the end of the summer, I traveled and learned languages.

I let only my closest friends know that I was home, some of them were out of school, on spring break. We would go out some nights and talk or go to one of those parties that always get thrown whenever college is out. We'd get something to eat, a drink, catch up with each other, that sort of thing. Sometimes we'd run into other people we knew.

This one particular day a friend called me, someone whose mom is plugged in to everybody. Although you didn't need to be that plugged in to get this news.

It was a Tuesday. I picked up the phone and said, "Hello?"

It was Ben. He said, "Hey…" I remember the way he said it. So normal. Then there was this pause and some breathing, like an obscene phone call, before he finally said, "Krissy killed herself."

· · ·

IT'S difficult to remember the exact reaction I had, time tends to sand away the edges of memory, making it less sharp and more finished. It was something less than shock and more than surprise. But not surprise in the way you might think. I was amazed that she *had* killed herself, not that she *could have*.

She had come home from college just for the weekend. And after dinner, somewhere between the house and the barn, she climbed in her dad's old pickup truck—he had died the year before—and hanged herself from a hand grip mounted on the ceiling just inside the door.

I GOT DRESSED, and I drove to the wake by myself. No music on. Just the sound of the wind whistling past the driver-side window I had opened a crack, and the melody of Krissy's voice as I replayed my memories of her.

WEEKS LATER, just before I left on my travels, I went by Krissy's grave. I cried, something only now that I'm thinking about this do I remember. I can see myself crouching down in front of the grave and weeping. Like most times when we weep, we are really grieving for ourselves, for the loss of the person, the parent, the friend, the lover.

Maybe if I had been able to talk to her. Maybe if I had been there for her, a friend to her, I would've seen this coming.

But I wasn't there. And I didn't see.

I FELL BACK into that place in the past where Krissy had been my lover. I felt a deep emotional loss. Mostly because this woman, who I had longed for from afar, never had a clue what she meant to me, how she had touched me.

But then, maybe she always knew.

THE WAKE WAS CROWDED with people from our town, people who had stayed, people off from school, and even some that made a special trip home. Her boyfriend sat at the front with her family, red-faced and crying. I paid my respects to Krissy, who looked so beautiful, but like Sebby, was so devoid of that which made her what she was. I heard her boyfriend saying over and over and over again, "I can't believe she did this. Why would she do this? I can't believe she did this."

I heard that sentiment all night. Why? Why would Krissy Simon kill herself? She seemed like the last person on earth, the last person in the world that would do this. I recall one girl in particular saying this, someone from my class, someone who had been a cheerleader with Krissy since Middle School. All the mourners around this girl began nodding and shaking their heads, not understanding either.

It was perhaps the wrong time, the wrong place to disagree, but I told them Krissy Simon was exactly the type of person to do this. She was alone in the world. Too many of us looked up to her. Too few of us tried to get close to her. Even fewer allowed her to get close to us. We were too busy being in awe of her or trying to impress her.

She was so accomplished, so far ahead of us that she had nothing she could do but fail. All she could do was disappoint us. Win another award? Of course, she would. Earn another scholarship? It's Krissy. Come in at the head of her class? Who would expect anything less? Be the sexiest, most confident woman at the dance? That was a given.

I guess it simply became too much.

And there was no one for her to turn to.

I understood somewhat.

Not *how* she could have, but *why* she might have done it. And not because I was a fellow outsider, but because I too sometimes felt the heavy burden of high expectation.

I had the high test scores like she did. Like her, I had people telling me I should be a straight-A student. Only I punted. I didn't go out to prove myself. Because whenever I did, the game became much harder, much less fun. I was learning what they were teaching. At least that much was true. But why put myself out there to come up short, if I could do next to nothing and get by well enough.

I wasn't tough enough to take the pressure.

Krissy made it look effortless, school, sports, partying, dating.

But after a while, it becomes increasingly difficult to keep up the kind of excellence that one needs to be a success in so many areas, let alone be a legend. And the world is very, very unforgiving to legends who fall from grace. And Krissy had the bar set so high that it was impossible for her to be good enough. What most people strived for, would be praised for, would seem like a failure for her.

I wish in some ways that I could have been more like her. And I wish she could have been more like me. Maybe I would have tried harder, pushed myself in those early years. My way hurt me, no doubt about it. I had to overcome my early failures. Come from behind. Who knows what I could have done, what anyone could have done with her will, with her drive.

And maybe *she* would have allowed herself to be fallible, to let herself make a mistake or two. Who knows, maybe she wanted to do that, wanted to allow herself to miss the mark occasionally. Maybe it was us who wouldn't allow her to be anything less than perfect.

KRISSY, me, and one other classmate didn't write our memories beside our pictures in the yearbook—the likes, dislikes, ambitions, all the customary crap. The words I had been pouring over in my bed as I looked at picture after picture. Snapshots of a moment. Words that didn't hold up over time. That hardly make any sense now.

The three of us, not knowing the other two had done the same, simply offered verse. Words that we had either written or found. Words that touched us and defined us.

The lyrical poem beside Krissy's smiling photo was strange and unsettling when I first read it, chilling when I went back and examined it after her death. It went something like this:

If you feel your going will leave an unfillable hole,
This will humble your soul.
Take a bucket. Fill it with water. Put your hand in it up to the wrist.
Pull it out. The remaining hole is a measure of how you'll be missed.
Splash all you please as you enter. Stir up the water galore.
Stop. You'll see in a minute. It looks the same as before.

I always wondered where Krissy would end up, where her life, her passions, her talent would bring her.

They brought her home...to her father's farm, to his old rusted-out pickup truck, to his side in a grave in a cemetery on the edge of a small town in the center of Connecticut.

.   .   .

DRIVING HOME, I rummaged through the old daydreams I had about Krissy. I used to imagine that we were part of a television series. There was this one daydream/episode at the end of eighth grade, the start of that summer, where I—and I can't tell you why I imaged this—but I had what could only be described as a cliffhanger ending, a season finale, something to get me through a summer without Krissy until school started again.

She missed the last day of school, missed the goodbyes and hugs, the yearbook signing, and promises to see each other over the summer. And I had missed her call the night before in the time before answering machines, a call I never knew was placed. Everyone wondered where Krissy was. No one had any idea.

Then the vision in my head followed her to this white, cloudy place, like an empty heaven where she strolled for a long time until she disappeared into the distance. And the last image was of a tombstone with her name on it, and the inscription: *To a Wonderful Daughter*.

She had committed suicide in this daydream episode. No note. No reason. We'd have to wait until next season for the answers.

When school reopened, and I could see Krissy every day once again, I started the new season of daydreams where I left off. But this time, her demise was only a dream. A heavy moment. Just a tiny peek into the romance teenagers have with death, in spite of, perhaps because we think ourselves invincible at that age. It was a dream within my fantasy, one that she told me—in my daydream—had shaken her, but made her glad to be alive.

I thought that up when I was in eighth grade. When I was thirteen, about to be fourteen.

I don't think I "knew" anything. I wasn't reading the future. Teenagers are always overly melodramatic. We think and write about death, in a deep, yet somehow trivialized way because we can't see ourselves ever getting there. Everything is big in those years, a pimple, a slight from a friend, young love, death, it's all so huge. It seems the same. No real difference between acne and dying. As we get older, we care less about the frivolous and write less about death and when we do, we write about it with more deference. Until we get close to our demise, and then we begin to write and talk about it again, because this time we know we're going there.

But I do think that even back then, I picked up an inherent sadness in Krissy.

I only wish she could see her pail of water now. Because since her warmth and light has been taken from us, the water has frozen so thoroughly it has left a hole where her hand had once been.

A deep, empty space that will take decades to fill, and many more to thaw.

14
THE PERILS OF VIENNESE BLEND

IT'S six in the morning, and I haven't gone to sleep when I stumble into Bellina's. I seem to be arriving just about everywhere these days at 6 A.M.

I walked here after spending all night at the White House in discussions with the President and about a half-dozen aides. The President, who often likes to stay up way past his bedtime into the middle of the night, was part of the debate until about 4:30 when his Chief of Staff—my friend Bobby McClain—made him go to sleep. He had a very important meeting with the Prime Minister of Kazakhstan in the morning.

I can still hear his last words as he was pushed out the door like a kid being sent to bed, "Why the hell am I meeting with the Kazakhstan Prime Minister again?"

I am stung by the smack of coffee grinds and their particularly harsh aroma. I don't know why I bother coming to a place like this. I don't drink coffee, I hate the smell and all I do is look down my nose at everyone else in the place, which I guess is the reason why I come. It's sort of like going to a tobacco industry convention and realizing that half the people there are going to die from lung cancer or some other horrible smoking-related disease. It gives you a false sense of superiority. I mean, hell, I could walk out the door and be run over by a chain-smoker who's blabbing on the cell phone to his dealer trying to score some smack while he sips at his thirty-two-ounce mocha java and tries to light his fiftieth cig of the morning. Even if he was paying attention, he'd never see me through all that fucking smoke.

I order my o.j. and flip through the papers off to the side of the counter that are meant to sort of ease you into the day. You wanna start out gradually. Getting up to speed, slowly revving up the brain by wading in the comics, diving next into the bra ads, then maybe, just maybe after the caffeine is hitting your bloodstream, you try and plunge into the front page. Oh, not all of it, you skip over anything that has to do with the entire continent of Africa (unless it's about the pyramids), skip anything with Central and South America, the Baltics, Bosnia, or Borneo. You'll read about Japan if we're kicking their ass at something. Europe's always good for a moment or two. But what you really want is just a nice juicy Beltway scandal.

I figure I've had enough bad news for one day, so I just pick up the funnies.

And then I see her. Immediately her name leaves my brain, as if all the blood has drained out of my head and gone a few floors down. It's the cute blonde, the one with the journal who got me started traipsing through the past.

Remembering names is one of my worst failings. In fact, it's Allison's job first and foremost to tell me the name of someone who I've met once last year in Iceland while I was freezing my ass off, which is only slightly more important than making certain that none of my ex-girlfriends get by her at the office.

The woman looks up and catches me staring at her again. Suzy... Sandra...what is it?

I have two conflicting thoughts, one, that this is a sign from God, the forces of Fate bringing us together once again for some higher purpose, for some greater good, and, two, I should turn around, sprint out the door, and not embarrass myself any further.

Being that I'm, as I stated earlier, a complete moron, I chose to believe that it was kismet. So, I walk right over to her and say in my deepest voice, "Remember me?"

For a moment there, I think I'm dead in the water. She looks up at me, no recognition, no emotion on her face. Great, I don't remember her name, she doesn't remember me at all. You know those moments when time seems to stand still, when you would give anything, all your money, all your possessions, even one arm and a kidney to get the clock moving again? Well, this is one of those times.

It's no more than a few seconds but, I swear, it seems as if it lasts as long as *Phantom of the Opera's* run on Broadway. Finally, after making me stand there, leaving me hanging, she lets slip the biggest, most gorgeous smile, I have ever seen, that is innocent and devilish all at once.

"Oh, you were making me sweat?"

"I thought it only fitting, what with our last encounter. Billy, right?"

"Very good memory..." Shit, shit, shit, I'm going down. Going down. Going down. Down under. Down Under!!! "Sydney!"

"What!"

I startle her.

"Um...I was just surprised to see you."

"Me, too. *Very*...surprised."

After her adrenaline subsides, she smiles that smile again. That one that got burned into my mind last time.

Thank fucking God I remembered her name.

"And what was wrong with our last encounter? I thought I was rather charming," I say.

"Oh, you did? I see. Well, then I guess it's true what they say: it really does depend on your point of view."

And then, from out of my well-educated, should-fucking-know-better mouth, comes another one of those "brilliant" strings of thoughts and words I wish I could stuff right back down my throat. "Well, from my point of view things look very, very good indeed."

It's a wonder the referee didn't stop the thing right then, put me out of my misery. But the ref seemed intent on letting this one go the distance. I guess, once you turn pro, you can't expect any of those easy stoppages. And what the hell, it's a lot of fun to watch.

"Have a seat," she says, despite my boneheaded statement.

"Are you sure?"

"You're not an ax murderer are you?"

"Okay, first of all, that's a really disturbing conversational transition." I pull out the chair across from her and sit. "And second, do you really expect an ax murderer to give you an honest answer?"

"Is that a yes or a no?"

"No. Not recently, at least."

"Well, that's something, I guess."

She stares down at my left hand unconsciously checking for a ring perhaps, or is that wishful thinking on my part? My hand is loosely resting around my glass of orange juice.

(By the way, do you know the Japanese word for orange juice? It's *orenji juusu*. I don't fucking get it either.)

"I see you're hitting the hard stuff again this morning," she says tapping one of her nails against my glass. I feel her finger glance over mine.

"Hey, this stuff is pretty damn acidic."

"Yeah, this place is known for its really strong o.j."

Her eyes move from my hand to my face. For some reason, I feel like I have just downed two hundred and seventy-three cups of coffee, my hands are shaking every so slightly, maybe it's her, maybe it's the lack of sleep, maybe it's the pressure.

The guy at the table behind her opens the front section of *The Washington Post* as he sits down to enjoy his Viennese Blend.

I see myself.

On the front page.

Frozen at the top of the AirStairs.

In Tom's coat.

The one I'm wearing right now.

It's a good shot of me.

I casually glance around and see the same picture a dozen more times on a dozen more papers, most of them the *Post*, a couple, *The Washington Times*. The headline on the *Post* reads: AMERICA WALKS OUT.

Sydney places her hand on top of mine, easing my jitteriness.

"Aren't you supposed to be in Europe or something?"

I give a little laugh. "Yes, Geneva." I glance at the picture of me again.

She looks at me. "You couldn't get a good enough glass of orange juice in Switzerland?"

Immediately, the reason for my return, the thing I haven't thought about for almost an hour, fills my head, and then my eyes, as tears well up inside them. "No," I wipe the corner of my eyes, "juice in the Alps really fucking sucks."

She has no idea what's wrong, but she squeezes my hand anyway and lets her soft, warm touch, and the silence do the healing.

After gazing at me for several moments, her eyes shifting focus between my left and right pupils, she breaks the silence and suggests that perhaps we can go somewhere else and talk.

Walking out of Bellina's, I cannot hold back my emotions any longer. I haven't cried like this since the Princess broke my Fat Track. Writing Sebby's eulogy, my tears were not as uncontrollable, even reading the eulogy, which by the end was covered and smudged by ink and tears, at least then I could speak.

The entire trek across the Mall to the hill the Washington Monument sits atop, I am unable to utter a single word.

I'm not sobbing. Not making a spectacle. It is simply me laid bare.

When we finally arrive at the marble benches at the foot of the Monument, the first busload of tourists are arriving. Dressed in sweatshirts and jeans and looking bleary-eyed from a night of traveling, they climb off the bus and make a bee-line for either the monument entrance, the bathrooms, or the hot dog cart.

Hot dogs at eight in the morning. The foundation of a healthy breakfast.

The only sounds are the flags flapping in the wind and the cry of children laughing and giggling and the shouts of parents yelling at their children to stop laughing and giggling so much.

Sydney looks around. I know she wants to ask me what it is that's bothering me. But she doesn't. She seems to sense that it's not me trying to be mysterious or difficult. It's not me wanting to keep her in the dark. I just can't speak. My mouth doesn't want to work. I can move it, but nothing will make the voyage from my brain to my vocal cords.

I turn my head and stare into her eyes. Her hair is being blown by the heavy breeze, the little blond strands catching the light so that her hair seems like a thousand sunsets. She doesn't reach for her own hair. Instead, she reaches for mine and pushes a lock of it over my ear.

Only then does she take her other hand and do the same to herself. She stops looking at me and stares out over the Mall at the buses that are arriving, at the children that are playing, at the Capital in the distance, at the White House.

"Do you want to talk about it?"

And suddenly, her words unlock something.

"He meant...he meant everything to me."

For an instant, I see a look of misunderstanding wash over her face. I can only imagine what she must be thinking, but if I had to take a guess, I would say that she's wondering if I'm talking about my lover who struggled valiantly against some AIDS-related illness. Again, I don't want the pause that is now taking place to mislead her in any way, but I'm still finding it difficult to gather my thoughts into something coherent or at least something I can explain.

She nods sympathetically and leans her forehead onto mine. I can feel the heat between us, and the proximity of her skin causes my headache, a headache that has been plaguing me for the past twenty-four hours, causes it to simply disappear.

"My grandfather. My grandfather just passed away."

Sydney curls up the corners of her mouth in a bittersweet smile, a new understanding taking place. A young boy runs over to us and shows us a penny that he's found on the ground.

"This is Abraham Lincoln."

"That's right," she says. "You're very smart. Do you know what Abraham Lincoln did?"

"Momma says he burned down my great grandpa's house because we wouldn't give him all our money. Now he's dead. And I got *his* money."

Sydney smiles at the boy, but as soon as he runs away, we burst into laughter. Which for me eventually blends with tears.

Now, the words are pouring out of me at an incredible pace. I tell her about my grandfather, about how Sebby was my rock when I was growing up. How he would reach into his pocket and pull out a couple of dollars and give whatever he had to his grandchildren, how he would laugh when the battery on his hearing aid went out and he couldn't understand a word you said, nor hear my grandmother shouting, "You're whistling again, Seb!" as the feedback looped and caused the device to whine.

And right in the middle of telling her these things, it happens. Something that makes me realize I'm getting back to normal. I was starting to take notice of her, how her hair looked in the wind, the way she interacted with the kids, and how much I wanted to, well, feel her arms wrapped around me.

"You've got a little bit of..." I raise my hand up to the corner of my mouth, indicating on my face where the big spot of mustard is on her face.

She licks it away, just subtly enough so I might actually think she doesn't mean to be sexy.

We had broken down and bought ourselves two hot dogs, mainly because all the tourists had them and we were curious what was so great that led people to move their heads like Ray Charles in delight, their cheeks bulging. As I suspected, it was just an Armour hot dog. No big deal. But we had fun playing with the mustard and onions and ketchup— none for me, a little for her.

My phone rings.

I'm in the city, so I get cell coverage here. I step away from her, not for privacy, but because I'm a bit embarrassed to have to answer it in front of her. Personal phones are rude, no doubt about it, but it might be important.

"Hello?"

And then I hear the unmistakable voice of Gunter Gerring on the line.

"So, are you in the middle of Siberia?"

"Kind of."

"I can never figure out where the hell you are with this thing."

"That's the idea, my friend. I might be a block from your house, you never know."

Gunter grunts. "Yeah, like that ever happens."

"Well, maybe if you lived someplace on the way to anyplace."

"I'll move just so you can visit." He pulls the phone away and yells. "I'll *tell* him, honey." He comes back to me. "Hey, I heard about your grandfather. Diane sends her sympathies. Did you get to make it back?"

Gunter's never been one for big emotional outbursts. The call itself is a massive display of compassion and affection.

"Yeah, I made it. I'm actually getting ready to fly back to Geneva."

I look over at Sydney. I'm in an etiquette dilemma. I've got Gunter pouring his heart out to me on the phone and this wonderful woman a few feet away licking condiments off her lips.

"That's good. They're supposed to be getting a huge snow storm in the Alps. Like the biggest in a hundred years. Have a nice flight," he says flatly, but with an edge of sarcasm. "I know how much you like bad weather while flying."

"I haven't heard anything about a storm."

"Always the last to know. Just don't say I didn't warn you." He pauses. "Sebby was a good man."

"That he was, Gunter." I look down at the ground. "Gunter," I pause, kicking at the grass with my foot, "thanks for the call."

"Hey, you know."

I knew.

. . .

"I'm a very big man in the Administration," I say, flirtatiously, as I waggle the phone.

"I'm sure you are," she says, specifically not looking below my belt.

I gaze at her, and suddenly I'm drawn in by her eyes. No, not her eyes exactly...

"You know, you have the most beautiful lashes," I tell her. And they are. Long and soft and much darker than her hair, they sweep me in. I don't usually notice lashes, eyes, yes, but lashes, no. But I want to reach out and... "Do you mind if I touch them?"

"Isn't it a little *early* for that?"

"Was that too forward of me? They just look so soft."

"They're dyed. No mascara."

She turns her head and leans almost imperceptibly toward me and I touch the feathery strands. A tingle runs from my fingertip down my arm.

"I prefer nighttime," she says, turning her head again to check her watch and confirm that it is, indeed, only 8 A.M.

"Really? So do I. But sometimes you take what you're given."

She runs her finger over her eyelid and across her lashes, smoothing what I have disturbed. "Sometimes, you're given what you take."

"Ooowww, I like that."

She looks at me for a moment. "That," she begins, her dramatic pause hanging in the air, "is because you like to take what's not yours."

"What makes you say that?"

"Hmmmmmm."

"I have a spotless record."

"That's because I imagine most don't mind the trespass."

"I thought that little turn of the head of yours was an *okay* to my request."

"Would it have mattered whether it was or not?"

"I don't know."

"Oh, don't disappointment me, Mr. Gerrick."

"No. I guess not."

"Thank you for being honest."

. . .

For the next twenty minutes, as we talked about Sebby and her father, and how much each meant to us, she spoke to me about love, and family, and the beauty and miracle of life. I forgot about the lashes and her pretty face, and I began to listen to her words. She had such a wonderful light about her. Several times during the conversation, we were interrupted by children and vendors, and every time, she genuinely didn't become annoyed.

Whatever storm was building across the Atlantic, the weather in Washington was mild for December. But it was chilly enough that I wanted to pull her close and cover the bare skin below her dress. I felt my hand instinctively reach out for her leg, finding a soft resting place on her knee as a warm shiver went down my spine.

"No, no, no," she said when her body responded and her leg raised up to push against my hand. She took in a deep breath of air.

"It's just my hand."

"Yes, but that's *my* leg."

"Your leg doesn't seem to mind."

"My leg doesn't get a vote in this."

I squeezed her knee gently, then removed my hand from her leg and let it graze her other thigh.

"And don't try getting the other leg to join in the rebellion."

"Rebellion? I like a good insurrection."

"So, you're hoping my body will revolt and give in to these advances."

"These are advances?" I said.

"Well, it certainly doesn't feel like you're withdrawing."

I feel her hips tense as she squeezes the space between her legs.

"Yikes." Okay, that sent about fifty percent of my blood to my cock. Which is why my next comment was from someone whose brain was running on half a tank. "I don't see a ring."

She looked at me and smiled. She must have felt pity for me. "I don't have to be married or engaged to not want your hand on my leg, do I?"

"No, but I would prefer it." I paused, enjoying the warmth of her body even though it was several inches away now. "Boyfriend?"

She shook her head. "Girlfriend."

I raised my eyebrows. "Mmmm. You *are* fun to play with."

"Not my girlfriend," she said. "*Your* girlfriend."

Ouch. That hurt.

15

PREPARE FOR BOARDING

"MY MOTHER TOLD me never to play with bad boys. They pull your hair."

I tried to look innocent as we walked across the Mall toward Constitution Avenue. "Why am I a bad man?"

"You have a girlfriend. And you're flirting with me."

"How do you *know* I have a girlfriend?"

"Really? So you don't?" She waited only a second, then continued. "And I'm sure she's incredibly beautiful, fabulously rich, and extremely well-connected."

I didn't say anything.

"He doesn't deny it. A point in your favor, by the way...even though you *were* flirting."

"I *always* flirt."

"With intent."

"We were at the Washington Monument. In public."

"Don't think I didn't pick up on the subliminal message of that locale."

I looked at her for a second. She was kidding, right? At least, I think she was kidding. That's the problem with bad little good girls. They look so...good that when they're joking, you can never really be sure...until they're laughing at you for thinking they were serious.

I tried a different tack.

"Like I was the only one flirting. And I bet you *do* have a boyfriend."

She stopped.

"No, I don't," she said, putting her index finger in front of my face, correcting me. "I have *several* boyfriends."

I gazed at her. She had a manner that was charming and engaging and open. "I don't doubt that at all."

She drew in a long breath. Her voice was soft and appealing as she asked, almost as an afterthought, "Where are we going?"

I hadn't been paying attention. The peculiar thing about Washington D.C. is that a neighborhood can change quickly and dramatically. The good parts of the District are only a block or two away from the bad parts.

I glanced around to get my bearings, 18th and F. We were okay. No need to panic.

My first time in D.C.—at least, the first time I wasn't being herded by grade school teachers and chaperones—I decided to go out for a little afternoon walk. I strolled out the front doors of the lobby and proceeded merrily down the street. After going two blocks, I turned a corner and immediately found myself smack dab in the middle of a gang shoot-out.

Thank God for those nightmare-inducing nuclear preparedness films from when I was a kid. "Billy knows what to do. Don't you, Billy? When he sees the flash of an atomic bomb, he knows...Duck and Cover!"

So, when I saw the flash from the Glock 9, I ducked and I covered.

For a while there, D.C. was the murder capital of the United States. What makes absolutely no sense is that you can't say we don't have enough cops on the street in D.C. Something like one out of every ten people you walk by are some sort of cop. There's the Metro Police, Treasury's Secret Service and Secret Service Uniform Division, Park Police, the Security Division of the State Department, the Transit Cops, Capital Security, Postal Inspectors, FBI, ATF, DEA, Military Police, not to mention myriad legions of undercover agents, like the ones protesting out in front of the White House.

Oh, c'mon, you think the United States government lets several dozen people sit just outside the gates of the Presidential residence at all hours of the day and night without having at least one guy amongst them holding up a sign saying, "Impeach the President?"

Please.

"I guess," I said, looking around. "I was automatically walking to my place."

"Lemme guess, Georgetown?"

I nodded. For some reason, I was embarrassed.

"I imagine you wanted to show me some of your etchings?"

"No, actually, my collection of axes."

Her eyes softened, and her mouth curled up into a smile. "My office is near Dupont Circle. I don't have to be there for a little while. As long as you get me there *in one piece*."

"Funny."

I realized something. We weren't that far. A block, maybe.

"You know, actually, all my stuff is at the White House."

"Yeah, I know, I leave my stuff there all the time. He likes it when I do that," she said, following me as I changed direction.

"No, really. I have to be on the SAM—" I caught myself, gov-speak. Special Air Mission is the military designation for a plane used exclusively for civilian leaders, like the one I flew back from Europe on. "I have to catch a plane on a State Department mission leaving at ten. They're making a special stop-over for me."

"You know, you really have much better excuses than most men." She paused for a moment, gazing at me. "I'll let you go. It was good to run into you again."

I tilted my head in the direction of the Mall. "Thanks for...you know..."

"I liked that. It's refreshing to see in a man." She ran her hands along my jacket lapel. "I'm just glad you had a craving for orange juice this morning."

We were now standing by the side entrance to the White House complex. For the gateway to one of the most powerful places on earth, it's rather unassuming.

"Listen, stay right here a moment. It'll really be much quicker if I just run in."

As she realized where we were, I showed my ID to the guard. He waved me in.

It finally hit her. People don't just *walk* into the White House.

I started to step inside the gate but stopped.

"Listen, this is going to sound a little crazy, but are you free for the rest of the day?"

"I thought you had to be six thousand miles away by dinner time."

"I'm supposed to be, but...are you? Free?"

"I don't have anything...I couldn't get out of, I guess." She blinked, glanced down at what she was wearing, and almost blushed.

"Why don't you come with me to Geneva?"

Sydney raised her eyebrow. She was no longer looking at me, she was studying me.

"That sounds more than a *little* crazy. Are you out of your mind?"

"No, I'm serious. Just fly over, drop me off in Geneva, pick up some diplomats in Rome, then BAM! you're back in D.C."

"Is that supposed to make it sound less crazy? You said the flight is at ten?" She looked at her watch. "It's seven-thirty. I can't just fly off to Europe. I don't have any luggage or clothes or anything."

"You don't need any clothes."

"Oh, really?" That eyebrow again.

I motioned to her outfit. "I'm saying you look great. And if you do need anything, we'll buy it...in *Europe*." I tried to make it sound like a bonus.

"You're sweet. Crazy, but sweet."

"Say yes." I wasn't pleading. I was asking her. "Do something different. One day out of thirty thousand."

"Thirty thousand? That's all I get?

"If you're lucky." I put my hand on her arm. "You don't say yes, you're gonna regret it as soon as I walk in there." I nodded toward the White House.

"I don't even have a valid passport."

"I can get you a passport in thirty minutes. The plane's on a diplomatic mission. You probably don't even need one. You're technically on American soil the whole time."

"You...are insane, you know that?"

"C'mon, when was the last time you did something really crazy?"

"I don't know, the time I walked out of Bellina's with you."

"Besides that."

"You can't really expect me to do this?" Her words were saying no, but I could tell by the tone of her voice that there was a fragile hint of uncertainty.

"C'mon. You want to get on that plane and come with me. You know it."

And then, the chink in the armor.

"How long would this whole thing take?"

There it is.

"I don't know maybe seventeen or eighteen hours."

"Eighteen?"

"It's no worse than flying to Bombay."

"You fly to India?"

"You really don't understand what I do."

"I don't *know* what you do."

"I'll tell you all about it on the way there. You'll be back home just in time for your one cup at Bellina's."

"You're absolutely serious?"

"Absolutely."

"I'm not going anywhere with you unless you can guarantee I'll be back here by six tomorrow morning."

I decided to call her bluff. I pulled out my phone and made a call to the transportation liaison at my office for an authorization to have a non-gov civilian fly with me. That done, I dialed the State Department. Asked them how long it would take for me to get an emergency passport for a U.S. citizen, then I got transferred to the Travel Office to verify the details about the flight I was hopping on, *exactly* where it was going, when it was returning, and what time it would be back in Washington.

I was only off by about an hour and a half. The plane would be returning to Andrews at about 6:30 A.M., which meant that Sydney could be back in her favorite chair at Bellina's by about 7:30.

For most people dealing with government service employees—even getting the simplest requests taken care of—is a nightmare. A quagmire of red tape, delay, and just plain bureaucratic lethargy.

But for a lucky few, a couple of phone calls can get just about anything done, and done quickly.

Sixteen minutes later, I had all the information and all the authorizations for Sydney Nathan to accompany me to Geneva.

SYDNEY TRIED to look serious for her first passport photo since college, but I kept making her laugh. Finally, after the woman taking the photos glared at me, Sydney clicked off a good one.

I sat there, watching her fill out the passport form, thinking, I can't believe she's doing this. I don't ever extend an invitation I don't mean, but still, very few people act on my spontaneous overtures. I guess so many of them have uttered false invites—invites they hope, pray, and expect will never be accepted—that they naturally assume everyone else does the same thing.

Then other thoughts started entering my head, like, what the fuck was I doing? I was about to take a woman, who was not Laura, who I did not really know, out of the country for a little Sunday drive.

This had disaster stamped all over the visa page.

I mean, let's look at this. I was obviously not going to call up Laura and say, "Hey, hon, mind if I fly off to Europe with some babe I picked up at the coffee shop?"

Her response, right after, "You don't drink coffee," would be, "Fuck you! I'm here helping your family grieve, and you're off *dating*?"

I would have to tell Laura eventually, because, well, because she would find out anyway, sooner or later. I'm not very good at sneaking around. I'm good at being straightforward, direct, blunt.

Something my little French kitten, Rafael, once told me sums it up.

"Billy," she said, her accent sending shivers down my neck, "the reason why you are successful is because you are like, how do you say, *comment dites-vous*, you are like a wonderfully soft piece of velvet wrapped around a very big hammer. You are pleasant to the eye and gentle to the touch, right up to the time you knock them over the head."

Le marteau de velours, she would call me.

This isn't to say I'm not a master of deception. It's my business to be cagey and clever, to not show my cards. That's what I'm paid for. Not to lie, but to conceal the point at which I will give in to a demand or to pressure. I play poker. And I win.

But in certain arenas, like playing with females, history has not been as kind to me. Like I said, I've been caught by others, while naked with, I don't know, three-quarters of the women I dated before college. Of course, I was naked with them a great deal and only caught a minuscule percentage of the time.

For instance, when we got caught by Gale's mother, it was, I'll admit, a bit unnerving. It was the first time we had been together. The second girl I had been with and the third time I'd had actual intercourse. A one, two, three punch that made me keenly aware that the stakes were much higher compared with getting snared doing some heavy petting.

(I consider the six-in-one-night with Jill Dohemann *one* time. If you ask Jill, it might even be less.)

Gale and I had a great winter, spending every afternoon wrapped together. And except for getting caught by her dad—a local Teamster, I might add—the *second* time we had sex, we were never interrupted during a performance again.

It was a few months later, well into my Senior year, when I had my first bitter taste of duplicity as my relationship with Gale came to a sudden and unexpected halt. And yet out of this carnage, I ended up dating one of the most mischievous, depraved, and amusing people I've ever met. Leslie Caron, who had this wicked little grin, this Cheshire Cat That Ate the Canary smile that more than anything said "fuck you" in a really delight-ful, playful, seductive way. Leslie was more than just someone to play with, she was someone you had to fight for.

She was the kind of evil goodness that you just couldn't keep your eyes or your hands off of. She'd walk into a room with her translucent green eyes and that much-too-sweet-to-be-innocent smile and you just had to have her.

I met Leslie while earning minimum wage at one of those major department stores that turn out to be pretty minor once you see the real things in the cities.

We hit it off immediately.

She came from the same town as Gale, who I was dating at the time. Leslie knew her, chided me for going out with someone so earnest and sincere. Someone so "wholesome."

"Hey, she had sex with me on our first date. It wasn't even a date. She picked me up and took me home." I had to acknowledge—"From a hospital."

"She wears flannel nightgowns, doesn't she?"

"So?"

"Aaaaaaaagh," Leslie let out a disgusted sigh. "Get away from me."

About four months after I split my head open and ended up in her bed, Gale informed me that the college guy she had been seeing before me, the guy who had broken her heart, the guy who had asked her to marry him, then jumped in the sack with the first dozen coeds he happened to bump into on campus, had, in fact, changed his mind and decided he wanted her back now. This information came out just hours before we were going to the big Spring Fling dance at her school when she let it slip... she was once again engaged to the guy.

Engaged. To be married. At seventeen.

Kinda put a damper on the evening.

She did offer to sleep with me one last time after we got home from the dance. But I said no—I thankfully had some dignity, some semblance of self-respect. I only let her give me head.

Leslie laughed straight in my face when she heard the story, and I had to take it. Mainly because, Leslie had warned me all along, since we started working together, that Gale was a deceiver who appeared to be truthful. Leslie, on the other hand, would tell me to my face, that someday she just might sleep with somebody else because that's the way she was, which was fickle. But she would tell me the moment she knew she was going to do it, unless that moment was actually the moment she was doing it. And in that case, she'd tell me as soon as she was done doing it.

I never got mad at Leslie for these jabs, never took it personally. I deserved it. More than that, they didn't seem so much her taking a hard shot at me, more a love tap. With Leslie, I got my first taste of someone who was able to give an insult, a cutting remark, and make you feel good about the attention.

I have this talent, somewhat. But it was Leslie who let me see how powerful and unique a gift it is.

"You wanna maybe go out sometime," she asked me one afternoon while we were folding towels in the linen department.

"You wanna?" I said.

She looked at me with her lips pursed in her *don't-give-me-that-shit* way. She had made the opening move, and she wasn't going to just let me knock it back into her court.

"You're probably right," she said after a moment. "We have to work together." She folded another towel. Half, half again, quarter.

"What about Brian?" The guy she was dating. Brian, who she talked about all the time as being beautiful, gorgeous, and stupid as a grapefruit.

"He's a fence post, Billy."

I remember her telling me how she liked to straddle banisters and railings and fences ever since she was a little girl. Was this a good thing or a bad thing?

"I heard you liked fence posts."

"Like 'em electric."

"You know I always thought you'd be fun to play with."

"Did you?"

"C'mon. You think I got them to schedule me in linens because I have a burning desire to sell sheets and pillowcases?"

She wasn't stupid.

Leslie knew the only reason I became one of the best salespeople in sheets and towels and draperies was because deep down, deeeeep down, I got a little rush and a not-so-little hard-on every time we worked together.

We had a lot of fun. Even more once we started dating.

Leslie was always candid with me about her penchant for duplicity. But even with her considerable skills, it was still nearly impossible to keep parents and other authorities from tripping over my sex life.

This one time, I was supposed to be going down to the beach with my guy friends—at least that's what I told my parents—but what I really was about to do was go down on Leslie as long as she and my jaw muscles would let me. The setup was perfect. Leslie's parents and her two younger brothers had taken off for the Caymans that morning. Her older brother, who seemed to always be auditioning for father-figure, wouldn't be back from the islands until late the next day. We had her huge house to ourselves. We could fuck, we could play chess naked, we could do anything we wanted for twenty-four whole hours.

The plan was this: That I would wait outside my house for her to pick me up. I didn't want to drive over myself because I didn't want any of her neighbors to see my car parked at the house overnight.

Only the Princess decided to come out and wait with me, something he had never done before. Why he chose this particular moment in history, I have no fucking idea, but he did, and I was going to be stuck with him until he ran out of things to say or I could annoy him sufficiently so that he would leave. For one of the few times in my life, I was unable to do the latter, and he, amazingly, was powerless to do the former. He was very chatty that afternoon.

"So, are you guys sleeping on the beach?"

"That's the general plan."

"You sure you're gonna be warm enough?"

Oh, yeah, I was thinking. I'm gonna be very warm. Nice and warm between the smooth, tan legs of Leslie Caron.

"Oh, sure. I'm gonna be fine. No problem. Not cold at all, Dad." I figured I should shut up immediately. My father might have been big, cranky, picky, unforgiving, a mumbler, an alcoholic, overly sensitive, but he was *not* stupid.

Okay, I thought to myself. What am I gonna do?

The Princess was never really someone who paid attention to detail unless it concerned flowers or booze. So, I figured, I could get away with being vague about our exact strategy. But in the heat of battle, I forgot that he was a camping fanatic as well. Not that he ever went, he just loved the thought of camping, had all the gear, knew all the best places. Actually going, taking his sons...never happened.

I bought some goodwill by asking him where he thought we should put up for the night.

He gave me exact directions. He liked to do that. My father holds colossal sums of information in his head on all kinds of places, which is fucking eerie because I couldn't conceive of him stopping his car and pulling over long enough to get out—he was always *going* somewhere. But he knew of this one spot that would've been perfect...if we had *actually* been going to the beach.

I mean, for years, I had been complaining that my father didn't talk to me enough, didn't spend ample time with me. And now, at the absolute worst moment, he decided to become a proud parent, the involved father. It was the best, most lengthy conversation we had had in years. Of course, I had virtually no idea what he was talking about because, to tell the truth, my concentration wasn't focused on him.

It was focused down the street, hoping to God that Leslie would be late and that my father would finally get bored with our tête-à-tête.

But then I saw it coming around the bend, the lights were unmistakably those of a BMW three-fucking-something-or-other, the kind of car Leslie drove, the kind of car you never saw on my street. After traveling the globe, and living in Washington, I'm no longer surprised at seeing BMWs or Mercedes or Rolls-Royces or even the million-dollar tanks dressed up as Cadillacs and Lincoln Town Cars. Those bulletproof, rocket-proof, bombproof, behemoths that ferry around the President, Vice President, and other dignitaries, even me sometimes. Oh, they look normal, but these damn things could drive through the fuselage of a 747 loaded with fuel, and the only thing that might even be slightly damaged are the flags on the hood.

Every once in a while, I wonder what it would have been like to be a teenager with access to one of those presidential limousines. Nothing too fancy, one of the old ones, just bulletproof glass, high-speed rims you could drive at 55 mph with the wheels shot out, maybe some armor plating. I mean, think of it. We thought we were invincible anyway, just imagine a bulletproof car. I could see us riding around the worst neighborhoods, begging for trouble. The thing is, all that would happen would be that this tank carrying me and the rest of my moron friends, a vehicle that weighs about twenty tons and gets one mile to the gallon would run out of gas right there in the middle of two warring gang factions in a turf battle.

"WASN'T THAT LESLIE?" the Princess asked me as she drove right by the two of us. Now, my dad had seen Leslie about a hundred times, either when she had come over to pick me up, or at JC Penney's where he would inadvertently walk by us on his way to having another half-dozen cups of coffee at the Friendly's diner in the mall, so, there was really no use in me lying and saying it wasn't her when clearly it was.

"Yeah, that was her."

He turned to me. "It's not just guys going down there, huh?" he said while he—God help me—nudged me in the ribs.

My father never told me anything useful about women. Plants sure. Stereo equipment, absolutely. Even cars. But women, that conversation never came up. Well, that's not exactly true, they—women—did come up. It usually took the form of my father craning his neck so far around to get a good look at a woman on the side of the road that he'd need a chiropractor in the morning, and saying something like, "Look at the bazookas on that one," or "Holy shit, how can she stand up?" or, my personal favorite, as he dropped me and Gunter off at a dance club: "Jesus Christ, looks like a lotta nice broads in there."

"You know, I'll go tell them that, Dad, I'm sure the broads'll be flattered."

Broads, bazookas, gravity-defying jugs, I had gotten it all, but I had never gotten the "elbow in the rib" from my father. I had heard about this, seen it in movies, witnessed comedians pantomiming it, but never actually had a bony appendage been stuck in my side. Not even a failed attempt.

My mouth was open, but only flies were going in and out of it. As I stared up at him, he nodded knowingly, looking at me over the tops of his glasses.

I faked a laugh. "Yeah, some of the girls are coming down. Supposed to be a surprise, but they're not sleeping overnight."

Oh, God. Another nudge.

"No, really, they're not. Apparently, they aren't into waking up with sand flea bites all over their bodies."

I don't know why I had this need to downplay my sex life, especially when it seemed to make him so happy to hear that *someone* in the family would be getting laid.

My dad seemed disappointed.

But not for long. Here came Leslie driving back the other way. She had turned around at the end of the street.

I looked her dead in the eye as she passed...right by.

"What's she doing?"

"I think she might be intimidated by you standing out here."

"Why?"

"I don't know...we're going off to the beach together..." I made a motion to him. Oh God, I can't believe I'm doing this. "...and she knows she might..." Oh, how can this be happening? "...might stay the night."

I don't think I have ever seen the ol' man so happy, so proud of his son.

Me being asked by the President personally to come and work for him didn't please my father as much.

So, on the third pass, I waved Leslie in. She was a little nervous, which, if you knew her, was rare. The Princess has an intimidating presence, not in a scary way, but in that big, manly, six-foot-three way.

I stuck my head inside the car. "He knows..." She nearly freaked, thinking I had blown the whistle on our long-planned night-long alone. "...about you driving me down to the beach."

She immediately calmed down and went to work on the Princess. She grinned her most devilish little grin, and said to him, "I'm sure the other girls will just be devastated you couldn't join us, Mr. Gerrick."

My father was putty in her hands.

16

A SMOOTH FLIGHT

OUR CONVERSATION, the one between Sydney and me, was interrupted only briefly by boarding (she had to go through a secondary security check).

"This is the craziest thing I've ever done," she said just after I was politely asked to leave the area.

"God, you've led a sheltered life."

WHILE HER CREDENTIALS were being checked, I walked out onto the tarmac. The plane was being refueled, its black tail number, 26000, stood out as the sun's brilliance illuminated the white paint. I spent half a minute looking around for another aircraft with its main door open, AirStairs rolled into place. But there wasn't one. The plane had the words UNITED STATES OF AMERICA on the fuselage just like the plane I'd flown out of Geneva. But where that was some random jet in the pool, this was one of the most fabled aircraft ever to fly.

I climbed the stairs slowly, gazing at the globally recognizable light blue, dark blue, silver and white paint job before getting on board.

One of the crew in a uniform that looked like standard-issue flight attendant attire except for the Air Force wings on her name tag, informed me that there were ready-to-eat meals, sandwiches, and snacks available.

As I looked over the interior, I tried to imagine seats and a wall hastily being ripped out because Jackie Kennedy wouldn't let them put her husband's casket in the cargo hold. Lyndon Johnson was sworn in right where I was standing. Nixon flew to China on this plane. It was no longer the primary plane used as Air Force One but was still used as a backup.

I decided on two beers rather than wine, for several reasons. It was 10 A.M. I didn't know if she was a white or a red kind of girl, and besides wine is a little too...romantic.

Beer meant buddies.

I could explain beer to Laura.

A few minutes after the rest of the passengers climbed on the aircraft, we left the ground. It's like that with government planes. Either you sit there for hours, waiting for someone—like me— to come on board, or you're in, you're up, you're off.

It was imperative I get back to Geneva, quickly. We'd be flying at fastest maintainable speed. We were two of only a handful of people on the plane, a plane that was detouring from its original destination (at the President's request) to drop me off in Switzerland before going on to Rome and then back to D.C.

Sydney drained the last of her beer as I finished telling her about Sebby and my grandmother, Annette, building the house by themselves, and how the Princess would squeal from the shower when we washed out our cereal bowls in the sink.

The conversation had shifted, and I noticed that I was dominating the discussion now, where before it was more balanced.

"You're not saying much," I said to her.

"It's because I love your voice."

"That's why I'm doing all the talking?"

She nodded. "Ah-huh, you didn't know that?"

"I thought maybe I was boring you."

She shook her head. "I love listening to it." She rubbed the sleeve of her shirt. "It gives me the chills," she added.

"That's funny, yours does the same thing to me."

"My voice?"

I nodded.

"I sound like I'm sixteen. If I'm lucky."

This time, my gesture was part nod, part shrug, part tilt of the head.

She smiled. "Then I guess I better start talking," she said, pausing for a moment to think. "What do you want me to say?"

"The beauty of it is, I have no idea," I whispered, putting my head back against the seat and turning toward her so that I was speaking into her ear without being obvious.

There were others on board, crew, passengers, but we were sitting on a couch-like seat in the forwardmost open compartment, and no one seemed very interested in us.

She closed her eyes and made the little noise you make when a tingle is running down the side of your body. A rush ran through me in response.

She leaned toward me, and in the sweetest, most innocent yet sexy voice said, "How 'bout...I can't believe I got on this plane with you."

WITHIN TEN MINUTES, my voice was half an octave higher and my normally cool exterior was being compromised by the turbulence we were encountering.

"God, I hate this."

She glanced over at me and placed her hand on top of mine. "Sitting next to me?"

"You know what I'm talking about."

She was doing better than me, but I could see the motion was getting to her. "Me too," she said.

"Really? You don't think I'm a complete pantywaist because I need antiperspirant on my palms right now?"

"Keep talking to me," she said. "How many miles have you flown?"

"About...I don't know...three million."

"Three million?" She stared at me. "Miles?"

"Something like that."

"*Something* like that? You hate to fly, and you've flown three million miles?" Any nervousness she had was completely annihilated by her shock.

"Well, generally these things are a bit smoother. That's how I like things, at least."

Her tone changed, softened. It didn't matter that the plane was jumping around.

"So you prefer things smooth?"

"Very."

"Not completely smooth, I hope."

She put her finger on the side of my face, feeling my skin along the jaw and up till she played with my sideburns.

"No, you need, you know, something. Otherwise, you look too young."

"I agree." She let her eyes fall on my carry-on bag. "I bet you're a blade man. Probably right in there."

Reaching down, I pulled out my razor from one of the inside pockets of my bag. She took it from me and studied it, glancing closely at the blades, then at my face.

We talked for a while longer. She asked a few questions about the conference, Sebby, and my grooming habits, then suddenly, she undid her seat belt, paused before getting up, and leaned forward. "I'll be right back. You know, the beer," she said, motioning that it was running through her.

When she returned ten minutes later, she handed me a drink, another beer she had gotten from the attendant. Sydney slid back into the seat gracefully.

There was a slightly mischievous grin on her face as she got comfortable. "You know what?"

"What?"

"I have a feeling the rest of the flight is going to be much, much smoother," she said as the plane hit another pocket of air and at the same moment placed my razor on the armrest between us.

I stared at Sydney, my eyebrows raised, then glanced down at the razor, which was moist.

"Oh, really?"

"Mmm-hmmph."

I continued to watch Sydney, who was now flipping happily through a magazine.

Slowly, I guided my left hand under the low, fabric armrest and inconspicuously removed the barrier with my forearm, while my fingers reached for her smooth legs.

The warm flesh of her thigh didn't feel any softer than before, which when I brushed against it earlier was very soft indeed. Seemingly reading my mind, she shook her head and said, "But you're getting warmer."

Which I was.

ABOUT THREE HOURS into the flight and somewhere over Newfoundland, the edge of my little finger had made its way up under her skirt and just inside the edge of her panties and was resting against the smooth, moist skin where her legs met her body.

Now, believe me, I'm smart enough to understand the physics and science regarding the newness of touch, that strange and wonderful tingle caused by a fresh caress as the aura around her body collides powerfully with mine. It's as natural as it is common. One of the reasons people get used to someone's embrace is that the human body has an incredible ability to withstand extreme conditions, to adapt. We become numb to pain and extreme cold as our bodies adjust to the surrounding environment. Without such a physical mechanism, we would be in a perpetual state of fear, of pain, of arousal, and nothing, no work, no hunting, no progress, nothing of any value would ever get done.

So, I appreciate the effect that an unfamiliar body has on mine, but this was something stunningly different. I mean, even if I factored in the novelty of her flesh, I was more than certain my nerves had never, and I mean never, been pushed to this extreme, to such incredible ecstasy, based solely on one of my fingers just barely having contact with a woman's pussy.

I LET that one finger stay right where it was for a long, long time before I decided to advance any further. It wasn't because I was afraid she would try to stop me. No, I wanted to enjoy the sensation for as long as I could.

She had taken a blade that had caressed my face and used it to make smooth the most personal part of her body, and I was going to appreciate that gesture as much as possible.

For the rest of the flight, as SAM 26000 jumped and pitched and bounced on the angry winds blowing over the North Atlantic, I did not feel a thing except for a few inches of territory between Sydney's legs. She had done quite an admirable job, especially considering the turbulence. The side of my hand told me that she had not shaved completely, just along the folds and a little above, leaving a cute patch of soft, straight hair. I slid my fingers through that fine hair and the yielding folds, a journey which was made much easier by her wetness. I let my finger disappear briefly inside of her, then drew it back out and over her clit.

I don't remember what I was thinking.

Probably because I wasn't thinking of anything but how my body was responding to hers.

I have rarely been able to be this focused about anything, and I let myself be consumed by it.

Too often thoughts rush into my head at the most inopportune times. But my mind was clear.

Her breathing, and mine, became heavy and warm. Several times I leaned over and whispered things into her ear that made her squirm or sigh, and made me shake with excitement.

I kept playing with her, kept pressing that sweet little button of hers, until, finally, as her body tensed up, she shuddered and rocked with a quiet, but explosive orgasm under the direction of my touch.

I could feel, which was confirmed when I looked down, that I was wet myself, dripping precum, my body acknowledging in its instinctual way, the proximity of a possible mating partner.

My face was flush and my heart raced as I pulled her closer to me.

Almost immediately after her body stopped twitching, Sydney began to sob uncontrollably.

I put arms around her and whispered, "Shhhh. It's okay."

Her body shook with emotion, and her tears burned into my heart like acid.

As I held her tightly, rocked her gently, I got angry with myself, squeezing my eyes shut, wondering why was I such an asshole. She was unsettled by this. Maybe she had betrayed one of those "boyfriends," maybe there was only *one,* and maybe he was the reason why she was so upset.

I pressed my head against her upper arm and cursed myself under by breath. For doing this...to her, to Laura. My body was still tingling from the encounter, and I was saddened that one of the purest, most perfect sensual experiences of my life was causing someone this much anguish.

But even in this regret, in this sharing of pain, I felt a deeper sense of something. And I was awed because I knew what it was, what it meant, and astonished I was feeling it on a plane six hours after running into this woman for only the second time in my life.

A FEW MINUTES LATER, she was still sobbing.

I knew why, but I asked her anyway, "Why are you crying?"

"Why do you think?"

I nodded my head, letting her know that I understood with a slight frown.

Only I didn't know.

She dropped her head and gathered herself.

"This happens sometimes," she said. "I don't know why exactly. Not often. Usually when I feel it so deep, emotionally." She wiped her eyes and stared at me with a gaze that pleaded and rewarded at the same time. "Sometimes, after making love, if it's really intense, I cry." She was quiet for a moment. "But this has never happened with someone just touching me."

17
DIPLOMATIC SIBERIA

THE PLANE TOUCHED down as a heavy snow was beginning to fall, which made the landing seem much more dramatic that it actually was. I mean, I knew that intellectually, but try getting my brain to listen. I held my breath just as I normally do, waiting for one of the wheels to fall off, the wing to crack in half, or a flock of birds to get sucked into the engine fans.

Geese don't follow Air Traffic Control.

We safely reached the terminal as the turbines wound down.

A minor issue had come up during the flight and the Captain announced before landing that he'd requested some maintenance be done on the aircraft in Geneva. I was looking forward to spending a few more hours more with Sydney, there'd be just enough time to rush her to my favorite restaurant in the city for a quick dinner. Let me clarify, the *only* restaurant in the city I really enjoy.

Like the Germans, the Swiss are precision-oriented people. Clocks, watches, beer, music, etc. Music may seem like a creative passion, but it's really one of mathematics and exactitude.

If you want to find love and great literature, art treasures and exquisite cuisine, go to Italy or France or Spain or Greece.

Geneva's not anywhere as bad as Zurich—the French influence helps —but you don't go to Switzerland for the food. Except the chocolate.

Now, there *are* reasons to visit Switzerland, least of which—after bad cuisine—is trying to find someone in the country that has any idea what the fuck they're talking about. This isn't to say the Swiss are stupid people, because they're not. Nor are they ignorant. They are educated and well-informed. More well-informed than most Americans. It's just that it doesn't matter in D.C. or Denver what someone in Chattanooga thinks about global politics, if they think about global politics at all.

The problem with the Swiss is that they have this long, proud history of compartmentalized communities and decentralized governance with four different languages and half a dozen different cultural sways, which has a lot to do with their equally long, equally proud history of being absolutely neutral, which has rendered them completely and entirely unable to distinguish right from wrong.

You're a Nazi with a ton of money, sure, you can deposit it here. International terrorist looking for a decent interest rate. C'mon over.

Their terrain combined with this inability to differentiate between good and evil has perhaps saved Switzerland from complete obliteration. With Hitler rolling tanks over and through the Tyrol Mountains, it's a wonder there still is such a thing as Swiss cheese anymore.

I mean, if you armed every man, woman and child in the country, the National Guard of *Delaware* would kick the *Yadalayheehoo* out of them.

That is, if you could find them. The Swiss are long-term thinkers. Instead of defending indefensible plains and cities, you know, where the people were, the army and political leaders in World War II withdrew to bunkers and forts deep in the mountains. Instead of being a juicy, easy-for-the-taking strategic link between Germany and Italy, they mined key bridges and tunnels connecting the two Axis powers, and made it clear, they'd blow them up if they ever got invaded.

And hey, we're neutral. You can drive right through without bothering to stop.

But this survival technique has also meant that the people of Suisse, as nice as they are, as fucking *beautiful* as they are, are an infuriatingly frustrating people to speak with. There's a slight arrogance to the only country in Central Europe to figure out how to avoid Hilter's insanity. And a strange indifference as well. Anyone who can say with a completely straight face that they don't have a bad thing to say about Churchill *or* Hitler is going to be thoroughly unable to pick a restaurant for dinner.

"I think this one's good. But that's one's good, too. And that other one...also good."

Wake up, people, none of your food is any good.

And your politics? Nobody likes a kiss-ass. Especially if you're kissing everybody's ass.

Even if it were *possible* in some alternate reality for you to argue that Adolf had some noble purpose in mind when he decided to get rid of Jews, gays, cripples and Catholics—oh, yeah, *my* people were part of the whole Holocaust thing, we just don't make a big deal out of it. I mean, we lost like two hundred people—even if you make that case, which would be an amazing feat in and of itself—the man was evil, the things he did were *bad*—even if you take Hitler's side, you *need* to have some sort of negative feelings about Churchill, right? The guy was trying to destroy your pal, *Der Führer.* I mean, an unkind word, at least.

Not the Swiss, no, they are unfettered by this seeming contradiction. In fact, it doesn't seem incongruous to them at all, that's just the way things are in the world. Some people win, some people lose, but everybody needs a bank to put their money in.

BUT GUNTER, as always, was right, and the storm heading toward the Alps was very mighty, indeed, and approaching more swiftly than predicted. The pilot decided it would be better to take off immediately and have the plane checked out in Rome.

Sydney and I stood at the glass door leading back out onto the runway, which offered an impressive viewpoint. One which, however, did not provide much protection from the cold. She rubbed her hands together, then put them under her arms. She had left her home this morning dressed in a skirt for an unseasonably warm December day in Washington, not a snowstorm in the Alps. And despite the oversized flight jacket I had borrowed from one of the crew members that hung adorably low on her small frame, she was still shivering.

"I wish we didn't have to rush this," she said, wrapping herself tighter in the jacket.

"They're worried about getting caught in the storm."

"I know." The words were said softly.

"I'm amazed you came this far."

"Me too." She looked at me, thoughtfully. "And I do have to get back." She pointed to her outfit. "I didn't quite pack for this trip."

"I thought with the delay, we'd at least be able to have dinner."

"You know, men usually buy me dinner *before* they try to feel me up."

"I picked up a sandwich for you."

"Yes, you did." She kissed my lips, then rested her mouth next to my ear and whispered, "I had a wonderful time. Thank you for my day off from reality. Definitely one of the thirty thousand I'll never forget."

I held her close. Her breath warm on my neck.

It was some time before she spoke. "I understand the situation and don't expect you to call me when you get back."

"I was about to ask you for your number."

She pulled away slowly, her eyes down as she studied the large metal zipper on the military jacket. Her expression was somewhat melancholy and distant. "Listen, Billy," she said, breathing deeply again. "Why don't we just not do that. I don't want to give you my number and then...not have you call. It would ruin this for me."

I nodded, then shook my head.

"But what if I *want* to get in touch with you?"

"You have a girlfriend. I don't want to be a part of screwing that up."

"What if you're supposed to screw it up?"

"Well, I don't want to." She was quiet, her fingers drifting along my shoulder. "I don't want you to think I didn't feel this, because I did. Very much."

"I felt it, too. And I think we should talk about that when this whole thing is over." I motioned inextricably in the general direction of the Intercontinental, about six miles away.

"No, no, no. I know what intimate feels like with you, I can't go backward and simply become interference. This has no place to go but spiraling down."

Sometimes words can feel like a punch to the stomach.

"You're sure about this?"

She nodded. "So, I guess this is where we say goodbye," she said, sounding like the *femme fatale* in an old movie. We were in the perfect setting for it. Our breath visible in the air. The mountains rising in the distance white with snow. A plane ready to depart within yards of where we stood.

She let her hand fall on my chest and slide down to my stomach.

The flight crew was making their way across the tarmac and up the steps into the plane. She glanced back at the jet briefly as the last person waved for her to come aboard.

The paint job. The snow. The 29000 on the tail. It sticks in my mind, even now.

"Goodbye, Billy, " she said.

I don't think I've ever heard one that sounded so final.

She reached up and kissed me on the lips again, then turned and pushed on the glass door, sending a blast of freezing cold air through me.

I shivered. I'm not exactly sure if it was from the frigid wind or watching her walk away from me.

At that moment, I wanted to run outside, grab her and stop her, keep her from getting on the plane, make her stay with me. But I had used up all my privileges by going home for Sebby's funeral. I couldn't endanger the negotiations any further.

At least, that's what I convinced myself.

I think I was more afraid that if I ran out there, she would simply turn to me again and say, "No."

As I watched Sydney climb on board, I thought about Jenna/Claire. Not taking decisive, determined, immediate action caused me to miss out on dating the most beautiful, approachable, intelligent, funny...*limber* teenage goddess imaginable.

But I learned a powerful and painful lesson from that mistake.

Then why wasn't I crawling naked across the frozen runway to seize Sydney by the arms, and keep her from leaving?

Perhaps because Sydney hadn't offered me her phone number, which I then let sit for three weeks without dialing. In fact, she had *refused* to give me her number.

I don't know if I recall having to make a more difficult decision than the one I made to turn my back on her and walk out of the airport into the waiting limousine, not bothering to watch the plane that had carried seven presidents—and one incredible woman—take off.

I had gotten her a passport in less than an hour, surely, I'd be able to find her phone number. Maybe she was playing hard to get, maybe she was creating an artificial barrier for me, something I had to overcome, so she would be sure I really did want to see her again.

Then again, maybe she was serious, that my involvement with Laura, which was not an insignificant detail, was too much trouble to deal with.

I felt a little like Scarlet O'Hara, I just couldn't think about it right now. I would think about this tomorrow. Tomorrow was another day. Right now I had a job to do and two hundred and sixty-three million people, more or less, were depending on me to do it well.

The ride back to the conference was uneventful, except for the snow that was beginning to accumulate as, what would become the worst blizzard in a century, moved ever closer.

ALLISON HAD MADE up a package for me, which she gave to the driver, who then proceeded to leave it on the roof of the limo. Luckily the pouch had frozen to the top of the vehicle. As I was being let in the back of the car, I spotted this large yellow, somewhat frosty enclosure with GERRICK written on the front.

"Oh, that's for you," the driver said when I brought the object to his attention. Then he ripped the packet from the metal, leaving behind one half of the manila envelope, and handing the rest to me proudly.

Why I said, "Thank you," I have no idea.

Ten years ago, I would have chewed the guy out, spitting fire and jet fuel about how sensitive these papers were and how stupid it was to leave them on the roof of a car, in public, and so on and so forth.

But over the years, I began to understand that unless a person works directly with you on a regular basis, why waste time trying to explain to them what they did wrong when a) they probably won't listen to you anyway, and b) the chance they'll have the opportunity to fuck up for you again is almost nil.

I say, live and let live like an imbecile.

This is particularly true of drivers. Because, after you've unloaded all your hostility and anger and resentment, drivers have to, well, drive...with you in the car. You don't want them having thoughts of wrapping the Lincoln or Mercedes—and you—around a very large tree.

Now, my dad never really learned this skill. The Princess has an almost remarkable ability to stick that very large foot into his mouth, seemingly at will. For the most part, I somehow get away with saying just about anything to just about anyone. I'm not really sure how this works, maybe it's because when I say something I don't usually have an agenda behind it. This is especially rare in my line of work, where almost everyone has some sort of hidden reason for doing something. I subscribe to the theory of "hide in plain sight." If you are so blatantly upfront with people, they'll be too distracted to seek any deeper meaning or see the ace you just pulled out of your sleeve.

I don't want to give the impression that I don't make any attempt to control what comes out of my mouth or edit my content in some manner, because I do. In fact, I tend to be more deferential to people *below* me on the societal ladder (God, that sounds awful), than I am to those *above* me.

Irreverence from below is spunky. Insolence from above is self-indulgent.

There are rules, however, when getting chummy with those in a position of power. Being heretical is one thing, being oblivious is something altogether different.

My father taught me this valuable lesson.

He went into work one Monday morning, years back, happy in the knowledge that his previous boss, who my dad had never gotten along with, had been transferred to another division, a *less important* division of the company. Something my father took great pleasure in since he thought the man was a complete idiot and was overjoyed that someone in the executive suites had finally realized this as well.

The Princess was introduced to his new boss. The guy was about my father's age, well-educated, but down to earth. He was very personable, and my dad immediately took to him. The man in return seemed interested in the Princess's opinions about the division, so much so, that he asked him to write up a short list of ideas and improvements that my father could present to management.

This was all in the first five minutes of their relationship. Things were looking up, career-wise.

But then came minute six.

My father, after extolling his views on the company, asked the man, who had been moved from a division out west, where he had chosen to live in the area.

His boss explained that he had found a very nice four-bedroom, three-and-a-half-bath house in West Hartford. West Hartford was the choice of many mid to upper-level managers in the Insurance Capital of the World.

Then my father said, and I quote, "That's a very nice area. Good schools. But I hear a lot of blacks are moving into the neighborhood."

To which his white Anglo-Saxon boss answered, "Yes...one of them is my wife."

So much for getting off on the right foot in your mouth.

My father could have been president of that company if only it weren't for that comment.

As I PORED over the icy documents, my driver made a point of hitting every bump, hole and snow drift we passed. I made a note in my day planner to tell Allison, never, ever, ever have this driver behind the wheel of any means of transportation where I am a passenger. Ever.

I read over the briefing. Still, I couldn't keep Sydney out of my mind. The headache that Sydney had temporarily cured came back with a vengeance. This hand-delivered bundle of mail in front of me was not a greeting card but a ransom note. I had introduced an Alp-sized mountain of tension into the negotiations, particularly when I left and returned to the United States.

Thank God Allison is meticulous. Without this summary, I would have walked into that conference, a smile on my face.

I would have been eaten alive.

I had opened the U.S. up to a firestorm of criticism because of my last-minute proposals, diversions meant to simply stall things until I got back. There were also rumblings from some of the U.S. negotiators. My own people. I was being blamed for bringing the talks to a grinding halt. I even got a call from Bobby McClain. One-half of the conversation was with Bobby, my friend. The other half with Bobby, the President's C.O.S. Basically, in both halves, he said, *I hope you know what the fuck you're doing.*

Off the record, he did tell me he was amazed how terrified everyone was that we might back out of this agreement. Which meant, we must be doing something right.

See, most of these other countries weren't used to the United States playing hardball. In the past, even when I had the best of intentions to get tough, political forces would conspire to undermine my strength at the bargaining table.

I mean, it wasn't really anything new, this had been going on for half a century, since the end of World War II. I've said it before, I'll say it again, we are perhaps the only victors in the modern era to pay for and rebuild the very nations that had risen up against us. Enemies that had struck first.

Ancient Rome, maybe, was the only other Empire in history to do something remotely similar. And even then, the Romans had been the aggressor in nearly every one of their campaigns. And they expected tribute in return.

Oh, we always talked tough. We were always going to kick some Labor-Exploiting/Trade-Barrier-Raising ass. Only when it came time to fuck, our formerly rock-hard dick went flaccid.

One of the first things that I did when I came to this job was to say to the President of the United States that there would be times when I would piss off some country or maybe even a whole Goddamn continent, and he was gonna get a call, maybe ten.

And not a pleasant one at that.

I might cause POTUS to take some heat in the short term, but my purpose was to win stronger trade agreements for the long term.

Over the past four years, the President has given me much more leeway than I ever expected. Something that has helped the cause tremendously, *and* enhanced my rep.

To me, it doesn't really matter how the agreement *looks*, I just want it to *be* better for my client.

And at the moment, my client was the United States of America. And more specifically, the President of the United States of America.

But something funny happened on the way to a funeral. I had inadvertently implied to all the other nations in the world that we were rethinking fifty years of policy. America was no longer going to roll over and play dead.

Here's how it went down: Tom Bowman showed up at a meeting of the top trade officials without me, of course. He made no comment during the entire gathering, other than cordial greetings. Meanwhile, he kept the rest of the team away from the bargaining talks that were going on down the hall. Imagine, the most powerful industrial nation in the world was a no-show.

Then after a bloc of developing countries staged one of those all-too-common last-minute reversals, which had the support of some First World nations, Tom quietly got up and left the room. A few moments later, Doug Powers joined the meeting in Tom's place. A few moments after that, Doug said these words: "Seeing as several other countries are interested in renegotiating parts of the agreement, the U.S. would like to add its voice and call for reopening talks on all aspects of the accord."

Newspapers, news channels, networks were all clamoring for answers.

On the eve of the biggest trade agreement in the history of mankind, the U.S. said *psych*.

I had been prepared to walk off the plane, come in and reverse course, saying there had been a misunderstanding of our position. I didn't relish the idea of backpedaling because it makes us seem indecisive and weak.

Only things had progressed at a much faster pace than even I had anticipated. And by the time I arrived back in Geneva, the story was a full-blown, worldwide crisis.

What we had done was not simply ask for a few outrageous items. We questioned—very respectfully—the entire validity of the process. Every step forward the U.S. made into foreign markets was counterbalanced by one and a half and sometimes two steps forward for most other countries doing business in the United States. I was a student of the game, had been for a long time. I got as excited about this shit as I did about fucking.

And I *really* like fucking.

I had studied all the data and had long ago come to the conclusion that if the United States had a level playing field with all countries, including those of the First World, we would have such a substantial trade surplus, it would be embarrassing.

I'm not saying it would always be like this, especially if we keep fucking around while the rest of the world gets its shit together. But in general, we have the creativity and capacity to do just about anything.

Now, of course, it was incumbent upon First World nations to make some concessions to underdeveloped countries because a nation whose economy we have destroyed by overwhelming their market, is a nation that can no longer purchase our goods and services, hence a country that is no longer one we trade with, but one we send aid to. And eventually becomes one that gets pissed off enough to begin exporting its pissed-offness to other parts of the world.

My phone bleeped, telling me I had a message. I'd never gotten a message before. Not on my phone. No one knew my net address. I didn't even know my electronic mail address. In fact, no one I knew even knew what electronic mail was. I take that back. Except for Doug Powers who spent nearly an entire eight-hour flight to Morocco telling me how easy it was to pick up women using America Online chat rooms.

"Where are these women?" I asked. I can't remember Doug ever taking a date to any function. Cramped his style, he said.

"All over. California, New York, Florida, Texas, Canada."

"So, it's *North* America Online," I said. "You know not one of those places is where you ever are, right?"

"It's spreading."

"Sounds like a disease."

Fifty button presses and a half-dozen scrolls later, I choose the blob on the LCD screen I guess was supposed to be some programmer's idea of an envelope. It was from cos@whitehouse.gov. The message from Bobby McClain read:

Don't fuck this up.

I had either stumbled on to something that could win us some incredible last-minute concessions—instead of the giveaway bonanza that customarily occurs—or I was going to be held responsible for the biggest screw-up in U.S. policy since we gave the Soviets control of Eastern Europe at Yalta.

Yeah, that worked out well.

America has been an idiot at the bargaining table for a long time. Cunning like a cow.

We keep coming back to the negotiating table time after time, seeking to extract concessions from our trading partners. And while these countries are happy to talk about taking effective action to give us the same benefits of "free trade" in their markets as they enjoy in ours, it just never seems to happen.

The more we negotiate, the worse our trade deficits become.

I had a chance to reverse this trend.

Maybe.

Or I could go down in flames.

I finished looking over the briefing papers just as we pulled up to the hotel, and the ever-present protesters lining the approach suddenly came to life as my car passed by.

As I got out of the limo, I could hear them shouting.

Protestors annoy me, and not for the reasons you might think. It's not that they are wrong or don't have some good points. No, I dislike them because they try to turn complicated issues into short phrases that fit nicely on a 24 x 36-inch poster board. Like most things that are important in life, in the world, global trade isn't black and white, doesn't fit into a neat box, and is rarely solved or even helped by people holding up "FUCK OFF WORLD BANK" placards.

Allison was waiting for me at the entrance. She didn't say a word, just followed me in. We had discussed what would happen next by phone from the car.

As I entered the lobby, I could feel all the eyes turn toward me. Camera crews and photographers jockeyed for position. My eyes have grown accustomed to not squinting or blinking at the harsh glare of lights or the rapid pop-pop-pop of a dozen flashes going off.

I walked up to a podium that had been placed to one side of the room. Tom joined me, standing off to my right. As I readied myself, shuffling some papers, trades poured into the lobby as if a dam had broken somewhere.

In a moment, the room was overflowing with bodies.

I looked up and out at everyone gathered, at no one in particular, and I began to speak.

"Fourteen months ago, the U.S. jump-started these talks with a bold plan and a new openness. Sensing America's desire for a worldwide trade agreement and taking advantage of the impending expiration of the President's Fast Track Authority, certain nations have quietly, yet consistently, tried to isolate the United States, delay and manipulate these proceedings in an attempt to force the U.S. into accepting an inadequate deal at this final hour. We have two days in which to complete negotiation of a fair and comprehensive treaty. This time, the United States will not sacrifice its sovereignty or economic well-being to make this a reality. We want what is best for all, not what is best for all but the United States."

I walked away from the podium. The room erupted. Reporters were shouting questions. "Is America walking away from free trade?" "Is this the return of Isolationism?"

I ignored them.

I headed toward the elevator. I wasn't able to keep my attention on the fervor I had created. I had a woman on my mind.

That heavenly Swiss maiden, the one not wearing any underwear on the original flight over, which seems like a lifetime ago, is not the woman I'm staring at now as I step into the elevator. It could be her sister, but then everyone in Switzerland could be somebody's sister. They all look exactly alike: blonde, fair-skinned, and disgustingly gorgeous. There's one passport picture for the entire nation.

I'm staring at this radiant woman, but I'm doing something unfamiliar. Instead of thinking, God, I'd like to see *her* without her underwear, I'm thinking how much I wish this beauty were Sydney.

I want Sydney to be here right now and not on a plane heading back to the States. The thought occurs to me, I have made a grave mistake letting her get on that aircraft.

But there's something else.

What's really eating at me is that when I told the President I wanted to come back to Washington to confer with him, I was the one who suggested—without directly saying it—that Laura stay behind. I mean, she could have flown back with me. We'd have had the entire flight together, and then, after my all-nighter with the Prez, I could have knocked on her door (she lives closer to the White House, then I do) and climbed into her warm bed for an hour or two until I had to catch my flight.

Yet I went back to Washington alone, knowing I would go to Bellina's, hoping I might run into Sydney.

I wasn't really expecting that to happen, but I wanted it to. It's hard to say at what exact moment I decided I wanted that, but as I stared into my grandfather's casket, remembering all the wonderful things we had done together, and he had done for me, that comment of his about how he always pictured me with someone like "the dancer" popped into my head again—subtle, but damning in the way it said so clearly: "I don't picture you with Laura."

On the way to the grave site, during the ceremony, as I watched them bury my most favorite person, I dwelled on Sebby's words.

Why would he say that? Then? When I had just told him about our "engagement."

He went on that day after the awning was repaired, as I helped him put away the ladder and the tools, to describe the kind of woman he saw me with. He gave details. Mentally, emotionally.

"It's good to have a woman like that."

He said it as if he was talking about Laura. It's not that she didn't have these traits. They just weren't all the amazing things I thought of when I thought of her.

And then, as I tossed a handful of dirt on his casket, I realized something. Something that stunned me, froze me in place until Dean dropped his bit of earth onto the mahogany sarcophagus, and the thud jolted me back to life.

I suddenly felt nauseous.

If you had asked me when I was sixteen or eighteen or twenty to describe the woman I pictured myself being married to, the woman I believed to be most compatible with me, I would have described her as...Sydney.

It was at Sebby's grave that I decided I would go to Bellina's.

The reason he knew, the reason Sebby could describe that person to me was that I had told him as much when I was seventeen. We were putting in a new window, the old one was damaged by the alternating freezing cold and stifling hot Connecticut weather—our time together fixing things always seemed to involve rotting wood. He turned to me and asked me about girls, about dating, about the future. He took me seriously, treated me like an adult and yet as an apprentice. I explained to him that day what I wanted.

And even though I had known her for only two glasses of orange juice and a plane flight to Europe, it was clear. What I wanted was Sydney.

Even when I couldn't remember her name.

She wasn't just some dalliance I had fondled in a weak moment, during a stressful time. No, she wasn't that.

I GET OFF THE ELEVATOR.

I feel the emotion rise up from my chest, culminating in a single tear that runs down my cheek. It is the realization that Sydney is the first woman I felt I could...

God, I almost say the word.

But I stop before it's too late, spoken, concrete.

The realization that I would quit my job, change my life, do anything to be with her is shocking to me.

I would complete my task here, that I knew. But after this, I would find her. And I would become something else, I don't know, husband, father, something, instead of just some frequent flyer nomad who is very, very good at arguing.

Unfortunately, distracted as I am, I don't see Francesca Thomas sneak up behind me.

"Guess who."

I'm in no mood. "King Kong. No, wait, Jesus of Nazareth."

"No, it's me, silly."

"I was so close."

I am even less enthused to see her when she informs me that I'm supposed to, no, I am *required* to attend a dinner that evening in the city. A little Good Cop to my previous day and a half of Bad. It's a gathering of career dips from all the countries with a consulate or embassy in Geneva. A mixer, if you will, so that when all the excitement is over and all the trades and pols are gone, they can call each other on the phone, get together for drinks and bore the shit out of each other.

"I don't have time for this. You understand what's going on here?"

"Anarchy," Allison says as she steps off the other elevator with Tom.

"Even more reason..."

"It's a personal request from the Secretary of State," Francesca says. "He thinks it may go a long way to averting another World War."

I scrunch up my face.

Tom pats me on my back. "You blew a huge hole in the side of this agreement. It's going down." He pauses. "Where's my fucking coat?"

I'm supposed to say a few words about how we will someday be one global market, so we might as well learn to become one people.

There won't be any trades, but the press will be there.

It'll act as a counterpoint to the shot I just fired downstairs.

I've given variations of this speech before.

But the live audience is different this time.

Diplomats.

"Fine, but I'm not eating with them."

Them. Talking to a diplomat is like talking to the Swiss, only they're not as good-looking.

I try to come up with something interesting that even they can understand.

It's not an easy task, considering these diplomats are complete morons who have simply failed their way upward from desk job to desk job to desk job until someone, somewhere, figures out that we gotta get rid of them, send them far away from anything important, as far away as we can, as soon as we can, before they do any real damage.

And that's how they become dips.

In Switzerland.

IT'S NOT AS bad as I thought. I'm in. I'm out. I'm back. In under an hour and forty-five minutes. I even broke down and ate a couple hors d'oeuvres. Tried some dip. May have even spoken to one.

I pass the protesters—don't these fucking people get tired?—and walk into the lobby.

Rafael aims straight for me. Doesn't she ever get tired? When she gets like this, there is no one else in the room. It's quite flattering, actually, the way she will focus on you, to the exclusion of all others around her. She wears her hair down tonight because she knows I like it that way sometimes. The entire outfit has been planned in advance right down to the matching bra and panties that, no doubt, she hopes I'll see later on. Another flattering gesture. The French are brilliant tacticians at using sex, seduction, a flirty smile to their advantage.

And I have to admit, I've never been one to struggle all that hard against their particular kind of arm twisting. Sometimes, it's all you can do to just sit back, relax, and enjoy the ride.

I'm relieved to find that even with all these emotions swirling around my head, about Sebby and Laura and Sydney, Rafael in a clingy black dress still creates a stirring in me.

I wonder if God had any idea what he was doing when he first put man and woman in the same garden at the same time. Either he has an incredible sense of humor or he just didn't know any better.

Everyone talks about the war between the sexes, men are from Mars, women from Venus, blah, blah, blah, blah, blah. Well, folks, the fucking war is over. We're just fighting over how to redraw the borders now.

Like I said, I'm relieved at the instinctual desire I'm experiencing, but it might become disrupting to the conference if every time Rafael comes bouncing into a room, I start walking around banging into people with the best thing the Princess ever gave me.

"So, are we on for dinner? We have things to..." Rafael draws a fingertip across her lower lip. "...discuss."

"I don't know if you've been paying attention, but I'm—" I glance at my watch. "—fifty-three hours away from completely fucking this conference up."

"Oowwww," she says. "They are just angry with you. Angry because everyone knows we cannot make this work without America."

She runs that same fingertip along my forearm. It's still moist.

"I don't know about this, Rafael."

"What 'tis not to know, Billy? It 'tis just an innocent little meal between good friends."

"Yes, good friends who used to spend entire days fucking each other."

"Where I come from, *mon chéri* , that 'tis just being good friends."

You got to love the French.

"I haven't been your *chéri* in quite a long time. *Mon cher* maybe."

"I think I know the right word better than you." The words are tinged with a hint of regret, which quickly dissipates. "Come, I didn't get to sleep with you the other night."

Grabbing my hand, she says this loud enough so that several of my colleagues can hear. I already have a reputation as a man who's been with several of the most sought-after women in the trade circle.

Rafael's continued affection for me only agitates the herd further.

I take a little too much pleasure from their envy.

I want those nubs sitting across from me tomorrow thinking about me banging the pretty Mademoiselle Perrieux, even if it's only a figment of their imagination. Because while they're getting pissed-off-jealous about me fucking her, I'll be fucking them.

"Okay. But we eat upstairs. In public."

"Of course." She smiles coyly. "How can we make a scene, if we are not seen?"

.   .   .

At dinner, Rafael was on her best behavior. Her hands remained on the table at all times. Her feet, however, did a bit of exploring that didn't stop with playing "footsie."

Unfortunately, the large thing humming in my pants was my cell phone in vibrate mode. I got up and excused myself. I take it as a personal insult when someone answers a phone at the dinner table. Unless it's brought over by a waiter. Then you're kind of a hot shit.

Standing in the hall leading to the restrooms, I finally answered the call.

Allison.

The evening session had just gotten underway, and already trouble was brewing.

By the time I got back to the table to apologize and explain to Rafael that she'd have to finish dinner alone, she was already getting up from her chair.

"I was paged as well," she said. "You have been a very bad boy, Billy."

"Hmmm," I said. "The agriculture subsidies?"

She nodded, her lashes lowering.

"I knew that would get you."

"And Italy and Turkey and..."

I leaned in and whispered in her ear. "I'll let you in on a little secret. I might—*might*—give a little on this. But you and everyone else are gonna have to give in to me on several other points."

"Billeee," she said, breathlessly. "I *always* give in to you. Yore irresistible."

I let out a little sigh.

"Let's go shake 'em up," I said as I held out my arm for her.

Rafael and I entered the conference room, arm in arm. If they weren't mad at me before, they were now. While they were arguing, I had been laying claim to this beauty...or so they thought.

A hundred and sixteen Trade Ministers and their staff crowded the long table decorated with flags in the cavernous room. I could feel the tension.

Immediately, Tom and Doug got me up to speed. Allison gave me her shorthand notes on the proceedings so far...and a cross look regarding Rafael.

I tried not to smile. Which got a lot easier when I saw him, sitting smugly across the table.

I turned to Tom. "What the hell is Beckett doing here?"

Tom didn't bother to look up at my former professor. "Last minute substitution. I hear he 'speaks for the entire EU.'" Tom actually made quotes with his fingers in the air.

Beckett had to be in his late seventies. He looked even more pompous now than he did at Wesleyan. Beckett and his "Win-Win" philosophy. His "compromise is the only way to guarantee an outcome" crap. Compromise only works if both sides start out at an equal distance from their desired goal. Beckett's idea of compromise is to inform everyone where we want to end up at the outset.

It may not make any sense, but you can't open negotiations with a reasonable request. If you do, it makes your endpoint the starting point for everyone else.

The U.S. let this man dictate our trade policy for nearly two decades even though he was a British citizen. If he had somehow screwed over America to help his Motherland, I might have forgiven him. But Beckett's policy ideas and strategies were so candy-ass and ineffective, Britain fared just as badly as we did.

Tom could sense my displeasure.

"You've got nothing to prove," he said.

"He gave me a 'C' in his class. A 'C.' Have the guts to hate me, flunk me. But don't call me average."

When I sat down, everything came to a complete stop, and the room fell silent. Rafael was seated directly across from me. She ran her finger from her clavicle down between her chest. Her feet were climbing up my leg.

Into the space of the silence, I said, "The corporate tax deduction for bribes has to go."

People were yelling. Beckett tried to rise above the din and manage the moment. "It's a cultural fact of doing business in some countries," he said.

"So is political assassination," I answered. Rafael was looking at me. Straight into, deep into my eyes as her foot slid between my legs, her toes caressing my cock through my pants. "Clearly, outside our agreement," I added, partly in response to Beckett, but mostly to Rafael's attack. I squeezed her foot, but this only made her smile. "If not a total ban, I, at least, want a phase-out," I stared back at Rafael, "in this agreement."

Cubrero stood up. His bony frame looked like a hanger for his five thousand dollar suit. How could something that expensive look so bad on a guy?

"Like your Batman and Robin Hood, you want to take from the poor and give to the rich," he said.

Okay, let's not even get into his complete ignorance of American and British culture. But it's hard to take a guy seriously who skims money from tragically poor people.

I shook my head. "No, I want to end corruption and level the playing field."

"You want to ruin us!"

Once again, the room was in chaos. People yelling at me, damning me, cursing me, hexing me.

For the first time, I was starting to realize the entire agreement really was in jeopardy, much more than I ever thought possible.

Bobby McClain was going to kill me.

And the President, as much as he loved me, as much as he thought I was a "great American" would piss on my lifeless body.

And if death seemed a little dramatic. I assure you, it was not.

Why? Because the talks for this agreement began eight years ago. Went through three Presidents and six Trade Reps. All of them working toward *this* day

The day where I would get to enjoy the glory. Where *my* President could stand behind a podium and declare economic victory for American workers and new opportunities for American business.

Instead, I was beginning to see myself as others would see me. The asshole who screwed up a sure thing, a done deal. The guy who misses the gimme. Boots the extra point wide. Can't score with a hooker.

I was going to be the butt of every political cartoonist in the country.

Gerrick Attends Another Funeral. Then there'd be a picture of me with a huge head and a tiny little body throwing dirt on a casket at the bottom of a hole with the inscription: *Free Trade.*

If we didn't get it done now. If the nations of the world left Geneva without a collective signature, we'd have to start all over again. Because the world was changing, and technologies were creating new problems and new opportunities for trade.

Eventually, we'd get an agreement. No doubt about that, but it would take another couple of years. The new technologies and new delivery systems aren't even discussed in this agreement.

And although it might be to our benefit to deal with these technologies and their effect on doing business now, the delay in implementation that would result would cost hundreds of billions of dollars in lost revenue and millions of jobs.

It's like buying a cell phone. They started out the size of small suitcases and cost about a third the price of a new car. If you waited, you could buy something much smaller for a lot less money. But if you waited a little longer, you could get something even smaller, even cheaper. But if you waited a little *longer*... At some point, you gotta break down and dive in. Otherwise, we'd all still be sending smoke signals, and you'd be forced to use the scraps of parchment you'd been keeping your important notes on for kindling.

Then where would you be?

Right next to me in an alley somewhere, sharing a cask of wine.

I wanted this agreement to happen on my watch. Wanted to be the one whose signature sealed the deal. And with every pointed finger, every screamed obscenity, I could sense it slipping away. I had confidence in myself and faith in my ability to control the situation. Maybe too much this time.

Without warning, the trade negotiator from Turkey, Ferit Erim, lunged across the table at me. The only reason he didn't make it to my throat was that he got caught up in those miniature ceremonial flags that they set in the middle of the table. I later found out he received twenty-seven stitches for his trouble.

But what "The Ferret" had started was not ended with his failed border crossing. Someone coming from the side hit me in the face. Instinctively and reflexively, I punched back.

Within seconds, we had a full-scale fistfight in the middle of the conference ballroom.

Someone grabbed Tom. Another person jumped on my back.

Allison whacked at the man on my back with a massive three-ringed binder until he slid to the ground. Tom tossed the guy holding him in a nice hybrid Jujitsu/wrestling move.

Fists were flying.

Sort of.

I mean, these were a bunch of career civil servants, political appointees, and economic theorists. It was a fucking miracle when one landed anything, even a finger on each other. Wild swings, awkward misses, there were plenty of those. But a good solid punch? Very rare.

While ducking a slow-speed right hand, I saw out of the corner of my eye Rafael walking out of the room. I couldn't tell if she was afraid of getting hit or just feeling superior.

Beckett, the pompous ass, tried to be the *lone voice of reason.*

"Everyone...this is no way—" he shouted. No one was listening to the windbag. "Compromise! is the only—"

Boom!

Beckett was knocked to the ground by two negotiators—one from Poland, one from Ukraine—in the prissiest fucking wrestling match I'd ever seen. They rolled around, arms flailing until all three landed at my feet.

I look down at Beckett.

"I *still* say, somebody's got to get *hit* with the big stick before everybody else is afraid of it."

With perfect timing, I flattened Cubrero—who was coming at me holding a crystal vase raised over his head—with one punch to the face.

According to some reports, as many as two dozen people had to be treated by medical personnel for cuts, bruises, panic, fractures, and sheer embarrassment.

I've never been good at fighting, well, not those premeditated, meet me behind the school at three o'clock kind of confrontations, anyway. Those require a deep-seated need to inflict pain and a strong anger-on-demand trait I simply don't possess.

Now, spontaneous battles, especially when I'm outsized and outmanned, those I'm much better at. Perhaps, it's because I had a bit of practice at this out-of-nowhere combat.

It was right about the time I started riding my bike pretty much anywhere I wanted to that my father and I began to really butt heads. It was a show worth watching, like two rams bashing skulls. His was definitely bigger, but mine was harder.

I think freedom is a wonderful thing. I also think it engenders a confidence that sometimes shows up in a face-to-face confrontation between father and son.

I don't know why, there was usually never any reason for my father to go off the handle other than he really wanted to be any place but where he was, especially if where he was was at home.

And I don't remember how it started, I'm sure there is some record about this somewhere in the universe in some databank as yet undiscovered.

The Princess was squealing like a stuck pig, which wasn't all that unusual, but he was being especially tough on my mom.

Now, since I was The Big Sonofabitch, I can always be counted on to piss my father off, but my mom...she rarely did anything that warranted the Princess's wrath. Except maybe washing her coffee cup in the morning while he was in the shower.

I started yelling for my dad to leave her alone. Calling him all kinds of names, hoping that I'd piss him off enough to come after me and instead of her.

I wasn't worried. I could outrun my father.

I was faster, could go longer.

Even if we had been the same age, I was built for speed, he was built for brawn—brawn, with a little yelling thrown in.

But the Princess surprised me.

My plan worked—he came after me, all right—but he didn't buy into my speed trap. Instead, he picked up a huge knife from the butcher block on the counter and, I swear to God, threw it at me.

Now, I know my father, know him well enough to recognize an instant of hesitation. He had pulled his punch. He didn't aim right at me. Even in his wild state, he had the control to fling the knife wide left.

I have had a knife thrown at me only one other time in my life.

That time was about one minute after the first time.

Neither time have I liked it.

After that first throw, I made the tactical decision before he could reload to run past my father. I had doors all around me that I could have ducked into, but they led to dead ends. I ran straight for him, charged him, but instead of barreling into him, I juked and knocked the butcher block to the ground, giving me a few precious seconds to sprint out of the kitchen and out the front door.

He followed me out with another knife. His huge frame burst through the screen door, slamming it into the rail of the steps. He again took aim and threw the knife at me, this time coming a lot closer, but still wide—I hoped—on purpose.

I picked up the knife and chucked it into the woods next to my house. Without a weapon, my father was still much, much bigger than me. I was giving up four or five inches and sixty pounds.

But I was pissed off. I just don't take having blades sailing toward my face very well, I guess. So, I rushed him again, this time hitting him with my body. But like I said, he was bigger.

He barely moved.

He got me in a headlock, with his forearm around my throat. I had a reputation as a slippery fighter. I have let myself be pushed into a defensive position, or, as in this case, be forced into it. I don't panic. I actually feel more comfortable this way. Because while my opponent is using both his hands and all his energy to hold me, I'm free to kick and elbow and stomp. I'm not tied down by having to restrain someone.

But this time, I didn't squirm or kick or hit.

I chose to save my strength and focus my energy on keeping my father's chokehold at bay, just enough so I could breathe. I wasn't afraid, I'm not sure why, perhaps, I knew deep down I was stronger than he thought I was.

My mother, however, who had now followed us outside, freaked out when she saw her husband strangling her eldest child.

She grabbed his arm and began tugging on it and screaming at him. I tried to explain to her that I was okay, that I was not being hurt, that the only thing keeping me from breathing were *her* hands on his arm pushing into my windpipe. She couldn't hear me the first few times because she was choking me.

"Leeeehhhh goooo."

Finally, she removed her hand. I sucked in a huge breath of needed air.

And with my father barking at me in my ear, my throat being squeezed, and replays of the knife tosses showing in my head, I reached my limit.

I had had just about enough of this.

I drove my feet into the ground and pushed, smashing my father back against the side of the house, then I used my defensive position, my leverage, and all one hundred and sixty-five pounds of me, to flip my two hundred and twenty-five-pound father over my shoulder and onto the ground.

I will never forget that moment. And not for the reason you might think.

It's that moment that comes for many kids, usually boys. A moment I'll dread when my children best me at something I believe to be my strongest attribute. It will be the passing of the baton.

I only hope it comes at a much lower price. And if I have the strength of mind, the wisdom, it will come more naturally.

I won't ever forget the look on my father's face as he realized he'd been thrown to the ground by his much smaller son.

It was a look of sheer astonishment and embarrassment.

He tried to downplay it. "I slipped," he said.

But we both knew what happened.

And far from being proud of my victory, I was devastated. I cried for two hours straight, balling my eyes out till I had no more tears, no more spit. Saying over and over, "I'm *so* sorry."

I had suspected for some time that I could probably defeat my father if he ever fulfilled one of his numerous threats to come at me. At least, I'd put up a good fight. But I never had said anything to him about it. Never boasted or dangled it over him.

Because that was what my father had left. His physical strength over me, over all of us. Life had worn away many of his qualities, had thwarted many of his dreams, but he still had something. A stupid, macho ideal, maybe, but it was something.

And then, in a second, I had ripped it all away.

RATHER THAN MAKE ME COCKY, that event taught me to never underestimate anyone, even if they appeared smaller or weaker. Which is why, when the five-foot, one-inch Japanese Deputy Minister of Trade tried to kick me in the balls, I was ready for him.

19

GOING DOWN UNDER

I HAVE pictures of myself with forty-seven heads of state—I'm not talking group shots, I'm talking one-on-one, just me and them—have been to fifty-some-odd countries, have made friends and lovers around the world, have had a tangible effect on not only the U.S. economy but the global market as well...

...and all I really ever wanted to be...was a rock star.

In fact, when I was in eighth grade, I played guitar in a rock and roll band called *Caribou*. Now, the fact that there never was any band named *Caribou*, nor did I have the slightest idea how to hold a guitar, let alone play one, didn't seem to matter to me. I was a great guitarist, and the lead singer of the band, which luckily for me never seemed to have any play-dates within driving distance of my town.

I might have mentioned that I had an upright piano in my bedroom, again something I couldn't play, but at least with a keyboard, I had the ability to bang out some chords, even bad ones so I could pretend as if I knew something about music.

You can't pretend to play guitar. It's kind of like pretending to play the trumpet. There are about twelve ways to make the instrument sound good and over 3,597,843 ways to make the thing sound like shit.

Over the years, I have perfected nearly a million of those techniques.

My very best friends in the world, Gunter included, tolerated these fantasies of mine, endured them without comment. Why, I don't know. But they did. Kindness, I guess. There was an elusive reference to it by Gunter one day at school, and from everyone else's reaction, I realized that they had known all along that I was lying. I didn't come out of my house for two days.

I had to deal with it sooner or later, so I steeled myself against the embarrassment and resumed my daily life. Thankfully, no one ever mentioned the subject to me again.

I guess no matter what you're doing in life or how well you're doing it, there's always something or someone you want to do differently.

I remembered the rock and roll thing when in the middle of the fight, I glanced into the hall and saw several members of a band carrying their instruments toward the hotel's nightclub. Drums, keyboards, bass, then, finally, the guitarist. And I thought, I could be that guy, setting up for my next gig. I could be that guy, playing tonight with all the women around him, screaming, dancing, wanting him. I could—

BAMMMMMM!

That's when I got hit with a left hook to the right eye.

This was the first brawl amongst trades in eleven years, since the time the German lead negotiator called Margaret Thatcher "a horse cunt"— not to her face, of course, she would have reared up and kicked him in the head, but to his counterparts—during a contentious session over Britain's in again/out again stance toward a super-state dominated from Brussels, a brawl which threatened to once and for all drive a stake through the heart of the tenuous and near-futile effort to begin negotiations on how to finally create one Europe, what—against enormous odds, and a lot of British grumbling—came to be what is officially, as of five weeks ago, the EU.

And when they all finally get their shit together and agree on how to fairly value each other's mostly (except for France and Germany's) fucked up currencies, the *euro* might actually give the dollar a run for its money.

Although, I'm still not convinced the Brits are all in for this "one continent" thing.

I WAS up in Allison's suite, which, as I said, was actually our command center. In fact, my assistant had the best accommodations of our delegation. Then again, we invaded her suite at all hours.

I was sitting on the couch, tending to my wounds, asking Tom how he thought we did, brawl-wise.

"I think we'll come away with better access to the Japanese financial sector," he said, sipping a drink and then using the cold glass to soothe a bruise on his cheek. "And the Indonesians are talking human rights for the first time."

Doug Powers entered the room. He had tissues sticking out of his nostrils. "We kicked ass!"

"Did we?" I said. There was a lot of pent-up anger in that room. It flashed instantly. This deal was on shaky ground.

Tom glanced over at me. "Oh, don't worry, you still may turn out to be the asshole who sinks this whole thing."

"Thanks."

He lifted his glass. "Don't mention it."

The reason the whole melee started, the reason I have a cut over my right eye, is because of a single misunderstanding.

And a lot of misunderstandings can happen when you're translating a sentence into a hundred languages.

In the town where I grew up, we were nearly all the same color, definitely spoke the same language, were just about all the same religion, and were mostly in the same tax bracket. Misinterpretations based on differences in background just didn't happen.

It wasn't until after I left home that I learned that not everyone shares a common knowledge.

One of my favorite exes, Kate, grew up in Norway as a young girl. She and her family came to America when she was twelve, just when she was starting to get the most perfect breasts on the planet.

The most important thing Kate taught me, besides numerous things about sex and openness, was something that has turned out to be even more valuable—that people who learn a language from a book or a class or in a foreign country, tend to take everything you say *literally*.

That's not to say they are naive or without nuance—they can read people as well as anyone. You simply must be careful about the words you use and be clear in how you phrase things because the meaning can easily be misconstrued.

The fact that English was not Kate's native tongue and that what lay under her sweater aroused many native tongues, did not engender the love and affection of her fellow female classmates when she arrived in America. This beautiful girl felt like an ugly duckling because other girls would make fun of her for being different.

I luckily never met Kate during those years. I met her a decade later in

Washington at some gala fundraiser for the Drought and Famine Victims in Ethiopia. It somehow didn't seem at all strange to the organizers of this function that the amount of food being served to prospective famine relief donors was obscene.

Never mind the disgraceful amount that would end up in the trash.

I glanced around the room at the guests as Aid Workers in jeans and work shirts stepped up to the podium and told the most horrible stories of death and disease and starvation. I watched the people as they listened and stuffed their faces with pâté, pork loin, prime rib, pasta, potatoes, and pie and nodded, *isn't that terrible?*

I noticed Kate because she was standing by someone I knew and because she wasn't eating anything. She held a plate in her hand with one hors d'oeuvre on it. It was just enough to stop people from asking her if she wanted anything to eat.

This technique is also useful if you don't want to indulge in alcohol at a party. Just make sure you have a half-full drink in your hands at all times. If it's too full, you will be bludgeoned by cries of "Why aren't you drinking?" If it's close to being empty, you'll have to endure endless refrains of "Can I get you another drink?"

Either she was eating sparingly to keep from joining America's obese, or she understood the absurdity of the proceedings. Whichever, I admired her determination.

I went over and introduced myself.

She had that Scandinavian casualness about anything having to do with sex.

In fact, we had sex the first night we went out a couple of weeks later.

It wasn't even a date.

She was always hot over some issue in the world—I think this one had to do with the treatment of citizens within the Soviet bloc (there was still a Soviet bloc at the time) or some fucking thing like that.

She had invited me, getting my number through our mutual friend, who obviously wanted to set us up. We had a nice conversation on the phone, and I agreed to come to the event.

Now, the night I met her, she was wearing glasses, had her hair pulled back and was wearing something far too businesslike for me to get any idea what lay underneath.

I wasn't prepared for the woman I met at the Campaign for the Good Treatment of Somebody event. She was dressed in jeans, which definitely gave me an idea of what was to come, no glasses, and her hair was straight and blunt cut. Very Scandinavian.

We went on to date each other exclusively for nearly a year.

One day, we were having an afternoon picnic out on this grassy embankment overlooking Georgetown. Just below us were two people playing tennis on a grass court. As I watched them volley, I told her how I had never played on grass.

Kate looked at me very strangely and sort of tilted her head to the side.

"You never played on grass?"

"No. Have you?"

"Oh, I played on grass all the time."

"Really? I didn't know you liked tennis that much."

A look of confusion streaked across her face.

"Tennis?"

THE BRAWL at the conference began because someone in the Turkish delegation overheard me joking with Tom that, at this rate, we could be here till Christmas. And that I was really looking forward to carving up the turkey.

Which was then mistold to Ferit Erim.

Misunderstandings...

They can lead to disagreements, which lead to arguments, which lead to wars.

MISINFORMATION IS ALMOST AS DANGEROUS.

I was resting on the couch with an ice pack on my eye. Allison came into the room, looking pale and stunned.

"You are one lucky son-of-a-bitch," she said to me.

"I wasn't the one who tried to make the ill-advised border crossing."

"Forget your schoolyard fracas. You know that State jet you came in on?"

"What about it?"

"Never made it to Rome."

"What?!"

"It went down in the mountains somewhere along the border between France and Italy."

My heart jumped, pounding in my chest so hard it hurt. The pulse in my head and neck raced. The lights and the sounds of the room collided and everything slowed to a crawl. A foggy crawl.

I heard my voice, but it sounded so far away.

"Where did you hear this?"

"Some of the dips were talking about it downstairs."

I ran out of the room and down the hall to the elevator and pressed the button ten or twenty times. Elevators are a lot like cops, they're never around when you need one. I decided to take the stairs. As I stormed through the door into the stairwell and began to descend, I heard the *bing* of the elevator reaching my floor ten seconds too late.

I raced down the steps, glad for the distraction. You can't be thinking too much about other things while you're charging down six flights of stairs. Otherwise, you might be tumbling down a flight or two.

Bursting into the lobby from the stairwell, I nearly took out the South African Minister of Trade. A few years back, I would have enjoyed knocking the hell out of a blond-haired Afrikaner, apologizing profusely, of course, but now that SA was majority-ruled, whether this guy was white or black didn't matter. Apartheid was dead, and the country's continued survival demanded that the world change its view of this land on the southern tip of the African continent.

"Sorry," I said as nicely as I could while sprinting past him.

I RAN into a group of low-level diplomats from Indonesia and asked them if they had seen their American counterparts. They pretty much had no idea what I was saying, their interpreter wasn't present, and kept pointing at me while saying, "*Orang Amerika!*"

Now, my mother's preferred method of communicating with people who do not understand English well is simply to speak louder. She would repeat the same sentence over and over, only with more volume each time.

I finally had to pull her aside one day.

"Mom, he's Portuguese, not deaf. But if you continue to scream at him, he will be."

Eventually, I got them to comprehend with gestures and hand signals and repeating, not unlike my mother, except quieter, "American. American."

They all started nodding. "*Amerika lainnya. Amerika lainnya.*" Oh, they were so happy, they understood that I was asking them for Americans other than myself.

Their answer was, with shoulders shrugging, "No."

I FOUND the American dips in the bar drinking with the Russians and the Australians. Now that's a frightening triumvirate to mix with alcohol. All we needed was for the Irish to show up and we could have ourselves a *real* example of how to throw a bar brawl.

I knew Ken Stockard from my numerous trips to The Hague. He was a good guy, very smart as dips go. The World Court was a tricky legal and political minefield.

Justice is a dicey thing, no matter how you try to cloak it in robes and powdered wigs and legalese. It all depends on your point of view. And it is infinitely more difficult for true justice to be done when you throw global politics into the mix.

The Hague is one of the tougher diplomatic assignments.

So, I felt pretty confident that Ken would, at the very least, be able to understand the words I was stringing together in the form of a question without requiring a request in triplicate.

He was laughing when I walked up to him, but he immediately stopped when he saw the look on my face.

"What is it, Billy?"

"Ken..." My hands were shaking, and I couldn't be sure, but I think my voice was as well. "I heard a SAM went down."

"Yeah," he said, the others quieting instantly. "In the storm."

"I was just on that plane. They made a special stopover here...to drop me off."

When I first heard, I had the briefest instant of relief that I wasn't on board, that I was safe, then I thought about Sydney, and I experienced terror and concern for her, and then a millisecond after that, I was hit with a profound sense of shame, shame for feeling relieved.

Coming down the stairs, I had struggled to keep from throwing up.

"Goddammit! Those people would be safe in Rome if I hadn't commandeered that flight..." I was talking out loud, but I wasn't speaking to anyone. I stopped and tried to compose myself. I focused on Ken and spoke to him, directly. "Are...are there any survi...sur—" I couldn't get the words out.

He put his arms around me, and I felt my legs go numb. I still had the scent of her on my skin.

"Billy…" Ken instantly seemed to sober up. "Everyone's alive."

I leaned my head down against the bar.

"The pilots are banged up pretty bad, and two women are hurt seriously, one is in critical condition."

I glanced back up at him. "Do you know who? Names?"

"The communiqué didn't identify anyone."

My head was pounding again. I tried to picture the people on the plane. Six women and three men, not including the pilots or Sydney and me. I saw one more woman get on in Switzerland. I knew I was playing a gruesome game of roulette in my head.

Eight women, two of them badly hurt.

I felt evil and callous for praying that it was someone I didn't know. But with or without my wishes, odds were that Sydney was not "the woman" that was critical. Still, two out of eight were injured seriously. Not great odds.

Either way, I had to go there.

I turned and asked Ken the question I didn't want to ask. "Where'd it go down?"

20

WHY THE FRENCH HATE US, REDUX

THERE ARE some things the French have no fucking idea about. Pizza is one of them. To the French, pizza is a flat piece of bread with sliced tomatoes on top. To Americans, this is an unfinished tomato sandwich. To the French, it's proof they aren't completely xenophobic about other cultures. To Americans, it's an unfinished tomato sandwich.

The second thing the French don't know anything about is cars, which leads us to the third thing they don't know anything about...highways.

The French don't build highways. They build little country roads with very impressive reflectors in the middle of them, on which small, poorly made French cars drive at unimaginable speeds in opposite directions only a few feet apart. Shitbox cars like Renault, which is sort of like driving 120 KPII in a roll of tin foil on bicycle tires.

The Germans, on the other hand, drive even faster but live longer because they build cars that are well-made with ample crush zones, unlike the French, who seem to only have two speeds to anything in their country. Off. And really, insanely extremely fast. The women are either drop-dead gorgeous or frighteningly hideous. Their cars might as well be made out of glass, or they are completely solid.

Like a rock. And not like the Chevy truck commercial. I'm talking like a *fucking* boulder.

Which, for a car, is not a good thing.

One time, a high school friend of mine's mother was backing out of the driveway in her imported Peugeot. She wasn't paying attention because she was thinking how chic it was to have a French car, because almost no one in America (who's still alive) drove one, when suddenly, she backed right into a telephone pole. Now, I don't know if you've ever hit a telephone pole, but they're pretty solid, meant to withstand terrific forces. Obviously, not as much as a Peugeot, however.

She broke the pole. Snapped it right in two. When my friend took a look at the car, there was nothing but a small dent in the rear fender.

He was very proud of this fact. I mean, a car that can hold together after knocking over a telephone pole, that's a car that will surely protect me in an accident, he thought. That was, until I showed him old footage from the Indianapolis 500, in the time before the cars were designed and built to disintegrate. See, when an object breaks apart, the energy goes with the parts. That way the cage containing the driver is subjected to a lot less force. It's kind of like how ice skaters spin quickly with their arms tight to their bodies, then, when they throw their arms out, they immediately slow down, almost to a stop.

The old Indy cars could survive flipping over, crashing into walls, you name it. Unfortunately, the drivers usually weren't as lucky.

My friend now owns a Ford.

Now, before you start thinking that I have something against the French. I don't. I hate the French, no more or less, than I hate anyone else. It's just that it's a little easier to make fun of the French because they incorrectly believe they are...yes...a world power. This is not to say that they are not an important player in the world, or the EEC or EU or the UN.

I'm simply saying, who rolled over like a lap dog in WWII? England? Russia? Liechtenstein? I...think it was the French. They're still a little sensitive about the subject. Kinda like how folks in the South are *really* patriotic and always talking about *real* American values. Like seceding from the Union, owning slaves, assassinating presidents, stuff like that.

So the French cover their insecurities by always being contrary. Whether it's about trade, farming practices, terrorist nations, if England, Germany, and America are for something, you could bet your *derrière*, the French are against it.

So there I was, a mess of conflicting emotions, hope, dread, affection, self-hatred, careening down this French highway in this shitbox of a

French car, albeit a very luxurious and expensive shitbox (and how did I get the *only* French rental car in Switzerland? Don't the Germans own that country?). I would be in Grenoble in less than an hour if the weather held up, but I wasn't going to Grenoble. I've always wanted to go there. There's an old acquaintance I'd love to look up.

In about twenty kilometers, I was going to turn off and head southeast, away from Grenoble. Not long after that, I would begin the slow drive up Mt. Pelvoux.

I told the concierge at the Intercontinental as I was sprinting by the front desk: Tell anyone who asks, I was going out for something. I'd be back in a little bit. It was the middle of the night. The hotel was quiet. Most people were asleep. Which meant I would only get called ten or twelve times by morning.

Going out for something. It seemed innocuous enough. No one questions going out for something.

My father used to go out for something and he'd come back after putting two hundred miles on his car. Whatever he was going out for, apparently wasn't available in our state.

My father liked to drive, there is no doubt about that. I don't mind driving, and sometimes it can even be relaxing, allowing you to clear your head.

But not this time.

While I was renting the car, while I was leaving Switzerland, while I was negotiating mountain roads, I had my ear locked to my phone, tracking down the local authorities with the help of information Ken gave me.

I couldn't get any news of what happened, well, not much anyway. Anyone who might know anything was out dealing with the problem. I did find out that the plane had tried to make a landing on a small, private runway. But the airstrip was too short even for the modified 707. The plane, coming in dangerously slow, and using the maximum reverse thrust, only stopped after smashing into a wall of snow at the end of the runway.

That was all I knew.

I woke up Allison and told her why I had stormed out of the room like a madman without saying a word. I asked her to call anyone she could think of for news and to call me back when she heard something. I couldn't do it any longer.

I told her that if she did find Sydney, that whatever she needed, food, clothes, medical bills, was to be put on my credit card.

She said she would stay up until she found out something.

I PASSED the sign telling me I was only four kilometers from the turnoff, but I'd been able to see the mountains for some time. The caps were covered in white and shrouded in clouds, which only partly obscured the bright moon. I was sure it was snowing hard up there right now. Sydney was up there somewhere. I kept saying to myself over and over, "She's okay," at the same time picturing the opposite.

I picked up my cell phone. I wanted to distract my mind from Sydney. No signal. I reached in back for the satellite phone. Unlatched the case. Perhaps the transceiver powerful enough to reach an orbiting satellite will toast my brain enough to help me forget.

"Hello."

"Hey, Mom." There's a certain comfort in hearing a mother's voice, even one that drives you crazy.

"Billy!" Her tone changed immediately. "Why are you calling me?"

"Gee, Mom, I was really worried about you, too. Thanks for asking."

"Laura isn't here. She's out with Anna shopping for food. She's very nice, Billy."

"Yes, she is." I switched ears. This was not the conversation I wanted to have. "How are you holding up?" This time, I got through to her.

"I'm okay." I could hear the pain in her voice. "Gramma's out of it."

"I know."

"That was nice what you said. At the church."

"Thanks."

"Well, I'll tell Laura you called."

"Mom, I didn't call for *her*. I called to talk to you."

I heard a heavy breath. "Why do you always call me from a car or a plane? You can't talk to me when you're sitting still?"

"I'm calling to talk to you. Does it really matter that I'm in motion?"

"It would be nice if I could have a relaxing conversation."

I shook my head. "It's not like you're the one driving. You're sitting in your chair." I knew exactly where she was. Parked. In the big recliner.

"It makes me nervous. Talking and driving."

"You're not driving!"

"Aren't you supposed to be in meetings?"

"I had to take a short trip into France. Something came up."

"France." I can hear the wheels turning. "Do you have Dominique's number in case you have a problem?"

"Mom, he's in a completely different part of the country."

"You should visit him...while you're there. It'd be nice."

"Yes, I should."

"Do you want his address?"

My mother has no concept of distance.

One summer I went out to Los Angeles. It was just after my senior year in high school, and I was visiting a friend who had moved there the year before. Ah, if I had only known about California girls a summer earlier, I would've had no trouble finding someone unchaste enough to play with me and my thick-headed friend.

Anyway, my mother, diligently seeking to protect her son at all times, gave me the address and phone number of a family friend two hours *north* of San Francisco. I tried to explain to my mother, that, although I appreciated the gesture, giving me the number of someone over six hundred miles away would be like giving me the phone number of someone in Canada when I go to school in Washington D.C.

She looked at me sort of funny. "Well, at least it's in the same state."

This somehow made sense to her.

In my book, six hundred miles is six hundred miles. It doesn't really make a difference to me whether I go through one state, two states, or three countries.

My mother often had these epiphanies of what she thought were brilliant assistance strategies. I never appreciated them at the time. I value them more now, and not just for the humor, which is a pleasure all its own, but because she really was trying.

I mean, that's all you can ask for, isn't it?

That the people around you, at least, try.

"Mother..." I said.

"Yes, William..."

"I just wanted to tell you...I love you."

"I love you, too, honey." A pause. "Are you sick or something and not telling me? A disease? Cancer?"

"I have to go, mother."

After saying our goodbyes, the thoughts came rushing back, swirling around in my head. Most of them about Sydney. Was she injured? Was she scared, traumatized? I felt responsible for her, for this. I suppressed the urge to call Allison yet again. She had no news. If she had anything to tell me, anything at all, she would've called me already.

Some of the thoughts I had were so selfish, they embarrassed me, even with no one else around. One of them was that if something horrible had happened to Sydney, it would come out that this "civilian" had been on the plane at my request.

The world would know.

Laura would know.

I saw another sign for Grenoble, and thankfully, my mind was diverted for a while.

See, I know a lot about that city even though I've never been there. In a way, Grenoble came to me, in the form of another French exchange student the year after I went to France, and hiked in Corsica with Dominique, and nearly had the fucking Skylab crash land on my tent.

News reports before leaving Nice said that the ailing space station was tumbling back to earth and was expected to hit the surface sometime over the next few days. We actually saw it re-enter the atmosphere on its final orbit, directly over our sleeping bags.

It was the most amazing sight, this bright streak across the sky.

But it was nothing compared to the fireworks I witnessed the next summer.

The Second Coming of the French to our house was quite different than the first. Where Dominique was shy and gracious, Laurence was outgoing and jaded. Where Dominique was conservative and from the north, Laurence was wild and from the south. Where Dominique had a very good heart, Laurence had incredible tits.

Lo-rrrronce, it was pronounced.

She hit my little town like a jet engine falling off a 747. I will never forget the feeling I got when I first saw her walk off the plane.

We'd been sent a picture of Laurence in the months previous to her visit. She was very cute and pretty for a fifteen-year-old. But something happened in the space of time between that photo being snapped and her walking off the Air France flight.

She had become...a sixteen-year-old.

And her body had become something altogether wholly unreal. It was several years before I had someone that beautiful and sexy sleeping in the same place and at the same time as me.

I have always found it odd that in the U.S., Dominique, who was male, is a female name, and Laurence, who, believe me, was female, is a male name. Ah, the French.

Laurence taught me like no American could have about dangling out a prize then pulling it back before it can be captured. It was furthering the lessons that Patrice had begun.

She was a master at this.

Overnight, I became the most popular guy in the surrounding towns. Every adolescent male within twenty miles throwing a party wanted Laurence to come, get drunk, take off her clothes and come again. She drove them crazy, all of them. I was getting invited to parties of people I didn't even know, from schools I didn't attend. If you knew someone I knew even tangentially, you knew about Laurence, and you made sure I knew about every party, beach trip, kegger you knew about.

And of course, being stupid Americans, she would play these guys like a piano. She pretended—Oscar-winning stuff—not to comprehend what they were talking about when they were coming on to her.

Consequently, these idiots would get more and more brazen with their words, thinking she had no idea what the hell they were saying. I can only assume these guys got some twisted pleasure out of doling out sexual innuendo and come-ons she was oblivious to.

Only she wasn't oblivious.

I knew she understood because every drive home, she would put her feet up on my dashboard, light up a cig and say, "Yore friens are so stooopid."

And I would have to agree. Because I was the one that ended up going home with her. Every time.

THE PHONE RANG. It was Allison.

The passengers on the plane had been taken to a nearby ski resort, which had the only medical facility on the mountain. Still no word on who was hurt. But all of them would be staying at the main hotel, the Auberge, on the northern face of the mountain until the weather lifted so they could fly them out (they weren't well enough to be transported by road was the unsaid, but not very subtle meaning). They were being cared for by the doctor on staff at the resort's medical facility. The injured women and the pilots were a priority, but the hotel staff couldn't say when they would be airlifted out. Allison left word at the front desk for Sydney. The manager assured her that they would give Sydney Nathan the message as soon as possible. Then Allison finally sweet-talked a policeman who said he would try and find out the names of the injured women.

I didn't feel much better. My head kept trying to get me to imagine the worst possible scenarios, but deep down, there was hope that Sydney was all right. There were always these two opposing forces battling inside of me. The pessimist, the optimist. The dreamer, the skeptic. The professional, and the sex-crazed lunatic.

I passed yet another sign for Grenoble.

Oooohhh, thank God for Laurence in a bikini.

My thoughts took a turn once again.

About halfway through Laurence's visit, my mother made a tactical error.

It wasn't her first, nor her last, but perhaps her most memorable.

She decided to take the family down to Hammonasset, one of the state beaches on the Connecticut coast. My father was driving somewhere for some fucking reason, of course, so he didn't attend the festivities. This was unfortunate. The Princess would have enjoyed the show, had he known—would have certainly given up the three hundred or so miles he racked up that day to see what was to come.

So there we were, my mother, the three Little Shits and me, and this gorgeous five-eight French girl in a bikini.

A bikini, I might add, that in the French style of the time, covered a minimal amount of her ample breasts, which was—for my mother— barely acceptable, yet did not cover all of her well-trimmed pubic hair, which was not.

It was a shock that my mother has yet to fully recover from.

I remember her face, my mother's, when Laurence slipped off her pants and stood up, wind blowing, hair flowing, the top of her pussy showing. I stopped watching my mom's face because I was more interested in the flash of heaven peeking over the top of the too-low bikini bottom at eye level only two feet away from me as I sat on the blanket.

"Com'in zee water," Laurence said to me, just before turning and jogging toward the ocean.

My   mother   tried   to   form   words,   but...well,   couldn't.

"Ummm...Law...um"

I, of course, immediately got up and headed to the surf as requested. *I* wasn't *stooopid.*

"Billy, tell her that she can't wear her bottom like that," my mom said to me.

"I'm not telling her. You tell her."

And with that, I was off.

I witnessed an amazing sight. Every straight man, hell, all the men on the beach stared after this beauty—a wake of heads turning as she passed. I watched several wives hit their husbands over the head, on the arm, in the stomach, for staring with their tongues hitting the sand.

Girlfriends broke up with boyfriends, wives uttered the word "alimony." It was pandemonium.

Like a nest of Africanized bees had been dropped smack in the center of the sun-worshiping throng.

Laurence and I peacefully swam and played together, just outside the reach of the vortex she had kicked up. She liked me, not necessarily in a sexual way, but she didn't look down on me or torture me (except with that body) the way she did everyone else. I always knew when she understood and when she didn't. When she was playing dumb and when she really didn't know something.

She respected that I guess.

It's one of those important things that you don't really think about:

Intuition.

Some people have it, some don't, some never will. If there's one trait that earns respect more than anything else from other trades, it's having a reputation for reading people. Because, even when you don't know the truth, the other side assumes you do and tips their hand more easily, which in turn strengthens your rep.

We had fun that day, Laurence and I. She embraced me in the water and squeezed herself against my body for a few moments, pressing her chest and pelvis hard against me. The coolness of the water. The heat from her body. The undulating waves swaying us back and forth. She bit her lower lip, blew me a kiss, then smiled and swam to shore where she was greeted with another wave of men staring, men drooling, men being bonked over the head.

My mother, God Bless her, tried her best to get Laurence to understand that her bikini was showing too much. But my mom, being my mom, couldn't or wouldn't use any word that could have possibly been of any help, like: pubic hair, crotch, vagina, pussy, etc. She just meandered aimlessly, trying to explain the situation using only words approved by the Archdiocese of Hartford, Connecticut.

"Um, you're bottom," she motioned toward the bikini, "it's...shows... too much." She lifted her hand up. "You know, up? Up?"

I looked at Laurence and caught her eye, letting her know I knew she understood. She stared at me for a long moment, her gaze intense, but playful—the waves crashing, the seagulls squawking—then finally, she turned and played dumb for my mother, torturing the poor woman into a full-on sweat.

I almost felt sorry for my mother.

But I was enjoying the show waaaaay too much.

LIKE I SAID, Laurence taught me the art of the tease. Putting something out there, then taking it back. Putting it out, taking it back. It's sort of what a magician does. Doing something with the right hand, while the left is pulling out the hare. Most people miss the subtlety of this. They think they see, stupidly watching the diversion, not realizing it's what they don't see that they need to be wary of.

In my job, I'm a lot like Laurence's bikini bottom.

21

MY MOTHER, THE GAS PEDDLER

I CAN ONLY IMAGINE if my mother were in the car right now. One hand would be on the dashboard, the other would be gripped tightly around the door handle so that she could, at a moment's notice, exit the vehicle post haste.

She has a certain way of crinkling up her face and contorting her lips, which I guess, in her mind, somehow makes me a safer driver.

I've tried to explain to her on many occasions that sitting there, looking like that is more of a distraction, and thus, a greater hazard than any danger we might encounter on the road. But no matter how many times I get her safely to her destination, she continues to insist that I "drive like a maniac."

This is from the woman whose idea of going the speed limit is staying five miles below it just in case her speedometer is somehow calibrated incorrectly. It doesn't seem to matter to her she's getting beeped at by twenty-seven cars behind her or that the twenty-seven drivers have become so frustrated and enraged by this slowpoke that at any moment they are going to attempt to pass her at all costs, crossing the double yellow line without regard for oncoming traffic, most likely causing a major pileup. And who will be to blame?

They will.

"I can't help it, Billy, that's just the way I drive," she said as a huge belch emanated from her body. I can't tell you where we were going because this scene could've been from an uncountable number of car rides before I got my license. Once I started driving, I never let her behind the wheel of a car I was in.

Any number of things can cause high-octane jet fuel to build up inside my mother's gastrointestinal tract. Broccoli, beans, milk, my driving.

My mother is an amorphous blob. I don't mean that as a physical description of her. It's more a *meta*physical description. The makeup of her spiritual core, if you will. Intellectually grabbing onto my mother is kind of like trying to hold onto a hundred-fifty-pound block of Jell-O. Even if you could manage to maintain control of it for a second, pretty much anything more than a handful is going to end up slipping away.

In a tornado, you're supposed to open the windows to let the force blow through your house rather than tear through it. In an earthquake, brick buildings will crumble where buildings made out of wood will twist and survive. My mother is a lot like that. Perhaps it's the reason why she and the Princess have been able to live together for so long. Another human being would have been destroyed by my father's antics. But time after time, hurricane after hurricane, my mother was still standing.

I am not nearly as malleable as she is, which is a good thing in my line of work, but I have on occasion withstood a storm by taking my cue from her, and resist the urge to resist it.

The belch from my mother permeated the interior of the car. I opened up the window to let some air in, waving away what smelled like a tuna, egg salad, and anchovy sandwich coming back up for a second run.

"I understand you want to drive safely—could you open your window? That you want to be a law-abiding citizen, mother. All very admirable. But I think your rights end where the front bumper of the car behind us meets the grill of the eighteen-wheeler coming the opposite way."

"Well, is it my fault if they drive like a maniac?"

"You mean, drive like your husband?"

I think I've mentioned about the third driveway my father had put in once I got my license. We also had to buy an extra car when I started driving. We already had *three* cars, but my father is not one to be caught with his pants down—unless he's hogging the only bathroom in our house.

Why is it that we had four cars and three drivers?

A spare.

Some people needed a spare tire, my father needed an entire spare car.

My father treated everything in his life like a NASA engineer. A system. A backup system. A redundant backup system.

Now, as it would happen, the Princess turned out to be a genius because between me crashing my car into the back of a school bus because I was trying to get to this girl's house before the bus did so I could drive her to school and maybe get her to go out with me, him running cars into the ground, and my mother wearing out brakes because she was worried about going two miles over the Goddamn speed limit, we always *needed* a spare.

I PULL over to look at the map. Allison has given me directions, and I want to make sure I'm following them correctly. I have this habit of writing down directions and never looking at them again. Sort of a game, to see if my memory really is as good as I think it is. But this is no time for brainteasers. The storm is getting worse, and I don't feel like getting stranded, especially since I'm getting no signal on my cellular phone and the satellite phone battery has gone dead. In my rush to leave, I grabbed the AC charger only, not the one for the car.

I unfold the sheet. All of these names and altitudes and symbols of terrain on the map, they're real places. Places with trees and honeysuckle and brooks and buildings and fathers and mothers and children and dogs. I've visited so many countries, traveled so many miles. The enormity of how far I've come hits me. I mentioned that I would move up from fourth to third-most miles traveled by a government official at the end of this trip. Well, in light of my little detour laying Sebby to rest, I've made that jump earlier than expected.

So many places.

Staring at the map, at the names, at the cities and towns and rivers and peaks, I realize there are so many places I will never go to. So much of this earth I will never see. And yet, there they are in front of me. It makes me feel humble, which is not something I choose to feel very often.

Strange places, beautiful places. Countries like Russia with its eleven time zones. "The Borsky Bunch" at 7 P.M. Eastern, 8 P.M. Central and 9 A.M. Siberian time. Puts a crimp in Prime Time when you're still eating breakfast. Then there are locales like Liechtenstein, a nation so small I defy you to find a map, globe, or atlas anywhere in the world *outside* Liechtenstein, where the name Liechtenstein fits within the borders. It's not even on most globes because the lines separating countries cover more real estate than the country has.

I was in Liechtenstein once, but I ran the stop sign and missed it.

I FOLD up the map and put it away, then stare out the window as the road begins to climb. I turn left at the sign pointing toward Mt. Pelvoux telling me 22km to St. Jean, 35km to Modane, and 48km to Sydney.

22

SYDNEY'S CAT, THE INVALID

THE ROAD less traveled was covered by heavily packed snow, and the pavement was getting icier as I climbed higher. My Renault *Le shitbox* was getting a little squirrelly on me, but I was doing my best to compensate. Besides, if I did plunge into a ravine, I wouldn't have to worry about that collision damage waiver. The car would be intact.

Me, not so much.

What I wouldn't give for a vehicle made by people who have to drive through ten-foot snow drifts to get to the factory. People in Detroit understand.

I've mentioned that my father loved Saabs, made by Swedes, folks who also know their snow. *The most reliable car built in the world*, according to him. That was until one day when the family was packing up for a day trip to the Big E, this huge New England fair that takes place annually in Massachusetts. The Big E was something the Princess enjoyed, there were flowers, there were beautiful young girls in tight T-shirts, there were broads there, too. He looked forward to it every year, even if he had to take along The Big Sonofabitch, The Little Shits, and the Ol' Ball-and-Chain.

We were running late, which was not unusual. The Princess went out to start the car, hoping that if he revved the engine loud enough to annoy the neighbors my mother would hurry her ass up to avoid the embarrassment. This tactic worked better than you might imagine. My father never worried about blowing an engine ("That's just a crock so you'll buy a bigger car with more power), but my mother worried all the time about what people thought. And he knew it.

But when the Princess turned the key, the damned thing wouldn't start. He tried pumping the gas peddle and then turning the key. He tried *not* pumping the pedal. Nothing. He tried using the clutch. He tried using more gas, less, then flooding it. You name it, he tried it. Nothing he did had any effect, except on his blood pressure.

Now I was still too young to drive at this time. However, we did have that third car in reserve. So we could have taken that one. In fact, we were already taking two cars because obviously my father wanted to be able to get pissed off, then take off, and not worry about stranding the rest of us.

He was thoughtful that way.

But the Saab ignition wouldn't turn over.

You never want to get within ten yards of the Princess when something of his isn't working. He takes it personally. Like the thing is persecuting him.

My dad had a habit of talking to inanimate objects: plants, cars, gardening tools, forks, knives, stoves, stereo equipment, bicycle chains, oil filters, garbage cans, you name it, treating them as though they were deliberately being stubborn and simply needed to be cursed at, cajoled, threatened, and/or "taught a lesson" until they "figured out who's boss."

So when the Saab wouldn't start after ten minutes of begging and swearing at it and banging on the dashboard, he went and did what any car care specialist would do. He went into the carport, picked up a sledgehammer, and proceeded to pound the living shit out of the car.

Me and Dean and Max must have watched him whacking that hood for eight, nine minutes. At which time, he lifted the hood and directly gave the engine a few dozen kisses with the sledgehammer. Anna came up behind us as we were staring out the window. She was sucking her thumb and calmly joined in the viewing.

"What's dad doing?"

"I guess he's trying to get it to turn over."

"Oh," she said through her thumb and a blanket that she toted with her everywhere.

I happened to think that the design of the car improved somewhat with my father's alterations, which is not to say by any means that he was pleased with his work of art. He stood there, out of breath, looking at his handy work. I was about ten at the time, and I remember distinctly gazing out at the crushed hood of the car wondering what the hell my father had hoped to accomplish by smashing in the engine, which seemed to me to be an integral part of the vehicle, or how he might even imagine that this physical abuse would somehow coax the car into starting for him.

"That'll teach the son of a bitch," he said.

That's right, next time that Saab thinks about not starting for him, it better know it's gonna get its ass—well, hood—whipped.

I heard the metal clang as the hammer hit the ground, then the sound of the front door as my father charged through it. He walked right passed me, and I said to him with a straight face, "Any luck starting the car?"

THE FINAL PUSH UP the mountain road was one long sheet of ice. The path cut into the granite had an endless supply of dangerous curves with sheer drops into dark ravines. A number of times, I came across boulders in my path. Slabs of stone that had cracked under the strain of the biting cold, tumbling down and rounding before falling onto the roadway. Some blocked more than half the pavement, making it difficult to slip by. Several cars had slid into embankments. The occupants looked shaken but safe. I could see lights from police and rescue vehicles coming up the mountain from the valley floor, so I didn't stop. I couldn't stop.

NEARING THE TOP, knowing I'm close now, I take a corner too quickly and lose control of the wheel. *Le shitbox* swerves and skids until it is just about to go over the edge of the cliff. The snow and the darkness make it hard to see how far down the bottom really is. But it's at least a hundred times farther than my body could withstand.

I'm pumping the brakes, resisting the urge to slam my foot to the floor and hold it there. Inches from going over the edge, all movement stops.

The car stalls.

I catch my breath.

Once my heart's no longer redlining, I press the gas and turn the ignition.

Nothing.

I can hear my father, "You flooded it."

"I did not flood it.

I try it again. No luck.

"You flooded it."

He's sitting in the passenger seat, staring at me.

"How come whenever I can't start a car, it's my fault, and when you can't, it's the car's?"

I remind him of the Saab vs. the Sledgehammer incident.

"That car was dead before I killed it," he says. "I put it out of its misery."

We're not in the Alps. Nowhere close. We are in my Pinto, and I'm sixteen and trying to get ready for my driving test.

"And," he adds, "I know how to drive, and you don't."

"Okay, listen. Let's look at this problem logically. I need you to be here so I can use my learner's permit. You need to teach me how to drive so you can drive to wherever the hell it is you drive to and not have to come back from those undiscovered reaches and pick me up from practice."

This line of argument appeals to my father because he nods.

"Now," I say, in a much more deferential tone, "Why don't you show me how to start the car...without flooding it."

I PULL up to the entrance of the Auberge and sit in the car for several minutes. My heart is racing, no longer from the drive but from the uncertainty that lies inside this magnificent resort.

I rest my head against the back of the seat, letting my mind calm down. I have rushed to this place, driven like a lunatic, risked my safety and my career to get here as soon as I could, and here I sit, stalling. I can vaguely see inside through the fogged glass on the front door of the building.

I undo my seat belt and climb out of the car.

The air is much thinner and a little too cold to fuel the storm. It's still coming down hard and accumulating at a rapid rate, but with nowhere near the force that the blizzard is hitting down the mountain. Still, the wind is strong, and it's difficult to keep my balance.

I knock the powder off my boots and step inside.

I lift my hand to my face and try to wipe away the cold. My hand is shaking. I am ten feet from the front desk, but I don't want to talk to them. I don't think I could talk right now.

A million things are running through my head. I asked her to come. I made her get on that plane. If something happened to her, I would never forgi—

Then I see her over by the fireplace, cupping a mug of something hot in her hands. She is wearing a very attractive sweater over a very comfortable-looking shirt. They're both new. I assume Allison got in touch with her and gave her my credit card because Sydney left the house this morning with a driver's license and twelve dollars in her pocket.

She seems warmed by the fire and by whatever she's drinking.

They say you learn a lot about a person when they're drunk. I couldn't disagree more. People are anything but themselves when they're drunk. All the inhibitions, all the guilt, all the years of trial and error, everything that makes up a life, that makes a person who and what they are is lost at the bottom of a bottle. The only thing you can learn from a person who is drunk is how they would act if they were rich. I mean really rich. That's why you never want to cross paths with a billionaire who's just downed a fifth of Stoli.

Actually, I find you learn much more about a person when you give them your credit card.

I'm told this is how most parents learn about their teenagers.

So far, I like what I've discovered about Sydney.

When she sees me, her face breaks into a wide smile, then she folds her hands across her body, trying to look stern as I come closer.

"This is your fault. You got me into this," she says, her cheeks rosy from the cold and the alcohol.

"Actually, my intention was to have you grounded in Geneva." I feel her body, even though we are not touching except for my hand on her back. "But this seems to have worked out better. I got you stuck in the middle of nowhere." I smile and lower my voice. "Now, I get to come rescue you."

"I need rescuing?"

"Absolutely. If only from boredom."

"Oh, really?" she says as a very good-looking ski instructor brings her another cup of what I later find out is hot chocolate—with two shots of Kahlúa in it.

She nods a thank you to the handsome man, then introduces me as the friend she's been waiting for. He gives me a hard glance, like I've roached his rap, moving in on him just when he thought he might cross the goal line. He tells her if she needs anything just let him know.

He then retreats.

"I see I'm not the only one trying to rescue you."

"Just the latest."

"I was hoping maybe the best looking, but wow," I say as I look at her most recent suitor.

She smiles, and her eyes glow in the amber light of the fire.

"I missed you," she says. "As soon as the plane took off, I thought, I'm never going to see him again." She takes another sip. "I almost didn't," she pauses, "Ever see *anyone* again."

"I'm so sorry about this, Sydney."

"I'm fine. Just a little shaken." Her body shudders as she thinks about it. "It was scary." She sighs and pivots the conversation. "Did you have any trouble on the way here?"

"Not at all," I motion to the bartender for a well-needed drink. "Geneva's less than a hundred and fifty kilometers away."

"You didn't need to come here."

"Yes, I did. Like you said, I got you into this."

"Oh my God. What's with the cut over the eye?"

"I got into a fight."

"How did you get into a fight in the middle of a diplomatic conference?"

"It's a *trade* conference. And you kind of had to be there. I was a little irritable."

"I guess so. Are you still irritable?"

"I'm much better, thank you. I doubt I'll lay a hand on anyone here."

"Well, that's too bad."

"I *can* make an exception."

She glances at her watch as she sips her drink.

"You keep checking the time."

"I just need to get home and prick the pussy."

I spit out some beer.

"Excuse me?"

Sydney lets out a long and wonderful laugh.

"I'm sorry." She can't stop laughing. "I have a diabetic cat."

"A cat...that needs insulin?"

"Right in the scruff of the neck, you—"

"Prick the pussy."

"That's what my neighbor calls it. And if I don't get home in...about ten hours, Flora is gonna go into shock."

Flora, it turns out, is this striped tabby, about eighteen-years-old, with clumps of hair missing from her body, that suffers from diabetes, arthritis, depression, uncontrolled bowel movements, has a tongue that hangs out from the side of her mouth because of a stroke two years ago, needs to be lifted over the toilet to piss, can't hear, can't sleep...oh, and only has one eye.

Since the cat can't hear, it doesn't meow, it screeches, making an ear-piercing, glass-shattering noise that sounds like the intersection of a tuberculotic cough and a skill saw. Aaaaaaaccccccccchhhhzzzzzzgggghhh.

You think a guard dog keeps prowlers away? This fucking thing scares the shit out of you, if only because you wonder what kind of disease does this animal carry and what kind of person would let this thing live?

I don't want answers to either one of those questions.

This cat long ago should have been put to death. For its own good.

"Listen, I don't even like cats," she explains. "It's my last boyfriend's. He wouldn't let me put it to sleep while we were living together and now that he's moved, I feel guilty about wanting to get rid of it."

Then I find out that one of the reasons she's no longer living with him is because he'd let the cat sleep with them every single night.

"Well, let him sleep with it now."

"He had to move to London. He made me promise him, I'd take care of it until he could send for it."

"When is that?"

"I don't know. He tried to have Flora sent to him, but the authorities wouldn't allow the cat into England."

"Neither would I."

"It's stupid. But I promised. They won't let it in the country. He won't let me gas it."

"Okay, this might sound a little callous, maybe even a little cruel, but let the pussy die! Put it out of its misery. That noise it makes isn't a greeting, it's a cry for help. It's saying KILL ME!!!!"

"If you saw this poor cat, you'd want to take care of it."

"Oh, I'd take care of it."

If Sydney had been my girlfriend, I would have put that tabby to sleep a long, long, long time ago. I can take the high-pitched screeching, the daily needle, even the human-assisted urination, but I will not have a smelly, ugly, one-eyed cat come between me and any woman's—especially Sydney's—naked body.

"THERE ARE NO MORE ROOMS, *Monsieur*. The storm," says the desk clerk at the Auberge. This seems to be happening a lot to me lately. Even when there's "no vacancy," there's always *room*.

The desk clerk sees my face, sees the look on it. I'm not sure if he's afraid of me or afraid of missing out on the big tip he knows this American might give him. Either way, he speaks. "But because of the emergency, we are setting up cots in the dining room for people who are stranded here."

Sydney glances at me. "That should be cozy."

I grumble something, then ask, "What about down the road?" He understands that I mean *down the mountain*.

"They say they're closing it within the hour."

"For how long?"

"I don't know. A storm like this? Typically, two or free days," he says in his French accent. So far, nothing about this diversion had been *free*. "But I wouldn't suggest leaving now. The storm is vuury bad. They say it's the worst in many years."

BELIEVE IT OR NOT, there is a Hertz Rent-a-car at the top of the mountain, that was open...with cars. They took my French shit-box— after charging me an extra "drop off" fee—and gave me the European equivalent of the Ford Explorer, a 4x4, that was a little smaller than its American cousin.

I spent the next forty minutes on one of the payphones in the lounge talking with Allison, Tom Bowman, and Francesca Thomas. I had woken them up, except Tom, who was in an all-night session negotiating the wording for the press release regarding the "misunderstanding" as the brawl was now being called. After getting a briefing from Tom, we discussed how to proceed with the negotiations. Especially with fresh news out of Washington that American unions and certain business coalitions were mounting legal attacks on NAFTA, which had been the other major item on my to-do list until last year. These legal maneuvers could cause NAFTA to be struck down. The argument behind these lawsuits—

quite a good one—was that the trade *agreement* was ratified by only a simple majority in the Senate. These parties claim the agreement is not an agreement at all, but a *treaty*. And treaties need to be passed by a supermajority, two-thirds of the Senate. I had long ago argued this point with the Administration so we could properly twist arms and get the number of Senators on board to meet this threshold.

What's the point of having a treaty clause in the Constitution if you don't have to follow it? Because, to me, if the North American Free Trade Agreement isn't a treaty, then I don't know what is.

This had complicated things further—even though it wasn't news to any of my team, I've been ranting about it for some time—but the frenzy I had created might actually turn out to be a benefit. The more concessions I could extract from our trading partners, the easier it would be to get super-majority approval. That way, regardless of how the Courts decided, this new trade agreement would stand.

"Billy, you're my friend," Tom said after the others got off the phone. "So, I can tell you." He paused. "You're *fucking* us here. I've got people running Mach ten with their hair on fire tryna clean up after your mess. What the fuck are you doing?"

"Tom, I'm not—"

"Your grandfather died. I understand that. I know what he meant to you, and I'm sorry. I really am. But this shit..." He took a long, deep breath. "You could've gotten on the phone and in two seconds had a dozen people flying down there to find out if this woman was all right."

I didn't even ask how he knew it was a woman.

"You know, my friend," he said into the silence, "sometimes you think you're just a little bit smarter than me. You need to stop that. You think, 'Oh, Tom, he's my buddy, he's my pal. He'll be okay with it.'" He paused. "I care about you. I *am* your friend. But I am not okay with it."

I could hear him breathing, calming himself, even through the hiss and crackle of the terrible connection.

"I am sorry about your grandfather," he said, finally.

"LISTEN," I said to get Sydney's attention, "You don't have to come with me, but I have to get back to Geneva." I drank her in for a moment. "I came to take you back, but now that I know you're okay, I'd feel better if you stayed here until the weather clears. I'll send someone for you."

She took my face in her hands. "What happened on the plane, that was beautiful and intimate and very, very sexy. I should've never let you done that. It wasn't playing fair."

"I'm a big boy. I knew what I was doing. Although, no, that wasn't playing fair."

She seemed to take my lighthearted comment hard. Not because of any tone in my voice, but because I think she was struggling with the consequences within herself.

We didn't say anything for a moment. She glanced outside at the snow-covered mountains bathed in moonlight, mountains that reminded me of gigantic versions of the ones I grew up with.

It was a full minute before she spoke.

"You can't control feelings. But you can control what you do with them."

The words burned through my chest and buried themselves in my heart. No one can command passion or emotion, I know that. It'll be there or not, whether you like it or not. But supposedly, people of good conscious can manage it. I guess I was more than a little embarrassed by my inability to regulate myself. I thought about Laura and sighed. What the fuck was I doing?

Sydney touched my face.

"You can't just throw everything away because you had your hands between some woman's legs."

"Even if they're yours?"

"Especially if they're mine. I should have never gotten on that plane."

"Why *did* you get on that plane?"

She shook her head and glanced at the fire, which was crackling and sparking at the moment as one of the hotel staff piled on several more logs. The weight of the new logs pushed some of the burning embers to the stone hearth. In a moment, the hot coals ignited the fresh wood.

I didn't know why she came, but I knew why I asked her to come.

"Sydney..."

"Don't say it. Please. Whatever it is. It's going to be hard enough going back to my life knowing you are out there in the world. And sometimes so very close to me. I just really want to go home."

"You can't just come crashing into my life—"

"Good choice of words."

"—and then walk out."

"You need to get to Geneva. I need to get home."

My hand absently caressed the cool marble head of a male statue that stood guard over the room, contemplating something very important it seemed. I wonder if he had ever been this confused. Probably, not. One of the advantages of having rocks in your head.

Then a moment of clarity.

Before I could say anything, she got up and walked toward the stairs. I finally caught up with her on the landing of the third floor near the spa. I pushed her back against the wall, and she looked up at me. I held her hands over her head with my hands. Then I brought one of my hands down and slowly began caressing her hips, one then the other, sliding my hand across her stomach as I moved between them.

"I need to understand this," I said. My breathing was very heavy. She tried to squirm away. "Don't move!"

She stopped squirming.

Which surprised and excited both of us.

"Do you love her?" she asked.

"What?"

Not what my mind was expecting.

"Do you *love* her?"

"Yes. I don't know. I guess."

"None of those answers are good enough for me to allow you to keep your hands where they are."

I didn't move my hands. In fact, I held her hip more tightly, my forearm pressing against her stomach.

She asked me again, a slight change to the wording, her breathing now as shallow and rapid as mine, "Are you *in love* with her?" she demanded. "Either you are, or you aren't, there is no guessing."

She did not take her eyes off of me.

I wanted to squeeze her, hold her, press her more firmly against the wall, but instead, I had to answer.

"Sydney," I said in a whisper. "I'm engaged to Laura."

The moment was broken, the heat between us evaporating in an instant. So delicate is the nature of such things.

I pulled my hand away and leaned back against the wall and let myself slide to the ground.

I was lost.

"I never proposed to her, I need you to understand that."

Sydney stood over me as I sat on the floor. I shook my head in response to her questioning look. I tried to explain to her about the handcuffs and the misunderstanding. It sounded absurd.

"We were in bed. And she says, 'I wanna have a baby.' I say, 'you gotta be married to do that.' She says, 'Exactly.' I say, 'Laura, you wanna *marry* me?' That was my proposal. That was it. A rhetorical question. I mean, I'm always leaving for someplace halfway around the world, I had this fucked up childhood, I'm not the easiest boyfriend, I doubt I'd be any better as a husband or a father. Why would she want that?"

"Maybe because she loves you."

The words were a fist to my stomach.

I knew this. I had felt it evolving over the last six months. But I had tried to ignore it. Not ignore it, hoping it would go away, but ignore it elegantly while I hoped to catch up with Laura, to close the gap between my feelings and hers.

"Why didn't you just say something?"

I sighed, the noise coming from deep within me, almost a laugh. "I know, it sounds so simple, doesn't it? Just say, no." I glanced at the floor between my legs. I knew my answer wasn't good enough, but it was all I had. "I got swept up in the moment. She was crying, tears of happiness. I felt it. And then after, I was busy preparing for the negotiations." I wanted to stop talking, to stop sounding like such an asshole, but I couldn't. I couldn't be anything but what I was with Sydney standing there, looking down at me. I needed her to know. Me, everything. Flaws and all. "And every time I started to question it, I thought, is this just some commitment-phobic male reaction? I mean, here's someone who is beautiful, interesting, someone everyone thinks is perfect. Christ, the President thinks she's perfect! Whose family is nothing like mine. And I want kids at some point. Maybe I could have a different life. Maybe I wouldn't screw up my marriage or my kids the way my parents did. Every time I saw her, she looked so...fucking *happy*." I put my hand to my forehead and wiped a bit of sweat from my skin. "I wanted to make her happy."

Sydney nodded and rested her hand on my head. "Then, I'm just a blip on the radar."

I laughed. It was tinged with sadness. "You're a Goddamn armada of ships coming in."

"Baby, you and I...we aren't at war." She knelt down to be at my level.

"But I don't want anything to do with stealing you from another woman."

I shook my head. "A person can't be stolen. They can be *won*. But not stolen."

I stared into her eyes. I didn't understand why I was feeling what I was feeling. It made no sense. It wasn't some physical attraction clouding my judgment, I knew those moments. No, this was—

"This is crazy," she said, finishing my thought. "Why are we even having this conversation?" She stood back up as a couple passed us in the hall. It would have been the perfect moment to walk away, but she didn't make any attempt to escape.

"Maybe because..." I began, echoing her phrasing a moment ago. "Maybe because we're supposed to be having it."

Sydney was watching me, studying my face, my expression, listening to my words, looking I think to find anything that seemed false. I understood. I would have done the same thing if I were her. Too many men have lied about such feelings. Too many lives have been scalded by the casual disregard for emotional consequence.

"You're engaged. Your fiancée is at your parents' house right now comforting your mother over the death of her father. What part of this doesn't sound horribly wrong?"

I nodded in agreement. I reached up and took her hand, the one resting on my head and held it. "Does it feel that way to you? Wrong?"

Sydney made a noise I can't quite describe. Something more than a groan and less than two planets colliding.

She didn't answer. She didn't have to.

I knew deep inside that I really did care about Laura, really did want her to be happy. Which was ironic because I started to realize that truly caring for her meant making sure she knew the truth.

But what if the truth was a lie or clouded in some way?

"I've been thinking a lot about this," I said as Sydney shifted and leaned back against the wall. "I haven't thought about much else since I left you at the airport." I took in a deep breath, closed my eyes and tried to slow down. "Laura is beautiful, charming, smart. Guys have always fallen in love with her. Guys are still falling in love with her."

Sydney waited impatiently for the inevitable *but*.

"But..." I stopped. "It's difficult to explain. It sounds so stupid—"

"Tell me."

Silence.

"Just say it," she whispered. She needed to hear it, whatever it was.

I took in another deep breath and held it in for a long moment, let the air inaudibly slip out of my lungs. "You..." I began. "You are what I've always dreamed about." The words sounded imbecilic to my ears, but I pressed on. "And I don't mean some fantasy. I mean, my real hopes and dreams."

I closed my eyes and watched my grandfather deal out a hand of gin rummy, watched his arthritic fingers flip the cards, one to me, one to him, one to me, another for him until we each had seven. I heard a voice, then I realized it was my own, but younger, telling Sebby about what I wanted in a woman. Saw the traits—the physical, the emotional, and all the million little things that make up a person—saw them in my mind come together to be what I already knew them to be. The woman in front of me.

"You're the woman I've always pictured myself ending up with."

She waited for me to finish, but I had nothing more to say.

"Is that the stupid part?"

I nodded my head.

"Why would that sound stupid?" she said, tenderly.

"Because I sound like a fourteen-year-old girl."

"Twelve."

For a moment she was there. She was with me, completely. Then...I lost her.

"I can't do this," she said. "I don't want to feel what I'm feeling anymore."

"How can you not want to feel this?"

"Billy, I feel...something so amazing. And then I get nauseous at the thought of you being with another woman, *being* another woman's, and I wanna run into a bathroom and throw up."

"Okay, that's not the feeling I'm talking about."

She leaned against me. Both of us sitting there, our mouths silent, our brains screaming at the top of their lungs.

She turned toward me after a moment.

"Tell me she's a bitch. Tell me she's some horrible person. Please."

But I couldn't.

"Then tell me you can't live without her. Say something, so I can walk out that door."

"Don't you think we should at least try to figure out what this is," I motioned between us, "before you walk away?"

She put the palm of her hand on my cheek. I was starting to like that feeling very much.

"I can't let you do this." She stood up. "Go to Geneva. Please, for me. Go."

23

THE FOUR-YEAR-OLD
PSYCHOLOGIST

WHEN I WAS ONE, I was walking and talking already. At least, I was saying a few words. By the time I was two, I was using complete sentences and formulating complex concepts. By age three, I was potty trained, shoelace trained, and miniature train trained.

And when I hit four years old, I became a doctor of psychology.

My mom was a few months pregnant with Dean in her stomach. I was very clear on the fact that this would be the last birthday I would spend in total peace, without siblings, with only people I had invited to be there. Except, of course, my parents, who seemed to be there whether I invited them or not.

I knew I'd be getting a baby brother or sister sometime between Thanksgiving and Christmas. I'd run around saying, Mom has a turkey in the oven. Oh, if I only knew how right I was. My mom wanted a girl, but I had the feeling it was a boy. I wasn't threatened by the addition of another child, wasn't worried that I would become less important. I had received a great deal of attention and never doubted for a moment that I would continue to get enough attention, even if I had to share my mother with an infant.

Oh, and I knew how to speak English, which is more than I can say for any newborn little brother. I mean, if the kid wet his pants, he cried. If he had to be burped, he cried. If he was hungry, he cried. If he was tired, he cried. Who the fuck knew what this kid wanted?

Me? I could point to things and ask. "Mother, may I have another piece of toast, please?"

You can almost *hear* the halo over my head.

Once my mother's stomach started growing in the middle stretch of the pregnancy, during the dog days of summer, she got tired easily and needed to sit down and rest. That's when we started our sessions. She'd lay on the couch, exhausted by a day of hard work. Not only did she do the laundry and cook dinner and work a few days a week, but she was also busy creating a small-scale human being inside of her. My father would come home wondering why dinner wasn't made and she'd say, "I'm sorry, I was busy today. I was making a finger." Then she'd give him one.

My mom would talk to me about everything. The world, my father, my grandparents, life, you name it.

I wonder sometimes if she talked to me that way because she *knew* I'd understand, or if she just started talking that way and that's how I *came* to understand. Hard to say.

She asked me complex questions. It took all the wisdom and knowledge I had compiled over the course of four years to answer these tough personal queries.

Now, when you're four years old and someone asks you a question, you say what you're thinking. No bullshit. That's all you know how to do. (Unless, of course, the question is "Did you break that lamp?" Hell, then you can lie, lie, lie, even if there's no one else in the house but you.)

So, I set up my sheepskin, and for a peanut butter and jelly sandwich (grape, only), I'd sit back and listen to my mother's life and relationship issues.

I began dispensing advice like you wouldn't believe.

On my father's bad behavior: leave him.

On his drinking: pour out all his alcohol.

On the fact that he didn't give her enough money to run the house: stop feeding him until he pays up.

You name it, I had a solution for it.

We'd be meandering along one of the downtown streets, and I'd be doling out oral instructions from the comfort of my stroller. A Lilliputian sage. A mobile information booth.

I'd even get out and push the damn thing myself whenever she'd remark, "Easy for you to say," just to prove I could empathize with her. Or remind her that I still wet the bed to demonstrate that I was not without my own struggles to overcome.

To give you a comparison, four years later, at about the same age I was then, Dean was being rushed to the hospital with a thermometer completely up his ass.

I CLIMBED into the 4x4 and put the key in the ignition. I sat there for—I don't know how long. It could've been a minute. It seemed like an hour.

My breath was fogging the windows, so I started the car, and once the glass became clear, I pulled out and left the Auberge and Sydney behind.

I tried to clear my mind of her, but I wasn't very successful. She kept crowding out all other thoughts.

When I got home, in my own house, in my own bed, things would be different. Time spent at home always numbed the suffering of travel madness.

The first time I went to France, those six weeks many summers ago, things were different when I came back, had inextricably changed. Two radio stations I listened to revamped their formats. A heat wave raged through most of August, and my town seemed altered in some subtle but meaningful way.

Maybe it wasn't anything external. Maybe it was me that had changed. Inside.

Fresh from my trip, we decided it was best that my father didn't try to teach me to drive after our first outing. Instead, I spent the rest of that summer under the tutelage of Seamus McRae.

Seamus was a short, round red-faced Irish driving school instructor who would pull up to my house two times a week, completely shit-faced, ready to school me in the fine art of drunk driving.

His bulbous red nose and cherry red cheeks would greet me from the passenger side window, having already slid over from the driver seat.

"Ooooooow, helllllllooooo, Mr. Gerrick." He had this lilt in his voice that drew out certain words. "Are youuuuuuuu oooowwww ready for your lesson?"

Not really. I was stone-cold sober.

How the hell was I supposed to learn how to drive drunk when I was already down a quart of booze on Seamus?

I would climb into the car, which reeked of Irish whiskey, shut the door, and immediately roll down the window.

For the next two hours, I would listen to the ruminations of an incoherent, alcoholic Irishman on safe passing distances, parallel parking tips, and the use of brakes during hazardous conditions.

Despite all this, I passed the written portion and the driving portion of my license test with a perfect score and spent the rest of the day driving around, visiting friends, and planning which girl I was going to ask out for the first ride in my car. Seamus, however, failed his blood-alcohol test at the DMV and spent the night in jail.

By the time I got to the start of the pass, they had already closed the road down the mountain.

I didn't bother arguing with the *gendarmes* blocking passage with their miniature police vehicle.

I turned around and headed back.

Deep inside, I was relieved and not just because I didn't relish the thought of navigating those steep, twisting, icy roads in the dark. I didn't want to leave Sydney tonight.

If the weather cleared by morning, I could still make it back to Geneva in time to save this thing.

It took me a while to find Sydney. She was having a drink in the bar while some American skier from the pro tour was trying to pick her up. She was surprised to see me, but I couldn't quite tell if she was disappointed, delighted, or relieved.

After several minutes of the skier ignoring the fact that I was there, she leaned forward and whispered something to him. He glanced up at me, and I nodded to him, trying to be friendly. His face flushed red, and I heard him say, "I'm sorry," more to me than to her.

Then he walked back to a table with several other ski boys and tried to make himself as small as possible.

"The pass was closed," I said.

"I know. They told us."

"You knew I was coming back?"

"Why do you think I ordered another drink?"

I heard laughter coming from the skiers as they were giving our amorous friend some shit about being sent packing.

"What did you say to him?"

"I told him you were my husband."

I got a tingle, a shiver down my spine at the thought of that.

"And that you thought he was cute and asked me to ask him if he was bi or at least open to it."

"You did not."

She nodded. "Serves you right."

I smiled at her—how easily she made me do that. And once again, I took in her outfit.

She noticed. "You like?"

"Mmmm hmmm."

"Free. Paid for by a very important, high ranking—" she whispered the next two words, "—government official, who gave me his credit card. I think he kinna likes me."

"I think he does."

She was loose, not pained like earlier. Maybe it was the alcohol. She leaned her head against mine and sighed with as much feeling as I have ever felt from another person. "I think he does."

More stranded travelers found their way to the lodge, and then to the bar, because of the road closure. Cots were being set up in the dining room. It was going to be very crowded. In fact, there weren't enough cots to go around. Some of us would have to sleep on the floor. I was tired. I needed sleep badly. Unfortunately, I've never slept well amongst strangers.

I believe if money can solve a problem, then there isn't a problem in the first place. All it is is a simple matter of negotiation, a haggling over the cost.

I scoped out possible targets. There were several good candidates, but the best seemed like three Italian hikers who had come off the trail to weather the storm. From the clothes they wore, it was pretty clear they had not expected to spend any time in civilization. They had originally thought they were lucky to get the last room for three hundred U.S. dollars. They were much less happy when the lodge announced it was putting people up in cots for free.

I felt these were my best prospects.

I approached the Italians from the south, attacking from the rear.

The negotiation went something like this:

I struck up a conversation with the three, expressing how nice it was for the resort to let people like ourselves who were stranded stay in the dining room at no charge.

"I guess we'll all be sleeping together tonight. Could be worse," I said, nodding with my head toward several gorgeous Scandinavian girls putting their gear near a row of cots being unfolded by the hotel staff, claiming them.

"Not us. We got a room," said one of the Italians, sounding completely depressed. It was more than the three hundred dollars they paid. It was the girls.

"That's great," I said, brightly with only a hint of jealousy. "My friend and I tried to get a room. Couldn't."

"We gotta the last one," said the depressed Italian. I wouldn't have left the guy alone with anything sharp.

His friend hit him. "Which we would no have got if we know we could stay for free!"

The third hiker finally spoke. "Next to them."

I picked out two cots with a good view of the Blondes keeping the hikers' interest.

"Yeah, that's too bad. Looks like it's gonna be a good show tonight. Although, I don't think my girlfriend's gonna find it as enjoyable."

I motioned toward Sydney, who had remained at the bar.

"You'll get a good night's sleep, though. You're lucky," I added.

They didn't agree.

"Maybe you could take it?" said one of the Italians as if it was his idea.

"The room?" I asked.

"Sí, sí, you know," the first Italian said, looking at Sydney, "Out here, that would be a waste of a *bella donna*," his voice going lower as he tried to sell me.

I patted the cot. "Oh, I don't know. She's not all that shy."

I could see the guys were starting to get heated up. Sex was all around them and they weren't getting any of it.

"Take-a the room," said one of them, blurting it out. "Justa pay us for it."

I pulled out my wallet. I only had two hundred and eighty dollars in American bills, the francs I needed to get down the mountain.

"I'll give you two hundred dollars cash. I need the rest."

"That's a—" the Italian was doing the math in his head. "A hundred less than we paid."

I looked over at the Scandinavian girls. "Is that one not wearing a bra?"

Their three heads swiveled in unison as if they just heard a gunshot. They clearly saw the nipples through the thin T-shirt.

They took one look at the girls, one look at Sydney, one look at the money, and immediately said they'd take the two hundred dollars.

Only one of them was going to get the bed. The other two would end up on the floor in sleeping bags. Waste of money. Waste of a chance—a slim one from the look of these guys' game—to hook up with some very pretty, very nearly naked women.

I handed them the cash.

They were grateful, for the money and the view.

I was grateful. I had a room.

WHEN SYDNEY REALIZED we'd be sleeping on cots, she ordered another drink. "I want to pass out." When I told her about getting a room, she immediately canceled the order.

Sydney was trying hard to hide the fact that she wasn't completely sober.

But being the son of an alcoholic father and a mother with the tolerance of a canary in a coal mine, I could tell a lightweight when I saw one.

My parents were always having people over the house every few Saturday nights. This was during that hard-drinking era, when everyone, including pregnant women, belted them down. Gunter was staying over this one particular evening. I was normally compelled to attend church on Sunday mornings, and I figured having Gunter over would absolve me of this wholly unholy duty. Only Gunter had this curious desire to visit a Catholic church. He'd never been to one. Gunter is a Congregationalist. His mother had told him, actually *warned* him, "Zey are going to vant you to kneel. You're not to kneel, vhatever they tell you. Do not do it."

Apparently, Congregationalists are very concerned about the health of their knees.

This only fueled his desire to see the inside of my church.

And here, I had had an airtight plan. Fucking Gunter.

So, that Saturday night, me and Gunter got to hang out in the kitchen and watch the drinks being made. And help serve them as well. My mom had *two* of the half-dozen drinks she allotted herself for the entire year that night. Two doesn't seem like a lot. Especially when you spread them over an evening. But my mother, she would get completely looped on two tiny glasses of wine, and then laugh herself into a near hysterical fit, where you'd have to make sure she didn't tip over her chair. She got hot flashes, too, and would fan herself wildly while she continued giggling.

This is a woman whose sneeze could crack glass, a sneeze that would echo so loudly in the church that everyone would turn around to see who had popped. She had a similar kind of laugh. Like a hyena on helium.

Hide your crystal ladies and gentlemen if you plan on giving her a stiff drink.

And please, God, don't let her tell a joke.

Because although my mother could crack me up with the sound of her laugh, I don't think I ever even chuckled at one of her jokes. As I mentioned, she has an uncanny talent for ruining comedy, either with bad timing or a forgotten punchline. Even when she did tell the joke in the proper order with the correct ending, somewhere in the distance, you heard a rim shot. Badoom Ching.

The reverse, however, is not true. I never had to give my mom a drink to get her going, get her into a fit of laughter. All I had to do to get my mother doing her asthmatic hyena act was to describe some idiotic thing my father had done, of which there were so many. I would continue telling the story until my mother was unable to breathe, or until she begged me to stop.

My mother doesn't actually laugh as much as she wheezes and screams hysterically.

"Oh, Billy, stop it. You're going have to call an ambulance for me if you keep it up."

The Princess, on the other hand, is nearly impossible to make laugh. I never quite know what's going on inside that massive brain of his, but it certainly isn't a comedy routine. I have occasionally told a joke in front of my family, a joke that gets everyone rolling, and my father will sit there and as flat as Kansas say, "Hmph. Funny."

See, booze doesn't go directly to my father's funny bone like it does for my mom. It makes a roundabout path, hitting the pissed-off bone, the burn-down-the-house bone, and usually ends up somewhere around the I-just-plain-can't-stand-to-look-at-your-stupid-face-anymore bone.

For alcohol to get to the Princess's funny bone takes a lot of drinks.

I *have* seen my father in various states of inebriation, states the size of Texas, states in which my father has done some pretty ridiculous, hurtful, and if the blood alcohol level was high enough, some hilarious things, but

I have never witnessed my father completely hammered. I mean, gone. Out of it.

Well, *once* I did.

My father had taken leave of us, walking to a neighbor's house. Most of the people in our neighborhood didn't hang out together. We'd see each other at church or sometimes during the holidays where we'd stop by and say hello and happy this holiday or that holiday, but almost never did my father or my family party with them.

I don't know what they were pouring at that house, or what they were slipping into those drinks, but my father was extremely well-lubricated by the time I got over there.

My father had originally stopped over to borrow their lawnmower. The Princess had done some of his notorious bodywork on our mower when it wouldn't start for him. It was similar to the work he did on his Saab a couple of years earlier. Although this time, he didn't use a sledgehammer. The sledgehammer, you see, was all the way around on the other side of the house in the carport. You couldn't call the Princess a lazy person, he would get pissed off and get out of a car and walk for miles and miles and miles for no other reason than he just didn't want to be in the car with us anymore. But you *could* say that he was practical and efficient as a demolitionist.

So, instead of marching the hundred yards to the carport and back, he simply stepped over to the cinder block retaining wall a few feet away that was presently keeping the front lawn from becoming part of the back lawn, a retaining wall that appeared near collapse—another one of those projects my father was always threatening to do.

He picked up one of the loose cement blocks and walked carefully, making sure he kept his back straight, and his knees bent, and then, upon reaching the offending mower, raised the cement mass over his head and crushed the motherfucker.

I don't think he found it as satisfying as killing his car. One shot, one blow, and the machine was history. It was pretty much over before it started. Like a heavyweight fight that's over after the first punch. I felt bad for him. I normally like people to get their money's worth.

By this time mowing the lawn was, for the most part, my domain. But I refused to subject myself to undue hazards by mowing right over large rocks and tree branches and parts of my Father's decaying greenhouse. Instead, I would go around them, leaving patches of uncut grass in my wake. If I had time, I'd go back and rake the area, then trim the grass, but our lawn was a little under two acres of Kentucky bluegrass, dandelions, and weeds, which got in my hair, my nose, my shoes, my underwear, and by the time I turned off that engine, I just wanted to be done with it.

The Princess would see the uncut patches, come out swearing, screaming that he had to do "everything" himself, then take the mower from me and terrorize the neighborhood by sending hundreds of rock fragments whizzing in every direction. It was like D-Day, shrapnel flying, people diving for cover.

But I had shut off the engine. And when he went to go start it up...it wouldn't.

My father's cinder block theatrics guaranteed the end of my workday, and I was getting ready to get on my bike and go visit my friends. However, the Princess had other ideas. He said I wasn't going to get off that easy, so he set off to the neighbors' to borrow their lawnmower.

Three hours passed, and we didn't have a clue what my father was up to. His car was still outside so he couldn't have gone very far. He didn't tell us which particular neighbor he was going to ask. It could've been one of six or seven people on our street. My mom was "ticked off"—her words—and sent me out on reconnaissance. Actually, as it turned out, it was more like a rescue mission.

I finally found my father over at the Arnold's house. Mr. Arnold, my dad, and the husband and wife who lived next door to the Arnold's were flat on their asses, busted drunk.

I'd seen my father heated, but not this hot. You could tell he was really drunk because he acted a lot like my mom with a glass and a half of sherry in her system. He was laughing himself silly.

And to be honest, watching the scene, I couldn't stop cackling myself. The laughter was contagious. My stomach and face hurt.

It took a while, but I finally got my father out of the big chair he was parked in and got him to come home. We were only about a hundred and fifty yards from the house, but with all the zigging and zagging that accompanied my father's trek toward our ancestral home, I figure we traveled upwards of a mile.

He was spewing information on a variety of unconnected subjects and commenting intelligently on things he normally had no idea what the fuck he was talking about. Fashion. Politics. The Middle East.

I have to admit, if this were how my father was every time he drank, I probably would have said, "Drink up, my man" each time he walked in the door.

Once I got him home, my dad, all two hundred twenty-five pounds and six-foot-three of him was lying on the floor with his feet on the seat of our rocking chair, looking like an Apollo astronaut preparing for lift off.

"God, I'm so fucked up."

This is the phrase my father repeated somewhere around two hundred thousand times.

No two of which were uttered *exactly* the same way.

SYDNEY WAS NOWHERE near that drunk when I brought her up to the room. As I lit a fire and turned down the lights, I heard her say, "No, no, nooooo," to the flickering flames.

"It's a nice room, I want to get the full ambiance," I said as sat on the floor next to her in front of the hearth.

"You can get the full ambiance from right over there." She pointed to the corner of the room farthest from her.

"That's not showing much hospitality."

"I am not a Bed & Breakfast."

But I didn't move. And after a few minutes, she stopped insisting.

Her cat-loving boyfriend's name came up, which surprised me, not because she mentioned him, but because, believe it or not, I know him, or rather, know *of* him. He's from a family whose name, in the form of a company, appears on my trade sheets every month.

Brendan Avery.

The name just drips with importance.

He seems relatively well-adjusted for someone who never has and never will have to worry about money. Ever. It's hard to tell what that knowledge will do to a person. I have several friends like Brendan, from wealthy families with driven fathers. One of my friends is a workaholic, even though she's worth more than any of her bosses. I guess she's trying to prove herself worthy of her success.

Another one of my wealthy friends excels at finding and buying failing businesses and running them into the ground.

It takes a lot more talent than you would think to take a few million dollars and turn it into a few thousand.

But it's something he's worked very hard at over the years.

Another person I know, who in every other way seemed normal, spent his twenties and most of his thirties reading things like the *I Ching* and meditating, only to wake up one day and realize he hadn't done anything with his life.

Wealth is often wasted on the rich.

Sydney's old beau has a passion for music. Even when he was working for his family's shipping business by throwing parties for the Washington crowd, he spent his off nights and days practicing his guitar and sitting in on bands whenever he could.

He went to England under the guise of learning the ropes of the *actual* shipping business in the London office, away from the pressure of his family and his father in New York and the parties in D.C., but we all assumed he was hanging out at Abby Road.

I knew all of this not from anything Sydney had said, but because my friend—the businessman with the brown thumb who buys companies and submarines them—went to the same prep school Brendan did. They've stayed close over the years.

In fact, I realized I knew a lot about Sydney Nathan, as well.

Rumor had it that Brendan asked his long-time girlfriend to marry him.

Apparently, the answer had been no.

It's strange to already have knowledge of intimate details about someone you're just getting to get to know. There's a sense of misgiving. As if you peered into their purse or looked through their dresser drawers while they were in the bathroom.

I wanted to break free of that feeling. To keep nothing from her. This was new for me.

"I heard Brendan was getting married."

"You know Brendan?" she said, pleasantly surprised, wearing that drunk smile that comes as you find you have something in common with someone random at a bar.

"I know the family."

"Yeah, so do I," she said, her smile fading. "The 'Family,'" she put quotes around the word, "had a date and a place all set before he even asked me." She shook her head. "I hate being taken for granted, no matter how noble the intention. But they're the Averys. They all just assumed I'd say yes. Why wouldn't I? Poor little me."

"Sort of takes the romance out of it."

"I was pissed." She stared into the fire. "He said he was going to work on his music, but I know they sent him to London because I refused their acquisition offer."

That's why she's kept the cat. Guilt.

We both were quiet as we watched and listened to the sap in the wood crackling and popping from the heat of the fire. The soft light coming from the flames made our shadows dance and our skin a golden amber that invited touch. I put my hand gently on her knee. She delicately knocked it away.

"No," she said, her head tilted in a pose of deep thought, the alcohol in her system giving more credence to everything than it really deserved. "Why do you continue to do that? Try and touch me?"

"Why do you continue to refuse it?"

"We've been through all this."

I'm not exactly sure how many women I've been with, but I am sure of one thing. In all those women, not once did I ever feel the way I did when I was touching Sydney. The strangest thing was, and I mean this, just the sensation of my fingers on her smooth wetness, resting there, barely moving on the moist folds of her pussy, and on the warm, pulsating button of her clitoris was more pleasurable than making love—penetration!—with the vast majority of the other women. And this isn't because these women weren't good in bed because most of them had been exquisite in the art of physical love. No, a unique chemistry was producing this.

"On the plane...I've never felt anything like that before," I confessed.

"Oh, my guess is you've felt a lot of things like that before," she said, cutting me slightly.

"I'm not kidding about this."

"Billy," she said, looking at me, the flame reflecting off her eyes, "Even if you weren't entangled, Brendan doesn't just have a cat at my house. He still has all his things there. This was just a little detour. Let's leave it at that."

One of the logs shifted and popped, sending sparks up the flue.

"That's not acceptable to me."

"This isn't a negotiation."

"I don't get a say in this?"

"You wanna broker a deal? Let's get Laura on the phone. The three of us can settle this. You're the expert. How do you think that bargaining's gonna go?"

I glanced down at my hands as they rested flat on the floor. I tried to search my mind for something in my past, some time when I had felt this helpless. I couldn't find anything remotely this painful, which surprised me. I always considered myself someone who had suffered all of his pain up-front, early on, getting most of my life's allotment out of the way while the prices were still low.

The only event I could compare to this was Jenna/Claire, and that was only an infinitesimal fraction of what I was feeling now. Then I was eighteen, my relationship with Jenna/Claire would've been a fun six months. This here, whichever way it turned out, this could be about the rest of my life.

She saw my face, saw the gears turning behind the calm exterior.

"What am I suppose to do?" she asked.

I took in a deep breath and let it out slowly, let a little of the frustration sneak out, hitching a ride with the air.

"It's not like I'm some school kid who just felt up his first girl. All I know is something felt different."

"That's because I went into the bathroom and..." She stopped.

"See, that right there. You went into an airplane bathroom at thirty-five thousand..."

"Forty-two thousand."

"Forty-two thousand feet, in the middle of that turbulence and shaved your—"

My omitted word hung in the air. The word doesn't sound the same, doesn't sound as sexy when it's blurted out. It needs to be whispered, to be growled, to be drawn out.

"Do you know how that makes me feel?"

"I wanted to do something for you." Her tone was somewhat confessional. "Something you would like. Something only for you."

"You had never done that before?"

She shook her head. "Not like that. I've never gotten on a plane with a complete stranger and nearly crashed into the Alps before." She glanced up at me. "I did that, too."

The fire crackled and hissed and eventually died out.

"One of us should sleep on the floor," she said after a long silence.

I sighed. "I won't *do* anything. I am able to control myself."

She gazed at me with this bittersweet look on her face.

"That would make me even more sad." Her voice sounded so weary, so tired.

And as I held her, as I caressed her, as I let my strength and my steadiness coax the fear, the anxiety, the events of the day from her body, as I allowed them to be cast out with each breath she took, she fell asleep in my arms within moments...

24

FOUR ALARM SNORING

I HAVE a lot of experience in the study of snoring. Three of the women I've dated long-term have been nasally challenged. As is Max, and both sets of grandparents.

So, I've developed an arsenal of weapons to combat this heinous assault on the slumber of people of good conscience.

I've had to. For my own survival.

Whenever things got weird over my house, which they often did, I'd usually be saved by an overnight at the Princess's parents.

Grampa Robert and Gramma Maggie were exquisite hosts. They had air conditioning, we didn't. They had fun kids living next door. We had the Addams Family down the street. I mean that figuratively *and* literally. They had the lovely Piper, who lived one house away, who was a year older than me, who I just pined after. We had a kid who had to have *all* his teeth pulled out by his senior year in high school.

Granted, we were six and seven at the time, but Piper was a babe and everything a guy wanted in a woman, at least, wanted at six years old. She was pretty. She had a great smile, some freckles. She liked to run and jump and play around. She didn't mind getting dirty.

Maybe the things I like in women haven't changed all that much.

If the Princess was the guy who brought coal into our house and picked his ass, his mother, Maggie, was almost entirely just a wide back and rotund buttocks to me. I don't think I saw ten minutes of her from the front—at least, not all at once. She was either standing at the stove cooking, or at the sink cleaning dishes. At the washer and dryer. Or driving with me in the back seat.

She died, this woman, mother of my father, at the very young age of sixty from cancer. It wasn't till many years later, when my uncle, my father's younger brother, died of colon cancer at fifty-nine, that I learned that Maggie had succumbed to the same disease.

Needless to say, I was at my doctor's office, ass in the air, the very next day, begging the man to climb up inside there and tell me everything was all right.

Maggie was only with us for a short time, I was just seven at the time of her death. In fact, I'm the only one of my siblings who remembers her.

Maggie...I remember you.

And it gets harder all the time to remember that face, because in a fit of rage after her death, my grandfather burned every one of her pictures in his fireplace.

But when Maggie was alive, which was the only time I was allowed to sleep over at my father's parents, I'd sleep in my grandmother's bed which was on the other side of the room from my grandfather's bed.

Maggie would kiss me goodnight, then go to the bed in the large and comfortable second-floor finished attic.

Robert would tip-toe over to the closet, reach up to the top shelf and pull down the fifth of whiskey *du jour*. He'd finish it, every last drop, and sometimes, he'd even crack open another one and get a head start on tomorrow's bottle.

Then he'd grumble "goodnight" to me—he wasn't the most emotive of men—and climb into bed. A moment later, the lights would be off.

Five minutes after that, my night of hell would begin.

These were not the demons that normally came to me in the night, things that when I needed to go down into the cellar for some reason after midnight would make me wake up Dean and send him—still about eighty-nine percent asleep—down the stairs ahead of me so any creature lying in wait would snatch him first.

I was such a good older brother.

No, this was something far more terrifying.

This was...the Snore.

A few minutes into his alcohol-aided slumber, my grandfather, the retired Fire Captain, would start revving up the Engine Company that seemed to be stuck in his throat.

It started out small, the little vibration of the tonsils on the exhale, the slight airy sucking sound on the inhale. Then it would move to Stage Two, vibrating tonsils and tongue on both the in and out. Stage Three came soon after. It was the sound of a lawnmower shoved down someone's esophagus.

I called to him, "Grampa, Grampa! You're snoring. You're snoring!"

Nothing.

So, I resorted to the only tactic I had at my disposal. Gramma's Kleenex.

First, I would tear off some tissue, roll it up and stick it into my ear canals to deafen the roar. Second, I would wad up Kleenex after Kleenex and pitch them toward his wide-open mouth.

I'd miss a few times, then, finally, one would drop into the gaping abyss.

It's amazing how a tissue down your throat cures the snores.

That's an ad campaign Kleenex should run.

THE SNORING that kept me up was loud and constant.

If only the clamor had been coming from this delicate creature with her head on my chest, I would have discovered a most elegant way to excise Sydney Nathan from my mind and my life. Because there was no way I was going to be with anyone who made my grandfather's snoring seem pleasant by comparison.

But the sound, instead, was emanating from the room next door, piercing the wood and plaster like X-rays through toilet paper.

Sydney seemed unfazed by the tumult. Which left me in something of a quandary. If I hit the wall or got up to knock on the door, I'd put an end to Sydney's slumber as well our noisy neighbor's, and although misery does indeed love company, misery doesn't like being woken up.

I wasn't prepared at that moment to face the reality of our situation. I couldn't stand another awkward pause or heavy sigh.

Not now. Not here.

Reaching over her body, which I wanted to touch so badly, I grabbed the TV remote, clicked it on, and then with the sound off, flipped through the channels.

Remember I was talking about coming to you live from inside the vagina of the world's hottest pop singer in the year 2094? I was off by a century. About halfway through my tour of the available satellite stations, I came across the Swedish equivalent of "Oprah." Which tonight was broadcasting footage of a woman as she had a pap smear. I actually was watching a live feed originating from inside of a woman's pussy.

I'm not quite sure where we, as a society, can go from here.

25

CHEMICAL DISTRACTION

SURPRISING AS THIS MAY SEEM, I fell asleep watching the show—perhaps the first time that's ever happened with the female anatomy splayed in front of my face.

I guess it's not all that surprising when you think of it because as much as I've enjoyed the benefits of sexual freedom born of their matter-of-fact liberalism, Europeans, especially the farther North and East you go, can do something I once thought impossible.

Make sex so fucking boring.

I'm not talking about the French or the Italians or the Spanish or the Portuguese or the Greeks. The French can make floor tile commercials sexy. The Dutch can broadcast a talk show where the hosts and guests are naked that makes you wish they had their clothes on.

The Vagtastic Voyage program turned out to be less Oprah and more a Scandinavian version of Cable in the Classroom. A show to be recorded and then replayed in sex education classes throughout Sweden.

To me, this is like teaching a baby how to walk by showing the little tot video of the 100m Finals at the Olympics.

Now, it's not like I'm puritanical—God has some pretty thick files on me if you doubt that statement—but judiciousness and moderation go a long way to keeping things engaging and stimulating.

I understand sex education for high school kids—even middle school kids. These are the ones about to dive head-first into turbulent waters.

Although, I racked my brain trying to figure out what, if any, good this program would have done me. Especially when this Sesame Street-like puppet came on the screen and pointed to a cotton swab brushing against something that looked like a rain-soaked old leather football helmet.

Seriously?

You don't need to know anything about bumping the cervix until after you turn pro.

So, what's with Elmo, the Gynecologist? Who is this for? We don't need sex education in *grammar* school. Not because they're too young, but because there already *is* sex education in grammar school.

Class goes something like this:

"Gerrick!"

"What!"

"Betcha don't know what a *pussy* is."

"Pffff. Sure I do."

"What is it?"

"I'm not gonna tell you."

"You don't know. Gerrick don't know what a *pussy* is."

"I do too."

"Then tell us."

"You guys just want me to tell you so *you'll* know what a pussy is."

Sing-song: "Gerrick don't know what a *pussy* is."

I was in fourth grade. I knew what tits were. Oh, did I know. My fourth-grade teacher Mrs. Denslo had a bulletproof bra that got stuck right in my face as she bawled me out in the hallway for doing something or other in her class.

I remember one time, we were learning about grammar and sentence structure. We had studied the subject and verbs extensively and now were working on the predicate.

Mrs. Denslo, I realize now, was a dominatrix at heart.

She was very, very exacting, but never in a shrewish, prim sort of way. That would have made her an Old Maid. And rarely does an Old Maid display the kind of howitzers Denslo was armed with.

No, somebody wore the boots in her family. And it wasn't *Mr.* Denslo.

In her exacting, I-have-need-to-control-you manner, Mrs. Denslo would run exercises from a book, in perfect order, beginning at one side of the room and snaking through the class.

She'd switch left to right, front to back—that was spicing it up for her. But once a pattern was set, it was followed exactly.

I was always amazed when we'd inevitably get to some kid who would look at her blankly, trying to come up with an answer on the spot, like the question was sprung on him. All you had to do was calculate the number of kids in the class, the number of exercises, the order strategy she was using that day, and you would know precisely, without a doubt, which problem you had to answer. And provided you weren't one of the first two or three kids in the pattern, you had plenty of time to come up with your answer—even if you had to ask the kid next to you for help.

I was also mystified how the rest of the kids in my class could sit there and answer seriously. Especially when you had all that time to think of something funny to say. I just don't know how they did it.

Parts of speech, object, subject, gerund, prepositional phrase, on and on. There was comedy to be mined in every single one of them.

So—anxious because I had waited so long, pent up with anticipation —when Mrs. Denslo asked me, "What's 'in the pool' Billy?"

I, of course, answered, "Water."

For which, I got two minutes of Denslo yelling something about "prepositional phrases" at me in the hallway with her big guns aimed right at my face.

I don't think I ever heard a word she said.

This began another round of concern about my ability to become a productive member of society.

My mother and the school's principal worried about my behavior. They were troubled that I was becoming a "problem again." That perhaps, this time, I might have to go somewhere else for help. The never-again-seen kid shrink I had tussled with earlier in my career at Goodwin Elementary, I think, had refused any contact with me. What they didn't understand is that I *wanted* to get in trouble. I *wanted* to be in that hallway with Mrs. Denslo as often as possible.

I wasn't out of control, I was turned on.

I mean, how often does a nine-year-old boy—or any guy for that matter—get some woman's nipples stuck teasingly in his face?

Now, call me prideful, but I couldn't admit I didn't know what a pussy was. And I couldn't very well do what we were instructed daily to do, which was, if you have a question, ask a teacher, even though I was kind of curious how Mrs. Denslo might answer.

She was always using visuals or diagramming something on the board to teach us.

Even now, a small part of me wishes I had asked.

But I was also pressed for time. Gary Farinelli and Donny Broderick were major influences in our school. Public opinion could be swayed one way or the other by a casual comment from them. I had until *maybe* the next recess period to come up with something.

Luckily, it was Friday afternoon. I at least had the weekend.

But Saturday came and went and even late into Sunday, I had no idea what a pussy was, and worse, no idea what to do about it. There was no internet at the time, at least not one a civilian could get on. I had tried the dictionary. That was no help. This huge, supposedly "unabridged" version of our language that could do major brain damage if dropped on you didn't even have words I *knew* existed, words I'd heard uncountable times coming out of the Princess's mouth.

What kind of reference tool is that?

I was in dire straits.

Then it happened.

I don't know how. But it did.

Friends of my parents stopped by for an unexpected visit. The quick social call turned into a couple of beers, then dinner. After dinner, me and their youngest son, who was my age, went on a walk down the street.

It was cool that night. Dark. No moon. The road was lit intermittently by mercury vapor street lights that in this part of my small town were spaced every four or five poles.

Jamie had an older brother. Several years older in fact. I knew if Farinelli and Broderick knew what a pussy was, Jamie had to know.

Still, I couldn't just ask him. Even though he was someone I had played with since I was a little kid, even though he didn't even live in our town, so no one would know, I didn't want to appear stupid or uncool.

So, I turned it around.

"I betcha don't know what a *pussy* is," I said as we passed under the light of one of the street lamps.

"Pffff. Sure I do."

"Then what is it?"

The moment of truth. Would he call my bluff or would he fold?

"It's right here on a girl," he said, grabbing his crotch.

"Yeah. That's right," I said, acknowledging his coolness at knowing something every fourth-grade boy should know.

We turned around and headed back toward my home not long after that. I couldn't suppress a smile that prompted my mother to ask, "What did you do?" when we got back inside the house.

I could hardly sleep.

Monday morning, I waited. I was chomping at the bit. I wanted to say something, wanted to stand on my desk and blurt out loud, "I KNOW WHAT A PUSSY IS!"

But I had to be cool. I had to resist temptation.

Then, after lunch, during recess, Gary Farinelli and Donny Broderick were standing around with a group of other kids. I purposely walked right by them, and when I got close, Gary yelled out, "Gerrick don't know what a *pussy* is."

Everyone laughed, even though I knew half those kids had no fucking clue what a pussy was either.

I stopped and turned around. "Gary..." I said, casually, as if I couldn't give a shit even though I was dying inside. "I told you...I do too know."

"You do not," chimed in Donny.

It was like they had one brain.

Between them.

"Do," I said.

"Do not."

I sighed. "Fine. You want me to tell what one is? I'll tell you what one is." I tried to sound sooooooo put out by the whole thing. "It's right *there* on a girl," I said as I reached out and whacked Gary Farinelli as hard as I could in the balls.

IT WAS SOMETIME LATER, the sky was still dark, that I felt her hand between my legs. I wasn't exactly sure what was happening initially. When you wake up and someone is feeling around down there, your twilight consciousness tells you they must simply be rooting around for their keys.

Now, despite the fact that I have often had to be on a plane at the crack of dawn to some far-off country, I'm not really a morning person.

Someone pours me into a car, spills me out at the terminal curbside. My body instinctively aims itself for the correct gate. I get shuffled to my seat, and then I sit like a vegetable till someone else tells me it's time to leave.

This isn't to say that if you try to negotiate something with me at 8 A.M., you would be any more likely to get a concession out of me than 8

P.M. Because not only am I much more tired in the morning, I'm also substantially more irritable.

But a woman's hand between my legs has, paradoxically, a simultaneous calming and stimulating effect on me.

My eyes tried to focus.

A clock that kept dizzily floating in front of me said: 4:06.

When my murky mind finally stumbled into awareness, and I realized what was happening, I quickly spun my head around.

I would have expected Sydney to be smiling or looking wanton, but instead, when I turned to face her, her expression was serious.

There was an almost unbearable moment of silent communication between us, by means of touch and glances, slight gestures and breathing.

I could hear the conversation in my head. Every bit of it. Finally, after all the unpronounced arguments had been made, I spoke.

"Sydney..."

She shook her head. "Shhhhh."

I stared at her. She nodded at me earnestly. I kissed her on the mouth and ran my hand along her hips and over her stomach. She had an incredible stomach which felt flat and firm and at the same time soft in my hands.

We were speechless again as I feasted on her body and she held my head tight against her. I tasted the skin at the middle of her chest, her nipples, slid up to her neck and then gently teased her mouth with my lips. She reached out and pulled my mouth to hers. She sucked on my lip and let her tongue dance in my mouth, then licked her own lips as she stared at mine.

I felt the tell-tale signs of precum escaping from my cock as I pressed against her body. Between her legs was burning hot and I was dizzy from the sensations and cravings that this closeness caused in me.

Her skin was on fire, and I wanted to be deep inside her, to be as close as a man and woman can get. The tip of my cock played just outside her warm, wetness.

"Billy, you're not wearing anything."

"Is there some lingerie you'd like to see me in?"

She laughed.

"You know what I mean."

"I've only been with Laura the past year. And we've both been tested twice. I'm clean."

"So am I. But that's not the issue."

Now, you must understand that in my Neanderthal way of thinking, all women, everywhere, are on The Pill. In fact, it has been since, well, since, a long time ago that I've been with someone that was not using an oral contraceptive. Sure, I've had sex with lots of women using a condom, but that was for protection against disease.

But with someone I wanted in my life, someone I knew I would be seeing for an extended period of time, I didn't use the same criteria. Because ultimately, truly being with a woman, to me, meant being completely *naked*.

A couple of women I dated found it uncomfortable to be on The Pill. In cases like that, you, of course, do what is best for both of you. But if a woman is using The Pill, and you are both tested and disease-free, I say skin is in.

"I just figured you were...you know..."

"That it is the most male chauvinist pig-headed statement I've heard in..."

"I know. It's horrible. I've got these two sides warring inside of me. The incredibly compassionate, sympathetic vulnerable side, and the idiotic, pig-headed Neanderthal."

I made a bam-bam motion with my hand.

"Well, at least you're honest about it. I guess that says something."

I kissed her softly on the mouth. "It's not gonna get me anywhere to lie about who I am to you."

"No. It's not. You don't have any..."

"You think I do this all the time?"

That made her feel better. And her look returned to one of desire. I got up and stared at her, how beautiful she looked.

"I'm gonna go downstairs," I said, eliciting confusion in her expression. "Hopefully, I'll have some good news for both of us."

"It's four-thirty in the morning."

"I have a pretty good idea where to score some condoms."

I RAN down the stairs as fast as I could. When I got to the lobby, the place was pretty much empty, the lights were low, and the last of the campfire stragglers had run out of conversation—which invariably occurs about an hour or two after the bar closes—and were heading to bed. I knew my best hope was to go back to the wellspring. I found the three hikers in the middle of the dining room. I smiled as I noticed they had moved their cots as close as they could to the group of Blondes that I had pointed out earlier. You have to love a guy for trying. You have to love three guys trying even more.

I had no doubt my Italian friends were awake, even though they were pretending to be sleeping very, very soundly. I knew this because at that moment the women were slipping out of their clothes and getting ready to climb under the covers. Now, as I said, these happened to be Scandinavian women, and Scandinavian women, and Scandinavian men for that matter, don't have the sexual hang-ups most people in the world have, or at least the hang-ups about sex that our Anglo-Romantic culture has.

There wasn't a lot of contrived modesty about these gorgeous, athletic women. There were flashes of this. Long glimpses of that. All delivered quite matter-of-factly.

Six women sharing three cots. They were sleeping together for comfort, to keep warm.

I've been lucky, most of the women I've been with were comfortable with their bodies and open about sex. According to numerous friends of mine, this is not true of all women. Which is a shame.

But you can't even compare the most uninhibited American woman to just about *any* Scandinavian woman. It's like apples and bowling balls.

My first introduction to Nordic females—long before Kate and her lessons on misinterpretation—was on my way to Corsica with my French host, Dominique, Patrice's boyfriend, Loren, and seven other guys. I was still a little nervous about the trip. I wasn't sure how much Loren knew about my fencing lessons with Patrice. We'd be leaving civilization. No phones. No hospitals. No American Express offices (sorry mom). And plenty of cliffs to get pushed over. But then, I was being so American. The French don't kill out of jealousy. Hell, they hardly kill at all. (See *French War Heroes*. Guitard Press, Paris [1952]. Paperback, 4 pages.)

The island of Corsica sits just off the coast of Italy, although it belongs to France (don't say that too loudly when you visit. If a local *happens* to overhear you saying anything kind about the French, just shout "Libre Corse" over and over. You should be fine.).

The ten of us were making our way down from Nancy to Nice by high-speed train where we would catch a ferry to the island, then hike into the mountains. We had two compartments on the train, not sleeping compartments, we couldn't afford those, but two seating compartments. Each one sat six people, so there was more than enough room to relax.

But I had never seen the French countryside, or any countryside other than my own, so I spent most of the time walking around the crowded train, looking out the windows, listening to my fellow travelers.

Young people with Eurail passes were packed into the halls, their faces next to the open windows trying to get some air. I was surprised to find that the French and the Germans and the Italians and the Spaniards were communicating in passable English. There were sidebars in any number of tongues, but English was the only language all of them had in common.

And this is how I came in contact with two dazzling Swedish females.

Swedish girls—who about ten minutes after I met them—asked me if I wanted to go somewhere and "*fuck around*." Now, this was a slightly different approach than the one Patrice had employed, where she tortured me with excruciatingly slow caresses for hours. In contrast, these girls were completely up-front about they wanted and what they were willing to do. It was an interesting comparison and one that I enjoyed being part of. But I have to say, that although cavorting in the baggage compartment with two beautiful and willing Swedish darlings was exquisite as well as athletic, just touching Patrice was far more pleasurable and much more fulfilling.

In fact, I would have to say that the only other time I felt anything close to what I had experienced with Sydney during the flight over was with Patrice in those moments after our fencing lesson.

THE PROBLEM as I saw it for the three Italian hikers was that they weren't being aggressive enough. *Wooing* doesn't work on Swedes. They see it as a waste of time, condescending, and a little too—*je nous se qua*— French for them. It's no secret that what the other person wants is sex. So why not just get to it. Fuck the pre-game warm-up. And just fuck.

I'm not exactly sure what the Scandinavians are in a rush to do post-sex, but whatever it is, they're very anxious to get started.

I sat down on the end of one of the hiker's cots.

"C'mon, wake up."

The Italians did their worst impression of three guys being woken up in the middle of the night.

"I need to ask you something." They glanced at me, only briefly taking their eyes off the fair-skinned maidens slipping out of their clothes. "Do any of you have any condoms?"

I think one of the guys almost choked on his tongue.

I sighed. Amateurs.

"C'mon. You're twenty-three, twenty-four for Christ's sake. You gotta have some somewhere. I'll give you three hundred francs. You'll almost break even on the room."

The kid whose bed I was sitting on sat straight up.

"I'm gonna use them," he said, tilting his head toward the passel of Blondes.

"Really?"

He nodded.

"What are you waiting for?" I whispered loudly. "One of them to hold up a sign with your name on it?"

He lowered his voice even further than mine, hoping I would join his attempt at discretion. "The right moment."

"They're Sweeeedish!" I looked at him in dismay, my body in a full shrug. I figured this was all I needed to say. Apparently not. He had a blank look on his face. "Okay, let me make this clear. These girls don't need a lot of wooing. *Capice?* You're going to say, 'Do you want to have sex?', they're going to say 'Yes' or 'No.' There's not going to be a big discussion."

Still nothing.

"Have you ever *met* Swedish girls before?"

He stared at me.

"Fine," I said. "I'll ask the women."

I walked over to one of the Blondes, who was about twenty-five years old and just pulling off her shirt. She saw me coming and stood there in her underwear, waiting for me. Like I was a ship, and she was the dock.

I glided in and stopped before bumping the pier.

I asked her if she had any condoms. She bent over and reached under the cot, giving me another, just as inviting, view of her body. She opened her bag and produced several different kinds, sizes, and colors of prophylactics, holding them out in her hand in a way that was meant to draw me closer to her.

"Why?" she said, pulling them away when I went to grab them. "Do you want to fuck?"

The Italian who had come close to choking on his tongue nearly coughed up a lung. It was even more entertaining to see the hikers' faces as I declined the proposition.

"I do...appreciate the offer," I said, slowly, my voice deeper. "But I already have someone waiting for me upstairs."

"Oh," she said, looking sadly disappointed, immediately getting a supportive hug from one of the other women, "Well, maybe after you're done with her," she said over the shoulder of her equally stunning friend.

"Maybe," I said.

She smiled and with a graceful recline onto the cot, reminded me again of what I was turning down or, in her mind, postponing.

AS I WALKED BACK UPSTAIRS, feeling even more aroused, not just from having a beautiful young woman hit on me, but because of the approaching destiny I was about to fulfill, I realized something.

I couldn't go through with it. Not tonight. I wanted to, but I had to think about this, and I wasn't in the best shape to do that. Laura was first and foremost in my mind. This would not be a mere dalliance, something I could dismiss as weakness. Even if I never saw Sydney again, I knew this would touch a place in my heart that would no longer be available to anyone else.

You have to understand, it's completely contrary to every fiber of my being, having a naked woman who I connect with in my bed and turning her down. I don't know, call me old-fashioned.

I leaned my head against the door and waited a moment before I went in. Was I being crazy? What if I was supposed to be here? In her bed, tonight.

I took in a deep breath and thought about telling her that I couldn't find a condom. Then I decided I needed to tell her the truth.

I pushed open the door to the suite.

I was only slightly surprised to see Sydney sitting in bed with a thick terry-cloth robe wrapped around her body, shaking her head.

"I'm sorry, Billy. I just couldn't..."

"Neither could I."

I showed her the condom I had gotten from the Swedish girl. And the brass room key stuck through it.

26
POTUS INTERRUPTUS

SYDNEY LAY asleep in the middle of the large, surprisingly comfortable mattress. The robe had come undone, the trapped body heat and the warmth of the nearby fire that I had rekindled making her unconsciously need to bare her skin.

I sat on the floor at the foot of the bed, watching the fire crackle and spark, letting her presence still be felt, but slowly, surely pulling myself back to the important task that had been long ago placed in my hands.

I asked one of the hotel staff to go to my vehicle and get the papers I had brought with me from Geneva.

My mind was not fully on the documents in front of me, but that's the difference between a professional and someone who just does something for the fun of it. Even when you're not into it. Even when you can't focus. Even when there's a half-naked woman in the bed just a few feet away...

...even then, you do what you have to do.

You perform.

It is the tiny, almost unmeasurable distinction between those who win and those who finish after.

I made marks in the margin. And scribbled notes onto a pad with the Auberge Resort logo on the top.

Sometime later, I heard movement, then a sweet series of moans as Sydney crawled down and peeked over the edge of the bed, and over my shoulder.

"Hey."

"Hey."

Meaningless words that held so much meaning.

"I fell asleep again." Her voice was girlish and tired and it cut through me, sending a lovely chill up my side.

"You had a rough day," I said. "I tried not to take it too personally."

"You shouldn't." She touched my face. "Sorry about before." As she said these words, she kissed me sweetly.

A lingering, gentle kiss.

Which only made us both more sorry.

She let out a long sigh. "Did you get a chance to get any sleep?"

I shook my head. "I've been going over job projections of various proposals, which normally would put me to sleep..."

She laughed.

Hearing that enchanting sound, I reached up and kissed her neck. That neck made me want to stop thinking about trade agreements and job losses and industry upheavals. I moved up to her lips. Mmmm. Soft.

And then suddenly, through the kiss—

"Aren't companies gonna just pick up and move to where workers get paid less?"

It took a moment for my brain to switch gears. I pulled away and looked at her. "That's...already happening."

"But," she paused and tried to formulate the thought through her drowsiness. "Won't opening everything up make it worse?"

A man. A woman. A fire. And she was worried about jobs. I got a feeling in my stomach. Like butterflies, only...

I half nodded, half shrugged. "Certain industries will be hurt. Others are going to be helped." I looked into her eyes and couldn't believe I was going to say what I said, which was: "The Europeans give Airbus huge subsidies that undercut Boeing. France limits the number of American television series that can be shown. Things like this cost us hundreds of billions of dollars each year."

"Hundreds of billions?" She was trying to get her head around such a staggering sum.

"At least."

Sydney thought about that for a moment, her forehead creasing up.

"So, what do you tell the person in one of those *certain industries* who loses their job?"

I stared into the fire. "I can't think about what might happen to some person in Peoria."

"How can you not think about it?"

I pulled her down off the bed so that she slid into my arms. She looked up at me, her head resting on my lap. Those eyes. "Because I have to think bigger, think what's best for *everyone*. If I allow myself to worry about one person, I might do nothing. And doing nothing is the worst thing of all. Because things might be worse in twenty years because of this agreement. But they'd be even worse than *that* without it."

I traced her face with my fingers, running them along her jaw and down under her chin, then up toward her hair. She kissed my fingers as they passed over her lips, her eyes searching mine.

"Do you love her?" she said.

I didn't stop caressing her even though her change of subject was again jarring. She had asked me this before. And I had given her the most lame, non-committal answer. I tried to do better this time.

"I love being with her."

"That's not the same."

"No." I said nothing for a moment. "I guess it's not."

Sydney nodded at me. And I stared back at her with a bittersweet feeling in my soul.

Partly to take the heat off of my relationship quandary, partly to learn more about this person I felt connected to but knew so little about, I said, "What about you? I know he didn't ask you properly—" I was something of an expert on improper proposals, but his presumptive bid couldn't be worse than my phantom offer. "—but Brendan seems like a good guy, good family."

"Good looking. Good in bed. Rich. Easy to get along with."

Even with her there in my arms, I was starting to feel jealous.

"Sounds like a loser. So, what's the problem?"

I ran my fingers through her hair.

"I don't know." She closed her eyes as I touched her stomach with my other hand. "Maybe it's that he couldn't get me to do in a year what you got me to do after a cup of coffee and a hot dog."

I reached down her body, moving further to that smoothness between her legs that I could feel through her sheer panties.

"Which I really do appreciate."

She slapped my hand away playfully. Then grabbed my wrist force-fully, letting me go no further.

"Get me on a plane to *Europe*," she said.

I smiled at my mistake.

I was feeling like I wanted to overpower her grasp, that I could have, maybe even should have, but...

"And these other guys?"

"Just guys."

The light from the fire danced in her eyes. Her expression said a thousand things.

She reached up and kissed me on the mouth, again so softly.

I could feel my hand, the one she held by the wrist, straining to touch her. The passion rising in both of us.

This time that extra condom, the one I didn't destroy, would get put to use. This time, the reasons to wait didn't seem as daunting, although there would be consequences. This time it felt natural.

As I went to slide my hand under her panties, there was a knock at the door.

Before I could stop her, before she could stop herself, she got up and answered it.

It was the hotel manager. His face was white. He held in his hand a single piece of paper. A fax. On it was a faded copy of the seal of the President of the United States of America.

He handed it to Sydney.

She handed it to me.

The message was simple.

The words centered on the page.

> *Get back. Now.*
> *—POTUS*

I looked at the hotel manager.

"Is the road open yet?"

"No, *Monsieur*."

He had been pleasant and courteous to me before, but now, his tone was much more deferential.

"Perhaps a few hours after sunup," he added.

"Thank you."

He nodded and closed the door behind him.

Sydney gazed into my eyes. Her lips were still wet from our kissing.

"You need to focus on that, not me."

Our eyes were locked for a long moment. Finally, she moved toward the bed. As she passed, I gently grabbed her wrist.

She looked down at my fingers wrapped around her arm but said nothing.

And I realized something. Something I needed to know. "What were you writing about in your journal when I first saw you?"

She raised her gaze to meet mine. And I could feel her. It made me take in a breath of air.

"That my father died before seeing me look at a man...the way my mother looked at him."

I watched her, unable to speak, as she climbed back into bed, taking the covers with her.

I got back to work.

This is what a professional does.

Even when he wishes, longs to do something—or someone—else.

27

DRIVING MYSELF CRAZY

I WOKE up because of the sunlight radiating onto my face, an orange blaze beyond my eyelids. The papers I'd been working on were spread out on the floor, beside me, underneath me. Except for one sheet that was stuck to my cheek, although I didn't realize it yet in my groggy stupor.

Sydney was standing by the window, admiring the blanket of new fallen snow.

"Isn't it beautiful," she said as she turned toward me.

I gazed at her and at the white background that lay behind her.

Like I've said before, I don't know how many times I have been to picturesque places like this. And in all those times, I've looked outside my window on barely a handful of occasions.

"Yes, it is," I said, only partly talking about the mountains and valleys and the snow because she seemed just as exquisite to me.

"You have a—" She motioned to my face where I found the summary sheet for latest IMF World Economic Outlook report.

I peeled the paper from my skin. "I've been looking for that."

Most people don't wake up pretty. It's not really their fault. Almost no one looks very good after having their face smashed into a pillow for seven or eight hours. It's even worse for those—I am one—who cannot be called a morning person.

Eight o'clock is the crack of dawn for me. Maybe it's that I do my best thinking at night. Maybe it's because I don't drink coffee. Maybe it's because the Princess never used to vacate the fucking bathroom until then at the earliest.

My hair is usually sticking up on end or glued to the side of my head (photos of this phenomenon have been published by not one, but two British tabloids), making me look like some crazed idiot escaped from a lunatic asylum who has somehow been able to afford the down payment and monthly mortgage on a really nice house in Georgetown.

But Sydney looked radiant and lovely, even in the harsh, unflattering sunlight. If I'd been born a woman, I'd have hated this bitch. Her dyed-dark eyelashes didn't have that morning smear about them. And her skin, although not flawless, was inviting to the touch.

Lucky for me, I was born a guy.

She strolled over to the end of the bed, bent down and kissed me softly on the mouth, then reached out and pulled up the edge of the large blanket she had placed over me at some point after I fell asleep on the floor.

"You need a little more rest. You want to get into bed?"

I moaned a 'no' and shook my head. If I moved, I'd wake up.

"Sleep." She pressed her lips against my forehead and in the warmth of that moment, I snuggled deeper under the thick blanket, followed her orders explicitly, and immediately fell back to sleep.

By the time I emerged from underneath the blanket sometime later and managed to get to my feet, Sydney had already left the room. There were traces of fog on the mirror when I finally made my way to the bathroom, so I knew she had taken a shower. I was more than a little disappointed I had missed that. And I told her as much after dragging myself downstairs where I found her sitting by the fire finishing a cup of coffee.

I was hungry, and she pointed me in the direction of food.

Most of the people that had slept in the dining room were up, which was good because that's where they were also serving breakfast.

And even though I was one of the later arrivals, I still had the distinct pleasure of eating my scrambled eggs four inches away from a pair of male feet poking out from underneath a blanket.

After the feet began to stir, I decided to return to where Sydney was enjoying the heat of the fire.

We sat across from each other as we went about the morning rituals of food and coffee and newspapers. There was only an initial moment of awkwardness, and it passed as quickly as she passed me the *European*. In fact, I felt a deeper closeness to her because we hadn't slept together.

"Did you get a good night's sleep?"

I studied her face to see if she was kidding, but she wasn't.

"You mean, after we tortured each other? Or after I decided whose job to kill?"

"Somebody's a little grumpy this morning," she said, raising an eyebrow at me.

"A little."

I get that way whenever I have to turn down having sex with a beautiful woman in order to spend time wiping out entire sectors of the American economy.

I needed a muffin.

THIS HAD BEEN the worst storm in almost a hundred years, but it had passed more quickly and farther to the north than predicted, and word came from the manager that the road was reopening a little after 8:30 in the morning.

He said that he would make sure that my vehicle was waiting out front.

Sydney changed her mind and now wanted to come with me. She no longer wanted to stay here alone. And besides, she'd have a much easier time getting a flight home from Geneva.

I was just glad for the company. And for the chance to spend more time with her.

We gathered up what little we had and climbed into the rented 4x4.

There was already a line to get down the mountain by the time they actually started letting cars through, which was closer to nine o'clock.

I, of course, got stuck behind the only idiot in Europe who had never driven on a mountain road before. This crankshaft felt extremely uncomfortable about going around any blind corner. So, what does he do? Drift toward the other side of the road so he could get a better look.

I swear, he nearly caused four carloads of people to fly off the edge of the cliff.

He's not only a menace to me and every other driver, but he's also got an "I'm Going to Euro-Disneyland" bumper sticker. To Europhiles and Francophiles, E.D. is high on the list of mankind's horrors.

The smiling mouse only adds to my misery.

I have been diagnosed with a genetic disorder. According to authorities, I have a defective gene in my DNA. It is the one that controls what happens when homo sapiens slide behind the wheel of a car. I don't act like an asshole on purpose, I really don't. And someday, God willing, scientists will have a cure. But until that day, automotive-induced animosity continues to shoot out of me like lava from Mt. Vesuvius.

Somewhere in my brain, the switches overheat.

And for a brief moment, as I navigate city streets and highways alike, I become my father.

According to D.C. Metro cops, I have on occasion gone almost four blocks without commenting on some idiot's driving.

But I'm usually not that good.

It's one of the reasons since joining the government, even more than security, they give me a driver.

This weakness in my character is somewhat counterbalanced by other mitigating factors. I'm now and again charming. I can tell a good story. And I'm able to remain extremely calm under the most adverse conditions. If there is danger, or if someone is in need of help, if a cool head is required, I rise to the occasion and remain focused no matter what is going on around me.

It's only when the sky is clear and the sun is shining and everything is hunky-dory that I get completely yanked by idiots bent on ruining my beautiful day because a related gene of their own makes it impossible for them to make a left-hand turn without FAA clearance and/or a cattle prod up their ass.

Or worse, they try a left-hand turn in a place clearly marked NO LEFT TURN while six dozen cars wait behind them, all but one of them in front of me, and the guy *behind me* is tailgating.

This is the same gene suspected to influence a person's ability to operate a shopping cart, causing them to park the cart wherever and whenever their little brains decide, usually blocking the end of an aisle while they spend ten minutes checking out the nutritional label on a pack of Ring Dings.

It's artery-clogging crap that will kill you! Does it really matter that it's low in fucking sodium?

"I'm seeing a whole new side of you," Sydney says as I yell at the driver in front of me for the twentieth time.

"Not my best side. Forgive me. He's an idiot."

"Yes, you've said that. Repeatedly." She grips the handle on the door a little tighter. "I'd love to see you stuck in gridlock."

"Oh, I handle that much better." She looks at me as if she doesn't believe me. "There's usually a lot more cops around."

"I see." She looks out the window for a long moment. "I'm not going to beat myself up over this."

"Don't take it personally. I can be a somewhat...difficult driver."

She blinks her eyes several times as if she can't believe I'm as stupid as I obviously seem to be.

"I had a really wonderful time last night."

"Oh, that. Me, too."

I put my hand on her leg. It feels great even through the thick clothing that she's wearing to keep herself warm.

"You can't do that, baby," she says softly, stopping my hand.

"Mmmmm, I like that."

"Yes, I like it, too, and that's why you can't do that."

"I wasn't talking about my hand on your leg, although I like that, too. I was talking about you calling me 'baby.'" I remove my hand and put it back on the wheel. "That's the second time you've called me that."

She looks at me strangely. Actually, her gaze is distant, as if she's replaying some memory, maybe one long in the past, searching for something. Her eyes refocus, and the connection to me is re-established.

"I've never called anyone that before," she says.

"I like it even better then."

She smiles, her eyes twinkling. I'm happy in this moment. Very happy.

"I want you..."

"Mmmmmm. Mmm-hmph."

"—to go back to your girlfriend and work this out."

"What?"

She repeats the sentence for me—as if I needed that.

"Am I not being clear here?" I motion between us with my hand.

"You're being clear, baby," she says with her eyebrow raised again.

"Good."

"To me," she adds with perfect timing. "I don't believe you're being clear to her."

I sigh heavily.

"She sounds darling to me. I just think you should really think about this before you do anything stupid."

"I have been thinking a lot about this."

"Good. That's a start."

She doesn't say another word, and I get the feeling she hopes I won't either for a while.

I GOT sick of being stuck in a traffic jam in the middle of the Alps, and I pulled off onto a side road, following a Mercedes that looked like it knew where it was going.

What ended up happening is that I accompanied this guy into the one place where Hell *had* frozen over.

The road was one lane in parts, curvy, with huge ravines off to the side. I was feeling more fear here than I had felt coming up the mountain, facing near whiteout conditions.

I had to affect an air of composure, so I didn't alarm Sydney any more than she already was. She didn't complain, didn't scream or cry. She simply made these tiny little noises whenever it seemed we'd be plunging to our deaths any second.

I wanted to pat her leg, but I didn't dare take my hand off the wheel.

Only one other time have I ever been this scared. It was also on French soil, in a car, on a mountain road.

I had been hiking in the mountains with Dominique, Loren, and my other French mates on Corsica for a little more than a week. It had been a thrilling and enlightening seven days so far. We had all bonded. I had not been pushed over one cliff.

We had been following what is called the GR-20, the *Grandes Randonnées* from Calenzana overlooking the port town of Calvi in the north down toward the lower half of the island.

Now, we were hitting the first sign of civilization in nine days. We had left the GR midway through the two-hundred-kilometer trail because I needed to catch a plane in Ajaccio on the western coast, birthplace of that somewhat short guy with the first known case of Napoleonic Complex.

More importantly, I needed a shower.

We had agreed to change our mode of transport from our feet to our thumbs for this part of the journey. If we hiked the rest of the way to the ocean, I would miss my flight to Paris. After the little side trip to the sandy beaches of Ajaccio, the others would return to the GR and continue southeast to Conca, near Porto-Vecchio then up the coast to Bastia where they would catch a ferry back across the Mediterranean to Nice.

I wanted to stay with them and complete the trip, but I was looking forward to my three-day stopover in the City of Lights before I had to head home.

So, the ten of us split into pairs to make it easier to hitch a ride down the mountain. Since I needed to make the plane, they let me and Dominique go with the first person who stopped.

This seemed like a good idea. That was, until the first person actually pulled over to the side of the narrow road and offered us a lift.

The guy, it appeared to me, didn't really want to give us a ride, didn't seem happy about it, anyway. Perhaps it was terms of his release from prison to perform community service which included picking up hitchhikers.

For whatever reason, he stopped.

He was driving what the French call a truck, but what any American would swear was a pizza delivery vehicle or the older sibling of those things meter maids tool around in.

As it turned out, he was going halfway to our destination, which was really great. We'd have no problem getting into the city in time—that is, if we weren't kidnapped and tortured first. It's not like he looked dangerous. It's just that he didn't look safe.

Dominique and I said our goodbyes to our travel companions (this was ostensibly because it was possible that not all would get to the meeting place before I had to leave, but I think it was really because everyone else feared we'd never be seen again), then we jumped into the truck...and prayed.

Before I could say, *merci beaucoup*, our psychotic chauffeur proceeded to stomp on the accelerator and careen down the curvy mountain road in his French tuna can.

I was the luckier of the two. I, at least, was strapped into the front seat. Sure, I had to tie my seatbelt together into a bow—it was missing one of the clasps—but I was fastened to something. Dominique, to his misfortune, was in the back of the...er...truck. No seat, no safety belt, only debris and heavy tools sliding around and smacking into him as we cornered at top speed.

I don't think I was able to utter a word for an hour.

I might have made *noises*, but Dominique can't confirm that.

We'd swerve around a bend, crossing over the—well, crossing over no line, since there wasn't room for one—but clearly into the space set aside for cars coming the other way.

Our good Samaritan would scream French epithets and honk his horn as if the *other* driver was in the wrong for being on the right side of the road.

I was riding with the Napoleonic version of my father.

They had these little *things* running all along the edge of the road, maybe ten centimeters high. They looked something like a miniature fence.

"What are those?"

"Guardrail."

"Guardrails?"

"Oui, to keep from falling over."

"Over the cliff?"

He nodded.

The only thing these things were going to do is blow out your tires just seconds before you plunge five hundred meters to your death.

"What kind of car is that supposed to stop?"

"Rabbit."

"A VW Rabbit?" The Volkswagen Rabbit—née Golf—was small. But not that small. "That wouldn't stop a bicycle."

"No, no. Not car. Bunny."

Apparently, in Corsica, they don't give a shit about people, but the bunny rabbits...

Every once in a while, I'd be staring over the edge of one of those five-hundred-meter drops, thinking I hope to God this guy isn't using drugs, alcohol, or French tires. He seemed to take pleasure in our terror, encouraged it by pointing out sights on the way.

But then, there are no sights in the mountains of Corsica, or rather, it's all sights. The only difference is that the picturesque vistas he chose to highlight almost invariably included the burned-out, abandoned debris of past car wrecks.

The Corsicans have an unusual sense of humor.

"Do you know where you're going?" These were the first words Sydney had spoken in some time.

"Why do you say that?" I tried not to sound defensive.

"You don't look very sure of yourself. Believe me, it's rare. I notice the difference."

"I'll take that as a compliment."

"Take it any way you want, as long as it takes me to an airport."

"You're serious about flying home right away."

"I should have been home yesterday."

I was looking at the road, which had become less dangerous. Flatter. Not as winding. "It's supposed to be this way...I think."

"That makes me feel much better. I thought you were an expert on these roads."

"What makes you say *that*?"

"The skill with which you dispense advice to other motorists."

"That's funny."

"Not really," she said. Then suddenly, she pointed forward. "Watch out!"

I turned around just in time to see a huge snow drift blocking the lane, formed by a mini-avalanche that appeared to have taken place only moments before. Two cars had already crashed into the embankment. One of them a French car, so, of course, the driver and the snow bank took most of the punishment.

Once past the danger, I pulled my "American" car (the Ford was made in Germany or Spain or Khartoum) over to the side of the road. I pretended not to be surprised by the frozen obstacle that had appeared out of nowhere, even though my heart was racing about two hundred beats a minute. I wasn't trying to show off in front of Sydney—look how cool I am under pressure—no, I realized from the tone of her warning that she had gotten a major scare. I didn't want her to feel any worse.

I squeezed her leg, just above the knee—God, she felt good—then reached for the map and tried to make sense of it. There had been a slight detour about twenty kilometers back. It wasn't well-marked.

I lowered the map and saw the disabled cars in the rearview mirror.

"I'm gonna go make sure those people are okay."

She nodded at me. "You're lost, aren't you?"

"Not really. Sort of. Just a little. Maybe they'll have a better idea where we are."

"That would be good."

So, I went over to the crumpled cars and discovered that the occupants were okay. I didn't need to take a pulse or check a pupil to know this because the drivers were having a heartfelt discussion over whose fault it was. Decibel level: 93. I decided to come from the point of view that it was a signage problem. Clearly, a lack of government oversight had led to their current predicament.

"The French!" agreed the Italian, which caused the German from the other vehicle to nod his head. Yes, indeed, the French were idiots when it came to cars and driving.

Which is the secret to all successful international negotiations. Blame someone not at the table.

"Do either of you know the way to Switzerland?"

The German pondered for a moment and said, "I think this is the road to Austria."

The Italian threw up his arms and started shaking his head, "No, no, no, no. This is the road. I have been here a thousand times. You," he said to me, "you drive until you reach another road, a big road, like this, then you take that straight into Ginevra."

The German shrugged. "All I know is this is the road to Austria. I do not know of this other road."

I watched as the Italian began to argue with the German. Well, actually, the Italian argued. The German, he just stood completely still, like he was thinking, *who was it licking der Fuhrer's boots in WWII?*

I think it was Italy.

It takes two to Tango. But it only takes one Italian to argue.

I decided to concern myself with the problem at hand. What to do and which way to go. Switzerland was in the direction the Italian had pointed. The question was could you get there from here in a car?

I went to school with these twins, Doug and Dan Dawson. They lived next door to school, right at the entrance to the parking lot at the end of the street. In fact, almost all of my friends during my Goodwin Elementary years lived within walking distance of school, which was lucky, since my house was six miles away from school and most of the kids I knew. So, whenever I wanted to see my friends, all I'd have to do was get in trouble with the Principal, be required to serve a thirty-minute detention after school, which meant I'd miss the bus, which meant I'd have at least three hours till my mom got home from work, since my grandmother, who as we know had a license, would not drive to pick me up.

I'd leave detention and visit my friends.

It was quite an ingenious plan if I do say so.

My best friend at that time, Ben, the one who called me to tell me of Krissy's suicide, lived right behind the school. During recess, sometimes we'd run through the thin line of trees if Gunter's mom wasn't watching, only she wasn't Gunter's mom then, at least not to us, she was just Mrs. Gerring, Nazi Recess Monitor.

This was a double bonus. Good lunch, snacks, a little TV, and if we could manage to get caught coming back onto school grounds by Frau Gerring, I'd get a detention—setting up my afternoon. All rolled into one simple step across the property line.

I had never seen twins before meeting the Dawsons.

Of course, I was only five when I first shared a classroom with them. I thought it was weird and cool all at the same time. As I got older and realized twins were not as unusual as I once believed, it was still more than a little strange to contemplate two separate humans forming out of one fertilized egg. I like having two brothers and a sister. No kid should be without a sibling. Sorry, Gunter. But I did thoroughly enjoy my four-plus years as an only child. I couldn't imagine what it would be like for there to be another me.

Twins, by their nature, are odd.

Most people couldn't tell Doug and Dan apart.

They were both tall and lanky, both were good athletes. They wore matching clothes, which annoyed me more than the fact that they started out looking alike. Supposedly, this is cute. It is not cute. It's proof *Your Mother Dresses You.*

Listen, most of the time, mothers control the wardrobes of their offspring, but you can usually *pretend* that's not the case. There's no pretending with matching outfits.

I now understand this dress-the-same-policy had more to do with managing human nature than being cute. If Doug and Dan got to pick out their own clothes, no matter who was wearing what, the other one would want it that day.

I *guarantee* it.

I had known Doug and Dan since Kindergarten, so it wasn't difficult for me to distinguish between them, no matter what they were wearing. It was all in their eyes.

Dan's were a bit more vacant than Doug's.

We ran track together in high school. Doug was great in the high jump, Dan in the long jump, both ran the mile and would often come in one right behind the other.

Cute, huh?

Our town didn't have a track, so all of our meets had to be at other schools. We'd climb in the bus and head out, week after week. There was never a home-field advantage for us. Most schools shipped their athletes around in old yellow school buses. Not our town. The owner of the bus company lived in town and more often than not, he'd send a tricked-out Greyhound-type coach for us to use.

Several times during our travels to other schools, the driver wouldn't have a clue how to get there. None whatsoever. The older kids would have to struggle to remember how we reached the location the year before.

Driving to one meet, up in Avon, one of our main rivals, we were completely and hopelessly lost. We came to a "T" in the road. We had three choices, turn left, turn right, or turn around.

We brought Doug and Dan up to the front and asked them which way they thought we should go. Both had been on the team the previous year, and they shared the same brain practically. (Like I said, it seemed Doug got to keep the brain more often than Dan.)

Doug looked both ways and at the blank yellow road sign straight ahead that basically said, don't come this way.

"I don't know. It doesn't look familiar," he said after pondering for a moment.

Dan piped in, "Sure, it does. It's to the right. I remember."

"To the right?" asked Doug. "Well, maybe it's to the right, but I don't know."

"Well, I do. We have to go to the right," Dan told the rest of us. Then to the driver, "Turn right."

"Yeah, I remember now," Doug finally agreed. "Turn right."

We turned left. Found the school a half mile down the road.

So as the Italian—having given up on the German—passionately tried to convince *me* that he, and he alone, knew the way, I got back into the rented 4x4 and turned the vehicle around.

Sydney watched me as I started heading back the way we came. "What are you doing?"

"Trying to get to Switzerland before Christmas."

"No, no, no, thata way," screamed the Italian as we passed him.

The words were muffled by the wonderful and very generous sound-proofing in the Ford.

"Didn't he just—"

I shook my head at Sydney.

Sometimes you just gotta know who *not* to trust.

ABOUT FIVE MINUTES LATER, Sydney turns to me. "I've got to do something about Flora."

"Again with the cat?" I'm still a little grumpy.

"She'll die."

"It should've done that a long time ago."

"Maybe," she says, agreeing. "But it's in my apartment, and if it dies there, it's gonna smell."

"From what I understand, it already does."

"You know, you're not a very nice man."

"I'm a bad man, remember? That's why you like me."

"Oh, is that what you think?"

I nod. "First, I didn't get to sleep with you—I understand why we didn't, it was a mutual decision, but it's still, you know, a little irritating. Second, if we were talking about a baby kitten or even a cat on its ninth life, okay. Pets are wonderful, but this thing is on its hundred and ninth existence. It must be killed."

"You really are irritated."

"I am. Not at you, just the—" I motion at her body.

"Does that thing work out here?"

I wonder what she's talking about until I see her pointing at my cell phone.

"I doubt it." We are in the middle of nowhere.

Her shoulders drop.

"Why, you gonna call my mother and tell her what kind of man I am? She already knows."

"I wanna call my neighbor and try to save this cat."

I slide her the small briefcase-sized combination radio wave/satellite phone.

"When they got my papers, I had them charge it."

She looks at it for a moment. It's somewhat strange in appearance when the antenna is extended. It looks like my phone has a hard-on.

"It's like an X-rated spy phone."

"It gets a little excited around beautiful women."

I get a half-cross/half-flattered look from her. "I just punch in the number?"

I nod. "Call anywhere, from anywhere," I say, sounding like an ad for the thing.

She punches the keypad and waits.

After a moment: "Chip, it's Sydney..."

"You have a neighbor named *Chip*?"

"Shhhhh." She waves for me to stop. "I know, I'm sorry. I didn't mean to scare you...I didn't realize the time. Yeah...Ah, well, I'm in France...It's a long story...Listen, I need you to give Flora her shots...I know. They're little needles." She listens for a moment. "I'll make it up to you..."

I raise an eyebrow. "Make it up to him?"

She eyes me. "I should be back, I don't know..." she glances at me for help.

"Maybe three days."

"Probably a day...I really appreciate it. You still have the key, right? Perfect...Okay...I'll see you when I get back. Thanks, Chip...Bye."

She hangs up the phone and slides it back toward me.

"So...Chip, the neighbor, has a key to your apartment?"

"Yeah," she says, shrugging.

"Really."

She stares at me for a moment. "It makes it much easier when he wants to come over and slip into my bed in the middle of the night. I don't have to get up."

I make a little grunting noise. "That's funny."

"You're jealous."

"I have no right to be jealous."

"But you are."

I don't answer.

A very sly little smile comes to her face. "Chip's just a friend."

"Well, let me know when there's an opening in your building. I'd like to be your friend, too."

"I don't think you'd have to wait for an opening."

"You know, Chip's gonna get the boot. Right after Flora."

"Oooww, you are jealous."

28

THE REASONS I SHOULDN'T BE A PARENT ARE APPARENT

OKAY, do you wanna know how Houdini did the trick?

Simple. The Italian was driving a French car, neutering his credibility right off the bat, *and* he was way too sure he was right. The well-dressed German in the very nice Mercedes smelled like a Dead concert. Perhaps he knew how to get home, but he was too stoned to know much else.

So, the choice was easy. None of the above.

It's a quirk of humanity that the more a person wants you to believe they know what they're talking about, the more I know they have no fucking clue what they're talking about.

And as far as being high, well, I know *that's* really good for the brain.

I never really did drugs. They never held any affinity for me. Maybe, the truth is, I don't hold any affinity for them.

There was this one summer when everyone in town was out of school and those already graduated returned for three months of partying.

I was hitting one of these parties with a bunch of people that I knew from the grade above mine. I wasn't best friends with any of them, but I liked to hang out and interact with a lot of different cliques. It made it easier whenever I needed to get out of the house but didn't want to go see my close friends. At these times I preferred people who wouldn't notice something was bothering me, or maybe ones who weren't concerned enough to ask me about it.

Anyway, I was mingling, making the rounds. I'd certainly had enough to drink to be impaired and fuzzy when I was offered marijuana in the form of a bong.

A big, huge purple glass bong with white wine in the bottom instead of water.

Chablis, I believe. Vintage unknown.

I have since learned that I am unable whatsoever to smoke pot because, bluntly, I get completely and utterly paranoid. Now, paranoia is a perfectly wonderful thing in its time and place. A certain amount of obsessive suspicion goes a long way to ensuring safety, success, and personal fulfillment. But when you start thinking people are talking about you, concealing information from you, and plotting against you when they are clearly—to any sound mind—doing nothing of the kind, paranoia is no longer your friend.

This one night, this evening of reefer madness, I watched three guys I knew as they schemed a secret plan. Something big. Every time I looked over at them, they were looking at me. I, of course, thought they must be talking about me. (It didn't occur to me they were looking at me because I kept *staring* at them.)

So, when they slipped out of the party early and went to their cars, I made my exit as well.

But I couldn't let them see me. I had to observe without being observed. They went out the kitchen door, the main door for this house. I went out the front door, the formal entrance. While they strolled pleasantly down the asphalt driveway, I crawled on my belly across the grass like a commando toward my car and slithered in the passenger side door so as not to arouse any suspicion.

When they drove off, I followed behind them keeping my head low —*very* low—below the level of the dash, lifting it now and then so I might have some idea where I was going.

It wasn't easy. I was driving with my lights off.

They were not going to see me.

They were not going to catch me spying on them.

After about five minutes of tailing the suspects, they suddenly pulled over to the side of the road.

Something was happening.

I drove past their car at a slow rate of speed, my head again down below the steering wheel. But I couldn't see anything because, like I said, my head was basically under the dash.

As I lifted my head a bit to glance in my rearview mirror, I saw the car had pulled back out. They came right up behind me and flashed their lights on and off.

I couldn't panic. I thought, maybe they're flashing me because my lights are off. But I was too smart for them. I turned on my lights and kept driving without looking.

Finally, they pulled up next to my car, yelling for me to stop. They got out of the four-door sedan and walked up to my window.

I tried to be really casual about the whole thing. I said, "Hey guys."

They asked me what I was doing. I looked at them blankly.

"*Why* are you following us?"

"Me?"

"You followed us out of the party."

I was so incredibly stoned I had no idea how they concluded it was me following them this whole time. Because I had successfully kept myself out of sight, I was sure. I was, of course, surrounded by an entire car. My car. A car that everyone knew was mine.

At the time, that didn't seem all that significant. These guys were *good*.

"Go back to the party before you get hurt."

Now I was really curious.

"Hurt?"

"You know how many people have accidents on this road. It's hard enough to drive it sober."

"While actually looking," said another.

Now, I thought these guys were making a big deal over this. I wasn't that drunk. I told them as much.

"Maybe not, but you are stoned."

"I resent that." Only I didn't say it that clearly. I think I showered one of them with saliva.

"Go back to the party."

"You just told me it was too dangerous to drive cause I was stoned." More showers, changing to rain.

"Fine. Gimme your keys," said one of them.

My mental capacity diminished, I was beaten. "No, no. I'll go back on my own."

Bested, I had nothing to lose. So I asked them. "What were you guys doing anyway?" They glanced at each other. "I thought maybe you were going to do something to me."

"Billy, if we wanted to do something to you, why would we have left the party? You were *at* the party."

I hadn't thought of this.

"Oh."

"You really wanna know?"

I nodded.

"Can you keep your mouth shut?"

I locked my lips and threw away the key.

"Fine. We're going to all piss in a jar and put it on the front steps of Mr. Ognos's house."

I giggled. "That's pretty funny."

Orin Ognos was a biology teacher at our school. His claim to fame, besides being a scientifically proven geek, was that he was President of the Connecticut Chapter of Zero Population Growth. ZPG is this really cool organization, which extols the belief that couples should have two and only two children. Mr. Ognos and his charges preached the gospel of curtailing overpopulation way before its time. So, when his wife got pregnant with their second child, snip-snip went the vasectomy scissors. Orin Ognos didn't even miss a beat, flew to a national conference thirty minutes after leaving the doctor's office.

And he kept on preaching for eight more months, until he was forced to resign in disgrace.

When his wife had *twins*.

"Now...go back to the party," one of the guys said.

"And don't move," said another.

"Which do you want me to do?"

The first guy looked at me, wanted to hit me, only didn't when he realized I wasn't making fun of him. I was just whacked. "Go to the party, *then* don't move!"

"Okay."

I turned the car around and headed back to the party where I stayed until morning because I was too stoned to drive.

It was completely humiliating. I mean, here I was driving down the street thinking no one could possibly have any idea who I am.

Why?

Because *I* couldn't see *them*.

It was one of my most dim-witted moments.

Even if they had been planning some horrible deed against me, it's hard to imagine that I could have ended up more humiliated than by what I did playing Stoned Commando.

Luckily, I had the presence to publicize the story myself before they could report it to anybody.

But I did keep my word. When it came to the part about what they were doing, I simply said, "They didn't tell me."

That was pretty much the last time I smoked pot, not counting the times subsequently that I would toke but not inhale, just so I wouldn't look like a complete pussy.

I did have one other pot scare.

One day I was coming home from school, I think I had just finished basketball practice—I was fifteen or sixteen, and the Princess brought me downstairs to take a look at something in his greenhouse. I hated that fucking greenhouse. Not only because I had to be in an enclosed room—an overly hot one—with my father alone, which meant that I had to search for something to speak to him about (plants being the most obvious topic of conversation happened to be my least favorite), it usually meant some sort of physical labor where I had to stick my hand in dirt and worms and transplant seedlings from small pots to larger pots. Or some other such horror.

I understand people like to "garden," and I respect that. But, like coffee, my father had a knack for making me dislike things.

I was especially concerned this particular day because the Princess was very excited about something. Whenever my father got excited about something, it usually meant one of two things: my mother was gonna get pissed off, or I was gonna be put to work.

Much to my surprise, it was option number three.

My father showed me a plant that I had never seen before and asked me if I knew what it was. I had a combat flashback to the Gary Farinelli/Donny Broderick pussy quiz. From the tone of my father's voice and the absolutely giddy look on his face, I had the feeling that even if I could identify the plant, I shouldn't admit to it.

"I—I have no idea."

He looked at me with a slight twinkle in his eye and said in an excited whisper, "It's *marijuana*."

My instinctual response was to get defensive.

I hate being caught doing something wrong. But what I really hate is being caught doing something wrong that I didn't even do.

Then reason returned an instant later.

I hated gardening.

Hated it.

Everyone knew that. The Princess never could have convinced my mom otherwise. It was clearly not *mine*.

Then it hit me.

Absolute terror surged through my body. At any moment my father was going to ask me to *smoke a joint with him!*

I prepared myself.

If he fired up a "fatty," I was going to bolt out that back door faster than a turkey the night before Thanksgiving.

I'm not going to get into the rest of the conversation because no one would believe me anyway.

There is just certain information in life that is better left unknown.

Period.

Even if you find secret confessions remotely interesting, there are just some...where there is no proper response you could give that doesn't make you sound like an idiot.

A girlfriend's father once took me out to lunch after I had been dating his daughter for a while. He said he wanted to get to know the man that was interested in his daughter. Read: *I wanna check out the asshole trying to poke my little girl.*

We had a wonderful lunch. We got along famously. We were smoking cigars and sipping cognac. I hate cigars. I detest cognac. But I'm a trooper.

Then this man put his arm around me and—I guess feeling a kinship to me in our moment of male bonding—decided to tell me about every single one of his extramarital affairs that he's had over the years. *Every* one.

I don't think you can truly understand the horror of having the father of your girlfriend telling you how he once boned the hostess that seated us.

THERE ARE two ancillary reasons for my writing all this down.

So I can look back on it and remember the kinds of stupid things I'm never, ever, ever, ever to share with my daughter's suitor.

And what it is I'm supposed to be forbidding my children to do.

In the latter case, I have little hope that this will have any effect on them.

But this might give me a chance to show my kids, when I can no longer remember myself, that their dad hasn't always been the uptight asshole who wishes to kill all joy and pleasure and anything remotely fun —that now stands before them screaming, "For the last time, no, you can not take the car tonight!"

"Yes! What is it!?"

It wasn't the friendly voice of a good son happy to hear from her that greeted my mother's call. I was in the presence of a beautiful woman, driving through some of the most magnificent landscapes and topography in all the world and I was in a really shitty mood.

I was letting down my country. I was in the process of fucking up my relationship. And I was lost again.

I take some solace in knowing that the Italian was wrong. We would have ended up in Austria as the German had said. But when at last, I found the right way to Geneva, the roads were still being cleared of snow. So, I thought I might *again* be able to bypass the long line of cars waiting for the work to be done by taking one of the unplowed side roads.

That's the trouble with having a 4x4: you actually think you know how to use one.

My mom was taken aback by my tone. And even as she tried to let me go, telling me I could just call her later, this only made me more uptight. Guilt does that. You feel bad that you're being a shit so you become more of a shit to somehow make up for it.

Makes sense to me.

"Mom, you have to understand, I'm under a helluva lot of pressure here. I know it doesn't compare with what you're going through. But I need to focus right now. I'll be home in a few days. We'll have all the time in the world to talk."

"You know," my mom said, "if I was on vacation, I would sound a lot happier, Mister."

My mother thinks anytime someone gets on a plane they're going on vacation.

"I'm not on vacation."

"It's Europe, then Hawaii. I wish I had your life."

So, my mother is partially correct.

In exactly three days, I was meeting up with six other couples in

Hawaii. All the women were friends of Laura's from college. I knew one, a cute lawyer from New York named Hanna. I've seen pictures of the rest, they all look similar. Slender, pretty, brilliant (until you get them all in the same room). The guys, I didn't know anything about them. Except that all of them were *husbands*. I wasn't looking forward to this. Paradise, yes. Five pairs of newlyweds, no. I even thought about trying to get my family to have a vacation at the same time, so I'd be able to beg out of this one. At least then, I'd be annoyed by people I could yell at.

Only that thought lasted about two seconds. There have only been two genuine vacations my family has ever taken. Day trips were difficult enough (see, The Big "E"/Saab redesign above). I don't think we ever went to the same place twice. I don't think anyone would let us.

The last time we tried—a trip to the Florida Keys—planning had gone on for months. Dates had to be agreed upon, accommodations made. Dates had to be changed. First, because Dean couldn't get away one week, then because I had a trade conference in Argentina, then finally, because the Princess would only go if we coincided the trip with the annual Flower Festival in Miami.

Did I mention I hate African Violets?

Then there was the fighting over who would have to sleep with the Princess. Now normally, you would think that would mean my mother, but that was the least likely scenario, unless of course, we wanted dad to land, *oow* and *ahh* over some fucking chrysanthemums, talk to a bunch of drunk flower growers, come back to the room, wait four minutes, get into a fight with mom and get on a plane and head home.

Without careful preparation and the utmost precautions, that would be my father's trip to Paradise.

The Princess isn't the Princess for nothing. Things need to be just right, special considerations must be made.

One of the sons will get stuck with Dad.

You see—and this might come as a surprise—the Princess can be a little difficult sometimes. Besides the fact that it took my father forever to get ready, that he'd occupy the bathroom so none of *us* could get ready, then blame us for taking so Goddamn long, he could take nearly an hour to just get a fucking car seat right. I don't mean car seat like a *baby* car seat. That would at least make sense, but there are no grandchildren as of yet, thus no babies (something my mother is not very happy about).

No, I'm talking about the positioning of the *driver's* seat.

The Princess, knowing that his ass was going to be stuck in a car, then a plane, then a rental car (this was the worst, and most painful, not just for his ass but for all of us) would spend sixty to ninety minutes positioning this seat "pad" made out of a million wooden balls that looked, more than anything, like some contrivance a retired mathematician might fashion out of old Abacuses to calculate his gas mileage. Or perhaps the as-yet-undiscovered device the Egyptians used to move giant limestone slabs across the desert to build the pyramids.

This contraption was somehow supposed to be more comfortable than the fabric seat that came with the car. How, exactly, I really don't know, just another one of the mysteries of the universe surrounding my father and locked inside his brain.

Years later, I tried to sit in one of those seat covers to see if it could be even remotely comfortable. It was not. All I got for my trouble were about six hundred tiny round bruises on my back. Of course, I didn't notice these welts—couldn't see them. They were brought to my attention by this incredibly beautiful, incredibly intelligent, incredibly eager woman that I was having my second date with, a date which started in a little nothing of an Italian restaurant, and somehow ended in the penthouse suite of the Waldorf Astoria on top of a sheet of plastic that she had draped over the bed so that we could play a sort of Naked Baby Oil Twister.

That was the plan, right up to the moment she screamed, "What the hell is on your back?"

"What the hell is on my back?"

"That's what I'm asking."

"Well, how the hell do I know?"

"Look at it. Look at your back. Oh my, God!!!"

"What about my back? Jesus Christ, what's wrong with it?"

I am not Linda Blair. I'm not able to throw up pea soup on command nor twist my head completely around. And the mirrors that seemed to be just about everywhere in this elegant suite helped absolutely, positively, not at all. My date finally had to videotape me and play it back in order for me to see what I looked like.

And as the realization hit me that she had *brought* a Sony Handycam with her on our date, and a plastic sheet and baby oil *and* a Twister spinner, I knew that because of these ugly welts—well, actually, because the hotel manager was pounding on our door eager to know what all the screaming was about—I was going to miss out on a very, very interesting evening.

By the way, you don't even want to know what happened on that trip to the Florida Keys.

I HATE BEING cool to my mother, hate being this son who is always away and rarely in her life. But it seems to happen anyway.

Making it worse, I was acting like an asshole in front of Sydney. Not that it would be okay to mistreat my mom if Sydney weren't here. I was just earning extra bonus asshole points.

"Well, call me when you have time to talk," my mom said, sounding hurt.

I clicked off the phone and stared at it.

I want my mom to be happy. I just wish she could be happy closer to me. My life is here and in Washington and in a hundred other places. None of which are very near the town where I grew up. Don't get me wrong, my mother and I have our differences. I'm not some Momma's Boy missing a bit of home cooking. It's really not that good anyway. And believe me, it may be the best thing for her sanity that I'm here and she's there, because I have made her life a living hell on numerous occasions. Mostly as a teenager. Whenever I wanted to go somewhere she wouldn't let me go or do something she wouldn't let me do, I would wear her down. Outlast her. Triumph by attrition.

It wasn't her fault that I prevailed. Parents simply don't have the stamina their kids do. Or, at least, that I do. I could repeat the words "but please mom, I wanna go" so many times that you would need a supercomputer to tabulate the exact number of miles it would take to string those sentences together one after another. I once came close to reaching Alpha Centauri, but she gave in too easily.

And unlike the Princess—who I would annoy without hesitation just for the hell of it—my mom was rarely deserving of such hostility. She might deny a request or suggest something stupid like going to McDonald's for a Happy Meal when you were fourteen years old, and even worse, suggesting that you invite your friends and a clown and make it a birthday party. But that was the extent of her shortcomings.

Most of her bewilderment revolved around having no idea what a fourteen-year-old boy thinks about. Unlike my father, she had never been one. She simply didn't understand. When we're not whacking off, stealing our father's Super Jugs magazines, or burning, blasting or blowing up anything that doesn't expressly say don't burn, blast or blow up, we were trying to figure out how to get an adult to buy us alcohol.

I didn't live in the most interesting of places.

In those formative semi-adult years, there were two main problems regarding the procurement and acquisition of alcoholic beverages. One, the actual acquisition of said alcoholic beverages, and two, the transportation and consumption of such beverages.

I became something of a local celebrity in my town when in the winter of my eighth grade, I came up with the "Booze Baggie" method of sneaking liquor past parents and teachers.

Adults thought so three-dimensionally, so logically. They always checked for bottles or cans, hard things. So I figured, pour the booze into a baggie (thank God for Ziplock technology), seal it up, and then wrap it around your ankle inside of your sock, or in the bra of a girl you knew padded, or (and only if you're drinking it yourself) stuff it in your pants. A cursory check would turn up nothing, and if they were feeling that close where they could distinguish that soft swell from a breast or a pair of balls as a baggie of Jim Beam, well, there was always screaming at the top of your lungs and calling them a perv.

For my fourteenth birthday party—which I might add, despite my mother's well-meaning attempts, did not take place at, near, or within sight of a McDonald's—I figured I had come up with a brilliant solution to the problem of getting beer. Just down the street from my house were a handful of pretty cool guys in their early twenties. A couple of them raced motorcycle dirt bikes professionally. They even had their own track down the street, which, whenever they weren't using it, we would ride our bikes on and race till we puked.

These two guys were my first stop.

I went up to the house and tried to look calm, my heart beating hard as I knocked on the front door. I peered inside the window after a few moments. No one seemed to be home. My brilliant strategy was beginning to collapse around me. I hadn't actually factored in the fact that these guys might not be sitting around just waiting for me to stop by. Adults are strange that way.

After ten minutes, I had to ditch them and go down the street to Jake's house. I was pretty sure Jake was home because I heard his motorcycle screaming down the street about half an hour ago. The only reason I didn't ask Jake right off was because, honestly, Jake scared the living shit out of me.

I stood at the end of Jake's property, which was actually his parents' property, and rehearsed what I would say. Then spent nearly twenty-five minutes honing the fifteen-second pitch I was going to make to him.

Luckily, in the meantime, Gunter and Ben arrived. I ran back to the house, explained to them the situation, and enlisted them in my plan.

Emboldened with a support team behind me, I strolled back to Jake's house, up the driveway, then up a meandering chain of slate islands that made up the front walk.

Now the reason Jake scared the shit out of me was he weighed almost, maybe a little over, three hundred pounds. He wore huge black boots, had a chain dangling from his belt loop, and was almost never seen without sunglasses and a black leather vest which was about two sizes too small for him and only served to make him look even more threatening.

Oh, and he was heavy into the Hell's Angels.

His mom came to the door. I hadn't counted on this either. Yeah, brilliant strategist in the making.

"Billy...how are you? I haven't seen you in such a long time. How is your mother?"

"She's really great, Mrs. Arnold."

The last time she'd seen me face to face, instead of riding past her on my bike, I was pouring my dad out their front door after he had gone over to borrow their lawnmower.

I could feel just the slightest bit of sweat forming on the peach fuzz mustache I was cultivating. And I shifted my weight casually, trying not to look like a kid who had just stolen ten packs of bubble gum.

"Is, ah, is Jake home?" I said this in a tone that suggested I often asked for Jake to come out and play.

It didn't at all seem strange to me at the time that this grown man lived with his parents.

Mrs. Arnold turned her head to the side and looked at me out of the corner of her eye. She wrinkled up her forehead. "Jake?"

"Uh-huh."

"I...I think so." She turned and yelled inside.

After a moment, Jake came to the door. I hadn't until that moment realized it, but his hand was exactly the size of my head.

He gazed down at the three of us. I can only now imagine what the hell he was thinking. Here were three kids, two fourteen-year-olds, and his thirteen-year-old neighbor who was about to leave behind that most awkward year that very night.

We must have looked pathetic.

"What can I do for you, gentlemen?"

He said gentlemen. This was gonna be easy. We were all *adults* here.

I motioned for him to come out onto the steps so that we could talk more privately. The three of us explained to Jake our situation, how grave a situation it really was, and how many cute girls were coming.

I guess we figured if he knew that we had a chance to get inside some girl's bra, he might be more inclined to help us.

Jake had this remarkably deep, confident voice that made him seem even bigger and stronger than he was. It was the type of voice that I can imagine biker chicks loved and anyone coming across him down a dark alley feared.

"I'm sorry fellas. I can't help you. I could get into some deep shit."

We asked him one more time as sweetly as we possibly could. He told us that he sympathized with us. And really did wish he could help, but he just couldn't risk it.

I knew that adults could get in trouble for buying kids alcohol. What I didn't know at the time was that Jake was on probation for manslaughter.

We slowly trudged back to my house, defeated. We had about thirty people, some of the coolest kids in school coming to my house in twenty minutes—Donny Broderick, Gary Farinelli, Krissy Simon—and I couldn't get any alcohol.

Not that all the kids drank, mind you. It was the point of the matter.

If you couldn't sneak booze, you lose.

I lowered my head in despair. All hope was lost. But then, from out of nowhere—a clear, perfect thought. *My dad's an alcoholic!*

Of course! There must be ten cases of beer stacked downstairs in the cellar. The Princess wasn't gonna notice if one was missing. And even if he did, there was still only a twenty-five percent chance he would say something to me. Partly because he wouldn't be completely sure I had done it, he *could* have drunk it. Partly because he would cut me some slack since he probably filched a couple of sixers from his father when he was a teenager. But mostly because if he brought up the subject in front of my mother, she was going to start in on him about a) drinking in the first place, b) having so many cases of Maximum Super lying around, which made it nearly impossible to get to the summer clothes, c) setting a poor example for his children, and d) not being smart enough to keep me and my friends from drinking his beer, because if that was *her* beer, she would have kept a close eye on it.

That discussion would be something my father would avoid.

In comparison, the worst that could happen to me was I might get grounded for a couple of months. A punishment that seemed insignificant when you stack it up against the glory of having provided beer for your friends.

See, this is another reason why parents lose when it comes to battling their kids, and an impetus for me to lay out in advance what kind of rule book I'm gonna be parenting from.

A couple of months is longer to a teenager than to an adult. The months start flying by at a faster pace the older you get. But even when you factor that in, a couple of months' punishment to save face? It was a no-brainer. And, you know what, the press might turn out to be a good thing.

"Where's Billy?"

"Oh, he's grounded, dude. That raging party he threw. Parents snagged him for bringing in beer."

"I heard that party raged."

"It raged."

"Aw, man, I missed it."

"You gotta stick your head in the loop, dude. Billy booted his entire summer for that party."

"Pretty cool. Was it worth it?"

"We *raged*."

ME AND BEN and Gunter dragged one of the cases out of the cellar, through the backyard, across the plank that spanned the stream running behind my house, then buried it under some leaves at the foot of a tree marked by paint denoting the Blue Trail.

The drawback of this scenario was that the beer started out warm, and since dried leaves did not cool as well as dry ice, it was going to stay that way. In retrospect, it turned out to be a stroke of genius, because warm beer, for some reason, gets you buzzed faster. Faster buzz. Less beer would be consumed. More chances we wouldn't run out. This was back when a case was a case, twenty-four beers, and not a "twelve-pack."

I think I've said the first time my father decided to hang out and get chatty with me was when Leslie Caron was coming over to pick me up and take me back to her place for a night and a day of sex.

Well, that wasn't entirely accurate. The Ms. Caron elbow-nudge incident was the second time. *This* was the first.

Dear Ol' Dad became the life of the party after he came down and suggested that we build a huge bonfire in the backyard. We were all, boys and girls alike fascinated. "Fire?!" Grunt, grunt, like cave dwellers.

Dad was an immediate hit. And as he stepped back to proudly view his burning work of art, coming from the woods and the Blue Trail came confirmation that the first group had found the beer.

"Here it is. And there's a whole shit load of it!!!" The words echoed off the nearby mountains after Karl Roget screamed them.

I was standing right next to the Princess. I happened to be looking at him, so I didn't have to make a sudden gesture to see his face. He glanced in the direction of the sound, then just as quickly looked back at the fire. He had heard the call of the desperate to taste drink, but he didn't say a word to me, except, "Pretty good fire we got raging here."

"Yeah, it's raging."

I PRESSED and held down the "3" on my phone. And as soon as I heard the voice on the other end, I said, "Listen, Mom, I'm really sorry. Okay? I'll call you back when I get to Geneva. I'm driving and I'm lost and I need to be back there saving this thing." I paused. "I love you. I'll talk to you as soon as I can."

As I clicked off the phone, I noticed Sydney looking at me. I nodded my head, knowing what she must be thinking.

"You just redeemed yourself, Gerrick. You just redeemed yourself."

AS WE CLIMBED out of the southwest and neared the peak, the morning glow had already begun to creep up from behind the towering Swiss Alps in the distance, a brilliant canvas of pink and blue and gray. It almost appeared as if the mountains were giving birth to the light, that it was emerging from within.

Clouds poured over the summits like a waterfall and all my stupid criticisms of the Swiss and the French and all other cheese-loving countries melted away.

We were not far from Switzerland now. We could see it. It seemed a beautiful place. A magnificent, majestic, almost magical patch of land.

Like looking upon Shangri-La.

The heavy white mist only added to the allure.

I still hadn't found my way back to the main road, where the numerous cars that I was too impatient to wait behind were already in Sweden by now. The unplowed road was becoming more difficult to navigate, the blanket of drifting snow impeding our progress.

We were cresting a summit, which I thought might give me a perspective, some idea where we were, when I saw them. There were two of them and they flew in very tight formation. The large predatory birds swooped down toward us.

At first, I couldn't tell what they were, but as they came closer, I identified them as AH-64 Apache helicopter gunships.

They were bristling with firepower. They were black. Unmarked.

The blades whipped and churned and kicked up the snow as one of the helicopters set down right in the middle of the road ahead of us while the other hovered overhead.

I slammed on the brakes, and the 4x4 slid to a stop.

Several well-dressed men in suits jumped out of the craft as if being dropped off for work on Wall Street, except we were on a deserted road in the thick of the Alps. I didn't see any guns, not on the men coming toward us, but I knew they were there, under their jackets. However, I could see several figures clutching rifles in both the helicopter on the ground and the one circling above.

And the Hellfires and the 30mm cannon made their point.

Sydney immediately began to panic. "Turn the car around!"

I didn't move.

"Turn the car around, Billy! They have guns!"

My first experience having heavily armed men heading toward me took place in Yugoslavia, when there still really was such a place, not some ever-shrinking republic, shedding parts of itself like a leper.

I was in Sarajevo on business. The country was falling apart, and the U.S. had quietly asked some American companies to entertain the possibility of investment and trade in the area, hoping that economic success would lead to political stability.

A plane carrying several American executives crashed into a mountain.

I was supposed to be on that plane. Not then, but after its stop in Zagreb. It was to pick me and my team up after we completed our talks in the former Olympic city and take us on to Belgrade.

It never made it.

Ongoing ethnic conflicts were causing a massive displacement of the various populations and a great deal of unrest. The place was a security nightmare. There had been some early and ultimately erroneous speculation that the plane had been targeted by a shoulder-fired missile.

So my team and I were ordered to travel by ground. We led a Range Rover caravan to Belgrade to speak with Serbian leaders, despite the upheaval.

This region was about to implode. We needed to act quickly. The plan was simple, to invest in the country, and without bringing attention to the fact, spread the factories and processes over the three main sectors, what are now Croatia, Bosnia, and Serbia (although, the Serbs still insist on calling their land Yugoslavia). The idea was that if you needed three factories in three different parts of the country to produce one product, then warring amongst the "partners" would be counter-productive.

Their interdependence would lead to cooperation.

This low-key approach has worked well in other parts of the world. In fact, mutual self-interest is one of the most cunning ways America spreads stability, democracy, and eventually freedom throughout the world.

Whenever we forget that, when we use brute force, the bludgeoning stick of our military, we fail to bring about the change we truly want.

Three plants. Three ethnic groups. One common goal. It is a more powerful motivator than the barrel of a gun.

But the leaders of this region were not interested in our plans. Like all civil wars, these were some of the most ghastly conflicts. Brother-in-law against brother-in-law, neighbor against neighbor. The more similar the enemy is, the more trivial the prejudice becomes.

Our Range Rovers were stopped on a lonely road in the middle of the mountains. Security personnel with guns and angry faces stood in our path. They searched our vehicles, our persons. They tore through papers and documents that had taken months to prepare. They confiscated watches and rings, and they paid extra attention inspecting Allison, checking inside her bra and under her skirt. It was difficult to watch. Not only because they were violating her, but because I had—at this early stage in our association—wanted to do these very same things to her. It made me nauseous to see how hostile a man's hand could be, especially if uninvited.

"Billy, do something." Sydney's voice was strained and fearful. She was shaking as the men walked closer.

I tried to sound as calm as I could. "Did I happen to mention that I am an at-risk person?"

"What?!"

"The U.S. Trade Representative is a Cabinet-level position. Technically, I have the rank of Ambassador. And as such, and because of the sometimes contentious nature of international economic policy..."

Her head was shaking like it was about to explode.

"I am considered a high-level risk."

"Oh, my God."

Sydney reached for the satellite phone, but it was out of power.

I put my hand on her leg to calm her down. She jumped when one of the suits rapped on my window.

"Sir, we've been looking for you all morning."

They had determined my location by knowing where I had started from, where they believed I was going to, and my well-documented loathing of traffic jams to narrow down the roads to be searched.

"We have located 'Temple,' over," said the one by my window into his sleeve.

"Roger, 'Temple' has been located," came the scratchy voice over the radio.

Sydney looked at me. I nodded it was okay. And much less embarrassing than it would have been a year ago.

I formerly was tagged "Casanova," but thankfully after Laura came on the scene, my moniker changed. I don't know why "Temple" is my codename. But the Secret Service has full discretion on these matters. Sometimes the designation is not at all flattering. For instance, I understand the President's brother has been christened by the Secret Service… "Headache."

I'd like to think my label is more complimentary. Temple of knowledge, perhaps. Or even the less favorable, but still apropos Temple from the Bible where the Money Changers traded goods and services and shekels.

More likely the name denotes the place the agents rub with their fingers after suffering "Headache."

We were asked politely to get out of the 4x4 by the agent just outside my window. He was six foot two and had intense eyes that were a little unnerving. I nodded to Sydney that it was all right for us to get out. She complied, even though she seemed shaky, and not at all sure it was the right decision.

As we were led to the waiting aircraft, two men approached the 4x4, while another checked under the vehicle with a mirror attached to a graphite pole about four feet long. He gave the two men the "thumbs up," and the men climbed inside and retrieve my papers, my cell phone, the satellite case, and Sydney's shopping bags.

I have a security detail. I'm supposed to, at the very least, keep them informed of my movements when the mission is outside of the country. When international tensions are high, I've had to put up with their presence around the clock. It's not as bad as my friend, the Secretary of State. He has to put up with protection all the time. They paved over his wife's flower garden to make room for all the vehicles. I'm usually shadowed by a couple of agents during a conference. When I'm back in the States, I'm more guarded about my privacy. The Service lets me get away with it, although they don't like it. They drive by my house every thirty to forty minutes. Make me check in all the time. And they maintain the alarm system.

Actually, I take them for granted, and I guess I shouldn't.

One of the agents lifted Sydney onto the helicopter then strapped her into the seat. I climbed on and did the harness myself. The agent checked it to make sure it was properly fastened. He motioned to the Army pilot with his finger to rev up the blades and take off, then situated himself in the seat across from me.

Sydney turned to me and shouted over the din of the blades. "Do you use this to impress the chicks?"

It was a little embarrassing to have a military helicopter have to come and take me home.

"I only bring out the Black Ops helicopters for special occasions," I yelled.

"It scared the hell out of me."

We were handed noise-canceling ear protection and told to put them on. Instantly, most of the sound was blocked out.

I tried to say, "I'm sorry," even though I couldn't hear myself, but she saw my lips. She understood.

The helicopter lifted off, creating another blizzard that whited everything out for a moment. Rising higher, the snow cleared, and the view became breathtaking.

It was peaceful. Almost tranquil. Our headgear creating a personal sanctuary for us.

I stared down at the rented 4x4, its doors open, abandoned in the middle of nowhere as it got smaller and more insignificant. In front of it, a smoke flare was sending a ribbon of green into the air. Someone would come and retrieve the car, but that was secondary. I was the primary concern.

I glanced up and took in the snowy peaks of the Alps silently passing by. I instinctively reached across the divide between Sydney and me, finding her hand already waiting at the halfway point, and we held hands the rest of the flight.

30

SILENCE IS GOLDENISH-GREEN

THE APACHE HELICOPTER we were in came to rest at the edge of the lake, while the other circled cautiously above. The blades kicked up snow into the eyes of agents and staff that came scurrying toward the helicopter in the ubiquitous pose of all people approaching this kind of craft: the head-down, walking-like-a-duck position.

There are some moments in life which resonate more than others. I've had the distinct pleasure of being a participant in a few relatively minor car accidents. In each of one of them, time seemed to stand still. In that place, every second lasts a minute. Details and meaning become apparent. Cognizant thought and actions are possible at intervals not conceivable in normal space-time.

In that moment of hyperreality, everything seems clear.

That's what it was like as Sydney and I were rushed into the hotel by the security detail, then joined at the door by Tom Bowman and Doug Powers.

Words and ideas were being tossed at me like handfuls of sand, and I managed to snare every grain, every granule with such ease that it felt like the world was moving in slow motion.

Allison pushed her way to me. Both Sydney and I were immediately given hot coffee, and I was handed a large notebook, containing an outline of all that had taken place in the late-night and morning sessions. Allison quieted the others with a look and a wave of her hand and ran through every item in the notebook, giving me a brief synopsis and relevant background on each situation.

I'd just been picked up by a helicopter in the middle of the Alps, which, by the way, doesn't happen to every government employee who happens to get lost. However, in the weeks leading up to the conference, there had been threats made against me. I was being treated like a six-year-old on his way to his first day of school.

If *The Washington Post* could see me now.

There is a vortex that materializes in the proximity of any high government official. The world seems to swirl around the individual like a whirlpool, and sometimes even those who are not part of the original entourage get sucked into the maelstrom. What's odd about these confluences is that they aren't consistent. At the moment, I seem to be the most important person in Geneva, at least, the most important person at this conference. And after the events of the past few days, and the fury I've churned up, I have no doubt that I am. That is why—as we walked toward the meeting rooms—I was leaving a wake of humanity behind me. If the Secretary of State were to show up, instantly my whirlwind would diminish by at least sixty percent. If the President were to saunter in that door right behind me, I'd have exactly three people around me. Allison and two Secret Service agents. And *their* job would be more about keeping *me* from harming *him*. The tempest would be circling the man with the eagle on his seal and the tiny American flag on his lapel.

But for now, I was the big deal.

I'm often amazed at this scene whenever I see others like myself, people who really aren't all that important, commanding so much attention, so much space. I especially love watching the Russian contingent that's been sniffing around the hotel. The Russian ambassador to Switzerland, Yuri Volkov, and the pack of dogs he tracks in have a sycophantic quality about them, even more than would be expected. Everyone is always kissing up to Yuri, or rather, kissing down to him, he's about five-foot-two. That's height and width.

By contrast, the Japanese delegation is more orderly. The Japanese advance more like a line of Confederate soldiers at the Battle of Gettysburg. Unless you have a very trained eye, you can't immediately distinguish the person in charge. The Japanese are very strange in this way, whereas the Russians seem to exult their leaders while secretly despising them.

But do not mistake...Hutseo Takai is in complete control.

The Russians...they're not even "observers" to GATT. More like lurkers.

Three months ago, six former Soviet republics led by Russia signed an agreement to form an economic union with a common currency, trying to mimic the EU and the eurozone. Three weeks ago, less than two months later, the agreement was in shambles after Russia "clarified" terms for the new ruble zone. Russia demanded that Armenia, Belarus, Kazakhstan, Tajikistan, and Uzbekistan hand over gold as collateral for any issued rubles. Sure, Moscow, I'll trust you with my gold. You've done such a great job in the past with it.

I was unable to say anything to Sydney the entire flight. The noise of the helicopter and our ear protection made it impossible to communicate verbally. But we did converse with our eyes, as we were doing now, being marched through the hotel.

When we reached the meeting rooms, there was an instant, a mere fraction where the bottleneck of slender door jambs gave her a moment to speak.

"It wasn't Peoria," she said.

I looked at her not yet understanding. "What?"

"That someone you can't worry about, it wasn't in Peoria. It was Crescent Falls. My father lost his job when they closed the GM plant. Then we lost our house." She seemed to be remembering. And in her eyes, I saw the pain. The pain of a cute little blonde girl being led away from her home. A father's anguish. A mother's tears. "Sometimes," she said, her voice a whisper, "it *is* about individuals."

I've cost thousands of people their jobs. I've given thousands of people their jobs.

I never once thought about any of them.

The instant was up. I was directed toward the ballroom and Sydney was held back. I turned to her as I was being led away, like a man going to the gas chamber, and told her not to leave until she was able to speak to me again.

She simply nodded.

Allison promised that she would take care of Sydney and make sure she was well entertained as soon as I was up to speed and situated.

My dirty little mind had a brief instant, an image of the two of them rolling around on a rubber sheet drenched in oil.

I think Allison knew exactly what I was thinking because she hit me in the shoulder with her fist and told me to concentrate on the nation's business.

"I am concentrating. And what was with the 'Apocalypse Now' Welcome Wagon?"

"Item seven." She pointed to the notebook she had handed me. "Actionable intelligence."

I flipped open the folder. The one-page cable had no letterhead but was marked URGENT and CLASSIFIED, and date stamped less than twelve hours ago. Not just a whisper of a threat against me. A credible threat against my life. The intel included information on my whereabouts, my movements, soft target points, vulnerabilities, and a timetable for completion: BEFORE FINAL VOTE. Felt Russian. Intimidation is their go-to move. But they didn't have any skin in the game. Maybe one of those countries unhappy that I'm pushing for a human rights exception.

"Item *seven*?"

She shrugged.

I closed the folder.

"It's bullshit," we said in unison.

This is why Allison is my assistant.

This was meant to harass me, frighten me, occupy my mind.

I got a rush of adrenaline. But it wasn't fear, it was anger.

"These people are idiots. Like if they succeeded, the U.S. would give up on our demands cause you took out one of our people? That would just make us only more resolute. You think Tom's gonna sit here in my place and give into them?"

"Oh, I would roll over and give them everything they ever wanted," Tom said with a smile.

I laughed. It felt good to do that. "Take the chair, scaredy-cat." I motioned inside.

The cyclone calmed as members of my team peeled off. I did not turn back to look—I was making my entrance—but I could feel that Sydney was watching me. I felt strong and confident. The lack of sleep did not bother me. I nodded to Rafael, Hutseo, and some of the other participants.

Tom went ahead and sat in the chair with the microphone and the plaque reading "United States" set in front of it. This had been planned out over the payphone at the Auberge when I suggested that Tom take the lead seat. It was a ploy of sorts, but not so much as to be obvious. There was no doubt I was the highest U.S. representative at the table, in the room, in the city, in the country, on the continent, everyone knew that.

Like I've said, Tom was the Current Permanent (what does that mean?) U.S. envoy to GATT, he legitimately had the right to sit there, but everyone would notice that I was *not* at the microphone.

This agreement wasn't in the bag. There were dangers and pitfalls ahead. Gathered here were the best minds, the most cunning negotiators who were trying to make this better for their country and worse for everyone else's.

And, of course, there was Beckett.

Saying yes to this treaty was a sticky proposition because unlike GATT, which had a resolution process that was arduous, drawn out and absolutely toothless, this agreement would create a bureaucracy that would have standing as an international body with real powers of enforcement.

Just the kind of authority that makes people in Montana grab their guns and people in D.C. press the 'Nay' button.

I walked up behind Rafael. Breathed in her ear.

"We've had a very fulfilling relationship, you and me."

"It 'az always been a pleasure."

She looked to the side, our eyes meeting, just barely.

"I need you on my side. Beckett's trying to corner me."

She smiled at the irony of her position.

"But I yam on 'is side." She paused. "And besides your sides, they seem occupied elsewhere." She flashed her eyes in the direction of the lobby.

I made a decision. One I'd have to explain to the President.

"I'll push off the agro subsidies till a later date. EU only, though. We'll set it in a side agreement that we'll disclose later this evening."

She didn't nod. She didn't have to.

"Let's keep this between us until then," I said.

And with that, it was done. I'd pissed in Beckett's sandbox. And taken away his shovel.

There was an empty seat next to Tom. Not one of the executive chairs, but one normally meant for staff. I sat there between him and Francesca, who was looking very pretty today. I glanced down and to the side, and she surreptitiously showed me a hint of the top of her thigh highs. I smiled, and so did she. This wasn't an attempt to seduce me. This was a playful gesture of friendship. A ritual. Something to make sure I was loosened up and ready to wage war.

This simple change in seating, to the side and slightly behind Tom in a smaller chair, did two things.

One, it kept me above the fray. I wasn't even going to bother arguing with the other countries. The U.S. position was clear. It was concise. It was in writing. We wanted fairness.

I might whisper something in Tom's ear if it got heated, but that would be used very, very judiciously. I couldn't get drawn in.

Two, this deflected any personal attacks. As long as I stayed out of it and Tom and the others talked about the "American Stance," it wasn't me who was messing things up. These were *our* policies and *our* beliefs.

Too often it becomes about the person and not the policies.

I love to give speeches. Especially at moments like this, when the agreement is within reach. When words and rhetoric do make a difference.

But I would not speak today. The day of my greatest achievement. Four years of hard work by me and my team. A decade of effort by thousands of American negotiators and staff. This day, I would say nothing.

That is, until, unfortunately, I did.

I LEANED FORWARD, pushing between Tom and Francesca. "We're going backwards," I said, shocking everyone.

I had been watching in frustration for several hours. The deadline was looming. The rest of the world could blather on for years, but at midnight, my President, my boss, lost the ability to negotiate a deal that would go before Congress as an up or down vote. That was the purpose of Fast Track Authority. So the little fingers of congressmen trying to save a broom factory in Missouri couldn't fuck around with the entire global economy.

But instead of getting closer, we were getting nowhere. If we were going anywhere, it was farther away.

On every side there was resistance. The goal in these final moments is to soften one of the major sides so the other sides will soften as well. But as with anything, if everyone stands firm, it strengthens everyone's resolve even more.

Every inch of ground I had already mentally claimed as mine, I felt it receding. I couldn't help but see the image of Sydney as a little girl getting evicted from her house.

"Airbus subsidies...still in," I said, knowing that Tom was burning a hole in the back of my head. "No opening of rice markets. Film quotas. Media limits. The fucking *bribery deduction*? This is where we were six months ago."

And here was where it happened. The mistake.

"We're talking about people's lives here," I said. "You can't expect me to agree to wipe out the jobs of thousands of workers. Now, we've got till midnight to break this log jam. After that, there's nothing I can do."

I sat back.

Beckett stood up. No one needed to be standing at the moment, we were all sitting around as near-equals, some more equal than others. Standing was simply unnecessary.

The ass.

He planted his feet. Cleared his throat.

"I'm glad to hear you finally talking about people's lives. I think your decision to postpone a final solution on agricultural subsidies for the EU is a start in the right direction."

I felt my face go dark, and I immediately turned to glare at Rafael.

She didn't look at me.

"That provision," I said, "which has not been finalized, would be in exchange for certain protections for—"

I didn't even get to say it before Hutseo jumped out of his chair, all five-foot-three of him.

"We also demand postponement to lifting agricultural protections. And security for our workers!"

Fuck. I was the "side" that had softened.

I GOT up from my seat immediately and headed toward the back of the room. Allison was already walking toward me. The look on her face told me everything I needed to know.

I was an idiot.

While the rest of the negotiations continued, Tom stepped away from the decorated table, all the snapped and broken flags from the fight had been fixed, any evidence of a brawl had long since been removed, polished away.

Tom was not happy with me. "Where the fuck are you going?"

"I just got caught with my pants down," I shook my head, not believing I could be so stupid.

Tom looked at me, "With as much as that dick has been out, I'm surprised it hasn't happened sooner."

"I need you to get Erlohof to call for the final vote. Now! Before we lose any more ground."

"What? We've still got things to negotiate."

He must have missed it. Must not have heard it. It's so easy to lose focus during these marathon sessions for a split second especially if you're pissed off about something and miss a word or an exchange that can cost you, your business, your country, dearly.

Allison said it for me. "He said it was about *people*."

If I had shot Tom in the face, he would have looked less surprised.

"People!" he shouted before he caught himself. "*Protectionism* is about saving a particular person's job. Choosing this guy over that one. Protectionism is the killer of innovation. You told me, in the battle of ideas, we win. It's about focusing on what we're best at. Inspiration, innovation, creation, and the money that attracts. The more money we bring in, the more money we have for jobs, for business. That's all that matters. More money in America. Because that means more money for Americans. Which gets back to people. You convinced me of that. You can lose a battle to win a war."

"Yes, but I've also told you...trickle down doesn't work. It's a nice theory, but it fails in the wild. It lowers the buying power of the middle and below because the top can pay inflated prices for things like houses and companies." I shake my head again. "Fuck! She got in my head. She made me think."

"Who? Who made you think? Some girl you're fucking? No one should make you think!"

I flashed an angry look at him.

"Where's Billy Gerrick? Where is he? The man who could get any woman he wanted into bed and still kill at the table the next day. I don't see him. Billy Gerrick, if he were here, would have had this done by now. What the hell happened to him?"

"He got engaged." The word fell out of my mouth. *Engaged*. In so many ways, that's what happened. Not only the obvious meaning of that word but all the little nuances. I had become engaged too deeply, in too many ways.

Tom looked confused. The call from Laura, asking him how tall he was. He couldn't put it together?

Allison wobbled her head, disappointed with me, with Tom, with everyone. As I turned to walk away, I saw her hand Tom two dozen more pages of bridesmaids' dresses that thankfully she had kept from me.

"Call a vote!" I yelled back at Tom.

BECKETT WAS STANDING by the side of the elegant staircase that led up to the mezzanine ringing the lobby.

He was waiting for me.

"Can you finally admit that your way is counterproductive?" he said in that superior tone of his. "Finally admit that arrogant application of coercion gets you nothing?"

Him calling me arrogant. Now, he was really trying to piss me off.

It was laughable. Not because I'm not arrogant. I am. I very much am, but because Beckett's conceit was a front.

And yet, here he was smiling, standing before me, finally getting the last word on his former pupil.

"What happened to 'Compromise is the only way to guarantee an outcome?'" I asked. "'Everybody wins,' rah-rah."

Beckett's assistant motioned to him. The vote had been called. My stomach flipped.

"You," he said, emphasizing that word as if I were some sort of disease, "have done everything in your power to destroy decades of accepted practices. You reap what you sow."

I glared at him.

"You know something? Your way was getting us nowhere," I stabbed him in the eyes with mine. "You understand that? If I didn't get tough two years ago, none of this would have happened. Everybody'd be stuck where they were, afraid, terrified, paralyzed. Your way sounds so positive. 'Win-win.' But you know what the problem with that is?"

He waited for the answer.

"It assumes that everyone thinks the same, has the same agenda, that we all will do the right thing. Some people are assholes, Beckett. You never factor that into your equations." I stopped because I knew he would never, could never see it. I moved on to something he could understand. "Forget whether or not everyone can or even wants to be 'one world.' We were deadlocked. And where were you? At a podium in a classroom in Middletown. While I was circling the globe, stitching this thing together. If you'd been in charge, we'd still be arguing over where to *have* this meeting, and if we were *really* lucky, what was going to be served for dinner that first night. My way got us here."

"Well," he said, forcing a smile, "here you are." He looked at his watch. "Out of time."

I saw her at the top of the stairs. She was wearing something simple. I don't even remember what it was. When Beckett realized I wasn't paying attention to him anymore, he turned and walked toward the ballroom to wait for the vote.

Sydney descended the steps, taking each one slowly. She was holding a copy of a French magazine. I wasn't on the cover, but I knew I was inside. I hadn't read the article—I got the thumbnail from Allison. Basically, I'm an asshole.

"I was reading about you," she said.

"Yeah, don't believe everything you read."

"My French is a little rusty, but *le marteau*, I kind of like that."

Rafael had said these words to me over and over again. *Le marteau de velours.* The velvet hammer.

"*Le marteau*..." I said. "What an idiot!" I smacked my palm to my forehead. I didn't mean to do such a cliché move, but it was my instinctual reaction.

I took Sydney by the shoulders, kissed her on the forehead.

"Thank you," I said. "See you after?"

She nodded, although I could see she was clearly unsure of what had just happened.

EVEN THOUGH NEARLY EVERYONE WHO would be voting had been in the room only moments before, it took over an hour to gather them together again.

It was past eleven-forty. Twenty minutes before the Sword of Damocles came down upon my head.

It made perfect sense.

The room was filled to capacity. This time, everyone was in attendance, not just the low-levels, not just the trade ministers and the negotiators, but everyone from the observers to the press secretaries to the guy in charge of the copier.

Jens Erlohof stood at the podium and looked out over the crowded ballroom. There was a sense of excitement in the room, a sense of history. As chairman of GATT, which this agreement was replacing, Erlohof was about to put himself out of a job.

Erlohof was a young-looking Swede in his early sixties. I liked him. He was smart, harmless. And like the GATT, he didn't have any teeth. You wouldn't know it, the fakes were so good, but they were all gone. He banged his gavel and then went on to read a series of statements that had been pre-written and pre-negotiated for use at this very moment in the process. The final moment.

When he had finished with the formalities, he took off his rimless glasses and said, "The vote must be unanimous among the parties to the agreement." Erlohof held silent for a beat. "On the matter of the Final Agreement, how do you say? Argentina?"

The Argentinian delegate with a sense of pride at being the first to answer, stood up and said, "Mr. Chairman, yes."

The Land Down Under was next.

"Australia?"

"Yes."

AND SO IT went down the alphabet.

My head was pounding. I had let myself make the one mistake I've always tried to protect against. Overconfidence. If there was anything I should have learned in my life, from my childhood, it was that you could be arrogant, you could even be self-assured, confident, but you could never, ever let yourself get *over*confident.

I compounded the error by losing focus.

As each of the countries voted in favor of the agreement, there was a growing sense of excitement in the room.

Even Tom, who I could tell was thinking of missed opportunities, of what we—what I—could have done better, was starting to loosen up.

I leaned into him. "I screwed this up."

"Yes, you did," he said. "On the bright side, no one'll know just how badly for *years*."

He was right, of course. It would take years, decades, for the mistakes —the ones we knew about and the ones we didn't—to take their toll on our economy. It gave me little comfort knowing that. In fact, knowing that made it worse.

Tom put a hand on my shoulder. He looked at his watch, which showed 11:48 P.M. "An agreement is a win for the President."

I pulled out Sebby's watch, slid my hand over it. Opened it.

God, I missed him.

Erlohof was rolling. "Trinidad and Tobago?"

"Yes."

I glanced across the table at Beckett. He was beaming, his face red with excitement.

"You finally beat me. You must be very pleased."

"United Kingdom?" Erlohof said.

Beckett glanced at Erlohof for an instant, then directly at me. "Yes," he said to both questions. Then discreetly he continued, "Despite your pretty speeches, Mr. Gerrick, about 'wanting what's best for all,' you have never cared about anything but winning."

He gazed at me triumphantly, and this time, I could see the professor, the theorist, the one who didn't get his hands dirty. It's so easy to spout off from behind a lectern. The real world is a lot more messy.

"Once more," Beckett lectured, "you have failed to learn from the past."

"United States of America?" Erlohof wasn't paying attention. Just saying the names now.

I stared at Beckett. "Maybe you're right."

Behind him, in the distance, I saw Sydney standing next to Allison amongst the people crowded at the edge of the room to witness this historic event. Our eyes met.

"But this...this is about the future." I turned to Tom. "Tom, what's the only rule I have that really matters?"

Erlohof was curious now. "The United States?"

"America first?" Tom said, whispering as if he wasn't sure.

Tom, Tom, Tom. I shook my head. It was *the* rule. "Always," I said, spacing my words out very deliberately.

"The United States?" Erlohof was getting impatient.

"...be willing..."

I did not take my eyes off of Beckett.

"...to walk away." I turned and looked at Erlohof, who nodded expectantly. "No," I said loudly. The word echoing in the now silent room.

I honestly don't know what I was expecting, but I certainly wasn't expecting such noiselessness. There had been a lot of screaming, a lot of angry words, a lot of heated discussions, even a full-on bar brawl during the past week. But in a room packed with men and women who made their living arguing with—or, at least, talking to—each other, the lack of words—of *any* sound—was eerie.

Faces of the delegates were turning red, yellow, and purple. Maru Patel of India who liked glittery makeup became a goldenish sort of green.

It sort of fit her.

Beckett, of course, was the first to pierce the silence.

"We have no time for your theatrics," he began with a shaky sense of confidence. "You have a deadline. Fast Track Authority ends at midnight. Accept it gracefully. I know it is your nature, but you can't *beat* everyone all the time. However, *with* an agreement, everyone wins. Win-win."

I got out of my seat, keeping my hands on the table. I looked up and down the length of it into the faces of the curious, the concerned, and in Diego's case, the sleeping.

I nodded my head slowly and returned my gaze to Beckett. "See, that's where you're mistaken." My voice was steady, deep. The voice I had used a thousand times as I angled to get a woman to sleep with me. "The deadline," I said, "is *yours*. When Fast Track expires, this is dead." I didn't say anything for a moment. "Even if we come up with a fair proposal tomorrow or the next day, Congress will demand changes that'll kill it. And with it, any chance of an agreement for years." I let the words sink in. There was no reason why the rest of the world couldn't come to an agreement. But they all knew what a pact without America meant. *Nothing*. "And this proposal, sir, is nowhere close to fair. And you may think I'm arrogant, that I believe I can fix anything with a few carrots and big stick because I may have mentioned in my final essay: there's no such thing as a bad deal, just bad negotiators. You may have the impression I believe otherwise, but you know what? No deal is *always* better than a bad deal."

The last sentence was straight from Beckett's book. I took great pleasure in that.

The trade minister from Germany spoke, "Whot iz unfair?"

"Does *he* still speak for the EU," I said, looking at the German and

Rafael and the other European Union negotiators, then motioning with my head toward Beckett.

Beckett didn't wait. "I speak for the European Communities," he said. So, fucking pompous.

"Great. Lift the limit on the number of non-European films that can be shown in France."

"The EC doesn't see these laws as trade barriers but as cultural preservation."

"They are quotas."

"Cultural preservation is a legitimate—"

"Then cut the Airbus subsidies," I said. "No culture there."

"That is a core industry that we—"

"Fine." I cut him off. "Remove the tax incentive to bribe foreign government officials." I continued rattling items off, no longer waiting for his responses.

Beckett was trying to keep up, I could see his face becoming redder and redder, but for a different reason now. Not flush with excitement but dark and moist with a growing sense of terror.

The clock continued to move forward. There were less than five minutes left until midnight.

I stared at Beckett. "You don't have the power to negotiate anything, do you?"

He started to speak but stopped. I realized...he honestly didn't know the answer.

I suddenly felt an extreme sense of mercy. I didn't want to crush Beckett. As much as I disliked him, thought he was a fool, there is no pleasure, no triumph in killing a fly, beating someone who is injured, bullying someone who can't fight back.

Unfortunately, what I had to say could not be left unspoken. It was too important, not to me personally, but to the reputation and future leverage of the United States for which I serve.

"They don't think any more of your theories than I do." I studied the faces of the other European ministers. I held my gaze on Rafael but continued speaking to Beckett. "You were a pawn." I reached into the soft briefcase that sat on the floor between me and Tom. "They used you, knew you would annoy me. Maybe even annoy me enough so I might not notice that Europe and Japan and the Developing Bloc have been colluding with each other since last June."

I pulled out a single, folded piece of white paper. I slid the page across the table to Rafael. I could tell from the look on her face she knew what was coming: a CIA report, detailing phone conversations between many of the parties sitting around the table, improperly discussing strategy in exactly the kind of underhanded way we had agreed to avoid.

There was nothing in the rules against parties speaking privately to each other. Even deals between parties were acceptable. But once agreements were made, they were to be made public. Isolating one country or a group secretly was out of bounds.

Throughout the CIA transcripts, the representatives of numerous nations and blocs of nations constantly debated over what to do about *me*. I had seen the reports but had been too caught up in Laura's dispatches—bridesmaids' dresses, flower ideas—to fully respond to what I was seeing.

Without removing my hand from the paper, I let Rafael lift the edge to take a peek at the page.

Her look betrayed nothing.

"I realize you had no idea," I said to Beckett.

I pulled the paper back.

Everyone else in the room was following the path of the white eight-and-a-half by eleven. The entire round trip took less than five seconds, and the paper was safely back in the briefcase.

I didn't risk an international incident by *actually* showing Rafael a page from a CIA document. That would have been foolish. Illegal. No, she knew everything she needed to know when she saw the handwritten words:

Le marteau de velours.

Erlohof was staring at me. His head was floundering as if to say, "Are you sure?"

I nodded. "The United States votes no."

Erlohof's shoulders slumped. There was no need for the Chairman to continue with the roll call. The agreement was dead without U.S. involvement. He stood there, however, not sure what to do next.

It was somewhat anti-climactic as everyone watched the hands on the clock reach midnight and the huge bells atop St. Gallen Cathedral began to toll.

They tolled for us.

"Ladies and gentlemen," I said as I walked out, leaving the room in stunned silence.

As I REACH THE LOBBY, I can hear a cacophony of sound emanating from the ballroom as the delegates finally realize what just happened.

Their world trade agreement—and with it, their world—had been knocked off its axis.

31

THE PRINCESS OF WAILS

I BREATHE IN DEEPLY. Feeling relief.

Rafael is the first person to reach me in the lobby.

I wonder how she is able to move so quickly without seemingly any effort.

"Very nice, *mon cher*," she says softly. I notice the difference in how she addresses me. "I had started to worry about you. That you had lost your touch." She kisses me on one cheek, then the other, slowly, with what I feel is a sense of regret. No, third cheek.

Rafael's slender hand slides down my arm. She does not say another word as she walks away.

Timing her approach perfectly, so she never breaks stride, never appears to be waiting for Rafael's exit, Sydney comes up to me. Her expression is soft, her eyes have a warm intensity to them.

"I didn't like the way she kissed you," she says, without a hint of anger or annoyance.

"I like that you didn't like the way she kissed me."

She is *with* me again.

"What you did in there...was it a good thing?"

I take a moment to answer. "I don't know." I am lost in her eyes. "It might have been the right thing, though."

Tom approaches with Allison. The rest of the team is lagging behind. No one likes to get too close to a nuclear meltdown. You worry about the fallout.

My hand goes to Sydney's upper arm. I stroke it gently as I speak. "I need to deal with this right now. Just a little longer."

She nods. "I'll be here."

I watch her glide away. I hate watching her do that. As I do, I speak to Tom without looking at him. "The Nikkei just opened. I want you to wait and let the news hit the markets. Then start quietly rounding people up." I glance at him now. "In the meantime, act like you're pissed at me."

"I *am* pissed at you."

I put my hand on his shoulder.

"What time is it, Tom?"

"Three minutes past *you're an asshole*, Billy." He takes a peek at the clock in the lobby as if he needs to make sure that I am, indeed, an asshole.

Yep, big hand and the little hand past the twelve.

"Allison, what time is it?"

Allison is smart. Too smart. I know she has to know.

"I guess. It depends on where you are."

I flip open my grandfather's watch.

"And if you are in, say, Washington, D.C. as opposed to Geneva...?"

Tom looks at me. He had been staring off to the side, cursing his friend in his mind.

"You really *are* an asshole."

I do my best to keep my grin under wraps as I glance down at Sebby's watch, still set to Eastern Standard Time. "Keep saying that over and over."

As I peel Allison and a few key negotiators away from the rest of the delegation, I can hear Tom repeating the epithet with increasing vigor each time.

AN HOUR LATER, about the time we should have all been drunk off our asses, the Intercontinental is buzzing in a much different way.

I've been on the phone with just about every person in the U.S. Government. I just hung up with Bobby McClain. It's a little after 7 P.M. there. The President won't be going to sleep tonight. So, if he accidentally starts a war tomorrow because he's grumpy and tired, I'll have that on my conscience.

I still haven't made an appearance downstairs. I've been working with my team behind the scenes, sending them out into the fractured groups that traditionally form: The EU. Japan and the Asian group. India and Brazil heading up the developing nations. The African Bloc.

Of course, the big pink dragon in the room isn't even *in* the room. At least, not officially. The People's Republic desperately wanted to be a founding member of this agreement, but I refused to reverse our stand. There's no way I'm letting China pretend it's some poor developing country that needs the same kind of protections Bangladesh needs.

It may be a developing country, but it's developing exponentially faster than any other country in the world behind iron-fisted, government-sanctioned protectionist walls.

Membership in this club is one of the few clubs we have to beat concessions out of them.

I give it five to ten years before they come around.

But I know the Hong Kong team is—I won't say looking forward to —wearily looking toward 1997 when control is handed over to the Mainland. I guarantee at least some of the Hong Kong negotiators are hearing whispers from Beijing.

We've all been blathering about Fast Track expiring, which isn't really true. Fast Track Authority doesn't actually expire until April 16th of next year. Under the law, the President must notify the House of Representatives and the Senate of his intention to enter into this agreement—an agreement that has been *finalized*—and publish notice of his intention and the agreement in the Federal Register *one hundred and twenty days before* the pact is to be signed to allow Congress time to digest the hundreds of pages of text before I put my signature on it and make it binding. Since the agreement must be signed by April 16, 1994, the day Fast Track expires, that means this accord will only enter into force without Congressional haggling if and only if the final decisions of the Trade Negotiating Committee are registered by midnight in D.C.

Tonight.

Allison walks into the suite, her suite, our base of operations. How does she get any sleep? Close the bedroom door? Eye mask? Earplugs? A fifth of vodka?

Allison has a frown on her face.

"What's going on?" I say to her.

"The dollar is rising. The Nikkei is down twelve percent on news the agreement is in trouble."

She should be smiling, but I don't think she likes this game as much as the rest of us.

"Wow." I'm blown back deeper into the large armchair I'm sitting in. I had figured a two or three-percent drop. Maybe five. But double digits... "Okay, how much is everyone hating life?"

A diving Nikkei would negatively affect Hong Kong, Bombay, and European financial markets when they opened. The cascade would eventually lead to New York, but the American exchanges had already gone lower this week *expecting* us to fuck this up. A rising dollar would bring in safe-haven investors, tempering the blow for New York and exacerbating it for everyone else.

"Nobody's jumping out of any windows yet. But they're checking to see if the latches open." Allison has a dark sense of humor. "But," she says, "it's driving some movement. The Koreans are floating limited rice imports if the Japanese agree to the same."

Even more shocking.

"What about the EU?"

"Tom's got them in a room. Everyone else is sitting on the fence waiting to see how that turns out." She looks at me. "They're waiting for you."

I WALKED INTO THE ROOM.

It was paneled. I had never noticed that before.

There was a different vibe in the room from anything I've ever felt. It wasn't fear. It was something else. I think, for the first time, they realized, I really didn't give a shit anymore.

Beckett was standing, clearly agitated.

"You, Mr. Gerrick, are an arrogant, tyrannical little boy. Who thinks beating his opponents into submission is the proper way to win."

I stared at him.

"I simply said, 'no,' Andrew."

I had never called him by his first name. Always Beckett. Even in school, I didn't use *professor* or *mister*. Just Beckett. He seemed taken aback by the familiarity.

"Isn't that the most basic right of every person, of every nation, the right to say, 'no?' 'No, thank you.' 'Not for us?' 'Not interested.' 'No.'"

I surveyed the rest of the people gathered.

"The markets are clearly speaking to us. We need to come to some sort of agreement. We should and we can hammer out right now a bilateral accord that is acceptable to both sides. Something I can take home and Congress will pass. Something we put in place no matter what the rest of the world decides. Everyone is waiting for Europe," I gazed at each of them, "and America to take the first step."

Beckett was still standing.

I turned to him. "Or does that seem too much like me bludgeoning you?"

"It 'tis not yet midnight in the U.S. I assume we can do this without interference?" asked Rafael.

I'm glad someone besides my assistant understands time zones.

"I've asked for clarification from the Comptroller General of the GAO and the legislative liaison," I told her. "We probably have a few hours, but we would need to have everything finalized and transmitted to Washington well before midnight to be absolutely sure. I will not agree to any items that don't have a reasonable chance of passing Congress, because they may try to make the legal point that it is, in fact, already *tomorrow*. Any agreement we finalize now will reflect that. The news is public. It's out. There's no backdating this. The faster we get this done, the less of an argument Congress will have. If this is going to creep past midnight in Washington, we might as well stop talking right now."

"I understand," she said.

"I'm tired. We all are. We need to do this right now, or I need to go to sleep."

Beckett put his hand on the door. "That's your idea of compromise? A pistol to the head? You want to kill this agreement? Consider it dead." He turned the handle and walked out.

The door creaked eerily before it finally slammed shut. We all watched it for several seconds. They were all staring at me when I looked up.

"How long do you think he's going to be?" I finally said to Rafael.

"Ohhh, I do not know, a few minutes, maybe?"

"Then let's get this done before he gets back."

There was a collective sigh and a general nodding of heads from the half-dozen others in the room.

They really didn't like him any more than I did.

It's always good during a negotiation to have one person that everyone hates. It bonds people together.

Up until now, *I* had been that person.

By the time Beckett finally, dramatically walked back in thinking he had somehow made his point, I had already worked out the broad strokes and left the room, leaving Tom to work out the final language.

ALLISON MET up with me in the hall just outside a restaurant where the Asian workgroup was holed up.

"Done," I said in answer to her look.

The trades from Australia, Hong Kong, Japan, Korea, New Zealand, The Philippines, Singapore, Thailand, and Vietnam were having drinks. The Australians and the Japanese were in the middle of an intense drinking game.

It was comical when they saw me, they held their shots of whatever the hell they were drinking an inch from their mouths.

"I just wanted you all to know, I just worked out a bilateral deal with the EU. So, we'll work out our deal at the APEC meeting...next year. Pleasure seeing all of you," I said, and then I motioned throwing back a shot. "*Campai!*"

I walked out.

THINGS KICKED INTO HIGH GEAR. Everyone was scrambling.

I got wind that one of the delegates from Indonesia was holding up progress with the developing nations, pulling the "two-minute drill."

But tonight, I wasn't having any of it.

I had been watching him all week, not focusing on him, but observing him *just in case.*

And what I had noticed about this guy, as strange as it seems, was that he reminded me of my father. Not in looks or size or anything like that, but it was something about the way that he maintained his papers at the table. There are plenty of anal retentives amongst the support personnel making sure everything's where it's supposed to be, and even some of the delegates are themselves very fastidious about their briefcases and documents.

No, this was something different. This had to do with someone being fussy about their things. Not anal. Fussy.

That may seem like a fine line of distinction, but I remember the way my father would act—still acts to this day—about his things and how he wants them set up.

My father had a workspace in the cellar where if you moved something five inches, he couldn't find it. He never actually *used* anything or did any *work* in the workplace, but he could tell.

It wasn't ever about neatness either. The thing was a mess. It was about spatial placement.

I can't begin to count the times I would be sitting in my room reading, or studying, or masturbating, or listening to music, and cutting through it all, I would hear this lamentable howl.

It was this ear-piercing, mind-numbing wail that would come from the depth of my father's gut. The shriek usually went something like this:

"Where the hell is my Goddamn *Blank*!!!"

Tools, gardening books, food items, it didn't matter.

The Princess could go ballistic if *his* mayonnaise wasn't right where he put it three days earlier. My father couldn't quite grasp the concept that he was not the only person in our house (see way, way, way above, regarding the bathroom). It never occurred to him that there were a dozen hands going in and out of the family fridge. He had put the mayonnaise at coordinate X,Y and it was no longer at X,Y.

My father had no real awareness that other people existed, not just in our house, but in all existence. I said that my grandfather, Robert, believed the world revolved around him. I don't believe my father thought that way about his place in the world. I simply think he felt he should be the only one in it.

People seemed to annoy the Princess, people in his way, people on the road, people with hands in the refrigerator moving his mayonnaise three fucking inches. Just plain people in general.

He would sit downstairs in our basement, alone in the dark, reading, just because he wanted to be somewhere, anywhere there was no one. And God forbid if someone did come within hailing distance of my father at these times.

My mother, God bless her, would blithely trudge downstairs with a huge load of laundry in her arms, only to be faced with—

"Jesus Christ, can't a person get any peace around here?"

You know Dad, she's washing your threadbare underwear, get over it.

I do understand this trait *somewhat*. I've always been someone who cherishes my alone time. But the extreme to which my father took this need is something still not understood by me, the rest of the family, and several prominent behavioral scientists.

Like I said, the huge workbench in the cellar was pretty much useless, not because there weren't some incredible tools there—my grandfather, the ex-carpenter, had given the Princess great equipment—but because my father wouldn't let anyone near the thing since we'd "fuck things up," and then he'd never be able to finish any of his projects.

Apparently, we fucked things up all the time.

Because almost none of his projects ever got finished.

There was this one undertaking where my father ordered and built a fuel injection system for one of his cars.

A Ford Pinto.

A Ford Pinto *station wagon*.

Gunter was over the day the thing finally got installed. It actually took two weeks to put together—the Princess liked to pace himself—where he couldn't use *his* car, he had to use mine.

"I gave you that car!"

"Yes, so I could drive it."

Gunter was picking me up on that Saturday afternoon since I had no means of transportation. He drove up in his dental-chair-green Ford Maverick, pulled in behind my mother's car (Gunter knew better than to ever block in the Princess's car, even if it wasn't working).

It happened that as I went outside to greet Gunter, my father was turning over the engine for the first time.

"You wanna feel something?" my father said.

Of course, I didn't want to feel anything, but before Gunter could realize what he was doing, he automatically said, "What?"

We got the whole lesson. Every detail on what my father had done and what it would mean to the car's performance.

He had a very viable increase of almost two percent, about one horse-power, raising it from a paltry ninety to a blazing ninety-one and change. But the Princess could feel that increase.

Oh, yeah. Big time.

And after being with him all these years, I actually believe he did feel it. Why? Because my father could discern a fluctuation in temperature of half a degree. Because he could sense if his tires needed one fucking pound of air.

He would drive the car to the gas station, pump another pound of air pressure in the Goodyears, get back in the car, swerve the steering wheel back and forth and basically make himself a road hazard for five minutes and then say—

"Can you feel that? This thing handles so much better."

It's a fucking Pinto dad, not a Ferrari.

I could go on for hours and hours and hours just about the idiosyncrasies he had regarding cars. It's enough to say that because my father could tell the difference in power and mileage between different kinds of gas, he would go to only one gas station unless he absolutely couldn't help it. Even if it meant going dozens of miles out of his way.

He likes what he likes what he likes.

And I don't mean buying one *brand*, I mean, a single gas station.

Buddy's Garage.

One day he got a bad tank of gas from Buddy—a guy my father seemed to know everything about, life, kids, business, the rest, and who, in return, I suspect only knew what octane gas my father put in his car. *Super* Premium, ninety-three octane.

One bad tank. And he never ever went back.

Any hitch or hiccup, any complication could stop the Princess like sand in an engine.

Huge undertakings were shelved because a single nut or a bolt went missing, a problem easily remedied by a trip to the hardware store. A tool misplaced—even for an hour or a few minutes—would result in a project's abandonment. The workbench, the cellar, the backyard, the greenhouse, the driveway were littered with half-finished endeavors never to be completed or revisited because some minor obstacle had presented itself.

So, as my Indonesian friend was attempting to throw a Grizzled Leaf Monkeywrench into the proceedings, I decided to put an end to it, quickly.

I WALKED into the room where the developing nations were meeting.

Colombia and the Swiss were the surrogates for the U.S. and EU within the group. I informed them that we had reached a side agreement and, as I had done a few moments before with the Asian workgroup, I told the room we'd pick this up sometime in the next year or so.

As I spoke, I accidentally knocked a few of the Indonesian trade's neatly piled papers to the ground.

I did it very naturally, pretending to push the papers out of the way so I could lean against the table and talk.

My Indonesian counterpart was so flustered and preoccupied with trying to put his papers back in order, that he spent the next ten minutes not paying attention to anything going on at the table.

I was able to further disrupt his personal space by continually having one of the Colombian aides pass him page after page after page of mostly irrelevant documentation, which not only made him more nuts, it also kept him from straightening up the original mess.

I greased the wheels of the most important and far-reaching multilateral trade agreement by jumbling up some guy's papers.

He ended up gathering his things and walking out, leaving his assistant to take over. After that, Indonesia, Brazil, India, and the rest of the developing bloc fell in line.

"COMPROMISE ON AIRBUS, agriculture subsidies. Phase out of the bribery deduction...givebacks on a whole range of issues. This is like a year's worth of work in two hours." Allison was shaking her head in disbelief. "What did you do in there?"

Tom glanced at me. "He caved on media content."

Allison was—something—surprised, concerned. "That was a top priority for the President."

"We're so dominant in media that I felt it was something we could put off for a bit, let the natural market forces handle it a little longer, in order to get what we got."

"You're sure about this?"

"I spoke with the President. He said if we scuttled this whole thing over the cultural exception for media everyone would think he really was sleeping with all those actresses the tabloids have been saying he's been sleeping with."

Tom sat back. "Jack-Jack was frothing at the mouth, told Billy, he'd destroy him."

"The head of the MPAA threatened you?" asked Allison.

"Oh, if he had a gun..."

"And wasn't like a hundred."

"...your boss would've been rubbed out like the bad guy in a movie."

Allison studied me with something approaching respect.

Quite an accomplishment.

"It won't matter anyway. What're the Germans gonna watch? French films? They'd rather shoot themselves in the head."

ERLOHOF HUDDLED outside the ballroom along with Rafael and the rest of the G7 negotiators as I walked up. Diego Costa was there, Brazil. So was Maru Patel, India.

We, the small gathering in the hallway, represented the major voting groups, and in essence, the success or failure of this entire process.

Erlohof didn't want to get in there and run the vote again unless there was a near-certain chance it was going to pass.

"So," he said. "Do we have a consensus?"

All of us looked exhausted.

"We believe everyone of consequence is in agreement," Beckett said, flatly.

Erlohof nodded, then started into the ballroom when I noticed—

"Where's Hutseo?"

Everyone stopped.

I glanced at Hutseo's deputy, Toshigawa—who had tried to kick me in the balls during the fight—this time speaking directly to him. "Where's Hutseo?"

Toshigawa gave a little bow, which meant absolutely nothing to me.

He did not come back up from the bent-over position. Not a good sign.

"Where...is...Hutseo?!"

I FINALLY TRACKED down Hutseo as he was scurrying into one of the elevators at the far end of the lobby. Seconds away from escape, he was now cornered. He had hit buttons for several of the floors—it didn't matter which ones—he just wanted up and out.

Only, no, no, no, he wasn't getting away that easily.

I had pushed this conference to the brink, sent it careening over the edge, and slowly, painfully, dragged it back to the mountaintop.

I pulled the emergency STOP button, causing the alarm bell to ring. It was annoying and loud.

Trapped, with nowhere to go, Hutseo backed up until he bumped into an empty brass luggage cart.

As I stepped closer, he retreated further by jumping *onto* the cart's red-carpeted base.

This had the added benefit of making Hutseo stand taller. He was now eye to eye with me.

I could feel he was emboldened by his new-found height.

"I cannot vote for this," he said, tilting forward. "I am sorry."

Again with the bowing.

Okay, now I was getting annoyed. I made a move toward Hutseo, but he backed away, just out of my reach. He was at the other end of the luggage cart, against the wall.

I spun the cart a hundred and eighty degrees so that Hutseo's back was momentary facing me. He quickly turned around.

We were face to face once more. He didn't bother to try retreating again. He knew I'd swing him around as many times as it took.

"If this is about your fucking rice…!" I screamed.

Hutseo was silent.

"Perhaps," he began after a moment, "if we drop that provision. You were willing to drop the agricul—"

"No, no!"

I started spinning the cart, first one way, then the other. I needed to get into the pocket of his suit, and when I went for it, he moved away.

It was time for a little more *sledge* and a little less *velvet*.

"Give me your phone!"

"What?"

"I want your phone."

I motioned for it.

"Why?"

"You're going to kill this entire fucking deal…" I was so mad I could hardly get the words out. "…because I'm trying to sell a couple of bags of rice in your country?!"

I finally got the cart sideways, now he was close enough, and I began patting down his suit. There! Left inside pocket.

I tore the phone out. It was the latest Japanese model, smaller than mine. I'll admit, I was a little jealous.

"What's your Prime Minister's number? I wanna call him! I want to hear him say, 'Yes, Mr. Ambassador, Hutseo is correct, Japan is willing to fuck over the entire planet'—not to mention every other industry in your country—'to make sure our *gohan* is one hundred percent homegrown!' I just want to hear him say it himself!"

Flashing through his speed dial list, I kept Hutseo at bay with a hand to his face.

I found the number, and while it was ringing, I began pulling the cart out of the elevator.

Hutseo did an admirable job attempting to look dignified, erecting something of a *Washington Crossing The Delaware* pose as I rolled him roughly across the lobby.

Someone answered in Japan.

"Hello," I said into the phone. "I would like to speak with the Prime Minister, please. Yes, it's an emergency. Tell him it's Ambassador William Gerrick from the UST—"

Hutseo reached out and flipped his phone closed.

"We should vote now."

32

THE DECIDING VOTE

NEGOTIATING IS HARD.

It's like war, only with more important things at stake.

I know that sounds strange, but think about it. Wars end. That is the nature of war. It cannot continue. Wars are fought over land, over love, over core beliefs. Good vs. Evil. Freedom vs. Tyranny.

We can understand these things.

But negotiation—negotiation is a constant state. And too many times we have bargained ourselves out of the very freedoms we have fought and died for, compromised one value to get another. Whether it's between nations or neighbors or husbands and wives, it doesn't matter.

Compromise is defined as *finding a middle course, a trade-off*, even *a sell-out*.

"You know why you kill at this," Tom whispered to me. "Because I honestly believe you don't care about anything. You really would've walked away."

I would've walked away. And not because I didn't care but because I cared in a different way.

Life is only about choices, about decisions. Our existence is defined by what we do. Day by day by day. No choice in life is insignificant. Only insufficiently thought out.

Sometimes, it's easy.

Sometimes, it's hard, like having to choose "upper deck or lower deck" —whether to get punched in the face or kicked in the balls. Slam into the little kid crossing the street or swerve into the truck coming the other way.

Choosing between the lesser of two evils is not difficult. It's choosing between the greater of two goods that is painful.

I don't know exactly when I decided.

I take that back, I know exactly when.

It was moments after we finalized the agreement, after all the chaos, the arguments, and high drama, much of which I had caused, first by going home for Sebby's funeral, then by slipping into France in the middle of the night to rescue Sydney, and finally by saying the simplest word in every language. No.

We, the delegations of the world, managed to finally arrive at an agreement that was equally offensive to everyone involved, so much so, that we were able to get unanimous consent on only the fourth vote.

> *By adopting the present Final Act, participants agree to adopt the Ministerial Declarations and Decisions; and to submit, as appropriate, the Agreement Establishing the Multilateral Trade Organization for the consideration of their respective competent authorities with a view to seeking approval of this Agreement in accordance with appropriate procedures of the participant concerned.*

With these mind-numbing words, it was done. Because we didn't have time to get everything to the printer, some of the last-minute revisions and the name of the new organization were handwritten on the documents. The Multilateral Trade Organization, the exact kind of needlessly obtuse moniker only a bureaucrat could dream up, had to go. Something called the MTO would too easily be mocked by critics as the Empty Organization, so Tom and I forced through a final change to the more dignified *World* Trade Organization.

And when I signed my name four months later in Morocco, the WTO was born.

In the euphoria surrounding the approval of the agreement, the jubilation of participating in such a monumental event, people were smiling and congratulating each other.

It was like the end of a war.

Or the end of a rock concert, just before the encore.

I had never seen anything quite like it. Much of the world was united for one brief moment, standing together as one people.

Cheering.

There were numerous spontaneous congratulatory speeches.

One of those impromptu addresses, by the lead delegate from Kenya, struck a chord in me. The tall, thin trade got up and said, "It is from now, East Africa shall be free from the chains that have held us back. This is a day that we have hoped for, we have dreamed of for many, many years."

And he wondered, what kind of world would this agreement spawn ten, twenty, fifty years from now?

Tom encouraged me to say something. I tried to decline, but it was the nod from Rafael that made me stand and say:

"This is the time of year, the season that so many of us and our cultures, our nations take time to celebrate joy and hope. It's not always easy to feel hope, but what we have done here tonight, what so many have been doing for eight years and even longer shows we can create a better, more open society. The new year brings with it a time to reflect, to start anew. This is a new step forward for all of us. It is not often that the world comes together, but when we do, we can achieve monumental results."

LIKE I WAS SAYING, there are no easy answers, no easy decisions in life. Opening one door means you're closing off a hundred others.

It's not that I hadn't questioned my relationship with Laura, or wondered whether she was the right one for me. It's normal, even healthy, to examine the choices we make.

It's the questions I *didn't* ask.

I don't think I truly explored the permutations of our personalities, how they would mesh and commingle and, God forbid, cohabitate. Never worried about those little habits, those annoying mannerisms, that become so incredibly magnified when you multiply them by forty or fifty years.

I realize now, I wasn't worried because, in the back of my mind, I somehow knew, I wouldn't ever be in that position.

It was when the delegate from Kenya said that—*fifty years*. What would the world be like? It was then that I made the decision. Because while everyone was laughing and shouting and slapping each other on the back, I closed my eyes and pictured myself on a balmy afternoon sitting with Laura and our two kids and their kids in a big backyard. And then another picture came into my mind, this time there were more grandchildren and more kids and the sun was setting and I turned my eyes away from the blinding light, and I was sitting next to Sydney. They were both nice pictures, both beautiful evenings slipping into night. But there was something different about one of them. I belonged in it.

It's not like I *didn't* belong in the other, it's just that I *wanted* to be in the one with the woman who crashed into a mountain to be with me again.

AND SO I got up without a word and headed to the back of the room, people grabbing for my hands, shaking them. I nodded. I was on autopilot. People slapped me on the back, some called out to me, trying to get my attention. But I just walked steadfastly out of the conference.

And there, I found this cute little honey blonde at the far end of one of the beautiful sitting rooms I had over the years repeatedly failed to notice. A space that reminded me, more than anything, of a very large, very elegant, yet very comfortable living room.

Sydney was not looking at me, but for some reason she glanced up, seeming to sense my presence.

I nodded my head. There was no doubt in any fiber of me. I had to make her mine. I had to, because when I looked at her face in that moment, I saw the future. And when I looked into her eyes, I saw God.

"Hi," I said.

"Hi," she responded, softly.

"I missed you. I kept thinking, I could be somewhere with you, instead of messing with Indonesians."

"I never enjoyed messing with Indonesians."

"I do sometimes."

She smiled at me with her mouth but didn't with her eyes. It was a sad smile anyway. Our time was coming to an end, we both could tell.

"I thought we could get something to eat. I hear there's this exceptional café that has a helipad out front. No waiting."

Again the smile without much happiness.

"I thought we might order in."

I tilted my head, not understanding. "Eat here in the hotel?"

"I got us a room. Much easier to come by now that everyone's leaving."

"I imagine it would be," I said suspiciously.

Shouldn't we be leaving, too?

She glanced up at me with eyes that were intense and demure in the same instant. "I think we should go up to the room now."

"Are you sure about this?"

She nodded. "I don't want to be *that* woman who breaks two people up." She slid a lock of hair over her ear. "On the other hand...I don't think I could deal with never sleeping with you, either."

Choices.

She again pushed her hair over her ear as if she'd forgotten she'd just done it. "I really don't care if this is the only time that we're together. I just want to be with you at least once."

I knew we were whispering, but it sounded like every word was echoing through the entire lobby.

"You don't need to do this, you know."

"I want to do this. I want to very badly."

Silence is such a poor description for what happens between sentences, between lovers. What are those moments made of? Not serenity, for sure. What do those thoughts mean, the ones that harbor just behind our eyes in the pause that takes place between our words? We glance. We nod. But there is something so much greater going on here.

"Sydney..." Again silence. "I want to be—"

She put her finger up to my lips. And shook her head. "Please, don't say another word. I want this to be just what it is. Nothing else."

SYDNEY LAY BACK against the foot of the sofa. The room was beautiful. Not any bigger than the rooms that I usually stayed in here, but definitely more intimate, not for business people but for lovers.

She pulled her hair back and tied it into some sort of knot. I'm always amazed at how women can just flip their hair or pull and twist a little of it and something will emerge, a bun, a braid, a tail, something that hadn't been there before.

The extent to which I do "something" to my hair is when I grab a baseball cap and cover it.

She pressed her lips against my neck and slid her tongue down to my shoulder, and kissed and sucked and nibbled all the way to the start of my arm.

I pushed her back and drew my finger over her lips, then traced down between her soft, lacy, seamless bra. I kissed her on the mouth as my hands found her thighs and smoothed along her hips and over her stomach.

We didn't say much. We had talked and talked and talked. On planes, in cars, in front of fires, over breakfast, in lobbies. We had spoken all that could be said up to this point.

I asked her if my hands were warm enough. She nodded, "Mmmhuh. But I could make them warmer if you wanted."

She did, not too much later.

I ran my palm down to her panties and squeezed the strip of tangled hair, cupping that warmest, most private of places in my hand. And I felt the heat flow from her moist pussy, through the thin fabric and into my palm.

The feel of her breath, the smell of her skin, the excruciating pleasure that comes from having to hold back unrestrainable passion. Her face flushed with the heat and I felt mine do the same.

We touched and stared into each other's eyes and explored each other's bodies. We had walked this path before, but there were different trails to follow, different scents to track.

We kissed.

So many ways, so long, in so many parts of the room.

Then I pushed her legs up, held them spread apart and surveyed the beautiful, smooth landscape that lay before me.

How many times had a looked at a woman this way? Her legs spread. The soft, tender folds peeking out from behind lacy fabric.

In all the uncountable times...

Never.

After a long, long moment, taking in her body, I eased myself down and pressed against Sydney. She instinctively pushed up her pelvis to meet mine, ever so subtly. She ran her hands over my shoulders and down my back, changing from the silky touch of her fingertips to the fine intensity of her nails as she moved further toward my hips.

I freed her breasts one at a time by sliding the straps of her delicate bra off her shoulders. And as our bodies moved in rhythm, the steady motion began to push her underwear to the side without any added help, till I could feel the underside of my cock naked against her moistness.

"Once," she whispered and let the tip of my cock slide a single time through the folds between her legs. Well, one time all the way from beginning to end. There were several other, shorter advances and retreats that apparently didn't count. "That's it...I said just once," she moaned as I tried to slip by unnoticed for the tenth pass. "Condom time."

I froze for a second. Not this again. What was I thinking? Why didn't I try to find some—

Then I relaxed as she pulled out two three-packs.

"Very nice."

"You're not the only one who was busy this evening," she murmured with a sweet smile.

"Six? Ambitious."

"Not really." She pulled out another pack. "This is ambitious."

"That's hospitalization."

"I doubt that."

SHE PULLED a condom out of the package and bent down, wrapping her warm mouth around the head of my cock, swirling her tongue in slick, fluid motions getting me very, very hard and slippery, preparing me for the sheath.

She gently slid the condom over the tip and slowly unrolled it down the length of me. Even before she was halfway through, I knew I was in trouble.

"What's wrong?"

I was looking down at my cock, which looked a lot like a—I won't even say the obvious sausage casing reference—like a three-hundred-pound woman in a size two bikini.

"I think it's cutting off my circulation."

"What?"

"I...think...it's cutting off my circulation!"

Sydney sprang into action. She tried to tug the condom off of me, but it only snapped back like a rubberband—SNNNAPPP!!—causing me to bite my tongue, which began bleeding onto the condom as I glanced down to see what was happening to my precious cargo.

"I gotta geth it owffth."

"What?"

"Offth." I didn't even feel the pain in my tongue. My pain receptors were all pointed South.

"Okay, I'll—"

"Don't!!! Touch it!!!"

"Let's be calm about this," she said. Easy for her to say, it wasn't her cock in some Chinese finger cuff. "Let's unroll it. Just like you put it on, we'll take it off."

She reversed her steps, unrolling the rubber a quarter of an inch at a time. One of my hairs got caught in the mix and I yelped.

"Sorry!"

"Where the hell thid you geth these? From Ompfahlomfas?"

She continued her work more carefully, licking me with her tongue to distract me. She disengaged her lips long enough to answer, "I went and I asked for the best-rated brand."

I glanced at the package. My eyes had seen it when she first pulled them out, but my *mind* hadn't.

"Okay, it's noooooot, oow, your fault. The Japanese make the best condoms on the planet, but they seem to love to shrink-wrap their fucking dicks."

Snap! It finally came off.

I was free.

SOMEONE ONCE TOLD me that repetition is the mother of skill.

Sort of, if at first, you don't succeed, try, try again.

I'm not sure if this works in all arenas. But I know for a fact that it works with parents. If a child can repeat over and over and over and over and over and over and over and over again, "I want to do *blank*," that child will be able to do *blank*.

Trust me.

My father was also very good at this technique. The man would repeat whatever something he wanted to purchase to my mother and the rest of us so many times that my mom would just say, "Fine, Sam, just get the G.D. thing."

Anyway, I'm not talking about the Princess, I'm talking about repeating things.

Here I am for the second time in as many nights trying to locate some condoms. I have some, but if I use them, it's highly likely my penis will fall off.

Again, it's unbelievable to me that I am a grown man groveling for prophylactics.

For some stupid reason, it seems like every time I go to buy, locate, or use a condom, it's the end of the fucking world.

Right from the beginning. From the first time I tried to buy one to a few minutes ago. Pure nightmare.

I'm sixteen, I go into a drugstore, and I think, okay, I'm going get one of these things. I really need to have one in my pocket just in case I happen to get lucky. Isn't that what we learned in scouts? *Be prepared.*

The place is full of women. Everywhere. Women with kids. Women buying those stupid napkins. Women who know my mother.

"Hi, Billy."

"Hi, Mrs. Samuels."

I don't know if women use prescription drugs more than men, but Christ, it seems like they do. Finally, after a half an hour of "browsing" (I know exactly what I want), and waiting for all these women to pay for their fucking drugs, doo-dads, and paraphernalia, I observe that the coast is clear.

The pharmacist is this really old guy, and I'm sure he's sold more than a few of these things to young guys over the years. Perhaps he's even used a condom once or twice himself. Who knows?

So, just as I'm about to get up to the register, I look away for one second, one fucking second, and all of a sudden, when I turn around, the pharmacist is gone and in his place is this very cute, very sweet sixteen-year-old girl. From my church.

I'm in hell. That's all there is to it. I'm in hell.

Then there was the time visiting Gunter and his wife.

It was New Year's Eve, and I was staying over a couple of nights after a solo post-college/pre-grad school trip to Central America where I had spent my entire Christmas staring at skinny "St. Claws" in shorts. They don't have Christmas trees in Central America. The yucca plant doesn't lend itself well to baubles and garland and little twinkling lights. But they do celebrate God and the coming of his Son. And the people there, the poor, the comfortable, the desperate, they see the approaching year with such hope, such shining hope, that I felt a twinge of sadness when I landed in America and saw all the cranky kids and crankier adults still complaining cause they didn't get the gift they wanted. And I realized that we have everything but cherish almost none of it.

Gunter and his wife, Diane, had assembled a wonderful group of people, some I knew, most I didn't. And when the night was over, and all the blowing of horns, kissing of usually forbidden lips and singing and wishing was done with, I ended up on the living room floor amongst the scattered out-of-towners, wrapped up in the prettiest, most eligible woman at the party, Mary Anne Brannen.

Nothing major happened, but even though it was cold outside, it was a warm, pleasurable night.

M.A. lived not that far from my parents, so a few days after the New Year's Eve celebration, she and I went out on an official date. It was pretty clear from the beginning that she and I would be having sex later in the evening. The chemistry between us was far too strong, and, remember, I had just gotten back from Christmas in Central America where I made the shrewd, yet difficult decision not to sleep with any of the beautiful women I met there. Central American brothers, fathers, and even aunts are known to pull out a gun or two when it comes to their *señoritas*.

And I was returning to school in a couple of days, so this would be our one and only chance to sleep together.

On the way home from dancing at a club, the subject of what might happen during the rest of the evening came up. She said, "Why don't we stop for something at the drugstore?"

Perfect. I was just hoping it wasn't her chlamydia prescription and was glad when she said, "No. Condoms, you asshole." In a really nice way.

We were both excited. I don't care how old you are, that moment when you know you're gonna be rolling naked with someone you like for the first time is just soooo exhilarating.

"Okay, I'm going in."

"Ooow," she said.

I got out of the car, reset myself so I wouldn't be scaring women and children, and went into the store.

It wasn't that late, about ten P.M. or so. It may have been earlier. We decided to skip out on the rest of our evening and go back to her place instead.

I was keyed up—of course I was. I was gonna get naked very, very soon.

I began searching the aisles, going up and then around and then back down and then around again, for condoms. Now, I wasn't going to *ask* where they kept the condoms. First, once again, this place was filled with women. Second, I'm a man. I don't need directions or guidance. I can track things down and locate them for myself.

Finally, I discovered the condoms.

They were in the farthest corner of the store, way, way in the back.

To me, condoms are one of those items that should be right in front, right beside the sugarless gum. An impulse purchase. No, these things were in a different area code. To make matters worse, they weren't even accessible to the customer. You had to ask the pharmacist for assistance. Which wouldn't have bothered me all that much—I'm an *adult* now—if there had been a pharmacist to ask.

I kept ringing the bell, and ringing the bell, trying to find someone who could help me. But apparently, the drug part of the drugstore closed down two hours before the rest of the place.

I ended up having to trudge back up front to the cashier.

And in the style of some older stores, and so very lucky for me, the cashier was raised above the customers, so they were looking down on their pathetic, sickly little patrons. After waiting my turn in line, and finally getting up to the register, I discretely asked the cashier if she could get someone to help me with the condoms in the back of the store. She nodded and proceeded to grab one of these giant microphones stuck atop a flexible metal snake. It made a loud squeaking and crunching noise as she pulled the mic to her lips and said, "Bob, I got a guy here who needs help getting condoms."

To which Bob, from somewhere, answered back over the intercom, "No problem, what kine he wanna see?"

The cashier looked at me.

"I'll just go back there and tell him myself."

"No, no, he'll bring 'em up to you. It's much faster. And it's our pleasure," which happened to be the slogan behind her. It's Our Pleasure To Serve You. "You want Trojans, Ramses, Ma—?

"Fine, yes, I'll take the Trojans."

"He gonna take the Trojans, Bob," she bellowed into the microphone.

"Ah, he want dem reservoir tip or regular?" This blared throughout the store. Now everyone was wondering who was buying condoms and wanted a look at them.

"Reservoir tip?" the cashier asked.

"What?"

"The ones with the little thing at the end."

The little thing? Are you fucking kidding me? Get me some fucking condoms.

"Fine. That would be...fine."

"Reservoir," she screeched into the mic.

"Lubricated? Or da ribbed?" came back the response. It seemed like he had turned up the volume.

The cashier was about to speak—

"Yes, great!" I was sweating.

"Which?"

"Both."

The cashier nodded and grabbed the microphone.

"Okay, Bob, bring up a package of Trojans reservoir tip, lubricated, and ribbed."

"Will do," answered Bob. "Spermicide?"

"No!" I said through gritted teeth.

"Nope."

"Three pack or twelve?" echoed through the store.

I wanted to buy a thousand so I never, ever had to go through this again, but I didn't want to scare the shit out of M.A.

"Three," I said, resigned.

"He say three."

A moment later, after the cashier had rung up the three other people who had been witness to my embarrassment, someone with the name Bob on his shirt came up to the front with my Trojans.

The cashier was just about to ring up my purchase when she realized there was no price on the package.

Bob had already gone back to his condom lair, so, once again, out came the mic.

"Bob, can I get a price check on these Trojans, lubricated and ribbed... ah, with the reservoir tip?"

"Will do." Silence. Interminable silence. "Was that the extra large size I gave you or the smaller ones?

"Ah, look like one of each."

"Oh. Well, den both're four eight-five."

Why did he ask if they were same?

"Thanks."

Yeah, thank you, Bob.

"So, you want the large or the small?"

This is like asking a woman how much she weighs.

I sighed. "Large."

She raised a skeptical eyebrow. Then finally, rang up the purchase.

Everyone in line was staring at me. One woman pulled her young child closer to her when I glanced in her direction. I fumbled with my money, dropped my car keys, and finally found my cash, didn't have enough, had to pay by check. By the time I got outside, I was drained and humiliated. Perhaps this is the reason condoms are one of the most shoplifted items. Kids would rather risk jail time than face the embarrassment of buying them.

To this day, I still have no idea how I was able to get into that car, go back to her place, and fuck this woman. Probably because I told her the story, which got us laughing so hard that we forgot all about being nervous once we ripped our clothes off.

I FOUND what I needed pretty quickly. I asked the concierge. Helpful fellow. Seemed to know a lot about the subject. He had someone reopen one of the stores in the hotel even though it was not yet six in the morning, and I was back upstairs in less than ten minutes.

Once again, opening the door, I found Sydney had gotten dressed. Only this time, I knew she wasn't saying no, just giving me some more obstacles. She was wearing black thigh-high stockings, and one of the Intercontinental's sumptuous robes...

...and nothing else.

I gazed at her and smiled and drank her in.

"You look beautiful."

She lifted her chin and stared with eyes half-closed, in a sidelong glance at me and the bag I held. "You look prepared."

33

JEOPARDY
(OR: AND THE ANSWER IS...)

THE ENTIRE NIGHT. The *entire* night.

We made love, we laughed, we talked, we cried a little, we mmmmmm fucked, we kissed, we held each other in long moments of silence.

People always say that men and women think differently about sex and love. I think people aren't as smart as they'd like to believe.

When true emotion and physicality bond in a moment of singularity —of feeling and touch, of passion and ecstasy—men and women may describe it differently, we may use words that sometimes make women think we don't understand, but the feeling is the same.

Is it love? That's not the point.

It's human. And that's all that matters.

I'M SHAVING, looking in the mirror at a tired but happy face. A low ceiling of fog hovers just above my head, the demarcation between moist air and clear is a boundary of frostiness cast on the glass. Sydney is in the shower, and the sound of water soothes me.

I run the blade across my face and enjoy the feel of the cutting edge slicing through my whiskers. For someone who doesn't like to shave, I love the shaving experience. The muted scrape of the razor sliding down my cheek and over my chin. The feel of my face, once rough from beard and dead skin, rejuvenated by the dangerous slash of a blade.

I glance to the side and see her reflection in the mirror. She is sitting on the floor of the clear glass shower, her knees to her chest. She is shaving, too. She had been doing her calf, but as I look, she is slowly drawing the blade between her legs, carefully removing two days of blonde, leaving a small tangle of hair.

My own blade freezes in place, and my heart skips a beat. "Oh, my God," I whisper.

She looks up to see me staring at her. She closes her legs just a fraction, almost imperceptibly.

I am surprised by the emotion that runs through me.

"No matter what happens," she says, "this I'll do because of you. That little patch of me will always be yours."

I put down my razor and go to her. I open the door to the shower, removing my towel, and kneel down beside her. I wrap my arms around her and squeeze her so tight. I don't want to let go. As the warm water rains down on us, she kisses me. I hold her face in my hands and just shake my head. I cannot believe that I have lived this long without feeling this.

I want to thank her, but I hear my grandfather Robert in my head, hear echoes of all the lessons that years of negotiations have taught me, never apologize, never give anything away, never get emotionally involved in a deal.

I gaze into her eyes.

"Thank you," I say. "Thank you so much for coming into my life." I touch her face. "No matter what."

"No matter what," she says.

WE WERE SITTING down at breakfast in the café, at a table with a view of the pool. There were still a good number of trades hanging around, which was normal. There were side agreements being worked out. Timetables being set for other, less comprehensive pacts. The thousands of things we put off to get this larger, primary agreement.

Most people were smiling. Although some of the euphoria had worn off as the trades realized they'd have to head home to deal with the hangover of the previous night, explaining all the negatives in the treaty (from each country's standpoint) to their political leaders. Some, like me, would have to testify before congresses and parliaments and assemblies, bodies of government that needed to ratify the agreement before it would become the law of the land and the law of the world. The work was not over, but for now, we could take a moment to savor the achievement.

But I wasn't really thinking about any of this at the time.

Sydney and I were looking into each other's eyes. Sitting across from one another, over some eggs and what the Europeans think is bacon.

It's a warm and wonderful memory. Basking in the light of day and in the warmth that was forged between us last night in bed. Sex is such a remarkable phenomenon. It can be casual and zipless, matter-of-fact and meaningless. It's still pretty good then. But it can also be so much more. A connection that words cannot characterize, nor ever bring about.

I felt an overwhelming sense of satisfaction. And not only in the way that's usually meant. But in my soul. We touched each other. Physically. Emotionally.

For a long time, neither of us noticed the waiter standing at our table, wondering if we needed anything else. Automatically, I said, "We're fine."

"*Monsieur...*"

"Yes?" I looked up. It was not the waiter, but a porter bearing a note. "This is for you."

I opened the folded paper.

"Jesus Christ!" I said, loud enough for half the room to turn and look at me.

"What is it?"

There was really no time to fully explain the three-word note from Allison. I stood, getting out of my chair. "I, ah, stay right here. Don't... move. Okay?"

"What's wrong?" She started to get up.

"Just eat your breakfast. I'll be right back."

"GODAMMIT. JESUS CHRIST. FUCK!" I probably said a myriad of other things, but that was basically the gist of the conversation I was having with myself. Godammit. Jesus Christ. Fuck!

I saw Allison standing with her back to me, looking into the lobby. When I came up behind her and put my hand on her shoulder, she jumped, scaring me even more than I scared her.

"Godammit!"

"Jesus Christ!"

"Fuck! Don't come up behind me like that," she said, going from the look on my face to the missive in my hand. "So, I guess you got my note."

I crumpled the paper even tighter than I already had, obscuring the eleven letters scrawled in Allison's perfect handwriting. "Laura is *here*?"

Allison nodded rapidly. "In the lobby. Over by the foliage, whatever the fuck that is. This is your fault," she said, pointing right at my chest. "And yours." Her finger wagged at my crotch.

"Hey, listen, I have been very, very good since Laura. Up until now."

"Well, you've made up for it."

"You're supposed to be an assistant. Start assisting."

She glared at me. We have a good relationship. I only pull rank whenever it's absolutely necessary. The rest of the time, she's in charge.

Allison said, "Okay, where is she?"

Allison's savage tone when she said "she" made me want to defend Sydney. But there were more important things at the moment. "She's in the café."

"Okay, you go deal with Laura, I'll take care of her."

Again with the tone.

"Don't say anything to Sydney about this," I said. "I want to tell her."

"Oh, don't worry. I'm not getting anywhere near this subject." She patted me on the arm. "Better warm up those trademark negotiating skills."

She marched down the hall. God only knows what she was going to tell Sydney. It wouldn't be the truth, that's for sure. Allison is an excellent bullshit artist, such a fine craftsman that you hate to obliterate such superb work with veracity.

I STRAIGHTENED UP, steeled myself and began navigating the lobby, wondering if I smelled of another woman, threading through the mass of people checking out of the hotel.

I moved directly toward Laura's position.

No wavering.

She got up and ran into my arms. She was happy and sad and so many other things.

"I wanted to surprise you. Give you some support with all that's been going on. But the storm made me miss it all," she said as she scanned the lobby speckled with faces of all colors and nations. "God, I missed you."

I squeezed her body closer to mine, and I could feel her heat even through the thick jacket and layers of clothing. "I missed you, too."

Believe it or not, I did.

I really did.

She kissed me on the mouth and drew me to her.

"I heard the conference went really well."

"Better than expected."

"You look pretty good," she said. "I figured you'd look like shit."

Instantly, I began to feel like shit. I was anxious and nervous and my palms started to sweat. I felt like everyone was staring at me, watching me, saying to themselves, look at him, smiling like that when he's got this other woman here in the hotel.

It's one thing to analyze my relationship with Laura, even talk about it with Sydney or think about it to myself. It's quite another thing to have her here, standing face-to-face with me.

"They're calling you one of the toughest negotiators America's ever had. They compared you with Ben Franklin."

Normally, this little stroke from the media would cause me to casually sprint over to a television. But I didn't really feel like a hero at the moment, since the key to my success had been the death of my grandfather and the destruction of an up-till-now successful relationship.

"Why don't we go up to the room," I said.

She smiled at me and raised her eyebrow. "I heard you worked fast, Mr. Franklin."

I pressed for the elevator door to close. C'mon, c'mon, c'mon. This was slow-motion torture. I couldn't possibly tell you what I was thinking. Sydney, Laura, Sebby. It was all a jumbled mass of crap and I just wanted it out of my head. If I had a hammer...

I'd have tapped my keg.

"How did it go at home after I left?" I asked.

"As well as it could, I guess. Did you call your mother?"

"Yes."

We got off on the top floor and started down the hall. I got her all the way up to the door of my room. I was just about to put the card key in the slot when I thought, what the hell, I've just spent the night with another woman in this room. I don't care if the place has been steam cleaned, scrubbed down and sanitized, Laura was gonna know.

For a nanosecond, I thought about falling to my knees, pretending to be ill. But that was so fucking lame, I would have told *myself* to get off the Goddamn floor and stop clowning around.

"Fuck," I said only a little too loudly. "This is my old room. The one they gave away after I got scalded."

"I'm just grateful it didn't harm anything," she said, touching the front of my pants.

I thought about using Sebby as a defense, fending her off with a fit of sorrow. But I couldn't do that to him. It was cheap.

And besides, I never like to discourage this kind of behavior in Laura.

Then again, I couldn't *fuck* her, I mean, that would be rather bad form.

I GET her down to the lobby. I tell her I want to check to make sure this is the right key card before heading back up. I go up to the desk clerk, which thank God, isn't the blond oaf. Only, it's worse. It's this ravishing blonde who I get along with really well. We had dinner once, innocent, although it could have been otherwise. She ended that evening by saying, "You know, I could just make myself a key to your room."

"Listen, Katrine, I need another room," I say quietly, whispering so no one can hear, including Katrine.

I have to say it again for her to hear me.

"Is there something wrong with your present room, Mr. Gerrick?" She's whispering, too.

"No," I say, almost inaudibly. I clear my throat. It's hard to talk like this. "I just need a second room."

She smiles and makes a little *hmmm* noise. "Now, I'm glad I stayed away from you." She raises one of her eyebrows.

I make a little grunt. "Please, Katrine...just...gimme a room key."

She hands one to me. "Four-fifteen," she whispers. Now louder: "Thank you for using the Intercontinental, Mr. Gerrick. *Again.*"

I growl at her.

I OPENED the door to Room 415 and let Laura in.

"You know, I really do love the rooms here," she said, taking in the decor and the layout.

"I'm just a guy, I don't think about it."

"Oh, you Billy, are anything but just a guy. You notice. You notice everything. You say you don't, but you do." She sighed and fell back on the bed. "I am really beat. I thought I'd be ripping your clothes off. And if we had gotten into that first room, I would have. But now..." She yawned.

Thank you, thank you, thank you. There is a God.

"You've been on a plane all night."

"I guess you're right. You're not too disappointed?"

"A little."

"I'm sorry. You deserve a reward," she said, beckoning me with her arms outstretched.

I didn't know what to do. I didn't know the *right* thing to do.

I had put Laura into a box in my mind. The stress of the negotiations, the shock of her wanting children *now*, had caused me to erect a wall between us. Between me and my feelings for her. It crumbled in her presence. I swallowed hard and felt the moisture pool in my eyes, which did not escape in tears.

She smiled bittersweetly as she noticed the emotion.

I lay on top of her, propped up on my elbows, and I caressed the side of her face from her temple down her cheek to her long, delicate neck.

We stayed like that for several minutes, until I heard her breathing become slow and regular.

"HIIIYAH," Sydney says with her brows raised and her eyes wide, like some Disneyland employee greeting me at the front gate. I notice that both my Champagne glass and hers are empty. "It was very strange, I was having a nice breakfast with this really sexy, interesting man who I went home with last night, then suddenly, he vanishes and his very perky secretary stops by just long enough to tell me to wait here before *she* disappears, and I end up sitting alone with a procession of guys from every corner of the globe, trying to pick up on me."

"It's nice to be wanted."

"It is. Somewhat. One guy named Sar...sarianian, or something—"

I realize who she's talking about. "Sahra Yossian."

"Yes. *Heeee* was really quite charming."

"He's charmingly worth twelve billion dollars."

"So, he really meant it when he said, 'Can I get you anything?'"

I nod.

"Damn."

"I'm really sorry."

"Hold on, I'm still getting over my breakup with Sarah."

"*Sabra*."

Her eyes closed, she holds up her hand, motioning for quiet. Three seconds later, she looks up at me. "I'm over it. So, now...tell me, what the hell happened to you?"

My eyes were focusing on the floor. "This is kind of hard to..." I'm completely tortured in my attempt to tell her. "Sydney, I, I didn't know—"

"Just say it!"

"Laura is here."

Her face changes. "Laura? Your *fiancée*?"

I nod my head. I have to force myself not to look away.

I watch as her expression alters again. "I'm such an idiot," she says. "What is she—?" Suddenly, a new question pops into her head. "What am *I* doing here?"

I touch her arm. Her body is shaking.

"She wanted to surprise me."

"Well, I don't know about you, but I sure am surprised." She starts looking around, I assume for Laura, only she has no idea what Laura looks like. "Where is she? Exactly."

"She's been flying all night. She's taking a nap."

And then, Sydney suddenly gets really annoyed. "In our bed?"

A shivering tingle runs down my spine. *Our* bed. It sounded so wonderful, so...

She's staring at me.

"No. No, I got another room. Don't worry I'm not going to sleep with her."

"Billy...she's the one you're engaged to. You should be saying that to her, 'Don't worry, I'm not going to sleep with her.'"

"This isn't funny."

"You think I'm getting pleasure out of this?" She turns her back to me in frustration. "What have we done? Oh, God." She holds a hand on either side of her head, beating herself up mentally for several moments. "Okay," she says, swinging back around, "I wanna go home. Now." She glances back toward the lobby. "Can I get into *our* room?"

"Yes."

"Good." She shakes her head and marches past me. After only a few feet, she stops. "I'm not upset, okay? I mean, I am, I'm pissed, but I'm not. I *wanted* to be there last night. I really did. I'm just pissed off right now."

I nod, stupidly. I think I understand what she means, but...who knows.

She disappears into the elevator.

I look around at the people passing by, the ones loitering in the lobby, the ones coming in from the cold. They don't seem to be noticing me, or what just happened. They have their own lives, their own problems.

They seem completely unaware of the Greek tragedy that is playing out before them. The drama. The horror. The comic irony.

This is one of the most difficult, confusing moments of my life, and all they see is a man standing alone by a potted plant.

"ARE MR. GERRICK'S BAGS DOWNSTAIRS," Laura asked over the phone. She had looked around the room and hadn't seen any of my things. They say girls are made of sugar and spice. I disagree. I think they're part sugar, part Sherlock Holmes.

"I believe they are being brought up to your room right now," one of the porters answered.

"From downstairs?"

"Ah, no, from his other room."

When Laura got off the phone, she put on her coat and headed toward my "other room."

SYDNEY IS PRETENDING to pack when I walk in. But all she needs is the small bag she got from one of the stores in the hotel to hold the clothes and items she's bought on the trip.

I can tell she had been sitting down thinking or maybe even crying until she heard me put the key card in the slot.

"Remember when I told you I didn't want to be *that* woman. That one that gets between you two?" she says, her fingertip wiping away the trace of a tear in the corner of her eye. "That's because I've been on the other end of it. Only it wasn't one woman, it was six or ten or who knows. He was like you. Intense. It was hard to be with him. It was hard to be without him. So, I believed him when he said he was sorry." With shaky hands, she pushes down the contents of the bag. "I guess I should just say, fuck it, all's fair, right? What's so special about her? Why should I be so nice?" She studies her handiwork and gives the clothes another pat. "But see...he always came *back* to me."

She zips the bag closed.

"Always."

LAURA GOT off the elevator and began walking toward the room.

When she got there, she stopped, her hand just an inch from the door. She heard a woman's voice and tried to listen in, but it was hard to make out what she was saying. She kept listening anyway.

SYDNEY THROWS the bag on the bed and glances at me. There is no anger in her face, no malice. There is only a sense of warmth and even tenderness.

"Are you ready?" she says.

I go to reach for the door.

"Are you ready to go to her and say that it's over?"

I stop before grabbing the handle.

"Are you sure you're ready and willing to just give up your relationship with her? Give it up and never, *ever* go back to her?"

"You can't ask me something like that right now."

She breathes in—it's more of a gasp. "This is exactly the time to ask you."

There's nothing I can say.

It's unlikely that I'm going to be able to make credible decisions in the heat of this moment. Whatever I say, even if I knew what to say, wouldn't mean anything.

At least, that's how I would feel if the tables were turned.

I realize this belief is not true for most people. They don't see it how I would. Any hesitation, any at all, and no matter how much you try to plead your case later, it won't carry any weight. In the moment, you wavered.

LAURA REACHED up and angrily knocked on the door. From inside, the woman answered, somewhat annoyed. "Who is it?"

"It's Laura."

There was a long, long pause and the sound of movement. Then finally, the door was opened just a crack.

"What is it, Laura?" The woman's voice was kinder now, not as irritated. Although, she seemed a bit anxious.

"Is Billy in there?"

"No."

"Are you sure?"

"He is not here. Although, I wish he were," she said, looking back into the room.

Laura would not be deterred. "May I come in please?"

Rafael unhooked the security lever on the door and pulled it wide open. She was wearing a sheet, which barely covered her bikini panties. As she sat on the bed, she let the sheet fall off her shoulders. Rafael didn't do this to show off her relatively perfect torso, nor make Laura more jealous that she already was of her. She wasn't like that. Strange as it may seem, she liked Laura. She did it because she felt no need for false modesty.

Laura looked around for signs of my presence or, at least, an indication that I had been there.

"Brigitte," Rafael said toward the closed bathroom door. "*Viens donc, ma cherie.*"

The door opened slowly, quietly and out walked Brigitte. About five-seven, slightly shorter than Rafael. Thick, brown hair. Strong brows. Hazel eyes. Her breasts were almost as perfect as Rafael's, but a little smaller. She was buttoning her shirt, finally hiding her bra. She had an anxious smile for Laura.

"*Veuillez descendre, je vous rencontrerai dans le café et commandez moi quelque chose à déjeuner .*" Rafael said to the young woman. "*Je serai là dans un moment.*"

Brigitte nodded her head, silently, put on her shoes and left the room to wait in the café where Rafael's breakfast would be waiting as well.

Rafael would later tell me that Laura turned and looked at her a little stunned at what she had just witnessed.

And Rafael answered the gaze, "You see what I am forced to do since your Billy will not play with me anymore?"

. . .

"WHAT IS IT YOU WANT? Do you even know?" Sydney says, grabbing her things. "You ask me to come with you. You go AWOL, drive a car in a blizzard to find me and now..."

"I want to be with you. I just want to be sure."

"*This* is how you act when you're *not* sure?" She stares at me. "I don't know if I'm prepared for how you'd act when you are sure."

"When I say, '*I'll never go back to her,*' I will mean that."

"And that's not the way you touch somebody you don't care about anymore."

Sydney started for the door.

"You saw her? When?"

"Allison was trying to keep me in the café, but I got past her into the hall. I saw you with a woman. I didn't know who she was. At first, I thought she was some government or delegate person. But the way you touched her arm..." She pauses, replaying the scene in her mind. "...I never would have guessed this was someone you were having all this angst over. Someone you weren't sure about. I just figured it was some other woman you had slept with."

Her words hurt me on several levels. How I talked about Laura. How cavalier she thought I was about women. Maybe once that had been true. Maybe...maybe it still was.

"Listen, Billy," she says softly. "You're not sure. That's all there is to it."

"But this meant something to me. Didn't it mean something to you?"

Holding her bag in her hand, she nods, then opens the door and walks out of the room as I say:

"I don't want to screw up the most important relationship of my life. I don't want to screw up my kids. I just don't want to screw up like my parents did. With their relationship. With me."

Sydney stops. Her expression changes to something like awe. "You don't get it, do you?" She studies me, shaking her head. "You really don't." It takes her a moment, as if she's debating whether to speak again or not. Finally, she does. "Your parents didn't ruin your life, Billy Gerrick." She motions to the hotel surrounding us, as if to say, *look where you are, look what you've done.* "They screwed you up just right."

She turns and leaves, heading toward the elevators.

. . .

THE SCENE at the back entrance of the hotel was short and bittersweet.

As I was about to put her into a car that would take her to the airport and to a plane home, I ran my hand along her jaw, staring at the contact point between my fingertips and her cheek. It's difficult to remember exactly what you are thinking at times, but I remember not wanting to let her go.

Not like the first time when she left to crash into a mountain only a few moments later. This time was more powerful, more deeply rooted. This time, there was something in the way she looked at me that made me want to go with her, or at least, make her stay. Make her stay with me.

Because this time, she was leaving with a piece of me.

I have been prepared by events in my life to handle almost anything.

The Economist made the ridiculous, unprovable claim that I am one of, if not *the* best arguer in the world. That was one paragraph before they called me an "insufferable bully."

I can argue.

But my job is to watch and to learn and to study people and actions and emotions so that I can get the best deal for my clients.

I am an observer first, then an arguer.

I'm not a lawyer. I don't deal in facts. Facts are truths that lie. That have meaning only in the moment and context they are uttered.

Truth is meaning without facts.

But the fact was, Sydney Nathan was leaving on a jet plane and truth be told, I couldn't do a damn thing to stop her.

ONE OF THE hardest things about watching her climb in the back of that limousine was the realization that I might never see her again. I didn't like the thought. Oh, I could find her, certainly. Use any number of resources at my disposal, but...

I have always let someone go if they wanted to leave.

A friend, a lover. Didn't matter.

But a part of me kept saying that this time I shouldn't, that I should get in the car with her, climb on that plane with her, and forget everything and all my responsibilities. And simply live my life with her, wherever that took us.

But upstairs in a room in the Intercontinental Hotel was another woman.

Someone once told me, when you first meet a woman, write down all the wonderful things about her, every nuance, her feel, her scent, darling things she says and does. Write down the way she laughs and the way she makes you laugh, the way she cries at movies, the way she playfully knocks your hand away from her upper thigh under the table at dinner with friends. Scrawl these things in a notebook, a journal, or even on scraps of paper and save them, because someday, someday not that far in the future, you're gonna need them as a reference.

We forget the best parts of our lovers.

Attributes that seemed incredible at the onset of love, we begin to take for granted. We get all bent out of shape when love matures and softens. It usually deepens too, but we don't care about that. It's on to the next new "love" because *that* is the way love is supposed to feel. It takes losing someone, or the possibility of losing them, or even the eager attention of a good-looking man flirting with my date for me to remember those things.

What if that's what had happened between Laura and me?

My brain, this organ that had brought me this far in life, had turned against me. What if I was wrong? What if this thing with Sydney was exactly what I was claiming it wasn't? New love. An unfamiliar touch.

I thought maybe I could stand here in the cold till spring, or maybe summer. Maybe it all might have blown over by then. And I wouldn't have to make a decision.

But there was a car waiting for me, for my signal, a tap on the roof.

Laura was waiting for me.

My future was waiting for me.

Marriage, kids, solitude. Who could tell?

Marriages have been arranged. Kingdoms have been torn apart and put together under the guise of marital bliss. Women have married for money, or security, or the man that could best provide for children, not always for true love. Men have traded in the love of a devoted wife for trophies, women who look good and make it easier to pretend we're not getting old. I guess the main difference was that now, I was aware of the game, the truth behind too many relationships.

The preachers say that you shall know the truth, and the truth shall set you free. I say —

You shall know the truth, and the truth shall make you cynical.

And you can't simply take yourself back, close your eyes and think about that time when you were a little boy or little girl, before you realized

Santa Claus worked for Macy's, before you realized the Tooth Fairy had been approved by the American Dental Association, or, for that matter, before you realized if everyone's paying attention, it's impossible to win or lose at tic tac toe.

I don't know about you, but I was happier then. And I don't mean to say that I'm not happy now. It's just that now I'm happy in spite of the world and not very often enough because of it.

That's a little heavy to lay at the feet of one person, but that's what I was thinking as I watched Sydney settle into the back seat.

I tapped on the roof

It seemed that all I did was watch this woman leave me.

Is it possible to fall in love with someone in two days?

I don't believe you can be *in* love in that time span. True love takes time. True love needs time. That's because true love must be based on everything, on the good, on the bad, on all the things in between. It can't simply be a pretty face in the window or a nice smile on a TV screen.

Human beings have been around for about a million years they tell us. And I suspect will be around at least a few thousand more. And in all that time, countries have come and gone, empires have risen and fallen, we've delved into the past, glanced into the future, we've brought the dead back to life, even stepped on the surface of another celestial body.

And with all that knowledge, all that information, we still can't explain love, don't have a clue what it really is, what it means, or how to raise our children to love and be loved without society shifting this way and that, saying dads shouldn't hug their daughters too tightly after a certain age, moms shouldn't show too much affection for their boys, or kids shouldn't see their parents making out or getting too physical with each other, or maybe they should, or who the fuck knows?

No wonder we talk so much about love, and rarely do enough of it.

I guess I've been as guilty as anyone.

And now that I knew it—knew love—it was driving away from me.

That's a lot to think about in the thirty seconds it took her to get from the rear of the hotel to the front gate where I couldn't see her any longer, but believe me, I've cut out ten pages of what was racing through my mind.

·   ·   ·

WHEN I GOT BACK inside the hotel, I went straight up to the other room, but Laura wasn't there. So I checked the phone. The light was blinking. I picked up the receiver and dialed. There were several messages for me. One from Francesca asking if I was going to the party tonight, another from the Swiss Trade Minister inviting me to the private party Francesca was talking about, a third from Rafael asking me to give her a call. And finally, one from Laura. Actually, one from Allison telling me that Laura was looking for me.

I erased them all.

THE ROOM SEEMED empty and lifeless. I went over to Laura's bag which had not yet been opened. I unzipped the main compartment and held one of her sweaters. It still had her smell on it. It seemed like months, months since I had truly held this woman in my arms, since I had made love to her and looked deep into her eyes. Suddenly, all the reasons that led me to fall in love with Laura came rushing back.

And I guess that's why it hurt my heart when I pulled my face away from her sweater. Knowing I had slept with Sydney. Knowing it wasn't just a thing that had happened.

Whatever the outcome, there was no going back. There wasn't any way for me to simply deny the truth. I felt something deep for Sydney.

And the love I felt for Laura, and the thought of having children with her, did not make up for the fact that there simply wasn't enough between us.

IT REALLY CAME DOWN to sex. Strange as that may seem, it really did. My relationship with Laura revolved around sex. Not that we had an inordinate amount of it—I would probably have more sex with Sydney over any given period of time—but with Laura, I was always waiting to get to the sex. My life was this: I was always thinking about the next city I was going to be in or the next time I could fuck her.

Sex wasn't an integral part, it was the major part of our relationship.

I know, *boo-hoo*.

The connection to Sydney was something different. In the shower, after seeing her shave for me, for *me,* we didn't have sex. I didn't push her up against the tile and press my body to hers. We just touched and kissed and mostly held hands.

It's that kind of bond you need in order to remain married for twenty or thirty or fifty years.

There would be time enough to push her up against the wall and fuck her. In the shower, in the hall, bent over the counter in the kitchen. But there had to be a balance. The dark and the light.

I returned the calls, speaking to the Swiss Trade Minister, leaving a message for Rafael, then finally getting Allison on the phone. My bags had made it up to the room. They were put in the corner. The porter had only taken out one suit. I don't know how he knew, but it was the exact suit I wanted to wear to the party.

Allison answered, and when she heard it was me, she giggled. Allison doesn't giggle. She'd been celebrating.

"What?"

"Oh, nothing."

"Where's Laura?"

Another little laugh.

"*What*?"

"She's down in the café."

"Thank you."

"With Rafael."

"What!?"

I COULD HEAR them before I could see them. The three women were laughing and talking loudly. I turned the corner and there they were. Laura, Rafael, and another woman, definitely French. She looked familiar, one of the support people under Rafael.

Rafael and Laura greeted me boisterously as I walked up to the table. The other woman just smiled and gave a silent giggle.

What was with the giggling today?

"May I join you?" I said, putting my hand on the remaining chair.

"Ooow, a foursome," said Rafael. "*Oui, oui, merci.*"

I grunted a laugh.

"Sit down, honey." Laura's face was pinking up, probably from the drink half-finished in front of her, or maybe it was the three empty glasses to her right.

I sat down and pulled in the chair. I nodded to several trades at other tables, who were staring at the four of us.

"I was telling your beautiful fiancée some stories about you," said Rafael.

"I'm sure." God only knows what. I had told Laura most everything about my past, at least, the parts I could remember. I'm sure Rafael with her elephantine memory would be able to recall many others I hadn't let Laura in on.

"She's very nice. *Très jolie*," Rafael said. The other two were laughing. Rafael was definitely the ringleader here.

"You've met Laura a dozen times before."

"Yes, but now I like her." She patted Laura's hand as it sat wrapped around her glass.

They were drunk, but I got the feeling Rafael was more sober than she pretended to be.

Synapses slowed by wine that was surely French, most likely expensive, and definitely strong, it took a moment for Rafael's words to get to Laura's gray matter. "Why didn't you like me before?"

"I'm very protective of your man here. I want him to be with the right woman."

"Oh," Laura said as if that was a perfectly logical answer.

Rafael looked at me. I wasn't sure what she was trying to say. She certainly knew about Sydney and my trek into France. Nothing gets past Rafael.

"I'm glad I have your approval," I said.

"You should be. Because as I told your fiancée," she dug in on that last word, kept fucking repeating it, "if she didn't, I would not allow you to keep saying no to me."

There was an uncomfortable moment, but she cut it short.

"You know Brigitte?"

"Yes, although, I don't believe we've ever been formally introduced."

"Hallo," she said in a heavy accent.

"I interrupted them about to…" Laura leaned closer to me and whispered, "…have sex."

I raised my eyebrows and glanced at Rafael. "Really?"

Rafael smiled. "Well, *again*." And while still looking at me, she kissed Brigitte at the very edge of the young woman's lips. It said: See what you missed?

. . .

"I DON'T TRUST HER."

"You just spent all afternoon with her."

Laura charged into the elevator. She waited for the door to close behind me.

"Because...I wanted to see what she was up to. I knew something was up when I got here."

I sighed. "She tried to get me to stay with her. I didn't. Okay?"

"She's such a Machiavellian little bitch."

"Wow." I leaned against the wall. "She didn't mean anything by it. She's French. It's what they do."

"I'm sure you wouldn't mind being French for a while." She stared at me.

Ting. The elevator opened.

WE ARRIVED at the party and I made my rounds. After having taken a nap, Laura woke up with a little hangover from her brunch date. I told her she didn't have to go. She said, "The best thing for a hangover is to just keep drinking. Besides, that slattern will be there."

"Slattern?" I was always looking up words in the dictionary after a heated discussion with Laura.

"Her."

Ah, Rafael.

Laura looked incredible. Allison had lent her a dress. It looked familiar to me, very familiar, and I was trying to remember when I had seen Allison wearing the elegant cocktail number. I found out later that Allison had gotten it from Rafael. A fact I failed to mention to Laura.

We danced a little. Then went off and gave our regards to our host. I brought Laura with me for that but spared her having to join me greeting the other trades. I did that alone.

At some point, Rafael pulled me into a corner and kissed me the way the French do, breaking any number of rules of our agreement. She held me for a moment, and we didn't say anything. As she pulled away, she said, "Zsolong, Billy."

It sounded like an ending.

I found Laura with Yuri and the *why-where-they-here again?* other

Russians. They were doing shots of vodka. Yuri was very impressed that she had not yet vomited, something he told me himself, slurring his words, making his stilted, inferior, couldn't-give-a-shit English even more atrocious.

I thanked him. I didn't know what else to do.

"Vwe vwill speak trade sum dey."

"Someday," I said.

Then I had a porter bring over a luggage cart, and we lifted Laura and the chair she was slumped in onto the cart and took her upstairs in the service elevator.

In the morning, I was awoken by a wild-haired female searching the room desperately for coffee.

I gently reminded Laura—a delicate touch is required to handle the uncaffeinated—that they don't provide coffee makers in European hotel rooms. That's an American thing.

I had a pot sent up.

At about ten, I asked for a car to take us to the airport.

It was the same car, same driver who had taken Sydney a day earlier.

We took a commercial flight.

I didn't want to fly back with the rest of the team. I didn't want them to have to feel uncomfortable around Laura. That's sometimes the worst aspect of these things. It's as unfair to the people around you as it is to the one you're cheating on.

There were a few other people from the delegation onboard, low-level staffers, people who wouldn't talk to me unless I spoke to them first. So, we were left to ourselves. I had my security detail radio ahead for someone to meet us and asked them to take the plane with Allison and the others. I could tell a couple of the guys were thinking I didn't want them to get anywhere near Laura because they knew something had gone on between Sydney and me, and they knew I knew they knew.

But really, I just wanted to have some time with her. I hadn't been with Laura, truly been with her in so long. Only she passed out as soon as we took off.

So, here I was, alone again.

As I watched her sleep, a powerful rush of emotion exploded inside me. All of the feelings I had for her came to the surface. And with it, the resistance, the questions, the fear washed away. I realized something in that moment—

I loved her.

I truly did love her.

AFTER GETTING off the plane and being walked through customs, we were met by a security detail.

The first thing Laura did was to purchase a half-dozen travel packs of Advil.

The second thing she did was throw them up all over one of the Secret Service agents.

34
REVISING MY PROPOSAL

THAT FIRST DAY BACK WAS—THANKFULLY—VERY busy. We landed and were driven into the District. After dropping Laura off at her place, I stopped in at the White House, then made the rounds on Capitol Hill, explaining to about a dozen key Senators and Representatives what the agreement meant for America, both good and bad.

It was felt by me and the Administration that I shouldn't try to candy-coat it since thousands of people from all sides of the political spectrum would pore over this fairly slim five-hundred-and-fifty-page document and spout its negatives anyway. Better they hear it early and directly from me. It would keep them from getting blindsided, and it would make the Administration look good, at least, for being honest with the Hill.

Laura was busy, too. She had to wrap some things up before our trip to Hawaii.

I thought often about Sydney, when I was pacing between the offices of our political leaders, some great, some insignificant, or being checked by security before entering the White House. Fragments of introspection. Brief moments of remembrance that were thankfully interrupted by the opening of a door, or the shake of an aide's hand.

Then I had a late dinner with Laura, had a wonderful time, and I didn't know what to think.

I did know one thing. I wasn't going to say anything to Laura until after the trip. She had been looking forward to this vacation for months. More than just to spend some uninterrupted time with me. Laura had more money than any of her bosses, but she worked as hard as anyone I've ever met. I knew she needed to slow down. Relax on a beach. And knowing Laura, she wouldn't go if I told her I needed some time to think. She just couldn't face all those married friends.

The next morning Laura and I climbed on a plane and flew to Dallas-Ft. Worth. All six couples would meet there and continue on together.

Sort of.

The woman in charge of the tickets, mother of two, put the guys on one flight and the women on another. Just in case one crashed, her kids would still have a parent.

I had my travel agent change that. It would be six women and me. And five guys who didn't know me, wondering what I was up to. Only Laura made me switch back because the four other guys not married to the woman wanted to change their flights as well.

I climbed aboard Air Testosterone.

It turned out to be a good thing. We all got to know each other without the pressure of being observed by the women as if we were primates in the wild. I don't know if guys are more themselves when not in the company of women or if they just act how they think other males expect them to be. It's probably a little of both.

When I initially agreed to go on this vacation, I didn't realize "going to Hawaii" meant "going to Oahu."

Oahu's the island you see on "Hawaii Five-O."

Honolulu is a city. It's got a murder rate. Sure, there are grand hotels and pretty beaches, but it's got people trying to kill each other. I could stay in D.C. if I wanted that kind of vacation.

I'll admit, I was somewhat pleasantly surprised, but only somewhat, by the island once we got there. There were many parts of it that were lush and very beautiful. They just weren't anywhere near the hotel.

If you ask me, the twelve of us spent too much time together. I mean, I didn't hate these people, most of them were nice enough, but I wanted, needed more time alone with Laura.

We did get to have one dinner, just the two of us. It was really wonderful to reconnect after the events of the past few weeks. It made me appreciate all the things I really loved about Laura. We held hands as we walked on the beach and talked about why we hadn't ever come to this place before. And even though we were having a pretty good time with her friends, it was the times we spent alone that were most special to her.

We even—after a long midnight stroll—made love in the warm, shallow waters at the end of a private beach.

I was *there*, really there with Laura.

And only once did I think about Sydney—on the walk back to the hotel.

THE DAY after re-enacting that famous scene in "From Here to Eternity," we all took a boat around to the other side of the island, where the guys and I went scuba diving at a fully submerged coral reef about a mile off North Shore.

It was teeming with life, colored fish, strange crustaceans, graceful old sea turtles.

I've always been very claustrophobic. Scuba diving was something I never thought I'd ever do. In fact, the first time I went, I almost didn't. It was a recreation dive, where you don't have to be certified. They just blab through a little course on the boat out to Cancun Island. It was Mexico, who knows what kind of liability insurance they didn't have. In fact, when I asked them if they were PADI certified, one of the guys said, "I not Patty. I, Manuel."

Feeling veeeeeery confident about the instruction had I just received and the equipment they assured me checked out "A-Okay," I was one of the last ones in the water. As we started to "walk" ourselves down the anchor line, I froze. I was maybe six feet from the surface. I mean, how lame is that? I've been ten feet under in a swimming pool for Christ's sake. Only two things kept me from chickening out. One, I couldn't yell for the instructor because, well, I had a thing in my mouth and he was down at the bottom, still not sure why I kept asking him if he was Patty, and two, the woman I was in Mexico with was two people ahead of me down the line on *her* very first dive. And if she could do it, I surely wasn't going to act like a pussy and climb back into the boat.

But this one, here in Hawaii, was my seventh dive.

Not only did I get through that first one, but I fell in love with it. It was one of the most freeing things I've ever done. I'm no longer as freaked out in close quarters anymore. If you have the chance, and you are like I was, I recommend heading thirty feet down and freeing yourself.

I went on a dive with Max in Florida last year. It was his first time. He had been a little weirded out in the beginning, which completely astounds me, since here was a guy who had jumped out of a plane at sixteen thousand feet on two different occasions, and he's getting panicked over being forty feet underwater.

One of the husbands had never gone diving before. He was kind of wishy-washy about the whole thing. And once the rest of us were in the water, he decided to snorkel on the surface in a few thousand dollars worth of gear while the rest of us proceeded on our dive.

Pussy.

The water was warm and immaculate. The sunlight shone down and lit up the coral like it was neon. We slowly cruised along that place where the reef met the ocean floor.

It's always astonishing to see the distinct line where barren sand ends and life begins.

Then, just about the time I was starting to get into the full Zen of diving, we ran across a most uncalming sight.

Our group floated perfectly still, trying as best we could to become as small as possible as a medium-sized thrasher shark swam by. The water was clear, and I was able to gaze into the shark's eyes as he passed me.

They were dead.

I've heard that before, but I didn't have a clue what that meant until I saw them. Black. Cloudless pools of nothingness.

I realized that all of the nasty, horrible people, trades, pols, dips, and despots, I've met along the way were innocuous in comparison to this creature.

I've always thought of myself as tough. I was nothing up against this.

It not only humbled me, it also gave me perspective on the folly that is humanity. We have our houses, we drive our cars, we work in air-conditioned, heated, climate-controlled structures, and we somehow think that we...*we* are masters of this world.

And maybe we are conquerors of the planet, but we are in no way masters of it.

My gaze was fixed on the shark as it mindlessly circled the area. Cruising and searching and patiently waiting for its tiny little brain to focus itself on something to eat.

Suddenly, I felt this huge creature slam into me from the side. My heart nearly stopped, and probably did for a second. There's no time to see your life flash before you in an instant like that. There's only shock.

I knew immediately it was one of the shark's buddies. As one distracted, the other attacked.

By the time my brain rebooted a second later, I realized, I was alive. The wind had been knocked out of me. There was no blood in the water. When I was able to finally see what it was that was attacking me, I looked into the creature's eyes. They didn't look dead. They looked stupid. I had been hit by a huge, meandering jackfish, notoriously blind, trying to swim through me to get to some tiny fish it was chasing. Tiny fish who had, by the way, decided to use me as a blocker.

I had to surface well before the rest of the group because I used most of my oxygen trying to get my heart rate back down below five hundred. I climbed on board the boat, stood on deck and unzipped my wetsuit halfway, pulling it over my shoulders and rolling it down to my waist.

Laura and the other women were sunning themselves on deck chairs, having drinks, and looking pretty damn good. Except for one of the women, who sat in the shade, in a hat, covered from head to toe in clothing.

Laura went snorkeling with me earlier in the day but said she wanted to relax in the sun instead of dive. The women were going to stay at the hotel and lay out on the beach there, but I convinced Laura to come along with us. Once she said yes, the others decided to join us as well.

As I breathed in the sweet, salty air, I stared at Laura. Sweat beaded up on her body and glistened in the sun. Her sunglasses hid her spectacular eyes, but that bit of mystery made her look even more attractive and inviting.

While the other women were trying to figure out who bought the last round of Mai Tais, Laura turned her head toward me and made a little noise, "Mmm mmmm," as she saw me.

She gave me a beautiful smile that ended with her subtly biting her lower lip. That and the hot sun warmed my shivering body. She had no idea how close I hadn't come to death. I mean, there've been no reported fatalities by jackfish—none that I could find, anyway, and I looked once we got back on shore—but still, the event made me reevaluate everything. How lucky I was to be in this tropical paradise and to have someone like Laura to share it with.

As the boat trekked back to Honolulu, I studied the land that was only a few hundred yards away. I would have rather gone to Maui or Kauai

—I hear they're much less urban—but I decided the part of the island we were passing was beautiful enough.

There were some large estates sitting at the water's edge. There were also groupings of small houses and even a few huts.

The sun was high in the sky. It was sometime a little after noon.

One of the guys—the chickenshit who didn't dive and watched the action safely from above—was regaling everyone on board with the story of the jackfish, and the hysterically funny, terrified expression on my face right after the fish that looked like a stunted tuna slammed me in the gut.

I was resting on the railing, looking over the side of the boat, not even bothered by the story—it was my side, by the way, my ribcage, not my gut—and thinking this was the way it was supposed to be. The warmth of the sun and the coolness of the moisture evaporating from my bathing suit. That satisfyingly tired sensation that washes over you after engaging in water sports. And most of all, being in a place like this with someone I loved very much.

Far from the pressure of Geneva and D.C., far from the frigid cold of the Alps and December in Washington, nearly stripped of all clothing, I began to thaw.

I put my hand into my swimsuit pocket and felt it. Technically, in the zippered compartment. It was Laura's engagement ring. A ring bought last week when it became clear she was serious. I didn't actually buy the ring. She did. But I paid the bill, so, I guess that sort of counts.

I'm a romantic, to the last.

She had done it for me, of course, because I was so busy.

She had previewed it for me on the flight to DFW, but the sparkling band made its public debut at dinner that first night. There were hugs and kisses, slaps on the back, playful warnings that I didn't know what I was getting into, and a slightly sick feeling in my stomach.

But that queasy sensation was long gone, replaced by...by butterflies.

I pulled out the ring and looked at it. It was simple and yet beautiful. A single teardrop diamond. She had taken it off when we went snorkeling in the morning, just off the beach from the hotel. She asked me to hold onto it for safekeeping. I had forgotten to give it back.

And now, looking out at the beauty of the islands and the ring and Laura, I realized, I had a rare opportunity. And I thought, *it's the right time to do it.* Do it the way it should be done. Propose. Only this time, I'd mean it.

So, I stuck the ring back in my pocket and conveniently forgot to return it once again.

After we got back into dock, I told Tammy, the one I liked best, that I needed to be alone with Laura for a little bit.

"But we have that thing planned," she said. Then as if covering for something, her face a little pink, she added, "It's our last night."

I realized that the "thing" was not only to enjoy our final evening in paradise but to properly celebrate the engagement of her best friend, the last to get married.

"Don't worry. We'll be there. Just maybe a little bit late."

IT WAS deep into the afternoon, and the sun was hanging low over the water when I called up for our rental car and drove, just the two of us, to one of the points I had seen when we were coming in on the boat.

We walked along the beach, which was even more beautiful up close. I didn't plan it this way, but just then, the sun began to sink over the horizon, reflecting off the water, creating a yellow brick road that spread out as it approached, inviting us to stroll into the fire.

We both stared into the light and were silent for a long time.

This was perfect.

The perfect place, the perfect time for me to ask her to marry me. A tropical beach at sunset with warm clear water lapping at our feet.

We sat down on some rocks and stared out at the ocean.

"Isn't it beautiful?" she said.

I smiled at her, then to myself. This was the moment.

I pulled out the ring and kept it hidden in the closed palm of my hand. I held her loosely by the wrists and studied her face. The words I was about to say—not the exact words, not some rehearsed speech devoid of meaning, but the emotional expression of a singular moment, a turning point—played in my mind. I opened my hand, revealing the ring, and I—

Hesitated.

I was looking at her. She was still gazing out toward the horizon.

I...I couldn't seem to do it.

She turned to me, and I said, "I just remembered I had this in my pocket."

"God, I didn't realize I wasn't wearing it. I gotta be more careful of that. I don't want to lose it."

"No," I said. "No, you don't."

We flew back to Washington the next morning.

LAURA and I have a standing date on Wednesdays. And whenever I'm actually in the country, she comes over to my place, and I make dinner for the two of us. Sometimes we order in. We lay in front of a roaring fireplace or a blasting air conditioner, and we eat, sometimes off each other's bodies, and we share a beer or wine, and we make love.

She calls Wednesday, affectionately, "Hump Day."

But that afternoon, I called to tell her that I was swamped and would be late for our rendezvous.

"How late?"

"I can't really say. Maybe between nine and ten."

"That late?" Laura asked. "Why don't I let myself in with my key, and I'll make dinner this week."

Laura likes my house. It's bigger than hers, more like a home.

But my place wasn't the right venue for this evening. Because this night, I had to tell her. I had to tell her the truth. And I needed Laura to be on her own turf, at her place. You may think I did this so I could make a quick exit. Or so I wouldn't have to deal with trying to get her out of my house. Those would be excellent reasons, but tonight had to be at her house since she needed some place she wouldn't have to leave. I would stay if she asked me. I would go if she asked me to leave. She could call a friend, or her sister, or mom to make the short drive across the Potomac.

It was also for this reason: my house had, ever since our discussion about children and getting married, started to change into *our* house.

The added insult of being asked to leave the home that had almost been hers was, I felt, a bit cruel.

I went over to Laura's apartment after sitting in my office with nothing to do from six until a little after nine P.M.

I knocked.

When she came and opened the door, she looked better than I expected her to. Was it her hair? New clothes? Or just that my eyes, which had over the past year plus become accustomed to her visage, were looking at her this last time for the first time once again?

She was a little annoyed with me for messing with our Wednesday night, and I couldn't help thinking, *Oh, just wait, you're gonna really be annoyed*.

YOU KNOW when you're about to do something wrong or upsetting, you figure everybody in the world can see it written right on your skull? And any sidelong glance from the other person only makes it worse, only makes it seem more obvious you're being obvious.

I went inside. The whole place seemed different to me. It was freaking me out a little. I try to find the humor in things, but this time, my gut was knotted up like Christmas lights the moment you take them off the tree. And my throat, well, that was closing up on me until I thought I might choke to death.

This evening wasn't going to be very amusing.

And yet, there were funny things going on. The idiot next door whose bloodhound would not shut up. The fact that on Jeopardy at that very moment someone was picking the category "Famous Adulterers for 100," not that Laura was watching the show, the neighbor with the crazy animal was.

And because his dog was yapping so loud, he had the volume on the TV cranked up to rock concert levels, so the entire neighborhood was treated to every word of the game show.

There was also a rather sizable piece of dried mucus hanging from Laura's left nostril. Just sitting there, defying gravity. The tiniest flaw on that flawless face. It was distracting, but I figured this probably wasn't the best time to reach out and pick her nose.

WE WENT into the kitchen where she was finishing up dinner. It was hard for me to look into her eyes. More than that, it was painful. I'm not trying to feel sorry for myself. Nor am I trying to justify my actions. This needed to be done, and done as soon as possible. I couldn't go on with this, not after my failure in Hawaii. Because in that moment, on that beach, I loved her more than I had ever loved her. If I couldn't do it then, when could I?

Laura looked at me as she stirred something on the stove. It took a moment for her mouth to catch up with her eyes, but her smile disappeared. And I knew what was coming.

Questions.

"Is there something wrong, Billy?"

"Laur…" I floundered. I rarely flounder. I may make the biggest ass of myself, I may be completely wrong at times, but when I do it, I do it all the way. I don't hesitate.

"Oh my God. Something *is* wrong." She searched through me like some high-tech bunker-penetrating spy device, seeking an answer. "Us?"

I blew out a little air and glanced off to the side. She stopped stirring whatever it was in the pot.

"Oh my God." Her hand went to her chest. "You slept with someone, didn't you?"

"What?"

"Who was it?"

"Where the hell did that come from?" I don't know why I said that. Of course, I had slept with someone. I guess I just wanted know how *she* knew that.

She gasped as it came to her. "Oh— That little French whore!"

"Laura, this has nothing to do with Rafael. It has nothing to do with me sleeping with *anyone*." I paused. Truth, Gerrick. You're here to tell her. Tell her the truth. "Well, that's not really true. It sort of does. I—" I kept rambling on.

"You *sort of* had sex? When? Over lunch today?"

"Okay, let me explain."

"When did this happen!?"

I lowered my voice. "Geneva."

And then came the body blow—

"I was up in Connecticut comforting your mother because her *dead* father was put into the *ground* and you're off fucking some trade bimbo?" She put her hand to her mouth. "Oh, God, while I was there?"

"Okay, this is not going at all like I had planned."

"Oh, you had a plan?"

Did I?

"Well, geez, I'm really sorry, Billy." She started throwing things, picking up a picture frame and hurling it at me. "Is this a little more of what you had in mind?"

"Laura—" A vase came flying at my face. "Laura, listen to me."

A dish.

There would not be any listening.

Out of this waifish woman was coming some very nasty, well-reasoned slurs, none of which she learned at Harvard Business School.

The indignity, the outrage, the slap across the face.

I was being called every horrible thing a human being can be called and a few things even most animals would be upset to be labeled.

I've said there has never been a breakup of mine that went, "*Blank*, this isn't working out, I really think we need to break up." "Okay."

History would not change this night.

I ended up staying an hour and fifty minutes, and most of the time was spent trying to explain the situation to Laura. Although the reasons were very clear for me, I knew that no matter what I said, it would do nothing to change her attitude, her understanding or her reaction to my leaving her.

I don't think anyone in the history of mankind who has been the object of a breakup has really given one rat's ass what the reasons are.

Even when they ask you.

It's not like she was going to turn around and go, "Oh, you know, that really does make sense. I can see how you would feel that way and want to leave me. Of course, Billy, I would have done the same thing."

Nope.

Not how it happened.

I HAD GONE from nearly asking her to marry me to asking for my freedom in two days.

So, when I finally left Laura's—backed out, actually—I was still worried about flying objects—her mom had arrived to comfort her.

Her family loved me. They would no longer after tonight.

I walked the streets, alone, my mind as much replaying recent events as it was empty.

By the time I got home, it was well after 2 A.M. I checked my messages, hoping perhaps—this is going to sound terrible—hoping Sydney had left word for me.

There were nine messages. None I wanted to hear. And only one that wasn't Laura telling me to fuck off.

The other was her mother telling me to fuck off.

I erased the messages, washed my face, then climbed into bed.

The phone rang five minutes later. I picked it up, waiting to be cursed at by Laura, or her mom, or maybe her sister this time. I'm afraid of Laura's sister. She's a ballet dancer. Which doesn't frighten me at all. It's that she's a prima ballerina who was once the U.S. National Open Hand Wushu champion that scares me.

But it wasn't any of them.

It was my mom, who was calling in the middle of the night because she couldn't sleep and knew I often stayed up late. She called just to tell me what a wonderful time she had having Laura over the house and how happy she was that Laura would soon be her daughter-in-law, part of the family.

You think I'm kidding.

I woke up feeling like I had gotten into a bar brawl the night before. My head was fuzzy, my eyelashes were pasted shut.

The covers felt heavy on my body, the weight of them cementing me to the mattress. I finally threw them off, climbed out of bed, and started to make myself something to eat. Sautéed some tomatoes, spinach, a little bit of broccoli. Cracked in some eggs. A little cheddar. Folded it into an omelet.

While I was waiting for my toast, I stared at my reflection in the chrome.

Who was I kidding? I didn't want any of this stuff. I wasn't hungry. I just wanted an excuse not to do what I really wanted to do. Go to Bellina's. Hope to run into her.

I tossed everything into the garbage.

I went to the coffee shop.

Went every day for a week.

At the start of the second week—I didn't realize I was being that obvious—one of the guys behind the counter handed me my juice and said, "I haven't seen her in here in a while."

"What?"

"The blonde. The one you met here."

This guy knows who I'm looking for, and I couldn't've picked this guy out in a lineup if you shoved a gun in my mouth.

"I haven't seen her in a couple of weeks," he said.

"Yeah?"

"You don't forget someone like that, man."

No, you don't.

"Thanks."

WALKING AWAY from Bellina's toward my office, I pulled out my phone and dialed. I waited for a moment, and when she answered, I felt relieved. There was something comforting about hearing her voice at that moment.

"Billy? Is that you? I just spoke to you last night. Is everything okay?"

"Yes," I said, "...and no."

"Is this a game show or something, which is it?"

I smiled and said, "Let me talk to Dad."

There was silence on the other end of the phone.

Now, you might think the lack of sound was because she was going to get him.

No.

It was shock. I don't think I've ever asked to speak with my father.

"Why?" she said suspiciously.

"Can you just get him, please?"

When she finally found him, hiding in the cellar in a vain attempt to get some peace and quiet, when he finally came to the phone, annoyed, grumbling, I simply said to him, "Dad, we need to talk."

I FLEW UP to New York to speak before a gathering of corporate executives to personally give them the details, the challenges, the pros and cons of the trade agreement.

We needed their support. At the very least, we needed them to keep quiet and not start whining publicly about what *wasn't* in the pact.

After it was over, after I caught a Knicks game with some GE execs, I got a car, ditched my security detail, and drove up to Connecticut to see my family.

My grandmother was still out of it. My mom was a little better. I spent time with them both, visited Sebby's grave, even got to see my siblings. But I had really come to talk to my father.

It was time for me to earn the gold pocket watch that Sebby had given me.

I found the Princess out in what remained of the greenhouse he had built when I was a kid. It had started out as discarded storm doors and unwanted windows pieced together and went through several iterations until it evolved into what it was: a wood-framed structure with an angled roof that was ten feet wide and twenty-eight feet long attached to the south side of our house. Actually, I think Sebby did almost as much work as the Princess did, but it was my dad's project. Sebby was simply the labor on this one.

It was cold.

The two layers of plastic sheeting that protected the greenhouse from the elements had deteriorated and torn in parts over time. Since the massacre of the African Violets, my father never had the same passion for working with plants at home. He worked at nurseries after he retired, got his fix that way, but he could leave it at the end of the day.

The place was more of a storage area now for his empty pots and tables, bags of soil and his gardening tools.

"Hey, Dad," I said.

He turned and looked at me. He was grabbing a couple of pots, holding both in one big hand.

"Hey, Billy."

He no longer had to think for a moment to come up with my name. I don't know if that was because he had been sober now for several years or because people on the news and in the local papers kept repeating my name over and over again with photos and video of me.

"Listen," I started out, pacing myself. "I want to talk...about you and me. Our—" I gestured between him and me. This wasn't easy. Communication between the two of us had always been awkward. Especially if neither one of us was drunk. "About all the shit between us."

"It's okay, Billy."

"No, it's not, Dad. We have to talk about this—" Then came more useless gestures from me trying to say *this thing between us.*

"It's all right, Billy." The Princess put his hand on my shoulder. Except for maybe that moment after Sebby's death, I can't remember the last time my father touched me. Even with age shrinking him somewhat, he was still taller than me by a couple of inches, still outweighed me. And then he did another something I can hardly remember him doing. He looked me in the eye. "I've already forgiven you."

I—

I couldn't have been more shocked if my dad started dancing around in a g-string.

"You've...forgiven...*me*? *You've* forgiven me? After all the shit you've pulled, all the screaming, the histrionics, the smashing of anything and everything I ever cared about—you...have forgiven me."

My father didn't remove his hand. I could see he was trying to put his feelings into words.

Language was not his canvas, unless you counted foul language. Then he could paint a masterpiece.

He gazed at me over his glasses. "I realized a long time ago...that you were never gonna forgive me." This was difficult for him. Not just the words but the meaning, the feeling. I could see the pain in his face. And if I didn't know better, I might have even believed he got choked up. It was only an instant, but it was there. "So, I forgave you for that."

I stared at him in disbelief, frozen for an instant in the freezing cold, suspended in time.

As my mind reeled at the incredulous nature of this moment, I turned and pushed through the broken door of the greenhouse that led to the backyard. The ground was hard and crunched under my feet. I wanted to walk around to the front, climb in my car and just leave. Leave this place. Leave it all behind.

On any other day, I might have. Any other day, this conversation would be one more wedge between the Princess and me.

Him...forgive *me*.

But I stopped.

I had come here to try and make peace with him. Because in a way it wasn't Laura I was afraid of, or marriage, or even kids, it was me I was worried about. Worried I'd become him.

I thought of Sydney and what she would think of me if I walked away right now.

Not very much.

I turned. He was not waiting for me to come back, wasn't looking at me with kindness in his eyes, wasn't holding his arms out like some scene in a movie. He was grabbing another pot. His back to me. I was gone for all he knew.

He did glance up when I walked back into the greenhouse.

It's hard not to notice when someone reenters through that door which is held in place by only one hinge and scrapes along the ground and needs to be yanked open and dragged closed.

I stood there, waiting for him to stand up straight. And when he did, I gave him a hug.

I could feel tears pooling in my eyes, could feel the emotion in me. From my dad, I felt a vague warmness. He patted my back.

"Give me time," I said. "Just give me some time."

I STAYED FOR CHRISTMAS.

My father walked out on dinner after we were more than thirty minutes into the meal. A record. And he didn't storm out either. He just got up, got in his car, and drove off to parts unknown. The McDonald's on West Main, most likely. He had lost his taste for Dunkin' Donuts.

BACK IN WASHINGTON, I rang in the New Year with friends and spent the beginning of 1994 going about the business of promoting the WTO and working on the dozen other regional and bilateral agreements that were already in progress.

I made a few phone calls and got her number.

A few days later, the phone to my ear, drinking a hot chocolate, I made the call. I was passing an old government office building that was being restored. There was a huge ceiling rising over the lobby, and I stopped to stare up at it, wondering about the craftsman that had originally made this, thinking of Sebby, pondering what his hands had made during the depression under the guise of the WPA. So many beautiful things we take for granted were built of that moment in history. Parks, monuments, buildings, bridges.

Sydney answered the phone.

I was so caught off-guard that I slammed my head into one of the pipes holding up the massive scaffolding.

"Fuck, fuck, fuck, fuck, fuck!!!"

There was a pause.

"Billy?"

ONE OF THE workers tried to see if I was okay, but I didn't want to risk hanging up the phone and having to call her back. I waved him off, even though he kept pointing at my head.

I realized a moment later why. I was bleeding. Not hospitalization-type bloodshed, but enough to make me seem like a crazy man who was gonna finish making calls until they finally pried the cell phone from his cold, dead fingers.

"It's done," I said.

"What's done?"

"Me and Laura. I ended it."

My head was oozing blood, and there was no response on the other end of the line.

"I'm sorry," she said.

I was confused for a moment because it took me a while to detect the unspoken "...to hear about that." I thought she would be excited or, at least, glad, but she didn't seem remotely either.

"Sydney?"

Nothing, then—

"I told you I didn't want this. Didn't want to come between you two."

"You didn't come between us. This may not make a difference to you, but it does to me. I was in Hawaii. I was walking on a beautiful beach, and I had the opportunity to ask her to marry me, to do it right. And I couldn't. You know why? Because it *wasn't* right." I squeezed my head harder where it was beginning to throb. "I want to see you."

"I don't date men on the rebound."

"Sydney, people are always on the rebound from *somebody*."

There was silence on the line. I wished I could see her face so I could read it. Speechless moments can convey so many things. Yet without the visuals to illustrate their meaning, these moments can be easily misread.

"I think we shouldn't talk for a while," she said, her voice softer than her words.

This time, the silence was mine.

"Call me when you're ready," she said, just before I heard the phone click.

I nodded. I was like the idiot monkey boy, unable to do anything. I was like one of those stupid toy dogs in the back of car windows, whose sole purpose is to constantly waggle their head up and down for no fucking reason at all.

I took my hand away from my head, and red drops began to stain the white concrete of the sidewalk.

IN APRIL, I flew to Morocco and formally signed the Final Act.

I stepped down from my post as U.S. Trade Rep six months and three weeks later once the bills necessary to align with the agreement passed Congress. The vote in the Senate was 76-24, a supermajority. So, go ahead, call it a treaty if you want.

I stood behind the President as he signed the bills into law. You can even see me in the photos. Three weeks later, on the first day of 1995, the World Trade Organization was officially established. By then, one hundred and twenty-three countries had signed on.

The successful conclusion of the Uruguay Round and the creation of the WTO was the crowning achievement for me. There would not be another treaty with as much impact or importance as this one for thirty or forty years, maybe longer. Maybe never. Because this was more than a treaty, more than an agreement, this was a living organization. Negotiation fatigue would probably keep everyone from doing much for a few years at least, but the Final Act already had mechanisms in place for further negotiations.

Moving toward a true global economy would shake the very foundations of industries, even countries. There would be unexpected consequences. Winners and losers.

This wasn't a flawless document. These little imperfections would fan out and get bigger and bigger.

As Tom said to me in Geneva, as he repeated on my last day as USTR,

"Look on the bright side, no one'll know how badly we fucked up for *years*."

It was the perfect time to leave.

Whenever I think about it, I feel a certain sadness. I miss the action, having the power of the President behind me. Sometimes, I still can't believe I was a Cabinet member. That the FBI cleared me.

In a few months, when I decide to get back to work, I'll make much more money in the private sector. But despite the hype, money doesn't always buy power.

Taking a little time off would be good for me.

Except for a short vacation here and there, I've worked non-stop since college. Every year, I promised myself *this* year I would take a break just as soon as I finished this one last project.

I had all these things planned. Places to see. Things I could never do because I was too caught up in life to live life.

Now, I had the time, the bank account, and the frequent flyer miles to go anywhere, do anything, be anyone I wanted.

Only what has happened since leaving my job is I have spent more time alone, more time thinking about how things haven't worked out the way I thought they would. And how very much I miss Sydney.

People are always saying that time heals all wounds. Time doesn't heal —it dulls, it dims. But it's no remedy.

Perhaps it does for some. Those people—those too many people—who find it all too easy to just forget. Forget about someone they once claimed to love, pretend they weren't ever really all that important, sweep the past away.

I couldn't do that with Laura. And I definitely couldn't do it with Sydney.

Since that phone call and the visible scar it's left, I've dated a number of women. Smart, witty, and beautiful. I'll be kissing them or having dinner with them or fucking them, and I'll be kissing her, dining with her, making love to her.

I think about Sydney a great deal, and I wonder, what if things had been different? There are times I've woken up in the middle of the night, sometimes alone, sometimes with someone else, and I would see her face. And then it would be gone. Into thin air, or into someone else's visage.

There have been so many mornings, afternoons, and evenings that I've simply wanted to talk to her, so many ideas I've wanted to share, things

I've wanted to say, questions I've wanted to ask her. The toughest part is knowing she's so close to me, less than a mile away, and yet so far away.

I have moments, and they come often, where I slide my hand along my leg and feel the fabric against my skin and think about touching her.

Most of my first dates never turn into a second, never mind a relationship. I guess I'm annoyed they aren't her, that they don't touch my soul the way she did.

I'm not asking for much, am I? Someone to love. Someone to love me. Someone that might ease my fears and at the same time, dilute my DNA.

Allison—who still talks to me four times a day to tell me the guy who's taken over for me is an idiot and to ask me questions about agreements in progress—said to me, "You know how long I've been hearing about this? Just fucking call her."

Call me when you're ready, she said.

What the hell does that mean? I was *calling* her!

Allison has been hearing about it for a while. I know it's been more than a year now. How much more, I don't know.

There's always that joke, "How long has it been?" someone asks. And the person answers, "Three months, eight days, and an odd number of hours. But who's counting?"

And everyone laughs.

But me, I honestly don't know.

Seems like a week.

Seems like ten years.

THERE'S this sign along I-95 heading out of D.C. where it says Baltimore 80 miles, New York City 212 miles. You continue driving for like an hour until you finally come across a second sign that tells you, Baltimore 21 miles, New York City 211.

Now, it doesn't take a brain surgeon to figure out that something's wrong here, that this doesn't make any kind of sense, that after driving sixty miles, I'm only one fucking mile closer to Manhattan.

And you know what's even stranger, it's been like that for years. No one's changed it. I mean, am I the only idiot to notice this?

Sometimes I feel like that sign, like I'm running on a treadmill. I've made all this progress in my life, have come so far, have scratched and clawed to get *here*, and still, I'm no closer to my destination.

Like I'm going nowhere...fast.

I was having dinner at Cafe Milano with Megan Anderson, someone who, throughout the years, I've always wanted to get together with, but always one or the other or both of us were dating someone, and it never seemed to work out.

She looked great in this stretchy, sort of flowing, kind of clingy black dress. Even better when she told me she had dumped her last boyfriend.

We had just finished ordering the entrees. We were in the middle of a great antipasto, and she was in the middle of a very funny story about the guy she'd just broken up with, this lawyer from Baltimore.

I'm staring into her eyes when it hits me.

It's Baltimore. It's fucking Baltimore.

All this time, I've been getting closer and closer to Baltimore. I'm almost there. I'm about to hit the city limits. Only I'm not *going* to Baltimore or Annapolis or anywhere else in the Goddamn state. I want to get to New York City. But I've been driving and driving and can't figure out why I'm not getting where I wanna be.

I haven't called Sydney again for any reason other than I've been afraid to. I've been terrified to tell her how I feel, that this...this *thing* between us is the most powerful feeling I've ever had. So potent, so vital, that I can't live without it.

And in this moment of clarity, as I stare at Megan's lips and can't hear a word she's saying, I realize there's something I'm even more terrified of than living without her. Not that she'd say, *No, Billy. I don't feel the same way.*

But that she would say *yes.*

She is where the future begins. She is where I become husband, father, all of the titles I've been afraid to receive, obligations I didn't think I could, or would take on.

See, I don't think I know how to be a family. How to raise kids. How to give everything inside of me. And yet, she creates such a sense of safety and understanding, I don't want to hold anything back from her.

I want to be the man that deserves to keep my Grandfather's watch.

But then I'd have no excuses, no one to blame but myself if it didn't work.

I have no idea how to make a home because I never *have* gone home again. Sure, I visit, I drop by for a funeral here and there, a holiday dinner, but ever since I was nineteen, I've been running away from that place as fast as my feet, my car, or a plane would take me.

Home. No matter where it's been.

I mean, here I am, this success, as far as the world is concerned, and it's because why? Because I've so triumphantly fled the scene of the crimes against me? Decamped from my birthplace and bolted without so much as a look back?

I always thought so.

But what if in the paradox of life, the irony is, it's the opposite? What if Sydney is right? What if it's not in spite of them but because my parents were completely nutty? Because my childhood was Dr. Seuss on acid. Because my Fat Track was smashed into tiny little pieces. Because I had to beg to find rides home, and be my mom's shrink, the eldest son, *The Big Sonofabitch*, and a million other things.

Maybe this is how you're supposed to raise kids. Maybe this is how a family is supposed to be.

When you think about it, how many people have you met with perfect childhoods? And who are these lucky few? They're some of the most perfectly boring adult human beings on the planet. Beings who, literally, put people to sleep. Better than Sominex. They don't have pain to draw on, they don't have misery to fill in the blanks in their personalities. All they have is sunshine. And as anyone who lives in the Sahara will tell you, too much fucking sunshine is a very, very, very bad thing.

Can this really be the secret to my success? To anyone's?

Was this all some master plan that my folks charted out for me even before my conception? Had they formulated, in advance, the proper mix of nuttiness, love, guilt, pain, fears, jokes, and cooking tips that would make me the man I am today?

It's a comforting thought, but knowing my parents as I do, I could have just as well turned out to be Charles Manson or the Unabomber.

They say behind every great man is a great woman. And vice versa. But the fact is, behind nearly every great success is a fucked-up, taunted child with a wacky upbringing who got even with little Jimmy Anderson—the bully in third grade—by buying little Jimmy's dad's company and selling it off piecemeal.

Take that, Jimmy, you little prick. How's it feel back in the mailroom?

Maybe it's my duty as a loving parent to fuck my kids up to a certain extent. Only I'm not certain to what extent that is.

I have been sculpted into a man, only not by the hands of Picasso or Rodin, but by the fingers and chisels of Robert and Maggie, Annette and Sebby, the Princess, my mother, Gunter, Laura, Krissy, Jill, Gale. Even Jenna/Clair.

Smoothed and finished by my father elbowing me in the ribs when he realized his son was gonna get laid. By my mother laughing hysterically at something stupid till we nearly had to call an ambulance. By my brothers, my sister, my friends, teachers, principals, Beckett, Sydney. A thousand other people. A cast of characters, some I would never see again or, like Sebby, couldn't ever see again. They're all locked away in my mind. They speak to me. Continue to teach me, give me answers. Something which I never really acknowledged before.

I always believed I had done this on my own.

Sebby, of course, but that the Princess—the *Princess*—could somehow be responsible for my success? It boggles the mind.

Perhaps Sebby said it best. Those kids he and my grandmother watched over for twenty years, the only thing different between them and me, between the streets and the alleys that led them to prison and the highways and airline routes that brought me to the White House and around the world, is that I had people who loved me, who cared for me, who gave me a *chance*.

Not perfect people. But people who loved me even when I haven't seemed to love them back.

Yes, Sydney. You are correct. I haven't been ruined. I've been fucked up just right.

Everything I am is the consequence of everything that has happened to me. The sorrows and joys, the loves and losses have fashioned me, forged me, filled in the blanks in my nature.

Yet since returning from Hawaii and putting Laura's toothbrush and makeup and shampoo in a bag with the clothes she kept at my place and sending them to her via messenger, all I've done is avoid doing something, possibly the most important something I would ever do.

I got out of my chair.

"Megan, I'm really sorry, but I...I need to leave."

"Are you okay?"

"I don't know. Here." I threw down my Visa card. "Just finish dinner, I'll...I'll call you."

I walked quickly toward the door before she could say a word, and as I passed the maitre d', I told him to take care of Megan.

I STOOD in the hallway and rang the doorbell.

When she opened the door a moment later, she looked beautiful. Even though she had no idea, couldn't possibly know I was coming over on a random evening.

I could tell Laura was surprised to see me.

We had run into each other a number of times since breaking up, but I had never come to her home.

I said something like "Hi" or "Hello" or "It's good to see you."

She stood there, one hand on the door, the other on the wall. She wanted me to come in, but she wanted me to have to ask for it. If I had been in the mood, this was exactly the kind of interplay I loved between us.

She didn't say anything.

It didn't matter.

I was the one who had something to say.

"I was wrong for the way everything went. It wasn't your fault. We both knew early on what we were creating, what we were building toward. A life together. Family. I changed the rules on you. And I'm sorry for doing that. I needed to tell you, I'm sorry."

I had so many other things I wanted to say. That I loved her. That I missed her. That I was so much less happy without her in my life. But I knew those words would open up the wounds that were still too fresh for her even now.

She remained silent throughout.

I found out later from a mutual friend, one of the few who would still speak to me, that witnessing—never mind *getting*—an apology from Billy Gerrick had left her unable to speak.

I WAS out of breath when I got to Sydney's door.

I banged on it. No answer. Kept banging.

I could hear the cat rubbing against the other side of the door as I continued to knock.

A door opened behind me and into the hall came a man that could only be described by one word:

"Chip, right?"

"Yes. Can I help you?" he said in the way a salesperson at a high-end Fifth Avenue clothier would if speaking to someone wearing white shorts and an "I♥NY" T-shirt.

"I'm looking for Sydney."

"She's not home."

"Do you know when she might be back?"

"Not for a while."

"Goddammit." I slid down against the wall. "I'm just going to sit here and wait for her if that's okay." I saw Chip look at me funny. "Don't worry, I'm a friend of hers."

"You're that Trade Guy, aren't you?" He immediately warmed up.

I glanced up at him. "Yeah. I'm the Trade Guy."

He looked me over. "Those news photos don't really do you justice."

"Thanks. I guess."

"You're gonna be waiting a while," he said. "She's left for London."

"London?"

He nodded.

I've been around the world, I don't know how many times, and London's always been a short hop in comparison to most of my trips, but it never seemed more remote, more distant than it did at that moment.

"When did she leave?"

He checked the old, beat-up Timex that was too big for his wrist. "Maybe four hours ago."

"Four hours ago? Jesus, you've got to be kidding me! Who flies to London on a Saturday night?"

The cat was clawing at the door. Chip grabbed a key from inside his apartment. "It's Valentine's Day on Tuesday." Then he opened the door to Sydney's apartment and Flora, the devil cat, jumped into his arms.

Aaaaaaakkkccchchhhhhhhhh. That was the cat's meow.

"That's a good girl," he said to the creature.

"When is she supposed to get back?"

"Actually, I don't think she knows. At least a couple of weeks."

"Do you know where she's staying?" I could be on a private charter in two hours, in London by morning.

"She's staying with her boy toy."

"Brendan Avery?"

"You know him?"

"Yeah...sort of."

"He's so yummy. And he's been trying *desperately* to get her to come live there for more than two years. I told her, honey, the man's gorgeous, he loves you, and he's rich! Perhaps we need to lower our standards just a wee bit. Finally, she said 'yes.'"

I petted Flora in his arms. The cat had a certain charm. Once you got over the smell.

"She's supposed to come back in maybe a few weeks to straighten things out, take Flora if she can. She told me she was thinking about giving notice to the landlord. I know she's gonna love it over there. They're so cute together, her and Brendan," he said this last part almost apologetically.

If I ever thought I had to worry about Chip in terms of competition, I had been mistaken.

"Thank you, Chip. You're a good guy. Take good care of Flora."

He smiled at me.

"If you talk to her..." I said as I backed down the hall. "...you don't need to bother telling her I stopped by."

As soon as I was out of the building, I hailed a cab and pulled out my phone. I climbed in the back of the cab and yelled, "National Airport," to the driver while on the phone I checked helicopter service from National to Dulles. Fifteen minutes. "Make it fast," I said as I put a hundred-dollar bill into the cash slot.

The money seemed to instantly make the cab travel more swiftly.

I dialed the Air Traffic desk at Dulles. Got someone who knew me. There were two carriers which flew to London.

"British Airways took off at six-fifty."

I glanced at my watch: 7:56.

"And United was scheduled to leave at 7:30 but has been delayed till—"

I crossed my fingers.

"Let's see. Hold on. Till...seven-fifty. I have it as taking off. No more flights until...United, one A.M."

I hung up the phone, told the driver to stop. Told him to keep the hundred.

And for one brief moment, as I climbed out of the cab, and into the street, into the cold and bitter night, I knew how Krissy Simon felt when she walked out of the house and across the muddy yard to her father's pickup.

But only for a moment.

I WALKED BACK to Cafe Milano where Megan was eating her meal alone.

You see people walk out of restaurants and leave behind a stunned someone in movies and TV all the time. But you never stay with the person left behind. The camera always follows the one that leaves.

Whatever reason caused the star to abandon the bit player is certainly more interesting than watching that someone eat pan-roasted herb-rubbed salmon filet in forced solitude.

But as I sheepishly walked back in, I saw the devastation that occurs. She was sitting there, picking at her food, not drinking the glass of wine in front of her.

She put down her fork when she saw me. I figured so she wouldn't be tempted to stab me with it. But she didn't make a scene. That wasn't Megan's style. She had gone on and finished the meal without me, trying to come up with an exit strategy that would not be too embarrassing.

It's funny that by not wanting to bring attention to herself, she'd done just that.

My meal was still sitting there, untouched where the waiter had left it. I picked up my fork and pushed the tepid food around.

"I'm sorry," I said. "It was important."

She nodded. "I think I'd like to go home now."

"I'll get the check."

"I paid it a long time ago."

I breathed in deeply and felt like an asshole. "Let's get you out of here."

I escorted her out of the restaurant and hailed a cab out front. I let her in the back and started to get in myself.

"I'll be fine," she said, looking up at me.

I nodded. "I really am sorry."

"Me too. I'll get over it."

I suddenly got in the cab. "Let me bring you home at least, Megan."

"Okay." She needed not to be alone again. Not so soon.

I closed the door, and we directed the cabby to her place.

When we got there, I had the cabby wait as I walked her up to her front door.

"You gonna be okay?"

"Are you gonna ever tell me why you left me there?"

I told her to hold on a moment. I went back down and paid the cabby, and sent him on his way.

And then I ran up the steps, and I told her.

"I'm glad you came back," she said.

"I can't take the credit. She wasn't home."

"You could've just gone to your place and sulked."

"And miss out on a chance to share the misery?"

"We've been really good friends a long time, Billy. Maybe that's just the way it's supposed to stay."

"But there's always been something, you know, *there*."

"I know. And I think the only reason you agreed to this dinner was because I asked—"

"—with intent. Very clear intent. This was supposed to be more than dinner."

"Yes," she said, nodding. "That was stupid."

"No, no, it wasn't."

"I just needed that thing you do, that you're so good at. Make me feel sexy, wanted, beautiful."

"You're blowing me off, aren't you?" I said.

"I think I'm actually being very understanding about this whole evening."

"You are. You are."

"I just don't think I'm ready for anything yet. As I was sitting there alone—"

"I really am sorry."

"—I was thinking, I need friends more than I need a man right now.

I'm learning so much about myself by being by myself. I've always been with a man. I don't know what it's like not to be with one."

"I know what you mean, not about being with a man, but...you know."

She smiled and said, "I'll see you later? Friend."

"Definitely, Friend."

"Good night, Billy."

"Good night, Megan."

She kissed me softly on the lips. "If you need someone to talk to about this..."

"Thanks."

I KNOW why Sydney did what she did.

It was the same reason why I hadn't busted down her front door months ago. I *wasn't* ready. I don't think I knew what "ready" even meant. She didn't want to be just any someone I ran to because my bed was suddenly empty.

I know I was ready two hours ago. Certainly a week ago. Maybe as long as a month. It's easy to look in the rearview mirror and see the turnoff you missed once you're past it.

Megan's the kind of woman you go out with when you're ready. It was the reason why she dumped that lawyer in Baltimore. Because he wasn't.

But I have to admit, on top of it all, it stings more than a little to lose Sydney to Brendan Avery.

I can't seem to get that name out of my head. In fact, when Brendan's father heard I was leaving the government, he called me out of the blue and offered me a job with Avery Shipping.

Thanks, God. Kick me while I'm down.

I politely declined the very generous offer.

It's not that Brendan's a bad guy, he just doesn't run very deep. Which isn't his fault. That's just the way he is. You know, perfect genes, perfect fucking childhood.

I called my mom. And after she said her requisite, "You always call me from the car phone," "I'm not in a car, mother," "You know what I mean," I told her I wanted to spend some time with the family. Except for some brief drive-bys, I haven't been up since last Christmas. Over a year ago. I wanted to do something. All of us together. Maybe we could even go down to Florida for a week.

She said, "But who's gonna bunk with your father?"

Who knows, maybe I will.

Sydney's doubts about me weren't unfounded. Then again, who can tell what might have happened if we'd gotten together right away. Maybe it would've worked. Maybe I would've destroyed us. Maybe she's better off with him.

There are a million reasons why someone in a relationship like I was with Laura shouldn't have gotten within ten miles of someone like Sydney, never should've let themselves get to the place where there was a dilemma.

I've had temptation in my life before, and I will have temptation in my life again, I'm sure.

Temptation, I can handle.

But sometimes, when the right woman walks into your life, you simply can't say, *No, I'm busy tonight*.

At least now, I was free. I had tried.

I had made a decision before it was made for me.

Or, at least, before I knew it was.

NEGOTIATING THE REST OF IT

LAURA'S FAMILY is from the South. She doesn't have an accent because she lived in California for much of her childhood—her dad was a professor at UCSD in San Diego. But the rest of the clan, uncles, aunts, cousins, and grandparents all hail from parts once burned and pillaged by us "Yankees."

It's a huge, wealthy, very attractive family that gathers together several times a year. Their most recent assembly, from what I understand, included a piñata for the kids that looked suspiciously a lot like me. More than a few of the adults took a whack at the effigy, I was told, which gave them a great deal of enjoyment, but made the kids start squealing for the grown-ups to stop hogging the candy trove, which started some yelling, which led to some time-outs, spankings, and other punishments.

I am to blame for much misery in the Sumner clan.

Her family was not happy when I decided to call off the engagement. There are several contiguous southern states that I am not welcome in.

I don't plan on passing through any of them for a while, let alone stopping there to seek some hospitality.

See, the number of guns in the South relative to the number of people is inordinately high. In fact, the Bureau of Alcohol, Tobacco, and Firearms (what a trio that is, get drunk, fire up a cig, and go out and shoot someone) estimates that there are twice as many guns in the former Confederate States as there are people. And in my own personal, more informal survey, I've found that the number of Sumners that can successfully tie a hanging knot is also higher than the average American family. They say it's all about skinning rabbits and putting up piñatas, but I still choose to avoid much of Dixie.

And even though I know Laura is dating now—Laura's the type of woman that'll never be without a date—the last three times I've seen her, not counting my visit this evening, she's looked unbelievably good, worn no underwear, and had problems keeping her hands off the inside of my thigh.

I have this sinking suspicion—and maybe it's just wishful thinking, or some sort of rationalization so I don't feel so bad—but I get the distinct impression that the only reason Laura touches me like that is not because she wants me back, but because she wants me to want her back.

That if we did get back together, she'd turn around and leave me inside of a month.

I DIDN'T TAKE A CAB. Instead, I walked back to my house from Megan's, studying the faces of the people who passed me on the street, searching for something.

The smell of an approaching storm was in the air. The barren trees were swaying in the growing wind, and if I read the sky right, we might see some snow soon.

The cold weather was late in the States. It had been the warmest year in half a millennium, so the experts said. I was glad we had stood firm on the eco exception, which allowed countries to put public health and safety and national environmental goals ahead of the general obligation not to raise trade restrictions. Meaning, we could continue to require that cars imported into the United States maintain a certain level of pollution control as long as we forced domestic producers to do the same.

Funny, but the agreement seemed like something I had done a lifetime ago.

To be honest, I hadn't noticed the belated cold weather. To me, it had been winter for more than a year. Ever since that storm over Europe. No spring or summer or fall. Just the chilly reception of each day drifting silently into the next like a blanket of snow into a drift, a protective wall. Yet, even in this self-imposed Arctic state, there had been growth. There had been life. A bloom of understanding. A flowering of wisdom.

I walked up the stone steps to my home. Pulled out my keys and finally looked up. And there she was.

"Hi," she said, quickly, quietly, like that was a normal thing to say.

I was frozen for a moment. I couldn't tell if I was breathing.

"Hi," I was able to finally get out. "I thought you were on a plane to London."

"Supposed to be. But when I got up to the counter to check in, I didn't have my passport."

"That's too bad," I said, not meaning it.

She smiled slightly, which disappeared as she reached out and touched her fingertips to my forehead, where the tiny scar lay from my collision with the scaffolding. "What happened to your face? Not another trade fight, I hope."

"Oh, you know, didn't see something coming. Didn't duck when I should have."

She caressed it slowly, then self-consciously pulled her hand away.

"I guess you came to see me, knowing how good I am at getting passports." It was an attempt to alleviate the awkwardness.

"See, the funny thing is, I had specifically not gotten a new passport so I couldn't get on a plane to London."

"That is funny." The irony, that I had given her the tool to leave me.

"I went home to get it—there's another flight after midnight."

"One o'clock," I said absently.

Her eyes avoided mine. "And Chip told me you stopped by. I thought it might be important." Then her voice changed. "How did you know where I live?" She wasn't annoyed, exactly, but she sounded…

"You know, I know a guy who knows a guy," I said.

"Yeah, I know. Same way you got my number?"

I nodded.

"So why did you come by?"

For an instant, I thought perhaps that in the intervening hour, I might have lost my nerve because the words didn't leap from my mouth, but they came soon enough.

"See, there's this sign on I-Ninety-Five on the way to Baltimore." I could see her forehead start to wrinkle up. "It's got the miles on it. It says Baltimore, eighty. New York City, two hundred and twelve. Then you drive for a while. And you come across another sign which says Baltimore, twenty-one miles. New York City, two hundred and eleven. Which is stupid because how can you drive fifty-nine miles and be only one mile closer to New Yor—"

"What the *hell* are you talking about?"

I stopped. Took a breath.

"Sometimes...you travel for a really, really, *really* long time..." I took her by the hands, held them tight. "And you end up right where you're supposed to be. Even when the signs tell you otherwise." I looked her in the eyes. "I don't want you to go."

She turned away, and I couldn't tell at first if she was angry or sad or about to cry.

"You were right," I said. "I wasn't ready."

She stared back at me. I could see it was sadness. "And what's different now?"

"My God, Sydney, everything's different." I felt the weight that had been pressing down on me lift. "I've been around the world. I've been with more women than I can count. And you know what? None of it means anything. Because you...you reach parts of me that no one, not one of them, has ever gotten close to." I touched her skin tenderly. "Some I almost forgot about. Most, I never knew existed."

She looked hurt, which surprised me. Tears were welling up in her eyes.

"Then why! Why didn't you tell her right away? Right there, in Geneva. How could you let me get in that car and leave? And how could you go to Hawaii with her?"

She slapped a weak hand on my chest, then slowly drew it away. She was crying.

"How could you do that? Like what happened between us didn't mean anything to you. Like it didn't change *everything*."

I didn't answer for a long time. Because I didn't have one.

At the time, it seemed the less hurtful thing to do, but looking back, it made the breakup far more painful to Laura.

"I don't know." I dropped my head. "I guess...I guess I was trying not to get caught up in the moment."

"It didn't feel like just a moment to me."

"No. It didn't."

I was quiet after answering. And I could tell that she was beginning to feel that coming to see me had been a bad idea.

I closed my eyes and struggled to find the words, trying to put it in a way that might make some sense. I needed to let her in, let her deep inside me.

"When I was nine years old," I started slowly, "my father smashed this Hot Wheels Fat Track I had gotten for Christmas because I didn't come to the table for dinner fast enough. It was the best gift I had ever gotten, and it was gone in a flash of anger completely out of my control. I cried for hours." I was there again, feeling it. "I loved that thing. Really loved it."

I looked at her, back in the present.

"You asked me, first time we met, what it was about my past I was afraid of. I've been afraid ever since that day of caring about anything so much I couldn't bear losing it."

I glanced down at the sidewalk, silent for a moment.

"And I got really good at it. Being always in control. So proud of myself for having risen above my pedestrian roots, my crazy childhood. Proud that I had made myself into something out of nothing. And then you—" My hand went up to caress her cheek, but I stopped it halfway to its destination. "You came along. You scared me. You made me see something was missing in my life. In my relationships. Not just with Laura, but with my family...myself."

She stared at me, searching my face, peering into my heart.

"I look into your eyes, Sydney, and I see that essence, that something —whatever that is—that makes us alive. That makes us whole." I glanced at the ground. What she makes me see, what she really makes me see...is that one lifetime isn't enough to experience all that she is. "Baby, when I'm with you, I'm home. Do you understand that? I feel like I'm home."

She blinked for the first time in several minutes.

Then the warmth that had washed over me suddenly grew cold. "And every time I realize that I don't have that, I get this feeling in my stomach and my chest—I don't know how to describe it. It's like, I don't know, like...loss."

"Emptiness," she whispered.

"Yes," I answered almost inaudibly.

We were both silent for almost an entire minute. I heard the distant roar, saw the blinking lights of a plane far overhead in the night sky.

"Do you feel this with him? Is that why you're going there?"

There was no response. It was only a second or two, but it was forever.

"I was *always* going there, Billy." She let the words sink in. "I said,

'No' when he asked me to marry him because I felt like we were being pushed into it. Like his family was asking me instead of him, so they could check off a box, get him a wife, get him settled down. But when he was leaving, and it was just him and me, he asked me to go to London with him. To be just us. The way we'd always been. No timetable or pressure. I told him I would. But it isn't like going to Baltimore, or even New York—it's *England*. I couldn't just leave my job. I needed time. To complete projects, to sort things out. To give him the chance to think about what he wanted instead of what his family wanted. He said he'd wait. I said it might be a while. I tried to come up with every reason why I wasn't really in love with him. I dated other men, didn't care about any of them." She glanced to the sky, maybe for strength, maybe for forgiveness. "I went to Geneva with you to prove to myself that this want and desire for more was just fantasy. That this beautiful, kind man waiting for me in London who loved me, who loved me for me, who looked at me the way my father looked at my mother...wasn't a fantasy, but real. That whatever doubts I had about him were trivial and more about me being afraid of not fitting into his world than about him."

I looked down the street, up at the night sky, anywhere but at her. Finally:

"I don't pretend to know how you feel about him. But I loved Laura, *loved* her a great deal, and it wasn't enough. I don't know why. It just wasn't. I didn't break up with her to be with you. I ended it because it wasn't right." I locked eyes with her. "I mean, Sydney, how much can you love the guy? You haven't gone to London before now."

"Billy, I've been to London four times over the past year."

That was one piece of information I didn't learn from the passport office.

"But this isn't about him right now."

"I know. It would take a lot less effort to be with Brendan Avery. I'm not an easy man to live with. I'm a bit more difficult."

"You are a *lot* more difficult!"

I nodded. "All I can tell you is, I'm a better man with you than without you, Sydney Nathan. A better man than I've ever been with anyone else. And I don't want to give up being this man. When you were writing in your journal, it wasn't about how someone looked at you. It was about how *you* looked at them. How do you look at him?"

She stared at me, then wiped her eyes, although I saw no visible tears. "Brendan is gonna be at the airport, wondering where the hell I—" She tried to move past me, but I stepped in front of her.

"Why did you come here tonight?"

She began to tear up. And her whole body started shaking. "Because," she began quietly, "Seeing you is painful. But not as much as not seeing you."

I grabbed her and pulled her to me, holding her in an embrace that embodied all the fear, frustration and emotion I had been keeping locked inside of me. Tears slid down the side of her face and met the ones pouring from my eyes as our cheeks came together.

And then the words came out, said like no other time in my life, with a new understanding of the power they held, power I had wielded recklessly in the past, but not now, not ever again.

"I love you," I said into her ear.

She kissed my mouth, passionately pressing her lips against mine. The kiss engrossed us, washed the world away, its problems, its uncertainty, its existence.

After a moment, she pulled away.

It was hardly a whisper, hardly the sound of a breath, but I heard it: "I have to go."

She ran into the street and hailed a cab. I tried to keep her from going, pleaded with her, begged her, but she said she had to do this. At the last moment, as the cab was pulling away, I pounded on the trunk, causing the driver to hit the brakes. I opened the door and climbed in. If she was determined to leave, if I was fated to lose her, I was going to fight until the last second, until that jetway door closed, until the plane pulled away from the gate.

Fifty minutes later, we arrived at the airport. She kissed me on the lips, this time, more gently—a kiss filled with sadness—said, "Goodbye," then handed her ticket to the woman at the gate and boarded the United 747. I watched her travel down the jetway, her back to me the whole way, never once looking back, lost sight of her as she turned the final corner, was sealed off from her as the jetway door closed.

A few moments after that, she was on her way to London.

I stood by the glass and watched the plane taxi to the end of the runway, featureless faces visible in its tiny windows. It stopped there for a moment, waited for the okay from the tower, and then took off.

After the plane's wheels left American soil, I looked away from the tarmac.

And as one of the gate crew went behind the counter and slid the card out, then another back in, changing the flight information to the next departure, I gave one last look at the terminal, absorbed every detail, every aspect, because I knew my life from here on would never be the same.

I turned and walked away...toward my future.

So, I'm standing here, something like three years later, having my hand broken by a beautiful woman lying on her back in the bed with her legs spread open. We're both sweating and breathing heavy, nearly out of breath.

But it isn't over yet. We're right in the middle of it.

It's a pleasurable, sexy moment, and a painful one as well, because of how firmly she's gripping me. I want to look down between her legs, but she doesn't want me to. I can feel her tightening up. She's getting really close. I don't know if I can hold out or how much longer I can take. This woman who thought it would be a really neat idea to have natural childbirth, no drugs, no nothing, just a lot of heavy breathing, and now that it's too late, is screaming for an epidural, Demerol, Fentanyl, anything, begging me to make them stop, pleading with me to keep them from doing what they're doing to her—if I care for her at all—and squeezing my hand till the bones are nothing but calcium dust, and generally being in about as bad a mood as I have ever seen her, as unpleasant as I think is possible for her, which, by the way, regardless of the circumstances, is still better than most women I've dated on a good day.

Knowing that in the next half-hour, maybe a little longer, maybe a little less, but soon, very soon, from out of one of my favorite parts of my wife's beautiful body will emerge a living, breathing somebody, a miniature human being. A mix of her and me.

I don't know whether it's going to be a boy or a girl yet—we decided against knowing. I have the feeling it's going to be a boy. We're heavy on boys on both sides of the family. But whichever sex it is, the doctors tell us it's going to be very healthy and just a little purple. And if all goes well, if all goes according to plan, the day after tomorrow, I'm going to take my lovely bride—who once took a flight to London because she didn't want to break up with a man over the phone—and lovely newborn child

(Matthew or Jessica, depending), and bring them home...and then Sydney Nathan Gerrick and I will begin the long, slow, and joyous process of fucking up this child's life.

And if we're lucky, fucking it up just right.

...

ACKNOWLEDGMENTS

This book has been a journey. A deep, years-long exploration of *a few of my favorite things*: Family and friendship. Relationships and personal growth. Sex and love. And the humor, joy, and pain that accompanies them.

I'd like to thank Mickey Kantor—a member of President Bill Clinton's cabinet and inner circle, the man who led the U.S. delegation that finally broke through the logjam to negotiate the most complex agreement the world has ever seen, creating the World Trade Organization in the process—for speaking to me about his experiences during that time. Mickey is one of those rare people: A straight-shooter with a sense of humor, a sense of the absurd, and a grasp of issues that would overwhelm all but the very few. A man who carried a very big stick and knew when to use it and when to keep it at his side.

I'd like to thank Barri Evins for forcing me to answer questions that always lead to better solutions. "Velvet" is no exception.

Thank you to Karen Simard for her advice and counsel, doing for me what Mickey Kantor did for the WTO, breaking the logjam that allowed this book to be born.

There is no way to explain the tenacity that Lisa Lindo has shown throughout the years bringing my projects to fruition. I have often asked her for the near-impossible. And she has delivered. Her guidance and efforts are the reason you're even reading this now.

And lastly, and most importantly, I'd like to thank my family. To the three generations in this book and one that follows in their footsteps and walks on ahead.

ABOUT THE AUTHOR

Edward Savio is an award-winning, best-selling author, and award-losing screenwriter. He has written numerous film projects for Walt Disney Studios, Sony Pictures Entertainment and others. He once nearly drove Val Kilmer over a cliff.

Other Books by Edward Savio
Adult Literary Fiction
Idiots in the Machine

Science Fiction
Alexander X
Ancient Among Us
League of Auld

Children's Literature
The Stupor Heroes vs. Dr. Earwax

Visit edwardsavio.com for bonus material.

facebook.com/edwardsaviowriter

x.com/edwardsavio

instagram.com/edwardsavio

tiktok.com/@edwardsavio

youtube.com/edwardsavio